T0322854

GLORIOUS PEOPLE

GLORIOUS PEOPLE

PUSHKIN PRESS

TRANSLATED FROM THE GERMAN BY
IMOGEN TAYLOR

SASHA SALZMANN

Pushkin Press
Somerset House, Strand
London WC2R 1LA

Glorious People was first published as *Im Menschen muss alles herrlich sein* by Suhrkamp Verlag in Germany, 2021

First published by Pushkin Press in 2024

Quotation from 'This is how you stand for a family photo' by Serhiy Zhadan is taken from *A New Orthography*, 2020 (translated from the Ukranian by John Hennessy and Ostap Kin), by permission of Lost Horse Press

Quotation from 'The Anthropology of Water' by Anne Carson is taken from *Plainwater*, by permission of Aragi Inc.

The translation of this work was supported by a grant from the Goethe-Institut

1 3 5 7 9 8 6 4 2

ISBN 13: 978-1-78227-948-8

Designed and typeset by Tetragon, London
Printed and bound in the United Kingdom by Clays Ltd, Elcograf S.p.A.

www.pushkinpress.com

The author would like to thank the German Literary Fund for supporting their work on this book.

A Note on Place Names

Throughout my translation of the novel, I have used transliterations based on Ukrainian place names rather than on the old Soviet-era Russian names. For those parts of the novel set in the Soviet Union this is perhaps anachronistic, but it is now, rightly, common usage.

IMOGEN TAYLOR

GLORIOUS PEOPLE

Every made-up story is based on true events.
And if I want to be believed, I must get things wrong.

SKIPPING STONES

OF COURSE I WANTED TO KNOW what had happened, what exactly took place before Edi was beaten up in the yard. She was lying on the grass, her hair all pale and dirty. My mother was kneeling beside her, Auntie Lena was yelling at them both, and all three were waving their arms around like they were casting out evil spirits. When they saw me they started to cry, one after the other, like a Russian doll, the tears of one turning into the tears of the next, and so on. First my mum let rip, then the others joined in, as if they were singing a howling, wailing round. I couldn't make head or tail of it.

OK, so it wasn't hard to guess why my mum came over all misty-eyed when she saw me standing there after the long radio silence—but Lena and Edi? They seemed to have some score to settle. Mother and daughter, one of them lying on the ground like the other's shadow, or the other way round: one of them growing up out of the other's feet, like a shrub with broken branches. Auntie Lena was wearing a green trouser suit that hung loosely on her body; I almost didn't recognize her. I'd worn her daughter's babygros, sat at her kitchen table revising for tests and exams, rung her doorbell in the middle of the night when things got too much at home—but that was a long time ago and for a moment I wasn't sure it was really Lena, standing there yelling at her cowering daughter: 'Why were you hanging around out here? What were you doing?'

Edi looked the worse for wear but not drunk, though she claimed in all seriousness that she'd seen a giraffe in the yard, wandering around between the tower blocks, nibbling at the grass, peering in at windows. This may be the former East, but as far as I know we've no giraffes round here. You don't get them in these parts.

She hadn't been here long; you only had to look at her hair and clothes to know that—especially her clothes. I'd never seen much of Edi, even when she still lived with her parents and I did my homework at their kitchen table. I was too young for her, and anyway she never came in to make herself a sandwich or a cup of tea when I was around. The door to her room had a milky glass panel, and through this I could see her switch her light on and off for no apparent reason, day and night. On and off, on and off. Once, the glass was broken; only a few jagged shards stuck out from the frame. No one mentioned it and I asked no questions and soon there was a new pane of glass, as if nothing had happened. Edi was pretty unobtrusive back then—black hair, black jeans, black top. If I saw her on the street I'd walk right past her, she dresses so brightly now. I only recognized her because her mum was standing next to her, shouting at her. And because it was my mum trying to make the peace. Over and over they launched into the same string of reproaches, Auntie Lena saying furiously to my mother, 'Why didn't you tell me—?' and my mother retorting, 'It's nobody's business if I'm dying.'

Not a good moment for me to enter the fray; she was mid-sentence when she caught sight of me and she stiffened, as if time had sprung a crack. SNAP. She looks at me, I look at her.

Her hair's gone grey and she had a crushed look to her, though she'd clearly made an effort with her appearance. She dyes her hair—has done for a while—and I dare say it had started out the evening neatly styled, but now it was straggly and dishevelled, and you could see the silver roots. The skin under her eyes sagged—but maybe that was because I was standing over her; everyone looks weird from that angle. She seemed small. Looking past the crown of her head, I could see her hands; there was dirt in the creases of her palms. She must have tried to pull Edi up on to her feet.

I wasn't surprised she was in town. Uncle Lev had told me she'd be at the party at the Jewish Community Centre—in fact, he'd paid me an official visit to inform me and to demand a family reconciliation, a big reunion. He came in a clean shirt, his nostrils flaring; he had the best intentions, but I had to disappoint him. When he saw that he wasn't getting anywhere, he tried to guilt-trip me—you can't break with your own mother; you have to love her no matter what—but I don't think I'm obliged either to love or not to love her; she's my mother and that's all there is to it. Things are what they are.

I'd gone out just because I felt like it that evening—wandered around, watched the evening strollers, nothing special. The streets smell different at dusk, sourer, and I like that, but this particular night I smelt burnt sugar and heard shouts, and I thought I'd go and investigate.

At first I was glad it wasn't my mother lying beaten up on the ground—then I realized that was the extent of what I felt. Live. Leave me in peace.

It looked as if there had been a small fire here a short while ago; we were standing next to a heap of charred paper—crinkly, soot-coated bundles tied up with string—rather beautiful, actually. I seem to remember the smell of Coke and bitter caramel; it tickled our noses and made Auntie Lena sneeze. Whoever had tried to have a little picnic here between the tower blocks had either been driven away or had to leave in a hurry, but none of the women would tell me how Edi fitted in, or why half the Jewish community *mishpocha* were hanging out of the second-floor windows gawping at us. The women were crying, but they didn't want to seem weak. That's socialist manners for you—flaunt your wounded emotions, but try to keep a grip on yourself.

All around us were balconies with identical flags fluttering at their railings, as if the people who lived there would forget where they were if they didn't have that little bit of cloth flapping in the wind. The funny thing is that for many of the residents—the ones I know, anyway—that flag has nothing to do with the emblems on their passports.

None of the women wanted to return to the party, but they couldn't be left out in the yard either, Edi dirty and bleached and battered, Lena with her eyes puffy from crying, and my dishevelled mother who'd just announced that it was nobody's business if she was dying. I asked them if they'd like to go back with me to freshen up and have a cup of tea. It seemed the right thing to do, to offer them a sit-down at my kitchen table. We walked quickly, without speaking, as if afraid of being followed. I could hear the rubbery squeak of my soles on the asphalt.

When we arrived, Auntie Lena made straight for the sink, held a flannel under the cold water and pressed it to Edi's forehead. I flicked the switch on the kettle, ignoring my mum's greedy looks, the way she stared at the sofa, taking in every crevice, as if to commit it all to memory. It was her first time here; she even looked lovingly at the open bags of crisps on the floor. I ignored, too, the hissing voice in my head telling me that the flat was small and dingy and dirty. The only free wall was covered by a massive *Path of Exile* poster with a dark, forbidding sky and spurts of blood. There was a smell of barbecue sauce from the box of chicken wings next to my keyboard. The curtains were drawn, the computer was on, battling nations zapped each other on the screen. The roar of the fan filled my lungs.

We said nothing for a while. I could tell that Mum's hands were trembling because the tea in her cup was rippled, as if tiny stones were skipping across the surface, but her face was calm and her eyes big and round, as if she couldn't believe she was seeing me. I couldn't believe it either.

You shouldn't criticize people for not being heroes, she had said the last time we'd argued—or maybe it wasn't the last time; our arguing had neither beginning nor end, it was an unbroken chain of resentful mutterings. They weren't even reproaches; they were just noise. But when I asked her why, if that was the case, she expected me to be someone I couldn't be, she had no answer. She wouldn't—or couldn't—answer any of my questions. And she had no questions for me—still doesn't.

She sat there with her silvery copper-beech hair alongside bleached Edi and her emerald-green mother, all three of them rocking their heads, ever so gently, almost imperceptibly, as if waves were coursing through their shoulders, as if electricity were running up their necks. The little stones continued to skip over the surface of the cooling tea, faster or slower, depending on their size—hop, hop, hop, sink.

We made an effort, talked a bit, exchanged coordinates—tentative words, clumsy dance steps. But not bad, considering.

I

Reflections of bright faces on my palms.
Women and men from the 70s like dead planets
illuminate the summer air.

SERHIY ZHADAN,
'This is how you stand for a family photo'
translated from the Ukrainian
by John Hennessy and Ostap Kin

THE SEVENTIES

Lena

FROM UP CLOSE, the wall looked green. Lena knew that if she took just one step back, she would see the stripes and patterns of the wallpaper—fine black lines like flower stalks running crosswise from floor to ceiling. But she didn't look up. Her mother had pulled her by the ear and planted her right here. Lena stared at the green patch; there was nothing else and the nothing made her eyes ache. She was bored and needed a pee; more than anything she was bored, but she'd sooner have burst than said a single word. She wouldn't wet herself—she was too old for that, almost a schoolgirl—and she wouldn't do her mother the favour of crying. Besides, she knew that Father would be home any minute; he would rescue her. He would shout at Mother for shouting at her, Lena would confess all, and then her parents would quarrel and she'd have the evening to herself, maybe go round to Yury's, or look at the book Father had brought home for her. She could read, she knew she could. She might not recognize all the letters, but when her father asked her, what does this say, she dug a tooth into her tongue, screwed up her eyes and almost always got it right. And Father was a teacher; he'd never lie to her. Soon she'd go to school like him, and then she'd be able to write her name and spell out the other children's names and the different types of animals and all the birds, which you could tell apart by the zigzag edges of their wings and the curve of their beaks. Maybe a few other words, too. She was looking forward to school; at last there'd be an end to the boredom and she wouldn't have to spend so much time alone, with her mother always away at the chemical plant, sending people running up and down the aisles, and her father stumbling from one classroom to the next. Maybe she'd see more of him when she started school—she might.

Lena bit her lower lip because she felt something warm and wet dribbling into her pants. Her fist tensed. She'd broken a cup, but not on purpose—Mother knew that. Lena had picked it up because it was beautiful—more beautiful than anything in their one-bed flat—and because there was a danger to touching it; nothing must happen to it, ever. It was made of thin, cold china with a curved handle in the shape of Father's ear—bulgy at the bottom and pointy at the top—and it had a blue lattice pattern broken at intervals by gold double bows that gleamed like fish scales. The rim and base were finely painted, as if the cup had been sewn together with gold thread, and it was clear as day to Lena that no one would ever drink out of this cup. It was an ornament and it stood in the glass cabinet next to a faun figurine that Lena didn't like to touch because it left dust on her fingers, and because she was afraid of its hairy goat's legs and cloven hooves. Lena wasn't sure if such animals really existed. Might she come across one in the woods? Did they all have curved pipes that they played to lure children like her and crooked horns next to their ears for skewering those children when they caught them? Lena tried not to look at the faun when she passed the cabinet. But the cup was different; sometimes she just had to hold it. It was filigree and shimmered like Mum's jewellery, which was well and truly out of reach because it was kept in a box right at the top of the cupboard—and because she shouldn't be interested in it anyway, Mum said. The cup shattered; she didn't know how, her hands hadn't been the least bit slippery. All Lena could remember were the screams—first hers and then her mother's—and the pain in her ear, and now the wallpaper that she'd been staring at for hours, days, an eternity.

She'd been holding herself so tense to keep from wetting herself that she hadn't heard her father come in. Now snatches of words drifted down the passage from the kitchen.

'...the Leningrad china...'

'...no way to discipline a child...'

'What do you know about discipline...'

'I'm a teacher...'

'And I'm her mother...'

Father was losing. Lena bit her lip even harder and raised her head; she hadn't noticed it drop on to her chest. She stared straight ahead at the wallpaper, trying to think of her grandmother, Mum's mum. *She* would have helped her out of this. She wasn't as soft and warm as Father, knew how to speak her mind and had a loud, clear voice, just like her daughter. Sometimes, when the two of them were talking, their words sounded like whip cracks. And now Mother was cracking the whip at Father and he was growing quieter and quieter, so that Lena could no longer hear him, though he was just the other side of the wall.

Soon Grandmother would come and fetch her. Summer lay ahead and that meant Sochi and the seaside and the house on the edge of town with its smell of musty wood, and the hazelnut trees whose branches Lena would shake. And once—or maybe more than once—she would climb into one of the trees, and her grandmother would plant her fists on her hips and call up to Lena and shake her out of the branches like a nut. A whole summer away from Mum. But not yet—Grandmother wouldn't come for a while yet. It might be days or even weeks. Lena felt a stinging in her pants.

Father was talking to her gently, his face up close to her ear. She could feel the warmth of him, but she held herself stiff; in spite of her wet pants and wet cheeks she said nothing and pushed his hand off her shoulder. Only when he crouched down beside her and asked if she'd like to go to the new technical museum with him at the weekend, just the two of them, to see the steam boilers and the gas turbines—only then did Lena relax with a sigh. She squinted across at him. His chin had gone stubbly again. When he'd left in the morning, his face had gleamed and smelt of cucumber water; now it was strewn with black dots and reeked of railway dust. His hair clung to his forehead; he smiled and ran his hands first over her eyes, then over his. Beneath the finely wrinkled skin, thick veins ran from his knuckles to his wrists. Lena loved the way they popped up and disappeared again, and most of all she loved the mass of little dark-brown spots that covered the backs of his hands—they were her favourite. On one of his hands they made a pattern like a flock of birds flying all the way down his fingers, and when he took her to the museum with the paintings and pointed at the pictures, she was more interested in his moles than in what was on the walls. She liked to watch them run together or flow apart as his hand moved; they were so alive, so much more absorbing than the serious-faced people and pastel-coloured landscapes. The landscapes looked very far away, but Father's hands were close, and sometimes Lena reached out to touch them. At other times she was content to watch them swing next to her cheek like pendulums.

The museum with the pictures was, in any case, only ever an excuse to get out of the flat, have a walk, stare up at the sky, escape the smell of *kvass* fermenting in jars on the kitchen windowsill. A technical museum full of machines was a very different proposition. It wasn't an excuse; it was a proper treat. There might even, her father said, be an old aeroplane, but Lena couldn't listen a second longer; before he could finish his sentence she ran past him to the bathroom and yanked the door shut behind her.

When at last she was on the toilet, waggling her feet which tingled with relief, she began to imagine shiny screw threads and huge drills, milling machines and saws—things she'd never seen at home in Horlivka but which she knew from Sochi, where there were mountains of sawdust everywhere; all summer she ran in and out between them with Artyom and Lika. Both children had long black hair, but the sawdust made them look almost as fair as Lena. The three of them teetered on the sides of the mounds, shaking themselves like the stray dogs on the estate and squealing when the sawdust flew in their eyes. The woodchips heaped up at the roadside got into everything too: scalps, mouths, socks. In Sochi, Lena was allowed out with her friends on her own, at least on the estate where her grandmother lived—where the hazelnuts grew.

Before Lena went to bed, Grandmother would chase her round the house and try to shake the sawdust out of her. Lena would shriek with delight, pulling off her pants and whirling them round her head, and Grandma would catch her and lift her up in the air, grumbling about the pale-yellow dust on the floor and the wood shavings that Lena left all over the house, but hugging her close as she scolded.

Grandmother's hands were rough on Lena's bare skin, because everything in Sochi was rough from the heat—and from the hazelnuts. Lena's hands started to itch when she stripped the leaves from the ripe brown nuts, ready to throw into one of the huge sacks that were almost as big as her. The jaggedy-edged leaves that covered the nuts like funnels weren't easy to peel off, but she didn't mind the prickly feeling in her fingertips because she knew that when she was done Grandmother would take her down to the promenade, where gleaming white paths led to cafés with blue-checked parasols and people in fancy clothes. Lena could never work out what they were dressed up for; they drank lemonade and read the papers, occasionally adjusting their belts or straightening their sunhats, taking no notice of the other customers. Some smoked, some stared past the hotel roofs at the sky. Their sunglasses didn't come off until the evening, and sometimes you would see the frames glinting even in the light of the street lamps. These people seemed never to work, never to have to pick hazelnuts, never to be in a rush to get anywhere; they sat there straight and stiff, or made a show of strolling around dreamily.

Lena laughed at their strange slowness when she passed them on her way to the candyfloss stall or the merry-go-round—more often the candyfloss stall; she wasn't keen on those painted plastic animals on a turntable. She stretched out her arms for the thin sticks and held them while Grandmother rolled her own trousers halfway up her calves and Lena's all the way to her knees. Then they stuffed their sandals into Grandmother's bag, tramped barefoot down the steps to the sand and stood with their feet in the water. Lena lifted every toe in turn and felt the tingly sensation between them, and when the candyfloss was all gone they plunged their sticky fingers into the Black Sea.

Lena always spotted the first of those strangely slow holidaymakers on the train to Sochi, after Grandmother came to fetch her for the summer. The roar of the wheels on the tracks gave Lena pins and needles, so while Grandmother queued for bedlinen from the guard, Lena scrambled up and down between the berths, scuttling over the bare mattresses like an ant and peering out of the window to see if she could see any trees yet—or still only factory hulks, their smokestacks stuffed with crooked plumes that looked as if they'd frozen solid. Grandmother had promised Lena a bottle of sugared milk if she didn't make too much noise, but the vendor hadn't come down the aisle with his tray yet and Grandmother wasn't back yet either. Lena heard the chink of tea glasses in the next compartment and the sound of people laughing. She played with the tickets that her grandmother had tucked into the rack, ran her fingers over the luggage net like someone strumming a musical instrument, and stared out at the long strips of colour as they left Horlivka behind them.

Some of the passengers wore carefully pressed three-piece suits and flowing dresses, even on the train. Outside the compartment door, which Grandmother had left open, a woman in an eggshell-coloured suit was leaning out of the lowered window. Lena couldn't see her face but she could smell the clove scent of her cigarette and imagined wide frog lips to go with it and eyelashes like thorns. When Grandmother came back with a bundle of sheets and pillowcases, the woman turned to make room for her and her lips were like a prune in her face, dry and puckered and dark purple. She'd painted herself, which was something Lena's mother would never do, but then this woman was going on holiday and Lena's mother never did that either—certainly, Lena had never known her to. All she knew was that her mother sometimes put in weekends at the chemical plant. Maybe before she was plant manager she'd worn make-up like this woman. Actually, Lena wasn't really going on holiday either; she was going to Sochi to work, to help Grandmother shake the hazelnut trees. It made her proud.

Twice a week, grandmother and granddaughter waited at a bus stop on the other side of the hazelnut estate, a bus stop that was marked not only by a signpost but by a crowd of people—women with children and sacks full of things to sell. Hazelnuts mostly, Lena guessed, or some other produce from their small gardens; all the sacks looked heavy. Lena was five and stood not much higher than the leather wallets the women wore strapped to their belts, so it was her job to wriggle past their hips and grab a seat on the bus before anyone else got on—preferably a window seat, so that Grandmother could hand her their sack of hazelnuts through the open window. It wasn't easy, pulling it through the frame, but it hadn't ripped yet. The thought terrified Lena; if the sack did rip, all their work would be for nothing—the picking and gathering, the itchy fingers. The nuts would rain down on to the ground and the bus would drive off without them. There was never room for everyone anyway; judging by the number of passengers on the bus, half those waiting were left behind at the bus stop, and only fifteen people at most got to sit down. The others had to stand between the seats or wait for the next bus, and that meant getting to the market too late for a shady place to pitch their stalls. Their vegetables would wilt and their skin would be roasted.

The faces of the women at the bus stop looked battered by the sun even first thing in the morning. Strands of hair had come loose from their plaits; their thighs smelt of sour cream. Seen from below, the women seemed to grimace as they peered down the road into the dust. Lena always thought she saw the bus coming before any of the others did—how else explain that she was always first on the step when it finally pulled up in front of them? As soon as the sack of nuts had been safely stowed and her grandmother had sat down beside her, she would slide back and forth on her seat, looking forward to the evening when everyone would have screamed themselves hoarse, filled their leather wallets and emptied their sacks—when they would roll up their oilcloths, smooth their hair with their damp hands and tame it with a rubber band or a headscarf. By then the whole market was in shade and beginning to cool down; squashed fruit lay between the stalls and a few shrivelled potatoes rolled around in the dust. Grandmother would press a rouble into Lena's hand and pack up her things. Lena's very own earnings. A whole coin for every trip to market, a coin stamped with signs and a bearded male profile, a coin that Lena spent on treating Grandmother to dinner. Their tummies rumbling and the empty jute sack dangling, they would head straight from market to the town centre, always to the same canteen on the ground floor of one of those tall buildings that seemed to shoot up into the sky. Lena would put her coin on the counter and ask for a plate of *pelmeni*, which she would set down on the table in front of Grandmother. It came with cream, but instead of pouring the cream over the mountain of dumplings they drank it straight from the pot, cooling the hot meat in their mouths.

Sometimes the neighbours had a barbecue on the estate to celebrate a birthday or wedding, and the table of grilled and roast meat was so long that all the children from the estate could sit underneath. Grandmother explained to Lena that people here sang before they ate the animals because it made the food holy—the effect was especially powerful if you did it with your eyes closed and your head bowed. Lena didn't join in the singing, but she looked at the murmuring mouths on the momentarily serious, withdrawn faces and, feeling the desire to do something herself, she kissed the corner of the tablecloth. Her grandmother never took her to church, but she often made the sign of the cross—something that Lena had never seen her mother or anyone else in Horlivka do. Sometimes she tried to copy the motions, but she didn't know which direction to start off in and ended up doing an uncoordinated finger dance, which made Lika and Artyom laugh.

Once, when she went to the mountains with Lika's parents and Artyom's mother, she tried to pray properly before eating, putting her hands together and bowing her head. The grown-ups had spread out rugs by the river, uncorked bottles and anchored the legs of the barbecue in the sand. Lena peeped at her friends and moved her lips with them as they said thank you for the food. When the *shashlik* was all gone, they said thank you again.

Lika and Artyom were a little taller and faster than Lena; they ran up the hill into the woods and thrust sticks into her hands so that she could protect herself against the otters. You had to bash the grass in front of you, Lika said. And if they didn't come, Artyom said, you could lean on your stick and hike like a real Pioneer.

Whenever Lena spent the summer in Sochi she expected to have to fight off vicious, poisonous animals, to be pulled into dank underground caves by gnomes, like in the books that were read to her at home, or encounter real fauns—big ones with hairy, musty-smelling goats' legs; maybe with pan pipes, maybe without, but definitely ready to use those curly horns of theirs to skewer small children who had lost their way. She examined the grass carefully for hoofprints the size of grown-up feet and often had a stone handy, so that she could throw it between the faun's wide-set eyes if she had to. She'd never come across an animal in the wild, not even a fox, but she dared the woodland sprites to come out by standing at dark hedges for longer than necessary, holding her face close to the twigs to see if she could smell something more than leaves and grass. Maybe musty hair. Sometimes, very rarely, she saw fireflies flash over the scrub. She decided they must be the gleaming eyes of much taller beings, but, not daring to reach out and touch them, she only stared back warily.

Until she stepped into the museum lobby and saw the turbine of an aeroplane right there in front of her, all she could think of was Artyom and Lika, their black manes and whether they'd grown longer again and whether this might be the summer when she would learn to swim at last—maybe in the mountain river, which she liked even better than the city beach. She'd recently seen a film about a shiny green creature, half-man half-beast, with fins on its legs and a crest on its head—a creature with both lungs and gills. It lived in the bay of a warm country and sometimes came frighteningly close to the shore, destroying fishing nets and sinking boats. Lena preferred clear, shallow water. But when she saw her father's distorted reflection in the steel engine case it made her sneeze with excitement. She forgot all about Amphibian Man, all about Artyom and Lika. The engines filled the enormous halls of the museum. Lena's father strode ahead as if he were in a hurry, but she'd never seen such huge propellers before and was determined not to rush; she barely listened when he spoke to her. In each of the vast rooms she circled the displays several times, hiding when her father called her and refusing to hold his hand. She was so mesmerized by the generator in a scale model of part of a power station that even the prospect of ice cream couldn't lure her away. It was only when Father threatened to leave without her that Lena ran after him, and as soon as they were outside and the magic of the machines began to wear off, she felt suspicious of his offer of ice cream—it was a bad sign when Father promised sweet things before lunch. In fact, he'd been strange all morning, talking all the time, his hands damp with sweat. He only talked like that when something wasn't right; the words seemed to pour out of him.

On an ordinary day he could sit at the window for hours on end without speaking, staring out at the mottled white trees across the road, as if something were happening that he couldn't afford to miss. Now he talked and talked, wiping the spit from the corners of his mouth with the back of his hand, telling Lena something about shoes—that you didn't wear your outdoor shoes inside the school building, but brought another pair to change into, in a drawstring bag that dangled from your satchel. And that there'd be a uniform for her and she'd have a white pinafore to wear on special days, and a black one for the other days. That she'd be a Pioneer when she was bigger and then a Komsomolet, but not just yet—first she'd be a Little Octobrist. She'd have a red badge in the shape of a star and would be able to help out in the community, watering plants in the classrooms, for example, because that was what Little Octobrists were good at—working for the collective. He warned her that there were rules for the Little Octobrists, the most important being to work hard, love your school and respect your elders. There was a lot more too, she'd soon find out, it would all be great fun. She'd paint and sing and read and do sums with lots of other children—and so this summer would be a bit different, she wouldn't be going to Sochi. By now they were standing outside the kiosk holding their cones, and Lena had just sucked half a scoop of ice cream into her mouth. She went hot and cold; she forgot to swallow.

'You'll have to prepare for school over the summer. I'll help you,' said Father, coming to the end of his monologue.

'And Grandmother?' Lena whispered. 'Won't I ever see her again?' Her thoughts were all over the place. *Hazelnut-trees-Artyom-and-Lika's-hair-and-gappy-teeth-the-market-the-beach-the-candyfloss-the-silly-slow-people-on-the-promenade-in-Sochi.*

'Grandma will come to Horlivka,' Father promised. 'She'll come and stay with us. She's found someone to look after her garden so she can be with you. She's looking forward to it. We'll put up a camp bed for her in the sitting room, she'll cook lunch for you every day, you'll see much more of her now.'

'But the hazelnuts won't grow without Grandmother!' Lena waved her arms about; the ice cream fell on her sandals and seeped between her toes. There was so much else she wanted to shout: *But Artyom and Lika will learn to swim without me! They'll see the green creature with gills and lungs rise up from the waves! All we have in Horlivka are fat black cats that cross your path from right to left and bring bad luck!*

But all she managed to get out was, 'Where will I get the money to treat Grandmother to *pelmeni*?'

'*Pelmeni*?' Her father's eyebrows shot up as if he were hearing the word for the first time. 'Money? What money?'

It was no good talking to him. Could you even get *pelmeni* in Horlivka, or would she now be trapped forever in the stinky kitchen with the *kvass* on the windowsill, condemned to eating noodles with grated cheese? And what did he mean, Grandma would sleep on a camp bed? There wasn't an inch of space in the sitting room. When you pulled out the sofa bed that Lena slept on it reached all the way to the legs of the dining table, leaving only a narrow passage on the other side along the front of the glass-doored cabinet with the faun figurine and the Leningrad porcelain. Maybe Grandmother would sleep on the cupboard next to the cabinet? But that was where the fancy vases were kept, and some boxes or other that Lena sensed rather than saw. In Sochi Lena had a room of her own, and you could play hide-and-seek in the musty cupboards. Here in Horlivka the drawers burst like overripe fruit when you so much as stretched out your fingers towards the handles, and there were suitcases in the bottom of her parents' wardrobe that she wasn't allowed to touch. Grandmother would have to sleep on top of Lena, squashing her with her wiry body; she would sit and doze in the kitchen with her head resting on the table; she would cower in the hall on the old chest hung with dusty rugs. Sensing that the whole business of school was more serious than she had realized, Lena decided not to cry. If her father had made up his mind to ruin her summer and the rest of her life, it was best to be on her guard. She was surrounded by traitors.

Father took a handkerchief from his jacket pocket, wiped the sticky mess from between her toes and asked if she'd like another ice cream, but Lena felt numb and also insulted that he was pretending everything was the same as ever. Why was the world still turning? Why were all these people walking past with their usual cheerful faces? Didn't they realize that nothing would ever be the same again? Didn't they realize how bad things were going to be?

In all the photos taken at the first-day-of-school ceremony Lena looked grim. Hundreds of girls and boys stood hand in hand in rows on the school steps, smiling at their parents, careful not to let go of each other's hands and wave. Their palms were cold and slippery, and Lena tried not to look left or right. Her white pinafore had been tied too tightly round her bum and hips, but she hadn't complained. She screwed up her eyes and concentrated on the slight itch where the ties chafed her flesh. Her hair was so short that she could no longer braid it into proper plaits—Grandma and Mother had argued over whether or not to cut it and, as so often, Grandma had won. Since coming to live with them, Grandmother had spent a lot of time sitting on the camp bed they'd bought for her, scratching the backs of her hands with her bitten fingernails till the skin was raw and then running the sore spots over her face like a cat washing itself. It was a habit Lena had never observed in her in Sochi.

Lena hadn't known her grandfather, and the few times she'd asked about him she'd got nothing out of the grown-ups; they'd only changed the subject or said things that made no sense. There had always been Grandmother without Grandfather—that was normal—but now, moving around the cramped flat in Horlivka, Grandmother seemed somehow incomplete. As if she were missing something, or someone. As if she were looking for something she'd had in her hands just a moment before. Another change was that there was no pleasing her any more. She was forever complaining that it was too stuffy in the flat, but if you opened the window it was too loud. She told Lena not to galumph around and disturb the neighbours, but if Lena crept past her on tiptoes she was told to 'walk like a normal person'. Every evening Grandmother stood at the stove, holding angry conversations with herself under her breath and running the wooden spoon round and round the edge of the saucepan. The pervasive smell of food and the angry whispers made the flat seem even smaller; the ceiling felt suddenly lower, and Lena would wake in the night and—secretly, so that no one would notice—she would peer at it to see if it had come closer in the dark. It was because of the smells and the anger, Lena decided, that her mother didn't come home from work until everyone was in bed. But even then there were fights.

Often all it took was a dry *You're back early*, or an *Oh, so you live here too?* Lena couldn't make out what the arguments were about—all she knew was that the voices started off soft and husky, then grew suddenly louder, as if a door had been flung open on a singing choir. It seemed to her further proof that school brought no good. She hadn't taken part in the fierce debate about her haircut; no one had consulted her. Mother and Grandmother had bickered over her head about what was best for *the child* while thick clumps of hair fell on to her slippers. The newspaper spread out under her chair was crumpled and yellow; it covered the whole of the kitchen floor, making it look like a lightly toasted crust of bread that would tickle your feet if you walked over it barefoot.

Before setting off for school they had pressed a bunch of flowers into Lena's hand, pulled her white socks up to her knees and told her to smile at the camera. She remained impassive, obediently took Grandmother's hand when Father had put the camera away again, and climbed without a word on to the bus that she would now be catching every day.

Tap-tap-tap-tap, her wide-mouthed shoes said as she approached the school building. Lena counted her steps, trying to slow down. She glanced up only once, as they passed the man with a goatee. The man's name, she knew, was Lenin, Vladimir Ilyich Lenin, a name you spoke with pride, breathed in awe. Lena tried to do just that in her very first lesson, when she was asked who the school was named after. She rose, positioned herself at the side of her desk and tried to breathe the name *Vladimir Ilyich Lenin* with the requisite pride and awe. The other children giggled. Then there was silence. The teacher asked again—this time a blond girl in the front row, who jumped up like a mattress spring, positioned herself, like Lena, at the side of her desk and solemnly declared, 'Yuri Gagarin!'. Then she turned her crescent-moon profile to the class, so that everyone could see at least half of her smug smile. The teacher nodded and asked both girls to sit down. Lena felt numb with shame and decided that in the next ten years she was to spend at this school she would never ever open her mouth again.

There was no avoiding the Little Octobrists' song; it was a fixture of the primary-school repertoire:

Little Octobrists near and far,
Active boys and girls we are!
Little Octobrist, listen here,
Soon you'll be a Pioneer!

But however often Lena sang it, *Pioneer* remained for her the name of the camera that her parents kept on top of the cupboard and had so far taken down only once, on her first day of school. It wasn't until the beginning of Year Three that Lena fully grasped the significance of becoming a Pioneer, when her mother announced that she would now be spending every summer at a camp, running around outside and learning to be part of a community, a collective. While she was away, Grandmother would return to Sochi to pick the hazelnuts and make sure everything was in order—she'd be back in time for the autumn term. The neighbour who was looking after her garden and living off the hazelnut crop was moving to the next village to live with her children. She had back trouble and all manner of aches and pains, and Grandmother needed to find someone to replace her. Besides, she missed her house and the garden.

Lena's mother sighed. 'If it was up to Mum, she'd stay there. She hates it here, hates living with me, hates our flat. We must be grateful that it doesn't stop her scrubbing the floors and keeping us in chicken soup. I hope you'll thank her when you're a big girl—she'll listen to you. *My* words go in one ear and out the other. She grumbles that she wants to go to church in Sochi again. I tell her she can go to church here. Then she sits down in the corner and sulks, as if she's been hard done by.'

Two black manes danced in front of Lena's eyes, shaking themselves like dogs. Mouths with gappy milk teeth appeared before her; thin arms, bronzed by the sun and the dust, flew through the air. Artyom and Lika rolled around in the sawdust while she stood next to them looking on—much older, ridiculously tall, wretchedly clean. She dug her fingernails into the palms of her hands and asked as calmly as she could why she couldn't go to Sochi with Grandmother, but her mother flew off the handle before she'd even finished speaking. 'You've no idea what it cost me to get you into that camp! It's usually only Party cadres' children who get a place at the Eaglet!'

No wonder, then, that she hated the ceremony where she was presented with her Pioneer's neckerchief. When the class was asked who had excelled in their duties and lessons and should be the first to receive the neckerchief, she pretended not to hear her name and didn't go to the front until the boy next to her, Vassili, gave her a push. Vassili was one of the last to be honoured; he stared vacuously and tried to smile, and Lena smiled back because he looked so funny with the red at his neck and the red of his hair—almost pretty.

When the school committee divided the Pioneers into work groups, she was pleased that she and Vassili were put in joint charge of waste-paper collection. She didn't like the smell that came from his shirt collar or the dandruff on his shoulders, but they'd been together since starting school and she was used to him. She'd often helped him with his homework, and once, when he'd come out of the school committee's office with a hanging head and yellow goo in his eyes, she had put her hand on his. He'd been reprimanded for poor marks. 'Lenin,' they had said, 'urged us to different conduct!'

Collecting waste paper was a serious business; their teacher kept an eagle eye on the amounts they turned in. Lena's father had smiled when she mimicked his fierce-faced colleague: the way she straightened her glasses, pursed her lips, stuck out her chin and instructed the Pioneers to be conscientious—the state, she had said, needed recyclable material. Lena hadn't quite understood his response: 'Every schoolchild in the Soviet Union owes the state fifteen kilos of waste paper a year and at least two schoolmates who haven't made the grade!' He laughed at his own words, as if something had stuck in his throat, and Lena's mother joined in. Only Grandmother shook her head and turned back to the steaming pan on the stove.

Joke or no, Lena and Vassili did the rounds of the entranceways, snapping up every scrap of paper they could find, ringing at people's doors for old newspapers and magazines, assuring them that their donations would help save the forests of the beloved homeland. The two children spurred each other on, tried to outdo each other.

It gave Lena a great deal more pleasure than the monthly shop with her father, for which he would wake her early in the morning, even earlier than on a school day. If it was cold they wore several jumpers on top of each other and a headscarf was tied around Lena's woolly hat, so that Grandmother's voice faded to a distant hum. Her father moved awkwardly in the dark streets. It seemed to Lena she could feel the crunch of snow all the way to her jaws, and the cold got into her felt boots in spite of her rubber galoshes. She walked close behind her father so as not to lose sight of him in the dark. The orange cones of the street lamps cast only small circles on the asphalt; they gave off little light and no warmth. Lena and her father tramped through them, their eyes on the ground to keep from slipping. Father rammed his feet into the snow as if he had thorns on his soles; this slowed him down and Lena kept walking into him.

Eventually, the sour smell of sweat and fresh meat made her look up. Her father got into one of the queues outside the grocer's shop and she joined the other. He gave her a wink; after that they pretended not to know each other. Sometimes they both got the ration of pork belly or knuckle they were entitled to; sometimes only Lena did. If neither of them had any luck and the shop woman folded her arms in front of the thronging crowd and let the empty fridges speak for themselves, they would take a packed bus to another shop where her father would enter into a whispered exchange with the shopkeeper—a woman who kneaded her big hands under her yellow floral apron, making a sound like sifting sand. Afterwards, Lena and her father would carry home the meat, salami and butter, and as soon as Lena had taken off her galoshes and felt boots she would fling herself on to the bed, exhausted by the cold and the strain. She dreamt of the warmer months to come—it didn't have to be Sochi, just as long as things got better again; even if her toes thawed it would be something. Maybe it wouldn't be the end of the world if she went to the Pioneer camp in June—at least she wouldn't have to queue for food any more. There would be meals served three times a day and it would be summer at last—warm enough to go in the water.

Lena decided to look forward to it, but when June came she got cramps in her belly.

'There are six beds in the compartment—you're in number thirty-seven. The seats are numbered clockwise. Can you show me which way the hands of the clock go?'

Lena drew a semicircle in the air with her fingers, then moved her hands back to her tense, swollen belly. It had been making gurgling noises ever since Grandmother had started folding and packing Lena's shirts and shorts the day before, reminding her over and over that she mustn't forget to change her socks every day. Lena had smelt her buttery breath and pondered the fact that no one she knew would be there. Not on the way there and not at the holiday camp either. The camp was hours from home; the Pioneers had to take an overnight train and then catch a bus into the forest—the Pioneer leaders would make sure they got on and off at the right stations. For six whole weeks Lena wouldn't be able to call out to anyone she knew. Her father, as usual, had nothing to say to this. Sometimes he sat on the stool and sometimes on the chair next to the stool, and the rest of the time he wandered aimlessly around the flat. Lena raised her head every time he brushed past her, but he paid no attention either to her or to the half-packed suitcase on the floor, an open mouth silently screaming, *AAAAAGHHHH!*

He and her mother did, however, see her on to the train the next day—though they spent most of the time in tense silence. The Pioneer leaders interspersed their guttural orders with whistle blasts as they directed the hordes of children to their carriages and compartments. 'Luggage under the seats! If you're on a top bunk use the overhead shelves, please! No pushing! No jostling! I said *be careful!* Hands off the windows!' The sleeping cars stretched endlessly along the tracks like a string of sausages. Lena stared at the ground until she was hoisted over the steps into the carriage, and once on the train she didn't go to the window to wave goodbye to her parents on the platform. The carriage reeked of old galoshes and the compartment was nothing like the berths where she and her grandmother had slept on the way to Sochi. No chance of sugared milk here, and no one to lay a hand on her ear to comfort her, no one to hug her tight. Her belly yowled and cramped.

The other five beds were not yet occupied and Lena hoped desperately that it would stay that way. Maybe she could go to sleep and not wake until the six weeks were past. She'd get off the train, walk home, hide under her grandmother's housedress and it would all be over. But the compartment was filling quickly; five pert little bums pushed past her face, and five children chattered away as if they'd known each other forever. Lena's head began to buzz, and by the time they changed on to the waiting buses the next day the buzz had become a rattle. She didn't want to make friends, didn't speak to anyone for the entire journey and was glad when the buses spat out their chewed-up freight at the foot of a hill.

The group leader chivvied the Pioneers up the hill, luggage and all, lined them up in rows and began her speech. Only those with top marks and distinction, she said, had the honour of spending precious summer weeks here at the Eaglet. This rather contradicted Lena's mother's claim that it was her good connections and not Lena's success at school that had got her into this elite camp, but it did explain why Vassili wasn't here. Lena stared through the rings of the blue metal gateway that led to the buildings and campground; it looked like a forgotten construction that should have been taken down years ago—a climbing frame, perhaps, left over from an obsolete playground. The woods came right to the edge of the camp. You couldn't see whether the fence ran all the way round the site; its warped mesh vanished into the dappled green of trees and juniper bushes. Lena fancied that somewhere in the distance she could hear the splash of a lake—maybe this summer she would learn to swim at last. Maybe shiny-scaled amphibian men with raised crests would come out of the lake and pull the children into the water.

Heroes Avenue, a narrow cement path leading from the archway to the holiday camp, was lined with the busts of young men. Most had short-cropped hair and some had peaked caps; only a few wore Pioneers' neckerchiefs of stone. They were set on concrete pedestals as tall as the children, who had to crane their necks to see them. The group leader patted her bun, straightened her mustard-coloured dress, which looked like trampled leaves after the long journey, and pointed out one or other of the statues—did anyone know what this young person was called—or this one? Dozens of pairs of eyes turned and stared. The main attraction was a boy with a high forehead and a square hairline far back on his head. He wore a boat-like forage cap perched at an angle and looked very, very serious—almost angry. His neckerchief was knotted tightly over the top button of his shirt, and if the statue had been more than a bust Lena was sure he'd be wearing a leather jacket. She'd seen this wide-eyed, straight-browed face somewhere before, but she couldn't think where and made no effort to remember his name. The group leader had, in any case, no patience with children who shouted out answers, and took it upon herself to explain that Pavel Morozov was a Pioneer hero who had defied the kulaks and paid for it with his life.

'Who knows what kulaks are?'

'Enemies!'

'That's right. But why?'

'Because they betrayed us.'

'Yes, and how did they betray us?'

Lena knew that the kulaks had been landowning peasants and she knew that ownership was forbidden, but this was the first she'd heard of children reporting their own parents to the kolkhozes for hoarding corn or livestock. Pavlik Morozov, it seemed, had done just that: he'd reported his father to the village chief for hoarding stocks of grain, and for this his grandfather had stabbed him to death along with his little brother when they were in the woods, picking berries. While the other Pioneers raced on down the avenue, Lena lingered a moment longer at Pavlik's cut-off bust. She stared into his lidless eyes and sneezed.

That night, Pavlik's high forehead hovered over the end of Lena's mattress and sneezed whenever she glanced up at him, a strange, open-eyed sneeze—*hachoo*. Lena got the hiccups she was so scared; her belly started to gurgle and cramp again. She could hear the girls in the next beds talking in low voices and tried to make out what they were saying, hoping that their murmuring would soothe her and make her forget that knife flashing in the cranberry bushes. But they didn't seem able to get Pavlik out of their heads either. They whispered that as well as being stabbed to death, he and his brother had been chopped up with big knives and eaten, because that was what the kulaks did—they killed their children and gobbled them up. They had an insatiable hunger and refused to share with the community, and so trucks had come and taken them away, and when their children were put into homes they turned out to be every bit as greedy as their parents, tearing the flesh from each other's bones and eating it, leaving their little brothers and sisters out in the snow to freeze to death, and then boiling up the corpses. Pavlik Morozov had been a rare exception.

Lena stayed awake all night, watching the bodies of the other Pioneers rise and fall under their blankets; in the dark dormitory it looked as if someone had dumped grey earth over their curled-up forms. The big white bedsteads had legs on castors and saggy-bellied mattresses as soft as bread. They stood far apart from one another, each shadow distinct. Some girls snuffled in their sleep; the girl next to Lena chirped like a cricket all night long.

Lena ran her hands over her upper arms to calm herself, up and down, up and down, as if trying to smooth her gooseflesh. When the reveille sounded she leapt out of bed. She was the first in the washroom and the first out on the parade ground, where she stood at a neatly swept fire pit and waited until the others joined her and the bugle at her ear blasted every last thought from her mind. The

Pioneer who had blown such a fierce reveille wore a loose-fitting shirt tucked clumsily into his shorts; Lena thought he looked like a half-inflated balloon letting out little puffs of air. Behind him, a huge board headed DAILY ROUTINE read:

1. *Get up 8 a.m.*
2. *Gymnastics 8–8.15 a.m.*
3. *Tidy dorms and lavatories 8.15–8.45 a.m.*
4. *Roll call and hoisting of flag 8.45–9 a.m.*
5. *Breakfast 9–9.30 a.m.*
6. *Free time 9.30–9.45 a.m.*
7. *Clean campsite 9.45–10 a.m.*

The next items were obscured by the bright red flag with gold fringe that hung from the bugle, but at number 10 the list resumed and Lena could read: *Free time*, and then, *11. Lunch*, *12. Afternoon nap*, *13. Tea*, *14. Group classes*, *15. Free time*, *16. Supper*, *17. Communal activities*, *18. Evening roll call and lowering of flag*, *19. Evening toilet*, *20. Bed.*

The camp had been cut out of the forest and was crossed with cement paths that splayed out from the parade ground like fat fingers. Some poked their fingertips into low-slung wooden shacks with lean-tos; others led on to the vegetable patches and fields beyond; one pointed further still at a plastic-covered greenhouse quivering in the heat. Lena followed the paths, reading the signs on the buildings in letters as big as her body: GIRLS, BOYS, LIBRARY. Between the long dais where the welcome speeches had been held and the sports field with its running track, football pitch and parallel bars a banner was strung up with the slogan WE ARE IN FAIRYLAND. Over the parade ground a billboard proclaimed, CHILDREN—THE CAMP BELONGS TO YOU! and beside it another sign warned against leaving the grounds. In the canteen, which was fully glazed on two sides, enormous letters had been stuck to the glass all along the windows on the left: W H E N I E A T I A M D E A F A N D D U M B.

Mealtime seating was by numbered teams; folded paper signs at the head of each long table ensured that no one sat with anyone who was older or younger than them. Lena saw the girls in her group kicking each other's knees and shins under the table and pulling each other's hair as soon as the patrolling Pioneer leaders moved away. The girl across the table from Lena scraped her brass dish with her spoon and stared into Lena's eyes—it felt like a warning. Lena imagined that she was invisible and thought of the seaside. If there were a lake here or even a river, none of this would be so bad.

NO UNSUPERVISED ENTRY, Lena read on a sign on the open door of the greenhouse, and crept a little closer. She'd followed a group of older children with swing bins to see where they were taking them—and anyway, ever since arriving at camp she'd been wanting to peep inside this structure of shimmering plastic stretched over wood, from which a strong smell of ripe tomatoes leaked out on to the grounds. Thick, humid air, soft as a cushion, hung at the open door. Lena dipped first her arms, then her face into the sultry heat before venturing in. Her head felt heavy inside, as if the damp air had seeped into her.

Giant tomato shoots grew into the aisles between the beds, thrusting their long, downy necks at her like animals she'd only seen in books. A few Pioneers were busy tying stems and branches to stakes. No one took any notice of Lena. The heat tickled her armpits, and beads of sweat ran down her temples under her short bob. She ventured a little further, inspecting the clusters of flowers, the fluted unripe fruits, the bulging red ones. One particularly lush plant had black branches, like the hairy legs of a giant spider probing the air. Lena stopped and leant into it; the stems grew up and up, and beneath the leaves a white forehead appeared, then thick arched eyebrows, broad nostrils and a very red mouth, as red as the Pioneer's kerchief that hung lopsidedly around the neck below. The person to whom the face belonged straightened herself and stared at Lena, like a plant coming to life. Her eyebrows were as dense and black as her hair—broad felt-tip lines on white porcelain. Her lips glistened, her cheeks glowed feverishly; she gazed at Lena with huge, yellow-gold eyes. Lena wanted to hold out a hand and ask her name, or say something that wouldn't sound childish or awkward, but her throat was burning, as if she'd swallowed something bitter, making her gulp and sneeze at once; she held her breath to avoid getting hiccups too, gasped with excitement, turned in a panic and stumbled outside.

She didn't see the porcelain-faced girl again until that evening in the dormitory—a lopsided silhouette, weaving her way between the beds with a marked limp, as if her body were full of sloshing water. Lena wondered why she hadn't spotted her before; she was very tall and very thin, and none of the other girls had such bushy hair or smelt of sea buckthorn, almost like certain days in Sochi. Lena could smell her from her bed. She reminded her a little of Lika, but Lika was a long time ago.

The girl made her way to the other end of the dorm and lowered herself on to her sagging mattress. Lena ambled over with feigned nonchalance, inspecting the pleats in the yellowing net curtains, examining the walls for cracks and patterns. When she turned cautiously to glance at the girl, she was looking at her intently.

'Alyona,' the girl said, as if she were calling Lena. Lena nodded and murmured her own name. Alyona beckoned to her.

‘What happened there?’ Lena asked, pointing at Alyona’s feet. One of them was strangely twisted.

‘Bad break, botched mend.’ From above, Alyona’s mouth looked like an upside-down crescent moon, the tips almost touching. Lena sat down beside her and studied her round, dimpled kneecaps, her calves.

‘Does it hurt?’

‘No. Want to touch?’

Lena felt the evening’s porridge rise in her throat. She shook her head. ‘Why would I want to do that?’

‘Everyone wants to touch my foot or pull my twisted toes. It doesn’t hurt, it’s just not quite right. Someone ran over it with a car and it healed crooked. But I can walk on it and run and dance—actually, I can do everything.’

Lena wanted to ask who in the world would run over a person’s foot, but she didn’t dare. She took a slow breath to suck the smell of sea buckthorn deeper into her lungs. Up close it was mingled with something sweet—perhaps raspberry. Alyona’s hair refused to be tamed by an elastic band; it leapt out in all directions, almost touching Lena’s earlobes, and again Lena saw quivering spiders’ legs reaching out to her. She wanted to ask Alyona why her grandmother didn’t give it a proper cut, but her mouth was strangely numb, like in the greenhouse, and for a while they sat without speaking. Then, by way of goodnight, Alyona asked if the team leader had assigned Lena a job yet, because if not she could do cleaning duty with her—scrubbing floors, dusting, sweeping the common rooms. Lena nodded, because she didn’t know how else to respond. Maybe, she thought, Alyona was a big shadow that would cover her up and make her invisible, so that everyone would leave her in peace. Maybe she could stay close to her—the thought reassured and excited her at once.

'Why haven't I seen you before? Where have you been all this time?' she asked as she turned to go.

'I had a temperature.' Alyona fixed oniony yellow-gold eyes on Lena. Her face was almost glassy in the half-dark. 'I threw up when I arrived, so they put me in the quarantine room. I'm all right now.'

Lena knew nothing of a quarantine room; all she'd come across were the plump, becapped women in lace-up ankle boots and white overalls who thrust a thermometer under the arm of every new arrival and tugged at their eyelids with cold fingers.

'But you're better now?'

'I get it a lot.'

'The throwing-up thing?'

'I'm always getting something, but I don't think about myself when it happens—I think about something else. Daddy says it goes away faster if you ignore it.'

Lena cocked her head to one side and tried to imagine sick gushing out of Alyona's chalky face. She decided that if she were there the next time it happened, she would put her hand on Alyona's forehead and hold her head. She'd never seen anyone vomit, but she imagined you had to hold them very tight.

The soapy water made her fingers itch; the dormitory floors seemed to go on and on. No one at home had taught Lena how to wring out a cloth, but she watched Alyona's mechanical movements as she bobbed and dipped along the floor like a cat arching and stretching. You gripped the cloth at both ends, twisted one wrist towards your chest and the other away from you—not both in the same direction—then shook it out and dropped it. Lena lunged forward over the floor with the cloth and dragged it back to her belly, breathing slowly through her nose and concentrating on the sequence of sounds and movements. Afterwards they lay side by side on the drying floorboards, waiting for the bugle blast to drive them on through the day. Lena's hands smarted, but it didn't stop her from sticking her fingers into Alyona's curls and swinging them gently to and fro.

The girls on kitchen duty came back to the dorm pushing and shoving each other, their arms covered in bruises and scratches. Lena was glad she hadn't been assigned to such a big group but could crawl across the floor next to Alyona, who was happy to work in silence and sometimes only rocked her head back and forth when Lena said something or asked a question. Despite the packed timetable on the parade-ground board, where they gathered for roll call twice daily, there were aeons of time at camp; it smothered them like the thick air in the greenhouse, with not a breath of wind to stir it. Even the chickens in the yard seemed to feel it; they were in no hurry to get anywhere and pecked impassively at the breadcrumbs the Pioneers threw them, unfazed when the younger kids tried to grab hold of their feathers. The cock didn't crow, or if he did his screech was drowned out by the bugle call which, only a few days into their stay, had lost its power to startle and now sounded soothing and wistful.

'What are you going to be when you're big?'

They were lying in the grass behind the dorms, the muggy heat weighing on them. Long green dandelion tongues tickled the soles of their feet and the soft skin under their arms; stinging nettles nodded overhead. They had raced off for the tall bushes together, Alyona hobbling and panting, so that Lena had to keep waiting for her. Then they'd slowed down and pretended to run their hands over the jagged, hairy leaves until they'd burst out laughing, flopped on to their backs in the grass and wild flowers, and rolled back and forth in a tangle of limbs, holding each other by the hips, crashing down an imaginary slope, screaming.

'I'm not going to *be* anything. Why would I want to *be* something?' Alyona sounded as if she were chewing on bitter stems.

Lena never knew when Alyona was joking and when she was in earnest. They had let go of each other; only their feet were touching.

'I'm plenty big enough anyway, look at me. I don't need to get any bigger.'

Lena rolled on to her belly and dragged herself over to Alyona on her elbows. All the children in her class knew what they were going to be, or ought to want to be—Lena had known for some time that she would study medicine. She'd never met anyone who didn't have plans.

'And what do your parents say when you tell them you're going to be nothing?'

'They're all right with it.' Alyona tried to turn her face to the grass and nuzzle the earth, but Lena pushed her face up close to Alyona's and nudged her with her nose like a dog.

'Are your parents as funny as you?'

'My father's a colonel.'

'And your mother? Doesn't she have a job?'

'Yes, but she's ill a lot; she's always away on rest cures. She spends more time on rest cures than at work.'

'And they say nothing when you say you want to be nothing?'

'No.'

'Nothing to nothing?'

There was no answer.

'Hey, what's wrong?'

'I itch all over.'

'But we didn't touch the nettles.'

'No, but you've got scabies and now I have too!' Alyona threw herself at Lena and started pinching her sides. Lena sneezed with surprise and prepared to retaliate.

That night Lena dreamt of a man at the wheel of a big vehicle she couldn't see properly because she was dazzled by the approaching headlamps. The car was hurtling along an asphalt track between fields, clattering over potholes. She and Alyona were standing in the middle of the road; the headlamps shone right through them, and Lena knew that the man at the wheel must be Alyona's father. His face was rigid, his mouth wide open and he had the same oniony-yellow eyes as Alyona. Alyona took a step towards the car, one of her clumsy, sloshing steps—then another, and another. Lena was woken by her own screams. The girl in the next bed—the one who chirped like a cricket—hissed at her to shut up. All that moaning and groaning every night—couldn't she spare them her nightmares?

But they weren't nightmares; most of her dreams were quite pleasant. It was just that, whatever else happened in them, she could never reach Alyona.

A large piece of woodland had been cleared to make the camp, but to get to the lake you had to wind your way in and out of trees, dodging wayward branches. Lena allowed herself to reach for Alyona's hand, so as not to be held up by the slippery roots and stones on the path—strangely, Alyona was at the front of the swimming group, leading the way; the bumps in the path seemed to offset her lurching gait and she strode ahead as if she couldn't wait to get in the water. But when they came to the shore and the other children charged into the lake, Alyona sat down on the grass and gazed upwards. Lena followed her gaze and saw a flock of birds sweeping over a sky so pale and sallow it reminded her of her father's hands. Then she turned to look at the other Pioneers, who were squealing with delight, jostling and splashing each other in a cordoned-off bit of lake edged with thick jute rope. The group leader blew her whistle and ordered them back out—no one should even think of going in the water until all uniforms were neatly folded and all shoes lined up in a row.

Lena rolled her socks slowly down her calves and put them on top of the shorts she had already taken off. She took her time over everything, shaking her shirt out at arm's length before folding it and adding it to the pile. Alyona was still in her shirt and shorts, lying on the grass with her arms tucked under her head. Her thick eyelashes flickered; she seemed to be staring into space and didn't reply when Lena asked if she wasn't coming in. Lena was tempted to tell her she couldn't swim, she needed help, she'd been looking forward to learning. But Alyona wasn't paying any attention to her. Although her eyes were wide open her gaze was turned inwards, as if there were a milky film over her pupils.

Lena looked at the lake. The cordoned-off area was so full that she hoped to avoid drowning for the simple reason that there wasn't room for it. She was aware of every blade of grass that she flattened underfoot on her way to the earthy shore. It seemed to her that she could hear her muscles move. Some of the older children had got beyond the rope and were chasing each other through the water, their arms thrashing—they were ordered back with long, hoarse blasts on the whistle. Someone shrieked with laughter, someone else howled like a dog; the children ducked each other and surfaced, gasping for air. Lena ventured in up to her knees and looked about her at the other Pioneers slapping the water with their arms. Spray splashed her shoulders. She ignored the taunts and braced her body to stop herself from walking straight back out and burying her face in Alyona's belly.

It looked as if everyone could swim but her—when she'd spent every summer in Sochi. She stretched out in the shallow water; stones jutted up from the mud into her knees. Then she ventured a little further, pulling herself along on her hands, but turned round when a wave splashed into her eyes and ears. She decided she'd had enough for one day and stumbled back across the grass, her arms wrapped around her shoulders; for the first time in her life she was aware of possessing a body that others looked at. She could feel them peering at her, whispering and giggling—maybe talking about her bent back or her crooked arms. She'd never had thoughts like that before; her mother had always taught her to disdain appearances. 'Only the stupid and the bourgeois care about such things,' she would say—and so Lena stopped herself from wondering if her legs were too short and settled down next to Alyona, struggling to untangle her knotted fingers. The sky sighed like an irritated lung—perhaps there was a plane, but Lena couldn't see one.

Alyona held an insect gripped between finger and thumb; she kept bringing it up to her face, as if the tip of her nose were a magnet attracting the spindly black legs and then repelling them again. The insect had a long body that wriggled like a worm, but it was fatter than a worm and shimmered green like the surface of a lake; its smooth, round eyes were too big for its head and stuck out on either side. It had long, oval, see-through wings, but Lena didn't see them until her face was right up close to Alyona's fingers.

'It won't make it much longer,' Alyona said. 'I found it in the grass—it's broken something.' She put the dragonfly on her thigh and stared at it. Lena noticed how tanned Alyona's legs were. Her face was still as white as porcelain, but the swathe of skin between the hem of her shorts and the tops of her long socks gleamed brown in the sun; her round knees, in particular, were the colour of hazelnut shells—and the place just above her knee, from which the dragonfly was making desperate efforts to launch itself.

Lena wasn't sure whether to be happy or sad when the six weeks were over and she was on the bus back to the railway station, her forehead pressed against the window. In the first days of camp she'd had plans to throw herself at her mother's feet when she got home, begging her in tears never to send her back to that terrible place with its Heroes Avenue and its filthy, splintery floorboards. But when she came to say goodbye to Alyona, she felt an ache behind her eyes and clung to her until Alyona pulled away and took a step back, smoothing her hair behind her ears. Alyona looked particularly lopsided when she was standing still. She didn't smile, but for once her cheeks were peachy pink and she smelt of salt; her neck was sweaty. She turned without a word and got on the other bus.

Lena spent the whole of the long journey back wondering which tack to take when her parents picked her up, but when she got off the train at Horlivka they weren't there—instead she spotted Grandmother in the crush on the platform. She was even thinner than before and even more taciturn. Lena decided to put off sounding unequivocally enthusiastic or despondent until they were home, but she forgot everything, even Alyona's sea-buckthorn smell and spider-leg hair, when she found her mother lying on the sofa in the sitting room in the middle of the day, a piece of wood clamped between her teeth. The curtains were drawn and Grandmother hadn't warned her, so at first Lena thought the room was empty—then she saw Mother, lying there quite still. Only the gentle rise and fall of the blanket under her chin told Lena that she was breathing. The piece of wood between her pale lips was almost the same colour as her face; it looked like an extension of her mouth, as if something were growing out of it.

Lena gave a scream and threw herself at the sofa. Grandmother hissed at her not to shriek like that—her mother had a bad headache and needed quiet. Lena had never heard of anyone in the family having a headache, or indeed any kind of ache; she'd always regarded her mother as a woman hewn in stone—a woman who never had anything wrong with her because she was all of a piece, not made up of parts that could be damaged or broken. Now she was screwing up her eyes so tight that the lashes almost vanished into the wrinkles. But she took the wooden spoon from her mouth and put her hand on Lena's face. The corners of her mouth turned up; she heaved herself into a sitting position, then sank straight back down again as if her bones were cotton wool. Lena reached for her arm, but didn't squeeze it; she slid on to the floor next to the sofa and sat there in silence until Rita had fallen asleep. Grandmother had disappeared into the kitchen, but no sound came from there. The wooden spoon was still lying next to the pillow, which reassured Lena. She picked it up and examined it for bite marks.

Sitting on the floor with the back of her head against the sofa, she switched between staring at the spoon and gazing aimlessly about the room. She could see the outline of the faun figurine in the cabinet. He was blowing into his pipes, peering at Lena and her mother through the dim light, hairy torso twisted, legs akimbo.

Go on, Lena thought, tensing her jaw so hard that her upper lip slid down over her lower lip. *Just you try!* The faun remained still and silent, but he took a long, deep breath—Lena saw his ribcage swell.

That evening, Lena overheard her father on the phone to his sister, asking for medicine. Lena's aunt lived in the capital, she knew that—and she knew, too, that she had an important job.

'Really, as expensive as that?' Lena heard her father say, and then, 'Oh no, probably just a migraine. But the pain's hideous and all we can get here are ampoules of water. You know how it is.'

Lena didn't know how it was and she knew nothing about migraines, but she asked around in school when the holidays were over. Someone said it was only a headache—her mother shouldn't make such a fuss—and someone else said you died of it because your eyes popped out of their sockets from all the pressure that built up in your head.

The next time the curtains were drawn in the sitting room in the middle of the day and Lena was told to be quiet, she tiptoed past her mother, glanced at her still face—no wooden spoon this time, only chapped, flaky lips—took the faun out of the glass-fronted cabinet and hid it behind the sacks of potatoes on the balcony. It was only early October and still mild, but she hoped the woodland god would have frozen to death by the end of the year.

Soon Lena was coming home from school to find Rita bent over piles of paper at the table by the window. She didn't always have her head in her hand, but the light creeping through the net curtains made her look yellow, and Lena pushed her chair as close to her mother's as it would go and said she couldn't do her homework unless she was right next to her like that, elbow to elbow.

When the first snow fell, an ambulance had to be sent for. Father and Grandmother called it one morning after a sleepless night, and it came in the evening; all that day, Lena sat outside the closed bedroom door, holding her breath as she listened to her mother's groans. As soon as the paramedics had carried her out on a stretcher Lena ran to the balcony, pushed aside the sacks of potatoes, grabbed the icy faun and dashed it against the corrugated-tin cladding. There was a sound like a shot as the ornament shattered, and it took Lena forever to gather up the pieces, crawling around on her hands and knees, crying for fear she'd missed even one little shard in the dark—because then the god might live on unscathed, concealed in the bristly, slush-covered runner. When at last she went into the kitchen to throw the pieces away, her nose red and her eyes stinging with cold, there was no one there to tell her off. A pan stood on the stove, but no smell came from it. Grandma had stopped cooking with herbs, so that although the flat sometimes smelt of butter, it no longer smelt of thyme or sage or grated cheese. 'Smells are bad for headaches,' Lena was told when she asked.

Sometimes, as Rita lay motionless on the sofa, a blanket drawn up to her chin, Lena saw her grandmother sitting there, sniffing at her. She would raise her daughter's hands to her nose, turning them this way and that; she would lift her arm and smell her armpits. You might almost have thought she was doing a very slow seated dance; you might almost have thought she was praying—and perhaps she was. Lena stood in the door, looking at her grandmother's face; it was hung with strands of white hair that had come loose from her plait, as if she'd shaken her head too fiercely. She saw her grandmother staring into Rita's face—at the twisted lips that reminded Lena of a big boil. She counted the years until she'd have her medical degree. She was only in Year Four; there were still another six to go.

The doctor treating Rita was called Oksana Tadeyevna and had thinly plucked eyebrows under a bleached fringe. Lena hated her high voice coming out of the phone and the way she had of stressing certain words as if she were telling a fairy story. Mother was no better since she'd started seeing her; the only difference was that she and Father now talked about money all the time—about spending less and putting aside some of their monthly wages, maybe even selling the jewellery. They'd never done that before. Every month, Oksana Tadeyevna had to be given a bottle of cognac or a box of chocolates, but most importantly she had to be given an envelope full of banknotes. What was more, the medicines she prescribed Rita were so expensive that Lena was sure she must be a fraud and a thief. No self-respecting socialist would charge three roubles for a packet of Cerebrolysin—her father only earned a hundred and twenty a month.

'How can ten ampoules cost that much?' he would ask. 'Even ampoules that improve brain circulation...' He kept his eyes fixed on the floral plastic tablecloth. Lena had never realized how small his head was—like a little bird's that was almost all beak. His hair was thin now under the peaked cap he had taken to wearing, sometimes even at table. It didn't help much. He looked scraggy, cap or no cap, and often peered about him in a lost way. Once he set off for work in the morning in his checked slippers; Lena caught up with him in the playground and helped him to change into his outdoor shoes, but he only smiled wanly and started to tell her about the slippers his mother used to make from old bedlinen. It seemed she'd supplied the whole village, even the detested neighbours who'd poisoned her dog—or tried to poison it, or complained about the barking. On and on Father rambled—then broke off abruptly and went on his way, without stopping to say goodbye.

On the last day of the year, Mother called Lena into the kitchen and asked her to take Oksana Tadeyevna a New Year's present. Lena felt dizzy when she saw the envelope of banknotes. She knew by now the meaning of the word 'bribery', but she'd never done anything like that herself, nor had she ever seen so much money at once, let alone walked around with it. Apart from anything else, it seemed wrong to her; it *felt* wrong. Just the thought of it made her queasy. She couldn't find the words to explain and began to stammer, but her mother interrupted her.

'You're grown up enough now,' she said—then went on, as if she hadn't noticed the tears in Lena's eyes. 'You don't just hand over the money—it doesn't work like that. First you go to the market, to Irakli Zevarovich's stall, and buy oranges and apples and whatever else he has, and then you take the doctor a big bag of fruit with the envelope in it.'

Lena searched frantically for words; she wanted to object, to refuse, but Oksana Tadeyevna was Mother's great hope—that much she'd understood. She was her only hope. For a moment Lena thought of asking why Father couldn't do it—he'd been grown up for years and surely had practice in such matters. But then it occurred to her that until she started studying medicine, going to the doctor for Rita was the only way she could help her.

Lena wrapped a scarf around her shoulders, pushed the envelope into the waistband of her trousers, pulled on her sheepskin coat, tugged her woolly hat over her forehead and left the flat in silence. The cold stung her nose and she would have covered her face with her hands if she hadn't been afraid to take her fingers out of her coat pockets, where they were keeping a close check on the envelope through the lining.

The people at the market reminded Lena of Artyom and Lika's parents; she liked to listen to their sing-song voices and hear them call to each other across the stalls. Maybe that was why her grandmother came here so often; maybe she, too, was reminded of Sochi. Here there was fruit even in winter. Irakli

Zevarovich waved from a distance as Lena pushed her way between the stalls.

'Hello, big girl. On your own today?' He had a sharply receding hairline—how could he bear not to wear a hat? The market may have been covered, but there were no walls to keep the wind out. The apples and oranges were as cold as snowballs—some of the fruit was covered with blankets.

Lena would have liked to point to her waistband, lean over the crates of fruit and tell Irakli Zevarovich in a whisper that she had a lot of money with her—she was on a secret mission and really was a big girl now; that's what you were if you delivered bribes to doctors. But she stopped herself from saying more than she should, and tried to look as grown up as possible as she asked for apples and oranges and paid with the money she'd had the foresight to slip into her coat pocket. The bag was heavier than she'd expected and the weight seemed to stretch her arm. She didn't want to leave; she'd rather have stayed and asked Irakli Zevarovich if he'd ever been to Sochi and if he happened to know Artyom and Lika. Maybe he could pass on a message to them, or even take her there sometime—maybe she could stay with him and help out on the stall; she had experience, after all, and would have done anything to avoid having to be polite to that nasal-voiced bat with the piss-coloured hair who was conning her mother and driving the family to ruin. But she couldn't tell him that. Her lips felt as if they'd frozen solid.

Outside the building where Oksana Tadeyevna lived, Lena cricked her neck and felt her jaws tense. She'd only ever seen places like this from a distance; it had never occurred to her that people actually lived in these concrete castles—that there was any life here at all. No washing hung at the windows, and each storey seemed so high that Lena could barely see the roof. She'd always been aware of these shiny-fronted buildings as part of the cityscape, but homes for her were what she'd grown up in—boxes that looked as if they'd been moulded in Plasticine, with small windows and cluttered balconies given over to store cupboards and sacks of potatoes. Lena slowly climbed the broad canopied steps to the front door and squinted up at the pillars. She let the bag of fruit trail on the ground, sure that it was clean.

When the grille of the lift snapped shut behind her she hurriedly unbuttoned her coat, pulled the envelope of cash from her waistband and shoved it in among the oranges. She didn't care that it looked as though it had been chewed.

Oksana Tadeyevna didn't ask her in. She took the bag at the door as if it were an ordinary postal delivery, set it down between her legs and counted the money then and there in front of Lena. To avoid having to watch her fingers flicking through the bundle of notes, and to hide the shame she felt, Lena stared past the doctor into her apartment, but she could only make out a few coat hooks in a long, unlit hall. From somewhere inside came the crackle of a television, or perhaps a record player. Oksana Tadeyevna's face was inscrutable. She nodded wordlessly and signalled to Lena that all was correct.

Lena had been told to say a word or two, something like *Happy New Year! My mother wishes you happiness and good health for the year ahead* or *All the best for the New Year. My mother is thinking of you*. But she knew she'd cry if she even opened her mouth, so she said nothing, and the doctor shut the door without saying goodbye.

Lena started to run. She sprinted down the stairs as if a fire had broken out behind her; she even fancied she could feel her back itching from the heat. So what if she'd always been taught to take the lift and warned away from the dark, dangerous stairs? Grown-ups were thieves and liars, you couldn't trust them anyway, so why not take the stairs? She ran down the hall, her rubber soles squeaking on the stone floor; she jumped out on to the icy avenue, skidded, lost her hat in the dirty snow, picked it up, but kept it in her fist as she ran on. She ran and ran until she collapsed on the low front steps of her shabby, dirty-blue Plasticine house, not moving until her bladder burned and her feet were numb in her felt boots.

For a few days it hurt so much to pee it made her cry. Her mother prescribed warm water and tea, and stroked her face when she sat at the kitchen table with the hot-water bottle pressed to her belly. Rita was at home more since the New Year and investing a lot of time in Lena's education—keeping a closer eye on her marks, coming into school more often to speak to her teachers.

Lena was still top of the class in most subjects. Only Ukrainian gave her trouble—she was always mixing it up with Russian. She knew Russian inside out, but no one around her spoke Ukrainian, and it was exasperating having to write essays in a language that resembled her mother tongue and yet had pitfalls all of its own. In an essay about the city of Dnipropetrovsk she wrote 'Dnepropetrovsk' throughout, because everyone pronounced it like that, even if they meant Dni-i-ipropetrovsk with a long i. Some even switched back and forth between i-i-i and e-e-e several times in one sentence; the difference was negligible, until you found yourself being marked down. It infuriated Lena—what was the fuss about? Who cared so much about one little letter?

Before the summer holidays, her mother announced that she wouldn't be having Ukrainian lessons any more. 'It's not important,' she said. 'No one needs Ukrainian these days. It's a relic. We have to move on.'

She'd lost a lot of weight over the previous months: her cheekbones jutted out of her face; the skin at her throat hung loose.

Lena stared at this sagging skin as her mother told her that she'd spoken to the headmistress and they'd agreed that in future it was all right for Lena to sit exams only in Russian grammar and literature. Ukrainian was a foreign language, and foreign languages were not compulsory. Lena nodded; she didn't know what use she'd ever have for Ukrainian anyway. It was only later in bed that she remembered once confessing to her grandmother that she liked the Ukrainian names of the months more than the Russian ones. They were called things like 'the cutting month' and 'the fierce month', instead of just January and February, which were mere markers of time with no real meaning. Grandmother had nodded; she didn't speak Ukrainian either.

Soon Grandmother was part of the furniture, a fixture in Lena's life. In the weeks when Lena was away at camp she returned to the estate in Sochi, but she was back when school started—arrived as stony-faced as ever, changed into her housedress, tied a clean scarf round her head and set about cooking. This went on for six summers until just after Lena's fourteenth birthday, when she announced that she was leaving for good. In October she baked a last Napoleon cake for Lena and combed her short hair; in November she said that was it—time for her to go.

'You've no use for me any more, and my garden needs me. Vika looks after the hazels—they bring in a bit of money, of course—but when I think of my vegetable patches, the raspberry canes, the plums… I'd like to try and cross two kinds of apple.'

She announced this at supper, as the four of them sat round the table eating sauerkraut soup. Rita stared blankly at her mother; Lena's father only nodded. A week later, he and Lena saw Grandmother on to the train. Autumn was coming to an end; the smell of snow was in the air and Lena shivered in her coat. She promised to visit

Grandmother, but knew, even as they hugged goodbye, that she didn't mean it.

She would miss the way Grandmother grumbled at her for not taking her dirty trousers into the bathroom, leaving them on the chair in their room instead although they were filthy with dust from the permanent building site outside the house. She would miss being kept awake by the clicking, chewing sounds she made at night, and her habit of counting out loud in the evenings as she rearranged her supply of soap under the sink. Worse than missing Grandmother, though, was the thought of going back to Sochi after all this time—returning to the old estate on the edge of town, standing by the gnarled vine at the front door and wanting never to leave again, but to stay forever in her long-gone childhood with the mountains of sawdust, the sooty-smelling firepit, the patches of flattened grass where the tables had stood.

Really Lena was too old for Pioneer camp, but because she wouldn't turn fifteen until a few weeks after the holidays she begged for a last summer at the Eaglet. 'It's good for the soul, Mum,' she said with a smile when her mother finally capitulated. 'Isn't that what you always said?' And she kissed her on the cheek.

Since that first enforced stay at the Eaglet Lena had seen Alyona every summer except one, when she'd refused to go to camp because of a sudden fear that her mother would no longer be there when she got back. She'd had no particular reason for thinking that—although Rita's condition hadn't improved, it hadn't worsened either. But a strange breathlessness had come over Lena; she had clung to her mother's side, staring at her greying hair, trying to keep track of the wrinkles around her mouth.

There was another change in Rita besides the silver hair. She was milder, less argumentative, and hugged Lena more often. There was also something different about her eyes. Once, Lena had felt that her look was sharp enough to slice through doors; now she merely stared at them as if they weren't there. There were times when she stared at Lena like that too.

Lena wondered when it would be best to reveal her plan to Alyona. She thought maybe she would wait until they were lying by the pond together, flimsy shirts over their swimsuits, toes buried in the grass, the sky above them flecked with birds like Dad's hands. Or she would whisper it to her in the evening by the bonfire, her voice no louder than the crackle of the flames—and Alyona would stare in amazement and ask lots of questions, then nod several times, mutely but firmly. Or Lena would lure her into the greenhouse where they'd first met and where it wouldn't be so obvious that she was blushing and sweating—she and Alyona would wander up and down between the rows of tomato beds, Alyona rocking her head back and forth like a nest too heavy for a branch, and it would gush out of Lena like a spur-of-the-moment idea, a casual suggestion, not a plan she'd been brooding over night after night, working it out to the last detail: the room they'd share in the hall of residence in Donetsk, the walks they'd go on together, the films they'd watch—and of course all the studying they'd do together for their exams.

In the end she decided to tell her straight away, the morning after their arrival, as soon as they woke up. She crossed the dorm to Alyona's bed and announced her plan, without preamble, like a talking clock. But all Alyona said was, 'I don't know that I want to go to university.'

For years, Lena had been struggling to keep up with Alyona. She was now a whole head taller than Lena and everything about her was more definite—her gestures more confident, her gaze almost always impenetrable. Even now, standing at the side of

Alyona's bed, her arms sticking out awkwardly, Lena felt as if she were the one looking up. It was early morning, but already the sun was pouring in at the pollen-covered windows; the Pioneers were calling out jokes to one another, shaking each other awake, pulling their socks up to their knees. Alyona sat cross-legged on the bed, her bare feet peeping out of her pyjama bottoms, her sharp knees angled past Lena—she seemed in no hurry to get to morning gymnastics. The skin of her face looked as thin as paper, as if there were no flesh under it; as always, it was porcelain-white. She was brushing her eyebrows the wrong way with her middle fingers—a new habit that drove Lena mad.

Alyona had become stranger every summer. On one occasion she'd tried to tell Lena who it was that had run over her foot and crippled it, but she'd only chewed the inside of her cheeks and eventually come out with, 'Having a good memory makes you lonely.' When Lena asked what she meant, she said, 'Sometimes it's easier to get over things if you don't think about them.' That was as much as Lena could prise out of her and she didn't push, although she hadn't begun to understand what Alyona was getting at.

Alyona smoothed out the creases in the sheet with her hands and already seemed to be somewhere else, in some deep inner place. Lena had often observed this in her. When Alyona disappeared inside herself, she even stopped smelling of sea buckthorn, and with every summer that passed she grew better at it, as if she'd spent all year at home practising. Lena sat down on the mattress with a bounce, hoping that the waves created by the sagging springs would bring her back. She searched frantically for something to say.

'So what *do* you want to do?' she said at last. 'An apprenticeship?' No colonel's daughter could work in a factory; the thought was preposterous.

Alyona shook her head and rummaged in the drawer of her bedside table, as if she considered the conversation over. The sound of her uncut nails scraping the wood infuriated Lena; she almost jumped up and headed for the parade ground without her. But then she looked into Alyona's round eyes and saw that they were full of tears. Her lips jutted out and her hair fell forward over her shoulders in a mess of curls, making her face even smaller and harder to see than usual. Clearly no one ever cut her hair. *Who do you think you are?* Lena wanted to shout. *Something better? And what are you thinking of doing with your life? What's the big idea? Don't you care that we might never see each other again?* All these things she wanted to yell, but she couldn't get out a single word. The bugle sounded for morning gymnastics. Alyona didn't move.

'I'd like to show you something,' she said, interrupting Lena's thoughts. She seemed unaware that their future was at stake. Unconcerned, or feigning unconcern, she took a slim book from the drawer and—head lowered, so that Lena couldn't see her face—she began to read aloud.

> *There can be no doubt that the bluebottle had a strongly marked personality. It had had enough of not being taken seriously in the world, and in particular by the philosopher who behaved as if he were lord of all creation. He was sitting alone, hard at work. He was writing: 'Stupidity is omnipotent, reason is impotent. What can even genius do against the million-headed hydra of stupidity?'*

Alyona looked up with a gaze that seemed to say, *Do you understand?*

Lena didn't. She wanted to jump to her feet, tear the book from Alyona's hands and dash it against the dormitory wall, screaming, *No! You're the one who doesn't understand! You don't understand anything!* But the taste of shame was sour on her tongue. Should she have known what Alyona was talking about? What did you do with your life if you didn't go to university? Why had no one talked to her about it? And what was all this about a bluebottle?

The bugle sounded again. They were alone in the dormitory now; soon the head count would begin. But Alyona read on, loud and clear, separating each sentence from the previous one, pausing in strange places. It infuriated Lena that she was so far away. She'd taken herself off and had no intention of waking up next to Lena every morning in the hall of residence and going to lectures with her—instead she was getting them both into trouble; if anyone noticed their absence at morning roll call, there would be consequences—someone might even ring their mothers, and where would they be then?

'What's going on here? What is this book?' Lena asked at last, unable to say any of the other things that were going through her head. There were footsteps in the corridor; someone was looking for them, calling their names. Beads of sweat stood on Alyona's forehead and collarbones; the bright sunlight made her look even paler than usual. She spun round, clutching the book in one hand; with the other she made a grab for Lena's wrist and pulled her behind the dormitory door.

You couldn't just disappear in a place like this; it was ridiculous. You couldn't just not join in. But Alyona's hair was growing into Lena's face and creeping into her mouth; her thighs were pressed against Lena's, her bare skin was on her arms. Lena held her breath and tried to control the trembling in her ribs and legs to stop herself from keeling over. The floor was cold on her bare feet, as if they were standing on tiles, not floorboards, and glow-worms danced before her eyes after the abrupt switch from sunlight to dusty darkness. Alyona still wasn't looking at Lena, but her lips moved next to hers, maybe to say *shhh*, maybe to say something else—they made no sound. Out in the yard, the bugle seemed to go on and on; there were screams, shouts. Had all hell broken loose already, just because of a couple of missing kids? Wedged between Alyona and the wall, Lena was close to tears; she'd suddenly realized it was almost over—any second now, Alyona would peel her skin from hers like cling film.

Lena thought of the punishments that awaited them: the floors they'd have to scrub, the letters to their parents, the black marks in the register—maybe they should just make a run for it now, it didn't matter where. *Don't leave me! Don't leave me!* They'd head for the woods first, then to the nearest town, where they'd call their parents to let them know they were all right. No more queuing for food in the cold with Father. No more being woken at night by Mother's groans. No more worrying that if you called the paramedics in the morning, they wouldn't come till evening, and that by then it might be too late. In her confusion, Lena hadn't noticed that Alyona had moved away from her and was peering round the door into the empty corridor. She pressed herself closer to the wall and kept breathing; she was sure that if she went to roll call now and everything went off as usual, she would shatter, burst, BOOM.

The summer passed like a mistake, as if Lena were constantly biting into a hollowed-out fruit—as if everything she saw and did were already a memory she was passing through and couldn't hold on to. The Pioneers' once-gleaming uniforms had been washed so often they looked as if they'd been painted in watercolours; the older children's in particular were too tight for their long, wiry bodies. The white gloss paint of the barracks was cracked on the window frames, peeling off in porous curls. Lena thought of Alyona's words, *Having a good memory makes you lonely*; after that she thought nothing much. The billboards and signs no longer looked big and threatening; the admonitory

W H E N I E A T I A M D E A F A N D D U M B was missing its first M, and the last D was hanging at an angle. No one seemed to care. There was never anyone in the greenhouse any more; the tomatoes grew all by themselves, hanging their overripe heads. Lena wandered up and down the aisles, the taste of salt on her upper lip. She ran her hands over the hairy stems and rubbed the leaves between the palms of her hands, relishing the fruity scent and the itch on her skin.

On the parade ground, watching children who barely reached her waist run around after the chickens, she felt pity for the first time in her life—because of all the time they would waste here, all the hurt that was still to come, all the emptiness when it was over. The anger made her tired; whenever she could, she pulled her cap down over her eyes and pretended to sleep.

MAY OUR CHILDREN OUR JOY OUR HAPPINESS LIVE ON A SUNNY PLANET. The slogan on the dance-room wall was painted in white letters on a red banner. Until this year's disco, Lena had always ignored it, making straight for the dance floor and watching the others or concentrating on her own feet—now she sat with her back to the wall, craning her chin. The couples danced as depicted and instructed on the sign at the entrance: a boy and girl, both with the same long, blond hair, held each other's hips and shoulders, while between them arrows and a ruler marked a distance of 0.5 metres. Above their heads it said, PIONEER, with an exclamation mark, and beneath their feet, which were frozen mid-step, KEEP YOUR DISTANCE, with another exclamation mark. Lena had stared at this warning for a long time before going in. The seat next to Alyona was free; there were more empty chairs in the far corner. A few couples were already swaying tentatively under the coloured lights—woodenly, like in the picture, keeping each other at arm's length, with dull smiles and stiff, averted gazes, as if seeking the approval of those sitting watching. The walls were covered with billowing cloth like the sails of a ship that might put to sea at any moment. Alyona stared at the ceiling. Lena sat down next to her. Neither of them spoke.

Stars of purple fall from the sky—
What shall we wish for tonight?
On the horizon, over our quarters,
Let the Altair star shine bright.

Shooting stars, shooting stars,
They bring luck, people say.
We are leaving this song as our keepsake
For new Eaglets to find someday.

The loudspeakers were on the other side of the room next to the improvised stage, but Lena knew the song by heart and despite the crackly speakers she heard every word. Afterwards came a slow brass number. The microphone stood alone on the rostrum; there would be no speech today. When they'd gathered here for a lecture a few weeks before, the Pioneer leader had held forth on the subject of pride and joy and viruses and pesticides, and told them not to forget to report to the sister for their compulsory medical. Lena had thought of her first conversation with Alyona, of the image she'd had of Alyona being sick, the knee Alyona had offered to let her touch, the toes she could have pulled if she'd wanted to. Now Alyona's knees were swaying gently back and forth, reflecting the red, yellow and blue fairy lights. On the chairs under the windows opposite some boys were sitting, staring across at Lena and Alyona, digging their elbows into each other's sides.

Before any of them could come over and ask them to dance, Lena jumped up and held out a hand to Alyona.

Alyona took it without looking up; she let Lena pull her to her feet and hobbled into the middle of the room with her. Lena knew how cold her hands were—cold and slippery with sweat—but she only tightened her grip on Alyona's fingers. With her other hand she pressed Alyona's ribs; she could feel each one through the white shirt of her Pioneer's uniform—like chicken bones, she thought. Lena tried to lead. With every step she noticed what different lengths Alyona's legs were; she shifted the weight from one foot to the other in a syncopated rhythm that cut across the beat. As so often these last weeks, Alyona's gaze was turned inwards, so Lena allowed herself to stare at her, trying to commit her face to memory. She had no photo of Alyona and would probably soon have forgotten what she looked like. Her ears, surrounded by frizzy curls, were bent at the tips; her nose lay flat between her cheekbones, jutting down towards curved lips. She hadn't combed her hair for the dance; it stood up just as it had that first day among the tomato plants, and she still smelt of that same mixture of Sochi and raspberries. She wasn't looking at Lena, but her face was turned towards her. Lena tried to work out if Alyona's eyes were closed or if she was only staring at her feet so as not to make a mistake, and all at once it seemed to her that she was taller than Alyona—or was Alyona hunching her back, curling in on herself like the peeling paint on the barracks? All Lena could see of her were bristly black eyelashes and those mussed-up eyebrows that divided her face in two. She was less than half a metre away.

THE EIGHTIES

Heroes Avenue

FROM UP CLOSE, this wall had once looked as green as the grass in the yard; now it was faded. The black lines of stalks unfurling into flowers were visible only up by the ceiling; down by the carpet the wallpaper was almost ashen yellow. Lena tried to get as close to the wall as possible without giving herself away. The flat was flimsily built; everyone here knew everything about each other, but these people who had arrived an hour ago and accepted the tea she'd made them—these people were pros; they'd been holding what her mother called 'discreet talks' all their lives. They could probably sit in a room with the secret service and discuss their important business in such impenetrable code that the agents wouldn't notice. Since Lena knew, however, what the negotiations were about—namely her and her future at the Medical University of Donetsk—and since she knew roughly how such 'discreet talks' went—you agreed on a sum, you received exam questions and, most importantly, you were guaranteed a place at university—it was curiosity more than anything that made her sit by the wall with a book and pretend to read.

The visitors were less prepossessing than Lena had imagined. She had pictured lecturers as imposing figures in dapper three-piece suits of sturdy tweed, peering knowingly through thick glasses perched on beak-like noses. The pair in the kitchen were more like mice, with narrow, naked faces; the shoulder pads of their jackets stuck out past their shoulders when they took off their leather coats. They probably weren't lecturers at all, but mere cogs in the administrative machinery.

From the moment they had appeared at the door, Rita sounded her old self again, firm and strident, as if they had no alternative but to nod and do as she told them. Even when she greeted them she made it clear she drove a hard bargain and was prepared to do everything in her power for her daughter. But when Lena heard the words *ten thousand roubles*, she jumped up from her chair. She couldn't even imagine that much money. What had she finished school with a distinction for? What was the point of that gold medal for outstanding achievement? Why had the headmistress said at the prizegiving ceremony that the future was hers—she just had to reach out and grab it?

She couldn't burst into the room while they were negotiating a price for her life, so she skulked around the hall until the mousy-faced men had left. As soon as they were out of the flat, she ran to her mother and clasped her hands.

'Mum, I can get into university by myself. I'm good—I even went to Moscow for the Physics Olympiad. Why would they turn me down?'

Her mother stared at the table in front of her and then out of the window. She looked neither at Lena nor at Lena's hands squeezing hers.

'They won't guarantee me anything—competition is too fierce,' she said at length, more to herself than to Lena. 'Even if we pay up, we only get the exam questions, and that doesn't mean a thing.'

'Then I'll just go to Dnipropetrovsk instead of Donetsk—that's OK. It's a bit further away, but it's a good university and I'll graduate as quickly as I can.'

A strange quiet filled the room. There was no clock, but something was ticking—or the ceiling lamp was buzzing, although it was switched off. An electric charge or tension—something in the air was rushing like blood in the ears. Lena bit her lower lip. She regretted what she'd just said, but more than that she regretted the urgency with which she'd spoken; it was a tacit confession of her fear that her mother's time was running out.

'Did I ever tell you I wanted to study medicine too?' Rita said, coming to her rescue.

Lena shook her head, determined to keep her mouth shut for the rest of the day.

'I went to Moscow to sit the entrance exam, and of course I failed, fair and square. My mother had no money for bribes, and I was like you—thought I couldn't go wrong. I knew everything inside out, I'd passed my exams with distinction. Just like you. Went up to Moscow from Sochi, a young girl with dreams of being a great scientist and making medical breakthroughs. I think I was serious about it. The professors must have wet themselves laughing when I turned up for the exam with no cash. But I didn't regret it. I didn't get in, of course. I went back and studied in Sochi, and look at me now—head of the chemical plant in Horlivka. Not bad, eh? I'm happy enough. What I mean is, you can always try something else. There are so many interesting professions.'

Lena didn't shout that trying something else was the last thing she intended to do. She bit back the remark that she'd had it up to here with Rita's sunken cheeks. The rings under her eyes. The sound of her retching, the groans at night. She said nothing. What could she say?

'This is what we'll do,' her mother went on. 'The ten thousand roubles are yours whatever happens, but we'll leave them under your pillow for the time being, and once you've graduated and know where you'll be working, we'll try to buy our way into the waiting list for the local housing co-op.'

The tears came so suddenly that Lena didn't have time to blink them back; she lowered her head, shook it a few times and told herself to stop. Her face was burning. She would have given anything to have the old Rita back, ordering her in iron tones to become a doctor at once, find a cure for her, make a career as a great socialist scientist, bring pride to the family. She wanted her the way she used to be, strict and unrelenting. There was something scary about this woman with the dull hair and the puckered lips, telling her to live her life and promising to take care of her future. Her mildness terrified Lena.

It was the same when Lena brought Vassili home. This was soon before she went to Dnipropetrovsk to sit the entrance exam for the Medical University, and it was the first time that Vassili had come to the flat not as a schoolfriend who needed help with his homework, but as a young man hoping to marry the only daughter of the house. He showed up, as the occasion warranted, in a suit and freshly pressed shirt, his face solemn, his handshake proffered with an earnestness no one had ever seen in him before. But Rita only gave a mild, absent smile and gestured to him to take a seat at the ready-laid table, without even asking what he intended to make of himself.

Father took charge of that side of things, quizzing the guest on his family (Russian? Ukrainian? Something else?), as if the young man with red hair in a side parting and a face as broad as a tomcat's were a stranger whose acquaintance they had yet to make. Vassili dutifully reeled off his pedigree like a socialist poem, but Lena had the impression that no one was really listening, so she interrupted him and announced that he was planning to join the navy. That, she thought, deserved a mention.

Vassili and she had seen each other in school every day for years, but one afternoon in their final year, when she was queuing for an ice cream behind the Technical Museum, he had approached her like a passing stranger. He crept up cautiously, as if afraid of being tactless, and asked if he might buy her a cone. She looked at him, taken aback, and wondered if, instead of the slow-witted Vassili she had known since Year One, this was perhaps a doppelgänger, a relative—someone who looked just the same, with jug ears and dandruff in his parting, but was in fact someone quite different, not the boy she'd spent the last ten years cramming with facts and formulae in preparation for one exam after another. Why was he sidling up to her like this, as if they'd never met? And where had he got the money for two ice-cream cones? She agreed to let him treat her, and he grew even odder and asked if she, too, sometimes went to the Technical Museum to see the insides of the ships which he thought at least as beautiful as the insides of a human being. Then he told her that he was planning to join the navy because he hoped to travel abroad and that he imagined the shimmering surface of the ocean like the belly of a huge lizard covered in goosebumps.

Lena bit into the sweet, milky ice cream and looked at her friend. Something about him was different; something had happened to him. They'd always grown at the same rate and still bickered like children, but they no longer chased each other around the playground, and at some point—Lena seemed to have missed the moment—Vassili must have shed his skin. He'd slithered out of his old self to stand before her as a man—a man she barely knew, she thought to herself, observing him now. He had a small row of spots on his chin and was staring at her wide-eyed. *Travel abroad? Lizards?* What was he talking about?

It was all very strange to her and, for that reason, interesting. All spring she let him treat her to ice creams, and soon after their school-leaving exams Vassili said it was time to talk to her parents. Lena didn't protest. She was surrounded by couples talking wedding plans with their parents.

'I've been accepted by the military academy in Leningrad,' he explained to his future in-laws.

'We've already looked at rings, but we're going to wait with the dress,' Lena added.

'Wouldn't want you putting on weight—it'll be three years till I'm finished!' Vassili said, reaching for the hard-boiled eggs filled with caviar. Orange slime clung to the bristly moustache he had recently started growing.

Lena looked at him, then at her mother, whose face she couldn't see against the light from the window, at her father, who was nodding silently to himself, and at the mound of pea and mayonnaise salad on her plate. First, she thought, she must pass the exam and get into university; the rest would come soon enough.

No one told Lena why she'd failed the entrance exam. She had taken the overnight train alone to Dnipropetrovsk and spent the following night, between the exam and the results, at a friend of a friend's on a camp bed in the hall. She hadn't wanted to put her mother through the long journey, and her father had been teaching as usual—not that she could imagine him making much of an impression on anyone these days, with his sunken shoulders and the flat cap that he rarely removed from his now very bald head. Lena sneezed on and off all through the journey and got no sleep; she was drenched in sweat when she got off the train in the June sun and caught the bus to the university. Her blouse clung unpleasantly to her back and breastbone, and the pen she wrote with slid back and forth in her damp hand—she did her best to ignore it. She tried, too, not to think about her mother's face, which appeared before her, sunken and grey, or her father's ears, drooping under his cap. Even Vassili flashed up before her, and she was surprised to find she was angry at him for not bothering to send so much as a telegram to wish her luck, making do with a phone call days before, which he'd ended with a terse 'Chin up'. Had he even said he was waiting for her? Lena blamed him, more than anything, for the failed exam—she couldn't think of any other reason. She was sure she hadn't messed up the written part; she'd had no trouble answering the questions. The oral part had been all right, too, but she hadn't spoken as fluently or confidently as usual; it was not impossible she had seemed distracted.

'You didn't get the full number of points.' That was all the information she was given. 'But it would be enough for dentistry. You can enrol in dentistry right away. For general practice you'd have to try again in a year.'

What good was dentistry to her? She needed to get into neurology as soon as possible. She stood up without a word and left the university building. On the steps outside, clusters of young people stood around with their parents. They were neatly dressed, the women in straight-cut skirts and airy white blouses, some of the men in suits. They all had clean shoes. Lena kept her eyes on the ground and spoke to no one. She fetched her overnight bag from the friend of a friend, and instead of catching the bus walked slowly down the hill to the station. She couldn't think straight. There was nothing to say. She had no plan B. Worst of all, she didn't have the words to explain to her parents what had happened.

But her parents barely reacted; they seemed unsurprised. As if they'd already suspected as much and had been rehearsing for some time, they began to make suggestions. Lena felt like a baby being distracted from a big jab she was about to get in her belly. She rejected everything they tried to tempt her with: physics, chemistry, biology—all the subjects she'd excelled at in school.

She suggested doing a year's nursing to gain experience and then trying again. It was the only idea she had.

'What do you mean, *experience*—wiping old people's bums?' Her father, as usual, spoke softly and came straight to the point.

'Someone has to,' Lena said, turning to face him, wishing that just once in his life he'd lose his temper and yell at her—that it was no good, that she could do better, what was it all for? School at five, Pioneer camp every summer, best in her year, gold medallist, and now suddenly it wasn't enough—

'No daughter of mine will mop puke up off a hospital floor.' Mother's words tore Lena from her thoughts. Her voice wasn't exactly loud either, but the brusque tone, at least, was soothing.

A few days later Rita took a bottle of Armenian cognac from the sideboard in the sitting room and told Lena which ward to report to in Horlivka State Hospital.

The senior consultant took the gift with a nod, offered Lena a seat and told her in the same breath that she would be working as his secretary; if she did her job well, he would call the University of Dnipropetrovsk in a year's time and she could consider herself accepted. Lena was revolted by his smug face and the huge hands that he waved about as if he were conducting an orchestra, but she'd already lost one year of her life so she thanked him and set about making herself invisible.

After a few weeks she noticed that she'd begun to keep an eye out for Alyona in the hospital corridors. It would have been an absurd coincidence—Alyona didn't even live in Horlivka; she had come to the Eaglet from Mariupol. But it was possible, because everything was possible—people found each other all over the world. Maybe she would come as a patient; maybe she'd had a car crash nearby and would be admitted to Lena's ward with slight injuries—just a few scratches and a bit of a shock. Or maybe she would come to visit a distant relative who was being treated here. It would be nice not to be so lonely—to have someone, anyone, to walk to the bus stop with after work. No one in the clinic ever asked Lena anything that wasn't connected with forms or holiday schedules. Only Svetlana, who was seventeen like Lena, sometimes nodded at her in the breaks, but even she eyed Lena with suspicion. Svetlana had to wash bedpans for a year before she could re-sit the entrance exam; her parents clearly hadn't had the right phone numbers to hand, or the right cognac or whatever the appropriate currency was.

But when May came, Svetlana asked Lena if she'd like a lift to Dnipropetrovsk for the entrance exam—her mother would drive them and they could stay with a friend of hers near the university. Lena's voice failed her when she accepted.

The little red Zhiguli smelt of fresh peppers, and a sack of walnuts clattered on the passenger seat, leaping into the air whenever they hurtled over a pothole. Lena jumped every time. They'd set off in the middle of the night; the hazy yellow of the street lamps swept across her face at irregular intervals. She tried to keep her eyes open so as not to miss the sunrise, and took careful sips of black tea from the thermos flask she had filled that morning while still half asleep—shocking-pink tulips on a turquoise ground.

'Did you have to bring peppers, Mum?' Svetlana breathed noisily in and out, sounding like the child she hadn't been for a long time. 'Couldn't you have packed bread and butter and salami? Peppers on an empty stomach give you bellyache.'

Her mother was younger than Lena's—she looked almost youthful in her mint-green shirt with the sleeves pushed up over her elbows, her blond ponytail hanging over the back of the driver's seat.

'It's to help you concentrate, girls!' she yelled, swivelling round to pass them a bright-red one. 'Eat as much as you can! They're full of vitamin C and all kinds of goodness. Brain food! They're good for the brain!'

Svetlana pulled a face and closed her eyes in disgust, but Lena broke the pepper in half and listened to the skin crunch between her teeth. From the rear-view mirror a picture dangled, no bigger than a playing card: a bearded man with shoulder-length hair held his hand sideways in front of his chest, index and middle finger raised. His head was slightly bowed, but his gaze was turned yearningly towards the sky. Lena knew who it was, of course, but she felt like talking to Svetlana's mother, so she asked if it was a friend of hers.

'That's right, a very close friend!' Svetlana's mother had to shout to make herself heard above the wind that was surging through the open windows. (The draught would help keep her awake on the seven-hour drive, she had explained as they set off, thrusting a scarf into Lena's hand.) 'If you pass the exam, *you'll* have to make friends with him too. I spent hours praying for you both yesterday.'

Lena thought of this the following day when the admissions committee congratulated her on passing. Now I have to go into some church and light something, she thought. Maybe I'll ring Grandma and ask her how you thank Jesus—or I'll kiss Svetlana's mother, maybe that counts too. A wave of heat spread through her body from her belly button; her face flushed hot and cold. There was no one at the door to tell of her triumph. Lena managed to leave the building calmly and discreetly, but once outside she began to run. She dashed back and forth across the university grounds, looking for the red Zhiguli, but she was too excited to search the car park so she ran down the hill into town, almost knocking over an old man who was leaning against a metal barrel on wheels marked *Wine* and staring through the heat at the tipsy flies circling the puddle at his feet. Lena asked where the nearest post office was; the wine vendor muttered something and pointed down a street. Lena hurried on, hearing her own heels on the pavement in a kind of gallop: *clack-clack-clack, clack-clack-clack.*

She couldn't bear the thought of joining the queue to the phone booths; it was more than she could manage to stand and wait patiently. 'My mother's ill!' she shouted. 'Please let me through—I have an urgent call to make.'

She was bundled to the front of the queue, breathless and dishevelled—people touched her shoulder as she passed. She put coins in the slot, still beating out a rhythm with her heels as if she were running. Her mother picked up almost immediately and she yelled louder than she'd ever yelled in her life, 'Mum, I passed! I got in! I'm going to be a doctor!'

At the other end of the line, her mother breathed out.

'I'm so pleased, Lena.' Over the bad connection her voice sounded very far away, but it didn't matter. 'We must remember to thank your consultant again.'

Then Lena heard something about a safe journey, but the words came to her as if through gale-force winds. The thought that she'd got the place because of her connections rather than her achievements was like a punch in the gut. She felt as though someone had spat in her mouth. No, not someone—her mother. If she could claim no responsibility for anything that happened to her, whether failure or success, mightn't she just as well put herself in the hands of the bearded man with the lethargic gaze and the raised fingers, and trust in his power to solve the problems of the world?

She allowed herself to be ushered out of the post office, pushed by hands that were a good deal less friendly than those that had touched her shoulder a few minutes before. The whole queue must have heard her phone call, but she ignored the muttered curses behind her. She didn't care. She sauntered back up the hill to the car park and immediately spotted the red Zhiguli. Svetlana's mother was leaning against it, smoking. When Lena drew nearer, she clamped the cigarette between her lips, pulled her ponytail higher and peered at Lena through clenched eyes. Messing up an exam wasn't the end of the world, she said—Lena could always study something else.

'I passed,' Lena mumbled.

'So what's that pout for? Anyone would think you'd broken a leg.'

Svetlana's mother's face grew round with joy. She squeezed Lena's arm and touched her cheek, and the smoke from her cigarette got in Lena's eyes. 'Sveta made it too. She'll be back any minute, then we can jump in the car and put some music on—what do you reckon? In fact, no, do you know what, we'll put it on now, I've got an Antonov tape in the glove compartment.' She clapped her hands and looked far younger than she could have been. 'Come on, let's put some lipstick on; I always do my face before I listen to music.' She whipped out the tape and a black tube, painted her lips carrot-orange without a mirror, then reached out an arm for Lena, grasping her chin to make her hold still. 'Eyeshadow too?' she asked, examining her work with satisfaction.

Lena held her breath. The closeness of this near stranger, her cloying perfume—it was all too much. The pressure in her lungs made her hiccup loudly; then she sneezed. She stared at the gleaming blue eyelids before her, drooping beneath the weight of the eyeshadow, or maybe with tiredness—all last night, while Lena had lain awake in bed, Svetlana's mother had sat up smoking with her friend in the tiny kitchen on the other side of the wall (Lena could smell the smoke on her). Now she had the long drive to Horlivka ahead of her—hour after hour on the bad roads. She would wind down the window to stay awake and munch on red peppers. Lena suddenly realized that this woman, too, must have her troubles; despite the cigarette in the corner of her mouth and the make-up in the glove compartment, she was no longer a young girl. The fatigue around her eyes gave her away.

Lena sat orange-lipped on the back seat, squinting at the picture of Jesus as it swung back and forth in front of the darkening countryside to the guitar chords of Yuri Antonov, while Svetlana and her mother belted out the words:

We're all chasing after wonders,
But the greatest one I know
Is the earth beneath the heavens
In the place that we call home.

Lena asked Jesus this and that, and thanked him matter-of-factly for letting her pass. But she soon tired of talking to a playing card and went back to looking out of the window, where the silhouettes of copper beeches were closing in on them.

No one, it seemed, got into Dnipropetrovsk University without connections; it was a big topic of discussion in the first semester.

That and the Jewish question. Exchanging notes on exam material was clearly less important than talking about who was Jewish—and how Jewish they were—and thus had parents with enough cash to send them to the right university. The surnames and patronymics of students like Katya, Marusya and Anton were relentlessly analysed; in her first week Lena heard one student say to another on her way to the communal bathroom, 'Yes, sure, his surname's Molokov, but his father's called Isaak, for goodness sake—you'd hardly *choose* to be called Anton Isaakovich, would you?'

All this talk of Jews was new to Lena; she didn't know what to make of it, so she raised the topic with Svetlana, who was in a room with her in the girls' block and had a Jewish father.

'All ordinary people have Jewish relatives,' Svetlana said. 'But that means that all ordinary people also have non-Jewish relatives. No healthy person is completely Jewish. It's like Lenin, only the other way round.'

Lena thought of the summer when she'd been so worried about her mother that she'd stayed at home in Horlivka instead of going to camp. The heat had driven people out of their little box-like prefab flats and they'd gathered in the yard to drink *kvass* in the shade of the buildings. There had been games of chess on hand-painted boards and walks in the nearby woods. Children ran wild between the houses, making toys out of everything they found and throwing sticks at figures they'd made out of building blocks.

Every day during that hot summer, Lena had watched a family on the second floor of their block, sitting on the balcony, reading, dressed in airy clothes. Once they'd settled themselves, they barely moved all morning. Pale sunhats shielded their faces, and their heads were bent, presumably over books in their laps. Lena wondered what the girl must feel, sandwiched there between her parents, head bowed like theirs—a smaller head with an equally large hat. Her face disappeared entirely beneath the brim; or that, at least, is how it seemed to Lena, down in the yard. The three of them were a row of pale splotches. When Lena asked why they never left their flat and came down to the yard like everyone else, her mother said, 'I don't know. Maybe they're Jewish.'

And that was all. No more was said on the subject and Lena didn't probe any further, because she didn't know what to ask. There was a lot of talk among the students about which of them had connections to Israel, who should be blamed for Zionism and to what extent, and whether—and in what way—cosmopolitanism was corrupt and imperialist. Lena listened, thinking to herself that it made perfect sense to buy one's way into a city as beautiful as Dnipropetrovsk, whether with a bit of help from Jesus or with the backing of cosmopolitanism. It was a golden city—she hadn't realized before. Of course she'd learnt at school that it was the birthplace of Leonid Ilyich Brezhnev, great chairman of the Presidium of the Supreme Soviet—he had, at any rate, been born not far away, somewhere on the Dnieper, and the city milked this for all it was worth. But she hadn't expected the shelves in the shops to be so well stocked—better than in any other town she knew. Butter and salami, even ham and cosmetics, were almost always available, and the cafés were as busy as in Sochi. Lena's memories of queuing for pork belly on dark, cold winter mornings seemed like something from another life. If you needed anything in Dnipropetrovsk, you just went to the market or the milk bar and came back with full bags. Leonid Ilyich had been dead a year when Lena started to study, but still new cinemas continued to open in his supposed birthplace, and the avenues were choked with cars.

'What a city!' Lena said when she rang her parents for their weekly chat.

'What's that she says?' her father called out in the background.

'Dnipropetrovsk,' her mother said. 'She says it's nice there. Nice.'

Lena's room in the hall of residence was about as large as the sitting room she'd shared with her grandmother as a child, but a good deal more crowded; she and Svetlana had to share with a third room-mate, Olga. The narrow spaces between the beds were filled with shoes and bags; the walls either side of the only wardrobe were covered in magazine cuttings and photos of loved ones back home; the three women's books and essays were spread out over two desks. If someone sniffed in the room next door, you heard it through the wall.

At the weekends, when the weather was fine, the others—and sometimes their visiting relatives, too—would go to an island in the Dnieper that was named after the Komsomol. They would come back and tell Lena about the well-kept paths, the monument to the poet Taras Shevchenko, the benches where you could sit looking up at the sky and forget about everything, breathing in the smell of the grass, the conifers, the river. Svetlana spat into her make-up box and rubbed her little green brush into the black goo. Why wouldn't Lena come with them, she asked, not for the first time, as she applied the mascara thickly, lash by lash. Lena waved the question aside.

One afternoon, though, she let herself be persuaded to go to the cinema with a few others from the hall of residence. They watched her mother's favourite film about three young women from the provinces who move to the capital to work in a factory, meet men, get pregnant, rise up to become managers or slide down into drudgery, get themselves dachas, chain-smoke, throw out their menfolk, fetch them back, throw them out again. Olga seemed to know the film by heart and waved a finger at the screen—'Look, girls, that's us!'—whenever the protagonists were shown in their beds in the hall of residence, chatting about life and love. One of the heroines was pursued by the same misfortune twice: she was socially mismatched with both her lovers. In the first part of the film, she wasn't good enough for the man who got her pregnant; in the second she was too well off for the man she loved. All three agreed that a woman shouldn't earn more than her husband—*what kind of a life would that be*—and Lena was suddenly glad that a marine earned more than a neurologist.

Vassili had come to see Lena only once since their engagement, and she had found herself pinned to a sofa in a way not unlike that inflicted on one of the film's heroines. The sofa, covered in a rough plaid blanket, belonged to friends of Vassili; she hadn't known of these people's existence until he put an arm around her at the station and told her he was taking her to their flat. It was in a part of town unfamiliar to Lena. The couple that opened the door to them asked about Vassili's training in Leningrad and told him to send their love to his parents, but they were otherwise off-hand and didn't stay to have tea with their guests. Lena wanted to look around a bit and resisted Vassili's advances, but Vassili didn't seem interested in talking after the long separation, and eventually she allowed her skirt to be hiked up and her pants pulled down. Vassili's craggy knuckles scraped across her skin as he pushed his hand between her thighs. He entered her without looking at her—he seemed to be watching only himself as he thrust his pelvis against her, grimly intent. Lena stared at the clammy strands of thick red hair above her; she was tempted to push them out of his face so she could see him better but she was afraid to move, afraid it would make the smarting pain even worse. The heavy groans coming from Vassili's throat grew louder, then broke off when he collapsed on top of her. He was hot and sweaty, his cheeks wet as if he'd been crying. Lena reached out and clawed the hem of the tablecloth that was trembling beside her like a curtain. Vassili's friends had left them a modest tea—*sushki* and jam, a little salami. Lena tugged at the cool, smooth material and the entire spread fell crashing to the floor.

None of that happened in the film. The scene in the film stopped when the couple lay down on the sofa. Lena felt something rip in her belly. She put two fingers on the inside of her left wrist, felt the rise and fall of a vein, and counted the beats.

Outside the cinema, men in red armbands were checking ID as people poured out on to the street. The cinemagoers stood in small clusters, rummaging in their pockets. These volunteer patrols were much discussed in the corridors of the hall of residence. The *druzhiniki* saw to it that Communist values were upheld and that no one sold fish on the street without a licence. Women, as well as men, were encouraged to join their ranks and ensure that Soviets worked when they should and associated with the right people—and that no Caucasian faces were seen in places where they had no business to be. Lena didn't know anyone, man or woman, who belonged to a volunteer group, and it was the first time she'd had the uneasy experience of having to submit to a random ID check.

A little way off, at the edge of the road, two volunteer guards were talking heatedly to an elderly man. He jerked his face nervously from one to the other, eyed the hand on his shoulder, scanned the distance. Was he looking for help? Lena couldn't tell. She wasn't sure, either, whether the guards had twisted the man's arms, but she saw him suddenly double over. The three of them were little more than silhouettes against the afternoon sun. The *druzhiniki* pointed at a parked car and all three set off towards it. Lena gave Svetlana a nudge and drew her attention to the scene.

'What a schlep!' Svetlana said. 'What a loser! I bet he skives off to the cinema when he should be working.' She lit a cigarette to give emphasis to her words, a recently acquired habit.

'Where will they take him?'

'Oh, they'll give him a good spanking and let him go.' Svetlana's mind was already on other things. Lena watched her tear the cigarette from her mouth and exhale peevishly.

Lena's stomach seized up. She needed to get away, back to her room and her books; she wanted to wrap the duvet round her feet and stare at a wall. She felt suddenly cold. Others in the hall of residence had complained of a surge in red armbands since Andropov—alcohol was more expensive too, and no longer available at all before noon. Luckily, Andropov was already dead and buried; his successor hadn't lasted long either. There was a joke going around that if you were old and sick and struggling to get by on your pension, you should apply to be head of the CPSU—you had every chance of being accepted. People were speculating whether things would be better under the new Secretary General, Gorbachev, and whether he'd hold out longer than a year.

Lena didn't care how long the various leaders held their posts or what new regulations were passed. She did nothing unlawful, barely drank—not even when there were parties in the hall of residence and all the doors were flung wide and the tables pushed together across the corridor so that everyone could sit round. She often stayed in her room alone, pleading work—and work she did—but when it all got too loud and she had a headache from the clink of glasses and the clatter of plates, she would wrap herself in her coat and go out. She would walk through the cones of light from the street lamps, trying to shake the feeling that time was running away from her. She saw her mother only rarely now, and Rita didn't allow herself to sound weak on the phone, let alone desperate, so Lena didn't either; she kept quiet about the panic she sometimes felt, forced herself to breathe deeply and calmly when she phoned her parents and told them only of her successes, and that she'd soon be home with her degree. Just hang on in there a little longer. Just a little. Please.

In only one semester at the Medical University, Lena had gathered enough information to prove what she'd known since childhood: Oksana Tadeyevna was a fraud who had misdiagnosed her mother. She'd always claimed that Rita had meningitis and that the only cure was the expensive drug in ampoules that was so hard to get hold of, but in fact you either died of meningitis very quickly or made a full recovery. An inflammation flares up and kills you or it doesn't, but Rita had been dying for over a decade from something that was gnawing at her flesh and sapping her strength. She never complained of nausea, but on Lena's rare visits to Horlivka Rita often got up to go to the toilet, leaving Lena and her father in front of the lavish spread that had been prepared for Lena's arrival. They heard her vomiting through the thin walls. Lena would look at her father as he raised his fork to his mouth in silence, his face grey and badly shaven, the stubble dotting the skin around his thin lips like ants. Too soon, Lena thought, it's too soon. Don't leave me on my own.

Rita came back to the table and tried to pick up her knife and fork. Lena moved closer to her and stroked her back. She hoped that something in her mother's wasting body would remember these small gestures that she used in place of words; Rita was getting more and more forgetful and Lena wasn't sure how to interpret this. Did it mean she felt abandoned and helpless, or was she withdrawing inside herself as the illness progressed, returning to her childhood, where the sense of helplessness was not yet so overpowering? Maybe she felt better there, even good.

Sometimes Rita spoke of the estate in Sochi where she'd grown up, as if Lena didn't know the house and the hazelnut trees from her own childhood. She told Lena that when she was little her mother would shoo her out of the house first thing to water the vegetables and pick gooseberries. For a long time, she said, until she was eleven or twelve, she always got into bed with her mother when she'd finished these chores. The bed was no more than a hard plinth padded with brightly coloured blankets, and the wooden walls were hung with rag rugs to keep out the cold which began creeping into the corners of the house every November. In the evenings Rita would stay out as late as possible, doing her homework on the grass. 'Mum was so beautiful. I'd see her through the kitchen window pottering about inside and I couldn't believe how beautiful she was.' Rita only smiled with the left side of her face now, but her eyes were clear and piercing. 'With that thick black plait down to her bum… You should have seen her. Sometimes I couldn't take my eyes off her.'

Lena was startled at how like Grandmother Rita was becoming—her gestures, even the way she walked. She saw before her the woman in the gaudy housedress, sitting hunched over, slowly scratching her hands, then running the back of one hand over her face, as if trying to wipe strands of hair from her forehead.

She'd died quickly, her father whispered into the phone. Gone to bed and fallen asleep. The things people always said. For the first time in her life Lena shouted at him, using all the bad words she could think of. He didn't react. She wanted them to argue at last. *Monsters-useless-arseholes-criminals-they-killed-the-wrong-woman.* Nothing. Her father didn't speak, didn't hang up. Lena stood at reception in the hall of residence, cursing away, tears running into her mouth. She pressed her thighs into the edge of the telephone table; the veneer rippled and then split. She stared at the long splinters sticking out until all was quiet. Then a high-pitched tone started up, followed by a roar, as if giant hands had been clapped over her ears. Lena clung to the receiver until the receptionist came and took it out of her hand. The roar gave way to a hooting sound that was still in her ears on the train back to Horlivka.

Something pulsed in her throat, as if a frog were about to burst out of her gullet and go splat on the train window. She'd only been studying for three years, and in that moment it felt as meaningless as the perpetual cycle of seasons: slush in the streets, lilac in the nose, hot dust in the air, the sour taste of new apples, steamed-up windows, and then snow again. Like cotton wool everywhere. Why should she put herself through another two years of that?

'I'm going to sue that charlatan!' she yelled when her father met her at the station. 'She used Mum's illness to get rich. We must apply for an autopsy.'

They were walking along the platform. Father shook his head in silence and let her rant.

The next day Lena was even more furious, and this time she turned her rage on him.

'If you don't have the guts, you must let me make the application.' Her voice trembled; her eyes felt as if someone were pressing on them from the inside. She clenched her fists.

'What's the use, Lena? What difference would it make?' He was still wearing the same peaked cap, the edges shiny with grease.

'We'd get her convicted. Who knows how many more lives she has on her conscience.'

'I don't want a scandal, child. It won't bring your mother back.' And that, as far as he was concerned, was that; he started talking about mushrooms. Lena was speechless. It would soon be time for morels, he said—he went down to the ash trees most weekends in the spring; you found some beauties there. He said things had changed at school. The pupils were bolder, cheekier—they stole his folders and looked inside—but he was patient with them and they put up with him; he wouldn't get himself thrown out. And if he did, he had his mushrooms—he'd got to be quite the expert.

'What mushrooms, Dad? It's winter! Are you actually aware of anything that's going on around you?' Lena jumped up and stormed out of the kitchen, knocking over her chair.

The next day she went to the clinic where she'd done her internship, and begged the consultant to perform an autopsy on her mother's body, even without an application from her father. She had no foreign liquor and certainly no money, and she knew there was no point crying to his smug face. That wasn't how things worked here—in fact, nothing worked at all. She was offered condolences; her hand was pressed in commiseration; she was ushered out of the office.

At the end of the corridor, she thought she saw her mother silhouetted against the window. Now I'm going mad, she thought. I am going mad. They'll have to section me. The grey light shone through Rita. She was tall and upright, her face an empty oval—nothing in it, no one there. Lena resisted the temptation to call out to her.

They barely managed to scrape together the money for the funeral; all the family savings had gone on medication. But Lena didn't want her mother in a state-assigned plot on the edge of the cemetery, next to the public toilets; she wanted her somewhere central, away from the stench, so she suggested that they take the money put aside by her parents for her hypothetical co-op flat, sometime, in some city—who knew where she'd be posted when she graduated, who knew whether she'd ever need more than the six square metres she was entitled to? Who knew anything? The last thing she wanted to think about was whether she would one day have room for a child's cot. Her mother needed somewhere now. There'd still be pillow money over.

It was the first time her father raised his voice: that money was for a flat—a place for her and Vassili when they were grown up enough to start a family. End of story. He didn't get up and leave the room, but he might as well have done; he was already somewhere else, and Lena felt that she'd lost both parents. She'd lost everyone. Rage drummed in her head and against her ribs far into the night, and just before she fell asleep she thought of Alyona.

Grandmother didn't arrive until the day of the funeral. Lena almost failed to recognize her beneath the heaps of wool in which she'd swaddled herself. Her sharp nose poked out and the tip of her grey plait peeped between the shawls. They hugged each other, then Grandmother sat down at a distance, muttering to herself and moving her fingers as if she were worrying an invisible rosary. Her eyes inched their way across the floor like cautious spiders.

Father had borrowed money from the neighbours, enough for a small ceremony. A few guests had come, Rita's colleagues from the chemical works and his from school; they slurped soup, knocked back the home-made schnapps and talked about pay, the desperate lack of garage space and the ubiquity of death. One man from their block who'd been sent north to clear up after the reactor exploded had died soon after coming home, not yet thirty. Another hadn't even made it back. Then there was the woman who washed the floors in the chemical works—she'd lost her husband somewhere up by Chernobyl and now she walked up and down the aisles cursing to herself: 'It's the worthless ones that get sent, the ones they can spare…' She was beyond help. There was always something. People died, didn't they?

Lena wanted to stop her ears with one of her grandmother's shawls. She'd meant to be angry at Grandmother for coming so late, leaving the family in the lurch, abandoning her daughter and granddaughter—but instead she sat on the floor at her feet, clawing the hem of her dress. She didn't move until Vassili, down from Leningrad for the funeral, asked her to go for a walk with him.

He'd been acting strangely all day, but Lena hadn't felt like dealing with him and certainly hadn't been in the mood for kissing and cuddling. He had kept his distance, as instructed all those years ago at camp on the sign outside the dance room: PIONEER (exclamation mark) KEEP YOUR DISTANCE (exclamation mark). He pulled her out of the flat, pressed her hand, and then, clearly realizing how uptight he must seem, he put an arm round her shoulders, planted a kiss on her forehead and guided her to the bench in the yard. He pulled his quilted jacket tighter and told her that he wanted to get married before the end of the year—he'd soon be finishing military academy and needed to tie the knot before they packed him off to Bolshaya Lopatka or Vladivostok or somewhere. Only men with family ties in Leningrad were allowed to stay. Lena looked at him absently, sensing what was coming.

'I'm not getting married so soon after my mother's death.'

'That's what I thought. So I found myself a new fiancée. In Leningrad.'

'How long's this been going on?'

'Forgive me.'

And that was that. He got up, leaving her on the bench, and off he went—perhaps he gave a last wave or a nod, but Lena was no longer looking at him. She sat there for a while, feeling the slush soak into her laces and the wetness creep into her shoes.

Horlivka in winter was flat and shapeless—only the edges of a few buildings stood out against the white sky like lines in a drawing. Lena wandered between the deserted market stalls with their corrugated-iron roofs; old newspapers clung to the metal tables and stands. No vegetables, no crying of wares, no oranges in the asphalt gutters—only the deep prints of square-tread soles in the slush. She hadn't seen Irakli Zevarovich for years, a decade, a whole life. He'd probably forgotten her, like everyone else. She could walk forever now, and no one would pay attention to her. Soon not even her friends would recognize her when they passed her on the street.

She walked to the concrete castle, sure that Oksana Tadeyevna still lived there. She hadn't come to the funeral, of course, and for that Lena was grateful. She would have torn her piss-yellow hair from her head in bloody clumps. Lena stared up at the Stalinka. It no longer looked imposing. The façade had lost something of its glory; it was stained, and the lowest of the marble steps was broken. Lena didn't walk up them.

She couldn't work it out. Was she moving slowly or had the sun got stuck somewhere and decided not to bother setting? By the time she arrived home her head was on fire; she hadn't been wearing a hat and had been out so long she was numb all over—only her forehead burned. Her father looked at her in alarm and asked if she'd been smoking. 'I tried,' Lena said. 'But the packet fell in the snow and the filters and matches were all wet.'

The guests had left; Grandmother had gone to lie down. Lena heard only the whistle of her own lungs. 'I couldn't light them. Guess I'll live longer.'

‘Let me make you some tea.’ Her father went ahead into the kitchen. And because Lena knew he wouldn’t dare ask why she’d been wandering around town for hours without her hat, she told him about her broken engagement, keeping it as brief as the break-up itself. He nodded and stirred sugar into her tea.

‘I’ll never forgive you for that.’ Lena pressed her lips to the hot rim of the cup.

‘It wasn’t to be, darling. You’ll find another.’

‘That’s not what I mean.’ She still couldn’t cry; her voice failed her. ‘I mean for not letting me find out the real cause of Mum’s death. We could have done something.’

‘No, we couldn’t. That’s what I’ve been trying to tell you. It was too late.’

His silhouette had changed; he looked like a stale bread ring when he stood up. Lena thought he would come to her and give her a hug or a slap in the face, but he walked right past her to the window and didn’t say another word all evening. He still hadn’t spoken when she left the following day.

On the train, Lena slept with her head on the window frame. She saw Vassili walking along the promenade of a city she didn’t know. It was a warm spring day and he was sauntering along in his naval uniform, hands clasped behind his back. The glittering water softened the light; he was smiling. When the ticket inspector woke Lena, she shouted at him as if *he* were Vassili. That the idiot could even feature in her dreams felt like an insult. She clawed and tugged at the calico curtain at her temple, trying to tear it down, but it only rattled its metal eyelets against the rail.

The winter ended with persistent rain; it sounded as if pigeons were scratching at the windows with their crusty feet, asking to be let in. A brief spell of sun in the morning had made Lena forget the possibility of showers and she had walked the short distance from the hall of residence to the head of institute's office in thin, leaky shoes. Now she was waggling her toes about inside wet socks, while Nadezhda Gennadyevna offered her condolences and then launched into a lengthy aside about the latest research on meningitis and epilepsy. She asked, almost in passing, if Lena suffered from migraines—and in the long pause that followed, she looked into Lena's face. Lena shook her head wordlessly, not daring to avert her gaze. Nadezhda Gennadyevna was wearing a pepper-and-salt suit; the waistband of the skirt squeezed her ample bosom up and out like a funnel. She always wore a silk scarf knotted at her throat; today's was apricot-coloured. She looked rested; her eyes and forehead shone. As she held forth she addressed the raised window blind, then the spines on the bookshelves. It was only when she abruptly suggested that Lena switch course that she looked her in the face again. This time Lena lowered her eyes. She wasn't surprised, but she heard a sound in her head like breaking wood, hollow and dusty. There's a funny smell in here, she thought, but what is it?

'I'm not going to throw you out, but it isn't advisable to study neurology when your own mother has died of a nervous disease.'

Lena wanted to object, but you didn't interrupt your senior. She stared at the silk knot under her supervisor's double chin and felt it pressing into her own throat. If she quit neurology, she'd never see Nadezhda Gennadyevna again—presumably she'd have to change halls of residence too. Maybe she'd just abandon everything. She'd pack her bags, ask Svetlana and Olga the way to the island with the Taras Shevchenko memorial, walk over the bridge and vanish.

Her wet toes felt like gnarled claws. She thought about the chill that things leave behind them.

Nadezhda Gennadyevna was the only professor who smoked. In the mornings, as the students hurried to their lectures, she would stand, cigarette in hand, outside the university building, calling out to them, chaffing them: what time did they call this, how would they ever pass their exams; they'd miss the future, their heads weren't screwed on right. It was her ritual. 'You don't look fit to sit an exam—were you burning the midnight oil last night, or were you out on the town?' Lena always said good morning, nodding and smiling, smoothing her blouse, patting her cheeks and the throbbing skin under her eyes, tidying her hair with her fingers. She had thought it would go on forever. She'd rush to lectures, chivvied by her supervisor; she'd graduate and go to her with a bottle of cognac to thank her for the chivvying—and one day, in years to come, they would be colleagues and stand together at receptions, holding glasses of sparkling wine, exchanging recipes for salads, talking about prospective trips. That was how she'd seen herself. As one of those people who lead mundane, comfortingly unremarkable lives.

'From now on, you'll see your mother in every patient who rolls her eyes in pain. You won't be able to think of anything else till the end of your life. Is that what you want?'

Lena had to reply—if a person of authority asks you a question, you have to say something. But she couldn't. She had no words or thoughts on anything. Only Vassili popped into her head. She wondered what his new fiancée looked like. Was she well off? Was her father a high-ranking functionary? Was her mother still alive? Did they all get together at the weekends? She looked at Nadezhda Gennadyevna, hoping she couldn't see her clenched jaws. Even if she'd known what to say, she couldn't have got a word out.

'I'm not saying you should drop medicine, but you should specialize in something that will allow you to forget your guilt. Otherwise you won't be able to work.'

And that was that. Lena knew she'd missed the moment to object. By a long way. The chain of announcements was over; now they had to be acted upon, because at some point (but when?) she had failed to open her mouth.

They said goodbye. Nadezhda Gennadyevna told Lena she would miss her; she was an excellent student. If she wanted help switching to any other institute in Human Medicine, she had only to say. The halls of residence on the other side of campus were said to be better anyway.

Olga and Svetlana agreed with Nadezhda Gennadyevna. They, too, found it sad to see Lena go, but they could always visit each other and have outings together and meet at the cinema. They patted Lena's hands and thought out loud for her as she lay on her bed staring at the ceiling.

'Do gynaecology—it's not a complicated subject and you'd earn good money.'

'No! Are you mad? After a few years at the operating table her calves would look like swollen gherkins full of worms. Do dermatology—they treat STDs too. All you have to do is prescribe ointments and tablets. Everyone has syphilis these days. You'd rake it in!'

Lena stayed in bed for days, letting her thoughts wash over her. She didn't go to lectures, turned up her nose at the chicken in aspic that Svetlana had found for her somewhere, wandered the corridors of the hall of residence (a shock to the night porter whose torch lit up her ghostly figure), scraped her thigh on the cracked veneer of the receptionist's table (hours after the receptionist had left for home) and stared at the mute telephone.

But at some point, she'd had enough. Enough of the numbness in her bones and the squashed face that looked out at her from the mirror, as if someone had given it a hard rub with the flat of their hand. Enough of the disgust she felt at everyone around her, the stupid afternoon daydreams, the feeling of being unable to grasp a single thought. She allowed herself to grieve until spring was well under way; then she went to Nadezhda Gennadyevna, asked to be transferred to the Institute of Dermatology, and told her she'd found a room in the hall of residence next to the institute. Nadezhda Gennadyevna squeezed her shoulder and wished her well—or something.

It grew warm in the city. Poplar wool flew into Lena's eyes and clung to her coat; she plucked it off her sleeves, gripping the soft clumps between her fingers, raising them to her face, holding them out to examine them.

'I knew I'd seen you before!' Lena's new room-mate cried, as they exchanged notes on school, Pioneer camp and university thus far. Lena, who was unpacking her clothes, looked up enquiringly and tried to smile back at the pear-shaped face beaming at her. The room was pure luxury. Two desks stood side by side at a big open window—so much space just for the two of them. Inna seemed to have been living here a while; the walls were covered with calendar pages and horoscopes. Light fell on the red and beige plaid blankets on the mattresses; Lena sat down on one of them, while Inna paced the room. 'You were at the Eaglet with me!'

Lena looked up at this vivacious young woman; she had no memory of Inna's blond mane, protruding teeth or ridiculously short nose. Nor did she recall her high sing-song voice—and she could have sworn that she herself had changed beyond recognition since her Pioneer days.

She nodded, surprised.

'The Eaglet! Those were great times, weren't they? That was before you had to paint your lips to be noticed. I like thinking back to those summers—you too? The salute every morning and evening, a bit of waffle from the leader, and then once you'd got kitchen duty out of the way, there was nothing but the lake and the chickens and blissful boredom.' Inna pranced around the room; she seemed to have trouble sitting still and keeping her mouth shut. Lena hoped it was only the excitement of a new room-mate, and that she was actually a calm, hard-working person who spoke very little. That was the kind of person Lena had decided to be—she wanted, if possible, never again to say a superfluous word to anyone.

'You were friends with the wonky girl, weren't you? The crazy one. She went to my school, in Mariupol.'

The memory of Alyona returned so suddenly that Lena felt as if a load of sawdust had been emptied into her lungs. She saw Alyona's wayward hair sticking out behind her ears and her fingers trying to tame it. Before she could say anything, though, Inna was babbling again. 'You know who I mean. What's-her-name. The one who burned her neckerchief.'

'Who did what?'

'You know, set fire to her neckerchief and waved it around till it singed her fingers. What was her name again? Alina? No, something Armenian... The weird-looking one who limped like Baba Yaga. She set fire to her Pioneer's neckerchief in school. I wasn't there, only heard about it afterwards. But I think it was pretty bad. Apparently she'd stopped talking, wouldn't answer the teachers or anything. So she was summoned to the headmaster's office, and when she got there she kicked over a table and... No idea where she got the matches... Can you believe it? In front of the entire committee! They must have thought she was going to set fire to herself and burn down the whole school.'

Lena didn't believe a word of the stories that this young woman was rattling off like a wind-up rabbit. People talked so much, they talked all the time. But absurd though Inna's story was, it was good to hear about Alyona. It meant she still existed; it meant that Inna might know where she was.

'They put her in the loony bin—didn't you know? Schizophrenia's a serious business. Now she's being pumped full of whatever psych-drugs it takes—apparently that helps with cases of ideological sabotage. You're the neurologist, you'll know.'

Lena wanted to jump up and hurl herself at Inna, but she couldn't move.

'Why schizophrenia? She—'

'Oh, come on, she wasn't normal! Burning your neckerchief's not normal! Why would you do that? What's the point? That's not something any sane person would do. It's delusional, you can treat that. There are methods. I think it's irresponsible not to help people who are sick… Why are you crying?'

Every bone in Lena's body seemed to give way; she no longer had a spine to hold her up or a neck to support her head, and her lungs were bursting—no room for air or screams, only a gasping rattle and a stream of saltwater running out of her eyes and nose. She tried not to sob too loudly, and alternately pressed her face into the pillow and stared at the wall. Inna crept round the bed and gave her a glass of water. 'Here, drink this. Drink, girl, come on. I'm not going anywhere till you've drunk something. Are you pregnant or what?'

That night Lena dreamt she was peeping around in a wood-lined room that must have been part of a dacha. Feeling very small and hardly daring to move, she clambered down from a cloth-covered plinth that was fixed with brackets to the roughly hewn planks of the wall. An old rag rug on the floorboards scratched her bare feet. She stood there, hesitating over whether to turn back—but back where? Her toes were a greyish white and didn't look like hers. The sun burned bright patches inside the house, and a soft clatter came from somewhere, perhaps from a neighbouring room, Lena wasn't sure, but she followed the sound, dazzled by the contrast between the summery brightness of the yard and the darkness of the interior. She felt her way along the wooden walls, rubbing splinters into her fingers; she passed through a room of enormous glass cabinets filled with porcelain ornaments and came to the kitchen. On an oak table stood the faun figurine. Lena picked it up; she wanted to put it away in one of the cabinets. But she couldn't move. She stood there staring at the figure in her hand—the hairy, twisted torso, the scary goat's hooves. The clatter was very close now. It was coming from the other end of the kitchen, but Lena didn't look that way—didn't look at Alyona, though she knew she was there, standing at the stove, stirring a metal pot. She realized now what was making the sound: it was a ladle going round and round the inside of the pan.

As if pulled by strings, her head was jerked round to the yard window, and she looked out through pollen-covered glass. The sun was shining on a big field covered in oblong mounds. No grass grew on the loose soil; it rose and fell steadily as if it were breathing. Like piano keys played by an invisible hand.

'Frogs, you know,' Alyona began, 'have extremely strong legs. They'll bounce out of anything. Flex their muscles and off they go—like rockets. *Whoosh.*' She was lisping, which she never had. Lena couldn't remember Alyona's voice, but it hadn't sounded like that. She still hadn't looked at Alyona, but she was sure she had her back to her. The continued clatter told her that she hadn't stopped stirring the pot. 'What I'm saying is, you have to boil them slowly. If you throw a frog into scalding water, it'll jump straight out and get away. Then you have to chase it around the kitchen and if you're not careful, you'll end up squashing it dead—you can't make soup out of that.' The sound of metal on metal stopped and Lena forced herself to look up. Alyona had a black plait, longer and thicker than any plait she'd had in real life, and she was wearing strange, rustic clothes—a floor-length skirt and a brown apron tied at the waist in a bow. 'But if you put the frog into tepid water and set the pan on a low flame, it won't notice what's happening. It'll think it's at home in its pond. Sometimes I speak soothingly to them; they look at me with their big eyes and I look back with mine. In the end, the muscles in their legs are so limp they can't even twitch.'

Alyona turned slowly. Her face was small and charred, her eyes stuck out on either side of her head like balloons. She rushed at Lena, as if she were flying. Lena stumbled backwards and before Alyona could get to her, she woke up.

'Are you having a nightmare?' she heard Inna say. 'Speak to me. Can I get you anything?'

She had got up and was sitting on the edge of Lena's bed. 'What's the matter? Are you going to cry again?'

THE NINETIES

Meat Grinder

'EVERYTHING ABOUT A PERSON must be glorious. Face, clothes, soul—even thoughts. Do you understand that? The way you look reflects the way you think!'

The senior consultant had gathered the entire team around him to watch as he humiliated a young doctor who had presumed to show up at the clinic in dark-blue jeans and a black polo-neck jumper. Lena stood at the back. The young man held his hands clasped behind him and appeared to be holding his breath, but he kept his shoulders braced and his eyes on his boss, who paused at the end of every sentence.

'If a doctor comes to work in sloppy or, even worse, Western-style attire, he will be taken for a gherkin seller and treated accordingly. He will lose his authority, he will lose his credibility and eventually he will lose his job, because who needs a doctor who doesn't have his patients' respect?'

This went on for some time; Lena tried not to look. The whole team was silent. When the rant was over, Lena went up to the young man and searched for words of encouragement, but he raised a defensive hand.

'I can't hear this Chekhov crap any longer. These retards quote

Uncle Vanya at every fucking turn. It's the same drivel my grandmother used to spout.' He glared at Lena, as if she were the one who'd come up with the line about glorious people. 'Reactionary fools who can't accept their time is past.' He cursed and turned away, leaving Lena standing there; the rest of her colleagues went their separate ways too.

Lena stared at the closed door of the senior consultant's office as if it were a back that had been turned on her; she regretted having opened her mouth. The paint on the door was no longer fresh, and the consultant, too, was of the old guard. Lena was so scared of his fits of temper that she avoided catching his eye. Perhaps that was why he liked her. He sometimes called her 'modest but determined' in front of the whole team, or praised her 'consistently neat and pleasing' appearance. He wished, he said, that all his staff would speak to their patients as attentively, and as firmly, as Lena Romanovna. This aroused her colleagues' suspicions. There were whispered speculations about the services she must have provided to gain such favour—the boss was married, but that didn't mean much. Even Lena was surprised that his generous treatment of her depended on no more than honest work. She didn't blame her colleagues for suspecting otherwise.

She couldn't have explained to them that it was sometimes nice just to hear a kind word from someone—it didn't matter who. The young men at the parties Inna took her to played the guitar and expected to receive praise, not give it; when they spoke, it was to hold forth about the political changes instigated by Gorbachev—Gorbachev this, Gorbachev that. They spoke about *avenues of opportunity*; they all wore blue jeans. Their shoes were generally filthy. Their eyes shone unpleasantly.

Every morning Lena checked in the mirror for silver streaks in her light-brown hair; she was prepared to start dyeing it at any time. She was only thirty-one, too early to go grey, but at university she'd seen a student lose her hair colour and two teeth within a few months of pregnancy—she'd barely been twenty. Lena was there when the child's father came to fetch his wife's things from the hall of residence after she'd given birth. He had a flabby mastiff with him called Sarah.

'Sarah?' Lena asked, when he introduced the dog to her.

'Yes,' he said. 'Sarah, like all fat Jewish girls.' And he grinned.

Every weekend Lena rang her father in Horlivka. In the past, their phone calls had been like shouting into a forest. They had flung words at each other and waited for an echo. Now that had changed; only her father spoke. His words flew towards her like sheets from a stack of paper in a gust of wind. She tried to swallow and breathe steadily; she watched herself grow more and more afraid that he would tell her how he really was, but he never did.

To her mother, meanwhile, she spoke daily. She told her about the cardboard shanty town that had gone up under the bridge she crossed on her way to work. People had built themselves shelters and put up improvised stalls; they seemed to be trading. From the bridge you couldn't tell what kind of people they were or what they were selling, but there was an almost constant throng of coats and headscarves. Signs on masts and tarpaulins flaunted illegible slogans. The golden city of Dnipropetrovsk.

Lena sat at the table in her living room, munching quark pancakes, chatting to her mother, shaking her head at the plans her parents had harboured of organizing a flat for her and Vassili. Back then it had been as likely as flying into space—sure, people did it, but how did they go about it? Now Lena had as much room for herself as her parents had had for the four of them. She arranged the furniture exactly as she remembered it from her childhood.

She leant her head against the wall, let her eyes roam over the floral carpet and felt grateful for the tight-fitting windows that kept out the icy wind. She didn't explain words like *estate agent*, *private ownership* or *apartment swap* to her mother—words that were buzzing like flies around the heated heads of people who were trying to make a life for themselves beyond socialism. She preferred to say, 'I think we should tidy up the cabinet, Mum, there's so much junk in there... Actually, the cabinet itself is junk, I should get myself a new one... I'm useless at darning, Mum, and I can't go to work in laddered tights. You may think it's a waste of money, but I earn enough to afford new ones... I know you prefer the other shoes, but this is what people are wearing right now. Please don't be cross...'

The shoes that Lena wore to work had only a hint of a heel; the senior consultant expressed disapproval at this when he called her into his office for a 'serious talk'. It didn't bode well, Lena thought, that he began with her shoes.

'You could afford to be bolder, you know. Heels raise a woman's authority.'

Lena made a mental inventory of the shoes in her possession, wondering if she owned a single pair that would satisfy him.

'Our clinic, Lena Romanovna, is like the outside world; there are two kinds of people here. Those who want to achieve something in life and those who believe that their birth was some sort of fluke—that they just happen to exist, the rest is out of their hands. They take life as it comes, you might say.'

He got up and walked over to the window; Lena could no longer see his expression against the light—even his thick moustache was only a notion.

'I don't believe the world is held up by people who think only of how to get from one month's wages to the next, but you see, the state is crumbling… people have to look out for themselves. It's understandable. Our country is stretched out on the operating table, slit open from belly to throat. These… upheavals, these changes will give us a growing number of people who are ready for anything. People who believe only in themselves—because what else can they believe in? You take what you can get—anything else would be foolish, wouldn't it?'

Lena understood the words, but she didn't know what her boss was getting at. His lecture reminded her a little of the waffle spouted by the boys she met at parties. She looked up at him, hoping it was still wisest to say nothing.

'Humans have always been this way—they're animals. If you don't keep them in check, they guzzle up everything around them and then starve because there's nothing left for them to eat. That's what's going to happen now, and I… I don't want you to go under in the carnage.'

Lena suddenly wondered how she'd react if he came closer and put a hand on her breast. Would she slap him in the face and run out, or would she stay? The nape of her neck was damp with sweat. She listened uneasily, her stomach muscles tense, ready for flight; she barely heard a thing until her boss said, '…so I'm putting you in charge of our private patients here at the clinic'.

Lena felt her eyebrows shoot up and her lips part, but still she said nothing.

'That's why I asked you here. To tell you that I'm assigning you to the private wing. You'll have your own surgery. We can discuss payment at a later date.'

And before Lena could thank him—before her stomach muscles could relax—she was dismissed with the words, 'So you might take a little more care with your appearance now. I want to see high heels, more expensive fabrics. Your patients will come to you in furs; you have to look the part.'

For the rest of the week, Lena felt numbed. Her boss had only asked her to do her bit; he hadn't overstepped the mark. She realized that he would keep the lion's share of the fees for himself, but she didn't mind. She told no one of her promotion; there were enough rumours as it was about their supposed secret relationship. Later, though, when she first entered her office-cum-surgery in the newly refurbished private wing, she was so happy she bit her fists.

The senior consultant had been right; Lena's patients came to her in furs. She'd had no idea the country contained such rich people. Even the Party officials she knew from television never wore anything fancier than dark three-piece suits with clunky black or brown shoes and perhaps, at a push, long leather coats flung over their shoulders. But from her first day as a consultant in the private wing of the clinic for dermatology and venereology, young men came to her in sharply cut suits and pointed patent-leather shoes, bringing with them women who wore skimpy minks over their silk dresses—little more than négligées.

Lena never asked more than was necessary; she stuck to the facts, her face impassive, as she recommended soothing vaginal rinses, prescribed antibiotic creams for penile sores and penicillin for urethritis, dispensed ointments for genital itching and palpated lymph glands in latex gloves. Her friends, she thought, had been right to urge her to take up dermatology: almost everyone had syphilis; she would earn good money.

A gold bangle set with garnets was soon dangling from her wrist; it looked good with her light-brown hair. She still wore very little make-up, but she asked a surgeon friend to pierce her ears for her.

'You're very late!' her friend said. 'Ten is the age for this. What have you been doing all this time?'

Lena put silver studs in the healing wounds and went looking for silk scarves of green and orange to drape around her neck like Nadezhda Gennadyevna.

Her patients arrived in cars she'd never heard of, but which had clearly been brought over the border from the West. They wore flashy watches; they came bearing gifts. Cognac and whisky, flowers and foreign chocolates were the inevitable accompaniments to their informal gifts of cash. Some patients gave her lambskin gloves or miniature landscape paintings inlaid with softly gleaming amber. A television was carried unpackaged past reception and deposited in her office. Lena returned the warm greetings, answered the polite enquiries into her father's health and then asked what brought the patient to her this time. Invitations were proffered. Most of these she declined, but she knew that after a third request she had to accept. She toured building sites with newly appointed directors, nodded appreciatively and raised her glass to the good fortune and success of one brand-new company after another, often without having a clue what they produced or distributed.

It didn't surprise her that the same men kept coming back; she generally knew by the time she wrote the first prescription that they weren't going to change their way of life—not even when threatened with impotence or blindness.

'That won't happen to me, will it, doctor?' they would say jokingly. 'You'll help me, won't you doctor? That's why I come to you.'

Lena would reply, as neutrally as she could, that she would do everything in her power, but that she strongly advised them to use condoms. She knew it was useless. It staggered her that these men kept coming back with their wives—always the same women, whom she was to examine as discreetly as possible for diseases their husbands had picked up elsewhere. More often than not, they undressed in silence. They didn't ask why they were constantly being brought to the dermatologist, or whether the rashes and itches and stabbing pains were serious. After examining them, Lena would scan their faces to see if they had anything in common—indifference, perhaps, or greed or simple-mindedness. But there seemed to be no resemblance between them, except that they were all proud and reserved. If they spoke at all, it was to talk about the books they were reading, or perhaps a film they had seen.

There was one young woman in particular whom Lena couldn't get out of her head. She was certainly under eighteen; Lena hoped she was over sixteen. Her 'boyfriend' had brought her to the clinic in his West German car. She called him that without a trace of naïveté; she knew the nature of their relationship, and she knew that Lena knew. She had light-brown, almost caramel-coloured hair that came to her waist, even in a high ponytail, and very thin legs that stuck out into the air past Lena's ears when she examined her. She was pregnant. The syphilitic bacteria could infect the unborn child, Lena explained to her; she must see a gynaecologist immediately. The young woman slipped back into her jeans, lit a cigarette and offered one to Lena. Lena took it, but refused her offer of a light. She endured the ash that the girl flicked on the floor; she endured the growing silence.

'I don't want your pity,' the girl said, when she came to the end of her cigarette and got up to leave. 'Can you promise not to pity me?'

'Of course,' Lena lied.

The cardboard shanty town had been cleared. One morning, Lena walked over the bridge and instead of the usual throng of people in worn coats and headscarves she saw only a battered bus with no wheels. Stray dogs sniffed at scraps of soggy cardboard on an endless stretch of wasteland. Soon the place was transformed into a building site—as if there weren't already enough. Lena wondered where the shanty dwellers had been sent.

Since her student years, the word *sovok* had been used to describe the situation they were all in. It meant 'dustpan'. Some said it was an abbreviation for 'Soviet occupation'; others preferred the suggestive image of the USSR as a giant receptacle for filth. All the trash of the world seemed to gather here, so sure, why not call the place a dustpan? But Lena didn't think either was accurate. As she looked down from the bridge at the noisy building site, it seemed to her that 'meat grinder' was the only term that described what was going on here.

'Wolf? Seriously? This thing on my face is called *wolf*?'

Lena found it hard to guess the age of the man in front of her. His file told her that he was her age, but with his loose red shirt, silly goatee and dishevelled black hair he seemed far younger. He had a leather jacket draped over his shoulders and sat with one leg over the other, arms dangling at the sides of the chair. His flippancy annoyed her—she had just prescribed him cortisone for an illness that was not to be taken lightly.

'Do you think that's funny?' she said coldly.

'Oh, come on, a Chechen with a disease called *wolf*? If you didn't look so nice, I'd think you were trying to insult me.'

There were no pictures in Lena's office, no photographs on the walls, no landscape paintings, no busts of poets or scholars on the shelves, but still she had the feeling that she and her patient were being watched—that they were not alone in the room, that their every move was under scrutiny. As if something—or someone—were waiting for them. The patient braced his shoulders; he seemed to feel the same. The sore patches on his face formed red ovals from the bridge of his nose over his cheekbones—a delicate pair of wings that looked strangely good on him.

'Chechen or not, you have lupus. It would be best if you took it seriously. The disease can attack organs as well as the skin—even blood vessels and the brain. Right now, you have a mild form; it's purely external. But you must take your medication.'

'Don't *you* think it's funny?'

'What?'

'That I have a wolf growing on my face?'

'It looks more like a butterfly, if that's any consolation.'

He fixed her with his eyes, turning his head to one side as if to observe her from another angle. He seemed about to speak, but apparently thought better of it; he looked suddenly older.

'Do you believe in God?'

'What makes you ask that?' Lena had been asked all kinds of questions in her year as a consultant, but this was a first.

'There's no justice in life, so I can't bring myself to believe in a higher power. If there was anything there, the world would be a different place. I'm a godless Muslim—but don't tell my mother, she'd slit my throat.'

'I don't think I'll have the opportunity to tell tales on you to your family.'

'Oh yes, you will—when you come and see us at the weekend. You will come, won't you?' Lena looked at him in alarm. 'I won't let you say no.'

Even the sun shining in at the window seemed to be watching them.

'I'm afraid that won't be possible.' Lena had noticed his perfume when she examined him; now it seemed stronger, as if he were coming closer, though in fact he hadn't moved from his chair.

'Come and have dinner with the family. We'll put a few tables together; some friends are coming too. You'll enjoy yourself. Don't worry, I'm not going to abduct you in a rolled-up carpet—we've been here a while; we live just round the corner.'

'Thank you, but I'm afraid it's not possible.' Lena tugged at the blouse under her doctor's coat to get rid of any unsightly creases. Did she have sweat stains under her arms? Was her breath fresh? What had she had for lunch? Winter had lurched into spring early this year—every morning Lena left the house in a warm jacket and by lunchtime she seemed to be wearing several layers too many. She hadn't checked her lipstick for some time. And she was bursting for the toilet.

'I suppose it's not posh enough for you, eating with a bunch of Chechens.'

'That's not fair.' She glanced at her watch, avoiding his eye. The waiting room must be heaving with patients, but he made no move to leave.

'Listen, I know what you're thinking. But we aren't all animals. Come and see for yourself. We won't butcher you. Promise.'

'I never said anything about animals.'

'You mentioned wolves.'

'That's the name of your illness.'

'Is that a yes? I'll call for you. Saturday?'

'It wouldn't be professional.'

The blood rose to Lena's head; she felt dizzy. In an age when doctors were gifted with television sets, it was ridiculous to invoke professional etiquette. The watch she had so pointedly consulted a moment before had also been a gift from a patient. The man in front of her knew all this, of course. Decorum was a thing of the past. She looked at the name on his file card: *Edil Azlanovich Tsurgan.*

'Listen, I've had a really bad day. Maybe that's what got me wondering about whether or not there's a god. I'm thinking: *Why me? Is this some kind of punishment? Is it my fault that nothing's worked out?* Now I have this rash on my face too, and it's sore as hell. But it's so nice, looking at you. You're the first good thing that's happened to me today. You're like a medicine that's already starting to work.'

He laughed, and Lena tried to suppress a smile. She wondered what his mother looked like. Was it from her that he'd inherited those big, wide-set eyes that were darting about the room, scanning every corner? Was she really the devout Muslim he made her out to be? He scratched his knee and then his head; he ran a hand through his hair as if trying to shake something off. His arms seemed as long as his legs—they went on and on. He smacked his lips as if he were chewing gum. He was probably waiting for Lena to reply. She breathed out, the way she'd learnt, so that he'd know his time was up.

'Then I don't need to come again?' he asked, as if alarmed at the thought.

'First you must take the medication, as we discussed.'

'I'll miss you, doctor.'

Lena wanted to say, 'I hardly think so,' but she couldn't get the words out.

'Won't you miss me?'

The right answer would have been, *I'm always glad to see my patients recover*, but again Lena missed her cue. She wondered what was the matter with her and noticed that one of her feet was cramping under the desk.

'How about the theatre? Would you come to the theatre with me? The ballet? The opera? Come on, you can't tell me you just sit here all day every day, examining people's ailing body parts. You must go out sometimes.'

In fact, Lena had never been to the opera, and although a patient had once given her theatre tickets, she hadn't used them. It had seemed weird to go alone, and she hadn't wanted to ask Inna because she was afraid of being laughed at. She could, of course, tell Edil that she had to look after her sick parents at the weekend, or that she was seeing friends or going away, but instead she stared at the angry butterfly on Edil's face and heard herself say, 'Only if you promise not to come in a loud Western-brand car and scare the neighbours!' She struggled to keep the words from skidding out of control.

'Why would they be scared? Because of the car or because of the fearsome Chechen?' Edil had leant forward and was trying to meet her eye. He smelt like a fifteen-year-old and he smiled like one too.

'For goodness' sake, stop it!' Lena meant to sound exasperated, but she ended up laughing and then sneezing.

'Bless you!' Edil said. 'You must stay healthy, too, doctor, not just me. Promise me you'll look after yourself?'

Edil pulled up in a red foreign car and sounded the horn until Lena flung open the window and gestured to him to stop. Other people, too, came to their windows.

It had taken her a long time to find something to wear that looked as if she'd thrown it on without agonizing over it. The pale-blue dress was scratchy under her armpits and tight across her chest; she hadn't worn it for a long time and had forgotten how warm the synthetic fabric was, but it was too late to change now. It had been an unproductive day; all Lena had done was to call her father and chatter away to him—about her work, the new furniture she was thinking of buying, her plans to visit him soon. He was so surprised at her chattiness that for a while he said nothing, only listened. Then he said, 'That's great. That sounds great. You sound great.' When they said goodbye, he told her how happy she'd made him. 'Today you sound... you know, like... like when you were little and I pushed you on the swing.'

Lena almost kicked off her high-heeled shoes and ignored Edil's hooting, but then she gave herself a shake and went out. He was leaning against the car boot, smiling all over his face. He waved at Lena as if she were on the deck of a docking ship and he were greeting her from the shore. 'Come on, let's go!'

Outrageous, Lena thought, he's behaving outrageously. But she was pleased to see that he'd shaved off his goatee.

They watched an adaptation of Gogol's story *The Nose*. Lena couldn't have said who the composer was; she heard only the rush of blood in her veins. At some point between arias, Edil reached for her hand as if it were the most natural thing in the world. He didn't take it timidly, or pretend that their fingers touched by chance; he squeezed it as if all were decided between them. Lena was appalled. She wondered how she'd react if he tried to kiss her during the applause at the end. She saw herself slapping him in the face and taking a taxi home.

But when Edil helped her into her coat in the cloakroom and briefly laid a hand on her waist, Lena realized that she would do nothing if this bad-mannered man kissed her, though she might be offended if he didn't.

He didn't. Instead he asked if she was hungry.

She began to stammer. 'Yes... no... it's late... I have to work tomorrow.'

Edil drove in silence to a Georgian restaurant in the centre of town. He cut the engine and said, 'It's Sunday tomorrow. You must eat something. You can't refuse me that.'

Lena felt wretched.

They barely spoke over the *khachapuri*. In her confusion, Lena had ordered two different kinds of water—Borjomi and a still mineral water—and then didn't know which to take when they came. She ended up snapping at the waiter. Her scratchy synthetic dress was making her very hot, and her feet were throbbing in shoes they weren't used to. *Heels raise a woman's*—oh, fuck that. When the main course arrived, Edil spilt garlic sauce from the *shkmeruli* on his white shirt; he cursed and seemed angry, shaking his wrist as if he'd burnt himself. Neither of them had dessert.

They barely spoke on the drive back either. The fan in the car was unusually loud; Lena hadn't noticed it earlier. Edil drove, without being asked, to the block where she lived and made no move when Lena went to open the car door. Determined not to let him see her trembling, she walked slowly round the front of the car and resisted looking through the windscreen, which in any case was almost impossible to see through. The headlamps dazzled her. Again she had the feeling she was being watched—that there were eyes on the balconies and at the windows, following her every move. She imagined the neighbours whispering to one another, moving mouths damp with spittle, open and shut, open and shut.

Lena was already halfway to the entrance when she heard the car door open behind her. She spun round but didn't move. Edil was still in the car.

'Thank you,' she called out softly. 'It was lovely.' Then she regretted this and nodded several times, in case he hadn't heard her—perhaps he could see her silhouette. He had none of her qualms and called out to her with no thought for the neighbours, asking if he couldn't persuade her to change her mind about dinner with his family, next weekend or the weekend after.

'Please come! Don't be shy, we'd love to see you. We'll stock up on Borjomi.'

Lena thought of the estate in Sochi—the long row of tables outside on the grass, next to where the animals were slaughtered; the children hiding under the tables, the marbles in their mouths, their grinning faces. One of those children had been her. She thought of Artyom pinching her calves, Lika's whinnying laugh. And her grandmother—where was she now?

Then Lena thought again of the other people in her block. She imagined them in the tiny rooms of their tiny flats, torn from their tiny beds by Edil's resonant tenor; she saw them creeping wide-eyed to the windows in their shapeless pyjamas and peeping out from behind the curtains.

She hurried back to the car and stood at the open door. Edil still hadn't got out, but now he stretched his long, long legs out in front of him, his arms dangling at his sides, his sharp shoulders braced against the seat. He raised his smooth, lean chin towards her, his face level with her breasts. The only thing she saw with any clarity were his big, wide-set eyes. She took his head in her hands and, hesitating to lean in and kiss him, she pressed his face against her dress.

We swore that we'd never stray from
Off the path or leave the way, but hey—
Fate had other plans…
And I will not lie to you-ou
We're all scared of what is new, but hey—

Edil screeched the words, sinking his fingers into the chords of an imaginary synthesizer. He did not in any way resemble Makarevich—didn't have the singer's square face or chin-length hair or deep, powerful voice. Edil sang in a keening wail that made Makarevich's perestroika anthem sound like a kind of ballad, but he gave himself to the chorus with such abandon—screwing up his eyes, jumping up and down on the mattress naked, using the pillow as a microphone—that Lena had to laugh.

Yes! There's a bend ahead!
And the engine revs!

'I'm going to have a shower,' she said, trying to check his elation. She pulled herself on trembling knees and weak arms to the edge of the mattress. Her belly sagged, her breasts were tender; she felt like a crawling baby about to crash to the floor. She would have liked to pull the duvet up to her chin and sleep into the afternoon, then phone Inna and tell her everything—no, not tell her, but giggle until she worked it out. In the clinic, people would compliment her on the brightness of her eyes. She hadn't looked in the mirror, but she was sure her cheeks were shiny as new apples.

'You should've heard us belting that out in the kolkhoz choir!' Edil launched into the chorus for the second time, pushing away from the mattress and coming to lie over Lena. He smelt bitter and sweet at once.

'When were you in a kolkhoz?' His face hung over hers and she reached up and kissed the tip of his nose.

'When I was at university. Weren't you a member? What's that face for? Didn't you know Chechens go to university? Did you think we all wander the countryside with our sabres drawn? I dug up potatoes and sent them to collective combines just like any other Soviet citizen, but now— *there's a bend ahead! / And the engine revs!*'

Lena grabbed his shoulders and pushed him away. It annoyed her that he could barely speak a sentence without some reference to his Chechen origins; she couldn't open her mouth without being accused of prejudice, of having no idea of his life or his family's life. Well, so what. It wasn't her fault if she didn't.

Her legs felt like jelly; she could hardly stand.

'What? Why are you looking so cross? Come here, don't have a shower. What do you want a shower for? The water's still cold.'

'I can't stand the way you go on about Chechnya. You're always telling me how I supposedly think about you and your family and how I supposedly see you.'

'So how do you see me?'

When you're in the room, it's so bright I have to squeeze my eyes shut, but I'm scared to rub them in case you think I'm helpless. But she didn't say that.

'As a man who's too handsome for his own good, a man who's thrilled that he's seduced his doctor and is now going to tell all his friends so that they can try and seduce me too—find out if I'm the kind of woman they think I am.'

'Are you scared you're going to have hordes of Chechens invading the clinic?'

'You have to stop this!' she yelled. Her voice skidded away from her and she stumbled back from the bed as if she'd lost her balance. She felt a rising panic that he would run off and leave her. Not long now and it would be over. One more wrong word and a whole chain of misunderstandings would be set off, spark by spark, and that would be it. OK, so it was going to happen anyway, it had to end at some point—but perhaps not now, not yet, not like this.

'What? What did I say?' Edil got up too. Again he seemed so much younger than Lena, and she almost burst out laughing, but he pressed his lips together and reached for his white shirt that was hanging over the chair like something dead. Lena thought what she'd been thinking ever since they'd met: soon he'll go, soon he'll be gone.

'I realize I don't—that you—I'm not blind—that someone like you—'

'What do you mean, *someone like me*? Like what?'

'You're—'

'Yes, Muslim, I'm Muslim. Come on, say it.'

'I can't talk to you.' Tears pricked Lena's eyes, but she wasn't going to let herself cry. Here in this room there was no one to watch her. The neighbours and all the other people she knew were far away; only she was staring at herself, staring bewildered at her pale face and the smeared make-up under her eyes, watching herself hold her breath, because she thought it was the only way of holding up time.

Everything that wasn't Edil felt like a waste. They hadn't been out since their night at the opera, but they met every evening in Lena's flat. Sometimes he'd be waiting outside the door when she got home from work; sometimes the doorbell rang when she was in the bathroom in her nightdress, getting ready for bed. He always smelt the same—like a fifteen-year-old. They didn't turn the light on, didn't eat, didn't drink. They held each other's mouths so they wouldn't wake the neighbours. During the day, Lena heard a constant buzzing sound; the world was like an old film running in the background.

She couldn't tell anyone what was happening. Couldn't tell anyone that she woke at night, gasping for breath, stood naked in front of her wardrobe mirror and watched herself stroking her own body, gently pressing on her throat to bring back the nights with Edil. That the heat between her legs was almost unbearable. That she went down on her knees and thrust her fingers into herself, still holding her own gaze in the wardrobe mirror, which now showed only the top of her head to her upper lip.

She couldn't tell anyone that she woke sick with fear that something might have happened to Edil. Fear that he might be gone.

Whenever they said goodbye, she told him to be careful. He would laugh in his boyish way and say, 'There isn't a war on.'

Edil was getting better. The rash seemed to be clearing; the disease hadn't spread to his organs. He had a strong back and powerful arms; he could pick her up with ease and press her against the bedroom wall, and yet… She still felt a nagging fear that something might happen to him, that he'd disappear, vanish, as if none of this had ever been. She became jumpy; things fell from her hands. She kept a close eye on her own physical reactions and dosed herself with vitamin pills so that she wouldn't fall ill and miss precious hours with him.

On the evenings when Edil couldn't make it to hers, Lena sometimes let Inna take her to parties. She couldn't bear sitting alone in the flat, staring at the ceiling or failing to read—flicking through a book without taking anything in. She would call her father and tell him she was going out, as if she were still living at home, as if they were close to each other. 'That's lovely,' he'd say, 'I'm glad.' She always hoped he would say something nice about the sound of her voice again and tell her he could hear how happy she was. But he never did.

Inna was besotted with the idea of *making a good match* and had undertaken to find someone for Lena, too. Lena played the innocent and pretended to be too tired and overworked to be interested, but it felt good to be in crowded rooms where the women smoked and laughed and the long-haired men still seemed like students, only with incipient paunches and gruffer voices. Most of them were married; most of them played the guitar; most of them talked about work and politics. Especially politics. They discussed the best way to pursue a career in these times of change; they hinted at shady deals. Their envy of those who were making money, or even millions, showed in the beads of sweat on their foreheads. They moved their arms in sweeping gestures to stress their own lack of opportunity—they hadn't had a chance to make the right decisions. They pulled helpless faces, as if uncertain whether they could still make something of their lives, or whether they'd missed the turning. *And the engine revs!*

The discussions sounded rehearsed and they always followed the same pattern; the only new topic was emigration. The Jews were leaving the country. People were talking about it everywhere. Anyone who could was moving to Israel or applying for exit visas to the United States. 'Boris has gone, Andrey and Vita are going...' The list of names grew longer and longer. 'Would you have thought they were hook-noses? No, me neither, but then we never checked to see if their dicks were circumcised.' In Lena's student days, being Jewish had been all about knowing people who could help you up the ladder and get you an attractive job—now it was all about exit visas. Who had an invitation to take off abroad, complete with perks? Apparently you got language lessons, an apartment, a job.

Inna was sprawled over an orange wing armchair as if blown there by a giant fan. Her narrow feet, in gold shoes, were crossed at the ankles, her folded arms daintily angled towards a man who was telling a joke. The green of her eyeshadow went wonderfully with her red-tinted blond hair. Lena couldn't understand why Inna hadn't found a husband yet; she was so intent on it, and Lena was sure she always got what she wanted. What she clearly didn't want was to slog away as a doctor all her life; she hardly mentioned her work as a dermatologist in the State Hospital.

'Aren't you one too, Daniel?' The group of jokers who had been talking excitedly about circumcised penises turned to a short, slight man in a roll-neck jumper. His close-cropped black beard and the straight cut of his floppy hair made his pale face look square.

He reminded Lena of the young Vladimir Vysotsky—she had a record of his where he looked like that on the cover, gripping his guitar for dear life and staring grimly into the camera. There was nothing grim, however, about Daniel in the roll-neck jumper—nor did he have Vysotsky's dusty voice, deep and evocative.

'Yes, Vova, I am. And if you were thinking of examining my cock, I'm not circumcised.'

Laughter rippled through the crowded room. The women on the windowsill clapped their hands. Someone made hissing sounds. Someone else asked, 'And why aren't you moving to the USA or Israel? Or are you planning to go soon?'

'Why would I want to go to the USA, when there are arseholes like you here?' Daniel said, and this time the laughter was even louder; people patted him appreciatively on the shoulder. He raised a glass of amber-coloured liquid to his lips, and Lena noticed that he was looking at her.

She slid off her chair next to the sideboard and mingled with the tireless talkers and drinkers, among them people from the Lebanon, Cuba, China, Vietnam. Lena looked into their cheerful faces and wondered why all these people could clink glasses with one another as if this were a student party at the University of Friendship Among Nations, when there was no way she could ever bring Edil to a party like this. Chechnya wasn't half as far as Vietnam or Cuba. Why shouldn't he come with her? What could go wrong? He might have to hear the odd remark about his genitals, but he could cope with that, he had a sense of humour. The real trouble would be that he'd go on for days afterwards about how awful her friends were, how they thought Chechens were this and Chechens were that… There was unrest in his country; his people wanted independence like everyone else—was it Lena's fault if things were going the way they were? It wasn't as if Edil had ever taken her anywhere with him. She'd never met any of his friends or family. He was probably embarrassed by her, too. This *too* startled her and she reached for a glass from the top of a mirrored cabinet. A black cat in a rose bush looked at her enquiringly from a framed embroidery on the wall.

A black cat on your way
Brings bad luck, people say.
But so far, in fact,
The unlucky one is the cat…

'Have we met?' It was Daniel's voice; Lena saw his pale face in the mirror, sprouting out of her neck. She shook her head. When she turned to face him, the smoke from his cigarette pricked her eyes; she blinked to prevent her make-up from smudging.

'Do you know this one? Two Jews meet. The first one says, "I'm emigrating, Abramovich. I'm going to Australia." "Australia?" Abramovich says, "but that's so far away!" And the first one says, "What do you mean, *far*? Far from where?"' Daniel chuckled at his own joke, but he didn't take his eyes off Lena.

'I thought you didn't want to emigrate,' she said.

'No, you're right, I don't. But when I saw you, I knew what my faraway is. Far from you would be far away.'

He asked if she'd like to dance. Lena wasn't sure how to say no—there was, in any case, such a crush that there was no way past him. She nodded.

'But only if you stop making jokes.'

'Promise.' He grabbed her hand. 'Do you know this one? Gorbachev is asked if he believes in hell. Of course, he says, but they won't let me in because they're afraid I'll dissolve it.'

Up close, Lena realized he was much older than she was—at least mid-thirties, maybe even forty. His beard covered most of his face, but his eyes pierced hers as if he were trying to tell her something.

A telegraph pole on the estate in Sochi had been hit by lightning; the phone line was down. Grandmother sent a telegram, a few brief words to let the family know. Not for the first time, Lena was struck by the similarity in tone between Grandmother and Rita; the message was a simple string of statements, each one ending with an implicit plea to be left in peace. Lena's father read it out to her over the phone, stumbling over the words—he was probably peering at it at arm's length. The council, Grandmother said, had left the charred pole and torn wires at the side of the road and was promising this and that—something, sometime. Lena imagined silently protesting sparks spraying from the tangle of cables over the gravel paths; she saw her grey-headed grandmother dragging an empty hazelnut sack along like a defective parachute.

For the time being, then, Grandmother had no phone. She could still receive letters, but Lena wrote as rarely as she had called. Before meeting Edil, she had blamed this on her exhausting twelve-hour shifts, but now she was honest with herself: she didn't know what there was to say—or rather, she knew there was a lot to say, but she couldn't face the thought of embellishing all those stories to make them palatable, or even comprehensible. She wanted to spend every minute with Edil; she didn't want to have to tell anyone anything or explain anything. No one understood anyway. People understood only what they already knew. They couldn't process new information. Although if anyone could, Lena often thought, it was Grandmother; she was probably the only person in the universe who wouldn't have minded her granddaughter obsessing over a Muslim. Things like that had never mattered to Grandmother. She concentrated her energy on her garden, the hazel trees, the pigeons' nests under the eaves.

Not long afterwards, another telegram came from Sochi, telling them that Grandmother had died. It had languished at the post office all weekend before reaching Father, and when he rang Lena early in the morning before she left for the clinic she had only a day until the funeral. She felt as if she'd been doused in hot oil. For a moment she thought burn blisters were popping all over her body; then her flesh ran cold. She vomited in the kitchen sink, wiped her mouth, called the clinic to arrange a stand-in, left a message for her boss telling him she'd be back at the end of the week, tossed clothes into a bag and dashed to the station without getting changed. She was wearing a yellow dress with a pleated skirt, flat shoes and a thin white coat. She would stand at her grandmother's grave in yellow and white.

A vendor with a tray of sugared milk pushed open the door and offered his wares into the silence of the compartment, then pushed it shut again, not understanding why the young woman huddled in the corner began to cry when he held up a bottle of the sweet drink. The autumn air crept through the rubber seal around the compartment window; Lena leant against the glass with her legs pulled up and felt the draught slice her skin. She cursed herself, because she'd known it would come to this—that Grandmother would die alone and she would hear too late. She cursed her father for not coming to the funeral—he had promised to think of her and to lay flowers on Rita's grave, for her mother's mother. Then she cursed herself again.

Lena tried to recall Artyom and Lika's faces, their long, black, sawdusty hair. They probably wore it short now—Artyom must, anyway—and they would have found themselves decent jobs, built houses, had children. Lena scratched the back of her head, like a teenager trying to get rid of dirt, or an adult trying to get rid of a memory. Her grandmother's face was a blur. Lena couldn't remember how long her hair had been the last time she'd seen her.

She thought of Edil and his big family. He was always complaining about them—his mother too strict, his four brothers and sisters always arguing over something, his father dissatisfied with everyone, wife and children—but it must be nice, she thought, to be so many. It must be nice not to have this nagging fear that the last of your family would die and leave you on your own.

Lena knew that her father often went to the cemetery; she imagined him at her mother's grave, taking off his cap, which he never took off anywhere else, running his hand over his bald head, telling his wife about his mushrooms, complaining that their daughter rarely phoned and never visited. And she imagined her mother answering with a shrug and saying, 'Leave the girl.'

The sound of the cast-iron wheels on the rails sawed away in her belly. She got up and vomited again, this time into a juddering metal toilet without a seat.

She couldn't have said whether Sochi had changed much; she had little memory of it. Everything looked strange and familiar at the same time. People were still wearing silly gaudy summer hats; it was warm and humid although it was mid-September; hydrangeas coloured the roadsides. There was a lot of building work. Some of the new buildings looked like miniature Greek temples; the fresh white of their walls glared in the hazy sun. The smell of conifers tickled Lena's nose. Her Sochi was not the city where coffee stalls lined the promenade offering flavoured syrups of every kind; her Sochi was candyfloss with Grandmother and sticky fingers in shallow water. Lena saw people in shabby, dirty jackets, one of them without shoes, weaving through the tables on the hotel terraces, holding out their hands to aloof tourists. Their worn bodies were part of a larger picture, but Lena wasn't sure whether they knew each other—whether there was a shanty town of wheel-less buses and mouldy cardboard shelters in Sochi where they came together at the end of the day and divvied up their booty.

When she saw that the hazel trees had been felled, she felt burn blisters pop all over her body again. 'What? They're gone? Why? When did that happen?' Lena didn't know if she'd screamed the words, or if her jaws had seized up in shock. Her grandmother's garden was a small oblong with an apple tree or two leaning towards the little house that now looked no bigger than a garage—a wooden shack reinforced with corrugated iron. Lena ran in and picked up the phone that was sitting in its old place, on a stool behind the front door. She felt a panicky fear that she would hear the hum of the dialling tone and have to accept that no lightning had struck—that the telegraph poles were all still there, sticking up into the milk-soup sky over the estate; that it was Grandmother who had cut the line to her granddaughter. That would have been harder to face than a force of nature. But there was no tone—just a rasping silence such as only dead things make.

Lena looked up. There were icons all over the walls and sideboard, shining like new. Lena wouldn't be able to say a prayer for her grandmother because she didn't know any. She hoped the neighbours would take charge of the prayers, as they'd taken charge of all the other aspects of the funeral. Choosing clothes for the burial, arranging the little service. Lena came as a guest.

Alarmed at the thought that her grandmother might have had to go short without the income from the hazelnuts, she enquired cautiously what people here lived on. 'We have all we need in our gardens,' the neighbours assured her. 'You don't see it because you come from the city.' They also told her that Grandmother had died suddenly and peacefully—she had wanted for nothing. 'She had us.' Their eyes zigzagged over Lena's white coat and yellow dress.

Lena emptied her bag on to the camp bed where she had once slept every summer and rummaged through her hastily packed clothes—city clothes that would look like mockery if she wore them here. She opened the wardrobe that took up an entire wall of the room and pulled out a quilted, earth-coloured coat. It was far too warm for the time of year, but long enough to hide her dress.

Until the funeral the next morning she sat quietly. She had pictured herself walking through the garden and shaking the branches of the hazel trees, but when she saw how small and bare the plot was—no more than a few paces to the neighbour's fence—she decided to stay in. She sat on the camp bed or on the kitchen chair where she'd so often sat in her dreams, and stared at the empty stove and the apron hook.

Grandmother was laid out in the church. Her lips looked as if they'd been sewn together and she lay shrunken and slightly raised on her hunched back. Someone had pushed a cushion under her head. She was dressed in a lilac blouse and a grey skirt; Lena had never seen her in such formal clothes. An icon the size of a playing card lay on her folded hands. She didn't look at all peaceful; she looked alert. Lena spoke to her in a whisper and then couldn't stop.

First she confessed her morning sickness, which had become too persistent to ignore. Then she told Grandmother all about Edil—suddenly it didn't seem so hard. She talked and talked.

She explained why she'd borrowed Grandmother's coat, and she apologized for the yellow dress and for the filthy state of her shoes after the journey. She asked Grandmother if it was all right to borrow her trousers and jumpers for a few days. She said she was planning to stay on for a bit and sort out the house. *I'll wear your boots and waistcoat, that'll be nice…* She stared at Grandmother's sunken cheeks, covered in deep wrinkles; it looked as if not only her mouth, but her whole face had been sewn up with big stitches. Even the coffin, even the few people who'd shown up, some of them (the priest, the singing women) with candles in their hands—everything looked as if it were held together by a rough seam that might burst at any moment.

Outside by the grave, Lena saw Artyom and Lika—she recognized them at once, but could only nod to them. It struck her that they were standing a long way apart. She watched them from the corner of her eye as the coffin was lowered into the earth; they were staring into space, as if they didn't know anyone there—as if they didn't know whose name it was on the wooden cross at the edge of the pit. Below the crossbar with the name was a sloping ledge bearing the years of birth and death, and pinned to the ledge was a photograph of Grandmother, in which little more than a faint oval was discernible. Incense rose, making Lena sneeze and her eyes water. When she looked up, the other mourners were no more than dark silhouettes.

That evening at Lika's, she sat at table with the family. Lika refused even to speak about Artyom; as far as she was concerned, she told Lena, he was dead.

'It never used to make a difference to you that he was Abkhazian and you were Georgian—' Lena protested, but Lika's husband interrupted her, and although the children were present he unleashed a torrent of expletives against that *filthy mob* of Abkhazian *renegades* who suddenly wanted their *fucking independence*.

'Everyone wants to be free these days. Every fart wants freedom and independence. *We are somebody*. Oh, you are, are you? Well, why don't you go and hang yourselves then, that way you really would be free!' He swept the air with his arms.

'That's enough,' Lika said. 'Calm down.' And she sent the children out of the room. They must have been about five or six. Lika hadn't called them over to introduce them to Lena; she had only pointed at them as if they were furniture, said their names and ordered them to the table.

'Let's not argue about politics.' Lika lit a thin cigarette and poured *chacha* into their glasses. 'Tell us about yourself. You're a distinguished doctor now, aren't you, so where's the distinguished husband? You have someone, don't you? You must be, what, twenty-four now?'

'Yes, I have someone.'

Lena cradled her glass of schnapps, wondering whether to down it. She looked about her; the walls of the room were covered with gold-framed pictures that seemed to be more about the frames than the paintings.

'And why hasn't he proposed yet? Tell us about him. Is he one of these *biznissmeni*, as the new Mafiosi like to call themselves? If he is, you can forget it—those types never marry; they just want to go to bed with you. Shall we find you someone in Tiflis? When Georgians are serious, they're really serious. A Georgian would build you a palace and give you children.'

'He's Jewish.' The words flew out; she hadn't planned to say that.

It was true that the joke-cracking Daniel hadn't left her side for the rest of that evening. Even when she'd said goodnight to Inna, who was getting one of the guitarists to teach her the chords of a pop song, Daniel had clung to Lena's hand. Inna smiled approvingly and called out after Lena to phone her. Then the door to the flat closed behind them and electric light gushed over the concrete stairs like dirty water. Lena knew what was coming and fought the impulse to turn and hammer at the door. The alcohol had loosened her limbs and numbed her brain, and between her and the door was Daniel, mellow and smiling, saying in his soft, unfamiliar voice that he would take her wherever she wanted to go. Why, then, had she climbed on to his lap and unbuttoned his trousers as soon as they were in his car? She was still trying to work it out. Maybe she hadn't wanted him in the flat, touching the bed that was hers and Edil's. Maybe she'd just wanted it over with. Daniel was decent; he didn't push her. There was sweat on his forehead, the only part of his face not covered in hair. His beard rasped against her collarbone when she leant over him.

All the time she thought of Edil and how angry she was at him—angry at his absence, angry at the way he never called, but only turned up when it suited him, sometimes with flowers, sometimes with a black look on his face. It infuriated her that she couldn't rely on him to be there when she needed him. Would he bring her tea in bed if she got sick? She doubted it. He seemed to miss her only when he had time. But here—here was a good guy who would drive her anywhere.

She looked into Lika's face and Lika looked back, waiting for Lena to go on with her story.

'He's an engineer,' Lena added falteringly. 'For kitchen appliances.'

'I see.' Lika helped herself to another glass of *chacha*.

'No, it's not like that...' Every second weighed on her tongue. 'I'm wondering whether I shouldn't stay here in Sochi. Ditch everything and devote myself to the garden. Have all of you close by and get away from those brutes that drag themselves into my surgery every bloody day to show me their genitals. Sometimes, you know, I look at those men's hands and their knuckles are scraped raw. You can see the open flesh and the dried blood; they don't even bother to bandage them. It's as if they want you to see—as if they're proud of it. All I know is, I mustn't show I'm scared. Just have to nod in the right places. Prescribe them ointments and antibiotics. Keep an eye on the time. Send them on their way.' Lena set her glass down. 'I never set eyes on the others—the old ones, the forgotten ones. They're rotting away, God knows where, in their dachas, their hovels. No one phones them up; they die alone. There are no doctors for them in this country; only the guys with the bloody knuckles get treatment in this country.'

Lika got up, made a desultory attempt at clearing the table and sat back down, folding her arms. Then she leapt to her feet again, rummaged around for cigarettes and lit one nervously. She began to speak, faster than before, her voice deeper.

'*This country*. Always *this country*. *This country* is what we make of it. I get what you're saying; I wasn't born yesterday. But you can't throw in a good job, fling on a headscarf and start selling fruit and veg on the market just because you can't face treating those dickheads any more, or because your Jew boy doesn't deliver the goods. Of course people are pigs—when weren't they? The only places where they're not pigs are the places you've never been. But you won't solve anything by coming here and creating a prettified version of a past you can't actually remember. What would you do here? Do you think things are better here? Do you really think we live off our gardens? If I were you, I'd nab that Jew boy right now and run off abroad with him. What else is a Jew good for? Or if you don't want to take him with you, buy yourself one of those documents saying you're a certified Ashkenazi and bugger off on your own. You can do that, you don't have kids yet. You're free. Maybe that's the definition of free: being able to leave. Look, the Abkhazians are up in arms, the Chechens are up in arms—and look what's happening in Azerbaijan. Everyone's up in arms. Either you know where you belong these days, or…' Lika looked suddenly alert; her eyes gleamed, like back on those summer afternoons when the sun had beaten down, rusty and angry, on their sawdusty faces. 'Growing old is a lose-lose situation. At the very latest when your breasts start to hang like sausages and your husband hooks up with a younger woman, you're going to lose what little self-respect you had. Growing old is basically knowing that you'll suffer loss. Do you have that much time to waste? Oh, and another thing: do me a favour and throw out that awful quilted coat. It's an insult that you can dress up in that old thing and think you look like one of us. This may be the sticks, but it's still Sochi.'

Lena didn't reply. They drank in silence and Lika smoked. She offered to show Lena the house. Lena racked her brain for a *do you remember…*, some anecdote connecting them, but nothing suitable came to mind. It felt as if Lika had put a ban on memories, but ahead Lena could see nothing with any clarity, nothing she could have talked about. The only things she was certain of lay in the past.

After saying goodbye, she hurried to a phone box. Edil picked up immediately.

'You know you can't call me at this time of night,' he said. 'What is it?'

'I'm pregnant.'

The silence at the other end of the line was so loud that Lena held the receiver away from her ear; she waited, breathing fast. She wished she could reach into the phone and yank his hair.

It was stuffy in the phone box; the plexiglass sides were covered in graffiti. Someone had scratched *Where are you?* into one of the panes.

'You do realize that isn't possible.' Edil spoke so slowly, she might almost have thought he hadn't said it. 'My mother's nagging me to get married as it is.'

'Then marry me.'

Silence.

Lena recalled a student party where she'd danced with a man from the Congo. There had been shouts of 'Dance! Dance! We're internationalists!' She wanted to yell down the phone at him. *Marry me! We're internationalists!* The thought made her laugh.

Edil still said nothing.

She laughed again. She almost said *please*, but stopped herself in time.

He didn't hang up. Lena, too, held the receiver in her hand for a while longer, but all she heard was a rushing sound, as loud and clear as if the black waves from the beach were rolling towards her through the night.

She crossed town to her grandmother's house, got into her childhood bed, stared at the ceiling and began to count backwards: ten, nine, eight, seven—she got in a muddle, gasped for air, tried to close her eyes—ten, nine, eight, seven—until her pulse was no longer racing and her breath no longer coming in staccato gasps—ten, nine… She got up and wandered around the house; she searched for memories to hold on to, pictures of her grandmother, but all she could see were pictures of saints; the place was full of them. Then, on the kitchen windowsill, Lena found a photograph of her five-year-old self. She had a serious look on her face and neat, light-brown plaits; the photo had been taken before Grandmother had defied Rita and cut Lena's hair in a pageboy for her first day at school. Now Grandmother and Rita were both dead, and Lena was growing her hair again. She wasn't smiling in the picture, but her cheeks were round and firm, as if she had apricots in her mouth. Lena couldn't remember the photo being taken; she must have been sent to a photographer. Nothing about the picture was natural; she was wearing a beige blouse buttoned to the top, like something from an era she'd never known. Grandmother must have put the picture up when Lena stopped calling regularly—before the line burned through and she gave up hoping that Lena would ever visit again.

That was that. Grandmother was gone; Lena was probably here on the estate for the last time. Her mother was no longer around either, and her father was laying freshly picked flowers on her grave—another place Lena hadn't visited for too long. *That was that.* The feeling had grown familiar over the years; she recognized it like a well-known tune. It had a sharp edge to it—the clang of a trap falling shut, jagged steel jaws that said, *That's that.*

Lena felt dizzy. She wasn't aware of falling, but when she came to there were glow-worms or tiny luminous flecks glinting above her, although there was nothing luminous on Grandmother's walls and it was too cool for fireflies. Something had come in, though; a whole swarm had gathered at the beams in the ceiling.

She was woken by the gall rising in her throat, bitter and burning. She was afraid she might choke on her own gastric juices and didn't know if it was safe to close her eyes. There was no one to call out to. Inside her head, a fat, hairy animal dragged itself, wobbling and spewing, from one temple to the other; she tasted its secretions on her tongue. She retched, but only bile came out. She thought of sticking her fingers down her throat and realized she needed all her strength just to prop herself up on the floor. She couldn't get up, but had to pee. Slowly she began to count the steps to the bathroom. Four to the door, another six or so down the passage past the table and then left; if she managed to get the bathroom door open, she wouldn't wet herself.

Had she fainted again? She had no idea how much time had passed, but here she was, groping her way along the wall. Splinters dug into her fingers. She shuffled towards the door and felt the smooth surface of the handle—already she could see the light from the street lamp outside the bathroom window shining into the passage. She swayed and reached for the wall, the edge of the table; the kaleidoscopic light of the street lamp went out as she hit the floor.

When Lena came to again, the left half of her face was stuck to the floorboards, smarting as if the floor were made of sandpaper. She rolled on to her back; the glow-worms were still there, hovering above her. She found herself wondering if this could be it. The fall hadn't been serious, but she couldn't get up; the signals from her brain weren't reaching her body—it was impossible not to wonder. And what then? What about the child inside her?

Lena saw her arms in the dark, like the spindly legs of an insect on its back. She laughed. Perhaps, she thought, she was turning into one of those creepy-crawlies on the ceiling. *Or maybe they'll drop down on me and gobble me up. I wouldn't mind—but get it over with, please.* She noticed, when she laughed, that her jaw was numb; she must have hit it when she fell. She laughed again, until she heard herself loud and clear. A ringing laugh. She watched herself get to her knees, push herself up on her arms and sit up; the sandpaper floor warmed her hands. She crawled into the dark on her knees, getting her balance. She leant against the wall and laughed; she put her hand to her sticky, sweaty face and felt her jaw. It seemed to be in one piece; no blood, nothing. Only the heavy breathing of something glowing on the ceiling.

On the train back, grainy light filled her compartment. Rocked to sleep by nausea, Lena dreamt she was sitting on the bed in her flat in Dnipropetrovsk; she saw herself undress in front of Edil. She had her back to him, the part of her she thought he liked best—she had always secretly suspected him of feeling repulsion for her soft belly and doughy thighs. She saw herself spread her arms in front of him; she saw that instead of coming closer, he left the room without a word. Her face was wet when she woke, her head heavier than the rest of her body. But still, she thought, still, he would be at the station when she arrived; he'd had the night to think things over. It was understandable that he hadn't immediately started suggesting names for the child.

When the conductor came swaying through the carriage and announced her station, his voice sounded familiar, the voice of a storyteller she knew. She thought of the horror story that Grandmother had once told her (but when had that been, and why did she remember it now?) about women who were thrown into a deep pond to find out whether they were virgins. Those who had lain with a man sank to the bottom. Those who were untouched floated to the surface and drifted back to the shore.

Edil was not on the platform. Nor was he in the arrivals hall. Instead, Daniel was waiting at the door to her block with a bunch of flowers.

'How did you know where I live?' she asked irritably; then she remembered that he had once dropped her home.

'And how did you know when I was coming back?'

'I didn't even know you were away. I come and ring for you every day, just on the off chance. And now I've caught you. Come to dinner with me—it's the least you can do after all the trouble I've gone to… Wait, do you know the one about the—'

'I'm so tired,' she said, cutting him off. But before pulling the door shut behind her, she made a date with him for another day. And that was that.

There was no way, Daniel's mother said before Lena had even sat down at table, that the flat where she lived with Daniel was big enough for three, let alone four. 'But people seem to have places of their own these days—doctors, anyway.'

'Mum,' Daniel said.

'No one asked you.'

'It's true, I do have a flat of my own,' Lena said, trying to ease things up. 'With plenty of space.'

'That's what I thought. Everything's different these days. People have more space.'

'They do seem to.'

'Tell me about your family, then. Which of them are Jewish?'

Lena still hadn't sat down.

Daniel's mother was a tall woman, long and sinuous, as if she were made of running water. Her head was oval, her cheeks seemed to go on and on, her nose was a slightly bent arrow pointing to her neck—a slender neck set off by a chain that spilt out over her cleavage. Her arms whipped the air like ropes as she dished up. All through the interrogation she had only glanced at Lena, as if she were deep in thought and debating something with herself; her blue eyes didn't come to rest on Lena until she broached the question of Jewish relatives.

'None of them, really,' Lena said truthfully.

'I see.' Her eyes went back to roaming over the sausage and fish salads.

Daniel poured red wine into crystal goblets and vodka into ornate shot glasses, then crooked his arm and raised his glass in a toast. 'Why do we drink? So we can forget, at least for a moment, that we live in the best place in the world.'

Lena saw his mother roll her eyes, raise a glass to her tomato-coloured lips, take a sip of red wine and then, without setting the glass down, chase it with vodka. She decided that she, too, would drink this evening. After only two glasses she was so relaxed that her hand drifted to Daniel's biceps whenever he made a joke; she laughed loudly and hoped she was the only one who thought it sounded like retching.

The conversation took a while to get going. *She said… he said… we used to think… I don't know where all this is going… downright terrifying sometimes… top us up, dear… where are you from again… ah yes, it's nice there… hard to know what we'll be left with… we'll be left with nothing!… nothing!… oh well then, here's to us… and our good health, of course…* Helpless clichés that slopped out without creating intimacy. Lena screwed up her eyes as if dazzled by a glaring light. Was she listening to herself talking or had someone left a tap running?

She'd been back for four weeks and Edil still hadn't called. She hadn't called him either, afraid that he wouldn't pick up. She had barely slept. Every night she would think she heard the phone, but as soon as she opened her eyes she knew she'd been imagining things; the only sound was the hum of the fridge. She forced herself to close her eyes, but they kept popping open. She switched on the television, vomited, switched it off again. She went to work; she strolled home. She didn't get in touch with Inna because Inna would have seen it all in her face. Soon the swell of her belly would be visible.

And now here she was at Daniel's mother's. They drank a bottle of wine between the three of them, and Daniel's mother complained that her son was still a bachelor at forty and didn't shave properly. 'He doesn't get it from his father; he was a respectable yid.' Daniel's job probably wasn't *what's looked for today*, but he was a decent person. 'Engineering used to be a respectable profession. A normal profession. People used to be normal. Today everything's different. Everyone's scrambling to get to the top so they can spit on the heads of the people at the bottom.' At least Daniel wasn't like that, even if he wasn't good for much.

They agreed that it would be just the three of them at the registry office. Who needed witnesses?

A couple of weeks later the marriage certificate was signed; they had lunch with Daniel's mother in the restaurant next door. Daniel moved in with Lena that same week. And that was that.

After a few weeks of nausea and leaden legs, Lena's pregnancy went without incident. Apart from her swelling belly, the only serious change she observed in herself was the occasional fit of forgetfulness—that and a clumsy exhaustion; she was forever knocking things over, as if she couldn't get a grasp of them. Everything else she'd been promised passed her by—no constipation, no piles, no heartburn. When she took maternity leave a month before her due date, she was still going for walks despite the bulk of her belly. Daniel was all for driving her everywhere, even short distances, but she would have none of it and told him she wanted to carry her body herself. He understood—or said he did.

The newborn didn't take after anyone; she was a small, fierce-looking bundle snuffling at Lena's breast when Daniel came to collect them from the clinic. Lena breathed quietly in time with her daughter and realized that she didn't have a single lullaby to sing to her. Good thing Daniel had such a large repertoire—if not of lullabies, then of tunes and rhymes and anecdotes. They weren't necessarily suitable for a babe in arms, but it didn't matter. What mattered was that he felt confident enough to tell stories and sing songs to the child without let-up, while Lena couldn't imagine uttering even a word of silly baby talk.

Daniel talked to Edita non-stop, sometimes stuttering when he tried to say too much at once. She was still only a snuffly baby, wailing for milk and filling her nappy, when he first claimed she'd said 'papa' to him.

> *Fried chick, boiled chick,*
> *But life's what chicks prefer!*
> *They caught him and arrested him*
> *And said, 'Your passport, sir.'*

Daniel mimicked a violin with his voice to accompany the chorus. Lena watched her husband carrying Edita around the flat. If only Rita could see them, she thought. Everything about the picture seemed just right; Rita would probably approve.

Look, Mum, they're mine, the pair of them. Now I'm the same as everyone else.

The new grandfather came to visit, bringing with him a Malyutka washing machine.

'Where did you find the money, Dad?' Lena exclaimed. And then: 'You didn't bring it on the sleeper, did you?'

'Your mother once said that the automatic washing machine was her best friend in her first years with a baby—and hers wasn't as advanced as this one. So I thought… I hope, of course, that you have better friends than this—and better ones than your mother had—but you know how it is with friends: they often have troubles of their own just when you need them. Anyway…it can't hurt.' He patted the white metal casing. 'I'd have brought it to the wedding, but you didn't invite me. I suppose it's out of fashion to celebrate with your parents. Never mind. We can make up for it now, eh?'

His eyes looked sticky, as if they were full of spit. The hair peeping out from under his cap smelt unwashed; his throat was stubbly. Lena hugged him and showed him into the kitchen. Daniel dished up potato salad with herring. Edita was still asleep; they decided not to wake her with their oohing and ahing, but to get on and eat.

'More beetroot, Roman Ilyich? More of this too? Can't have you sitting there with an empty glass. Let me top you up.'

Roman Ilyich smiled awkwardly and stared across the table as if he didn't know what to do. He pushed his cap to the back of his head and then pulled it down over his forehead; he ran his hands up and down over his wrinkled face, as if washing it with sandy fingers; then he breathed out heavily and began to tell Daniel about the woods near Horlivka, where he went for long walks every weekend, watching birds on their nests, foraging for mushrooms in the leaves. He said he liked to wander off the beaten track and get lost—'though you can't really get lost in the woods; it's more that you walk for a while without being quite sure where you are'.

Lena tried to imagine her father sitting at a bus stop with a basket of mushrooms on his lap. Had he become one of those men who sat absent-mindedly on benches, talking to themselves? Apparently he had.

'You must come and visit,' he said, without a hint of doubt in his voice. 'I'll show you the best walks to the clearing. The view from there is just—my goodness!'

'Do you know how much you look like your dad?' Daniel said that night in bed, whispering so as not to wake Roman Ilyich, who was asleep on the sofa in the next room.

'Really?' Lena said. Did she? She couldn't get to sleep.

'Your crow's feet. And the set of your eyes. You smile the same way too, with only half your face. Has no one ever told you that before?'

Daniel's mother didn't come often—once every two weeks at most. Daniel would phone her at weekends and ask for recipes. He spent a lot of time in the kitchen and wanted to know what 'his girls' liked to eat, although Edita was still living on breast milk. For Daniel, that was irrelevant—didn't the milk come from the body he cooked for every weekend?

'My mother says I'm too stupid for gefilte fish, so I'll make you quark turnovers!' Daniel called cheerfully from the stove. He whistled as he cooked—tunes from old Soviet films that had disappeared from television except on public holidays.

Edita slept a lot, only crying when she was hungry. This worried Lena; she was too quiet a baby, too undemanding. Purple veins showed beneath her skin at the temples and on the flat back of her head where tufts of silky black hair grew.

'She's so dark,' Daniel's mother said disapprovingly. 'God forbid she takes after my father Yasha; he was a caricature of a yid.'

As far as friends went, Lena's father was proved wrong: Inna had called regularly since Edita's birth and often turned up unannounced, laden with gifts; she would scatter toys in the cot and on the chest of drawers, as if she'd taken it upon herself to re-equip the flat. She massaged Lena's breasts when they were painful, spoke soothingly to her, rubbed her sore nipples with ointment and instructed her to wear cabbage leaves in her bra. Lena watched her leaning anxiously over the baby; her voice, when she advised Lena, was uncontrolled, always too loud or too quiet—clearly she was genuinely worried, and perhaps that was what it was to love.

Summer worked its way deeper and deeper into the flat, and when it reached its most humid, Edita turned blue. Her body seemed to be sore all over; her skin looked transparent. They had to carry her day and night because she screamed frantically whenever they tried to put her down. She gasped for air, wheezing and coughing, and Lena didn't know how to touch or comfort her without hurting her. In the end, Inna insisted they take her to hospital; motherly care alone was not going to make her better. And so, after a sleepless night, Daniel bundled Lena and the babe into the car and sped to the clinic with them. The staff took Edita from Lena, deftly examined her and told Lena that swollen mucous membranes were narrowing the child's airways; they would have to act swiftly and she would have to leave. Lena tugged at the clasp of her handbag and pulled out an envelope of cash that she'd taken from the sideboard drawer in their hurried departure without consulting Daniel. She handed the money to the doctor.

'I'll stay here on the ward with my daughter.'

The doctor stared at her for a moment; then she pocketed the envelope without looking inside. Lena had no idea what state her hair was in or whether her make-up was smudged, but although it was too hot for more than a light blouse and skirt, she was dressed in an extravagant trouser suit. The common consensus these days, in this country, was that expensive clothes meant *don't mess with me*, and Lena was determined not to look like a supplicant, but like someone who couldn't be turned away. She was sweating, her head throbbing like a muscle. The doctor's cheeks were so hollow they seemed to touch on the inside. She was tall and very slim, and Lena had to crane her neck to look her in the eye. Determined not to squint up at her like a frog on the floor, she settled for addressing the necklace at the doctor's swanlike throat.

'You know as well as I do that this infection can be fatal if the windpipe swells shut. Also, that she risks choking if she lies down. She needs to be kept upright, and the nurses here won't manage that. Let me stay here; I'll carry her until she's out of danger.'

The answer was predictable: 'There are no beds here for mothers.'

But she had pocketed the fat envelope.

Lena told herself this was no Oksana Tadeyevna. She saw her father on the phone evening after evening, saying nothing into the receiver, while the voice at the other end of the line demanded more and more money for a treatment that never happened. She braced herself to bombard the doctor with medical terms in order to prove her authority, but before she could draw breath the doctor waved her on to the ward. It was crammed with cots, one of them empty, with a chair beside it.

'You can stay here with your daughter. That's all I can offer you at the moment.'

Lena laid Edita in the cot, threw off her jacket, picked Edita up again and sat down with her on the chair. It felt as if she sat there for days. Time stopped; all she saw was Edita's pale, feverish face and the intravenous drip in a vein in her head. Edita dug her soft fists into her chin as cramps racked her body. Lena paced the ward with her, rocking her; she made a conscious effort not to look at the other babies, whose mothers were waiting out in the corridors, scratching their arms bloody.

When a narrow camp bed was wheeled in for Lena, she collapsed on to it, and a humming fatigue spread through her body. The fat, hairy animal was back, dragging itself from one side of her head to the other. She must have slept briefly; she was woken by the smell of disinfectant, a bleeping machine, Edita's screams. Her tongue cleaved to the roof of her mouth as if she were eating rotten apples.

The next day, in the evening, she went out briefly to meet Daniel on the street in front of the hospital. Although it was dusk, the air was still warm. Daniel looked dishevelled. His colleagues had let him leave early so that he could buy chocolates for the nurses.

'Kyiv cake, bring a Kyiv cake tomorrow,' Lena stammered, as she took the bag of chocolates from him. 'And cash for the doctors—I think I need more.'

Daniel said he'd have to sell the jewellery they'd bought as an investment; it might take some days.

'Then borrow it,' Lena said. 'Borrow from Inna. Call your mother.'

She looked into his drawn face, wondering whether to confess that it was she who had brought this misfortune upon them; it was her fault that Edita might die, her fault that he was wasting his life in love with the wrong woman. She didn't think of him when he wasn't there, not for a moment. When she wasn't trying to drive Edil's face from her mind, she was searching for words to explain to her mother what was happening. She failed at both. She would have liked to pray, but that was even more impossible.

When Edita's skin began to recover its clover-honey colour a few days later, the doctor came into the ward and closed the door behind her—it was only then that Lena realized it had been open all the time. The doctor kept it brief; she advised Lena to take her daughter and get out. There was a viral infection going round; two babies in the next room were already infected and Edita might not survive if she caught it.

'Believe me, she's more likely to recover at home than here. She's almost over the croup—another few days and she'll be out of the woods. If you want her to live, you'd better pack your bags.'

For the first time, the doctor wasn't wearing a necklace. The skin between her collarbones was scaly, and her hollow cheeks looked as if they'd been rubbed with sandpaper.

Daniel came to pick them up. He carried Edita, and Lena followed, still in the same trouser suit; she felt like a wrung-out dishcloth. For days, she and Daniel continued to carry the child around the flat, listening to her breath, inspecting her back, trying not to think about where they would take her if she had a relapse. Lena looked searchingly into Edita's face, and then one day Edita looked back and seemed to recognize her.

When Lena returned to work at the beginning of the New Year, she discovered that three doctors had handed in their notice. 'Emigrated,' she was told. 'Jews, you know.' She stowed this information at the back of her mind—she wouldn't miss her colleagues—but when she happened to mention it to Daniel over dinner that evening, he seized on it as if he'd been waiting all along for this chance to talk about emigration. He knew all the necessary steps, all the niceties of the procedure—he even knew how good they'd have it abroad. Lena wouldn't hear of it.

'We almost lost our daughter,' Daniel said eventually, as if to clinch it.

'What's that supposed to mean? Everything's better in the West?'

They argued, and Lena ended things by saying that she wouldn't get as good a job anywhere else, and as she was the main breadwinner and they all lived in her flat, it was her decision. Full stop. Daniel said nothing, but Lena soon realized he wasn't going to give in so easily. More and more, he talked over dinner about friends or colleagues who had moved to Germany and rated Berlin the best place in the world. Lena thought this naïvc.

'Everything's such a mess here!' Daniel would yell.

'Not where I am,' Lena would say, putting an end to the discussion.

That winter they watched *Window to Paris*, a fantasy comedy film that the whole country was talking about. An impoverished music teacher climbs through a window in his communal flat in St Petersburg and finds himself in Montmartre. He wanders around Paris, makes music, falls in love. The audience laughed a great deal, especially during the scene when the dishevelled, clown-like music teacher bumps into a Russian friend who has emigrated to the West. This friend, chic in a European-style pinstriped suit and designer sunglasses, is full of yearning for his Soviet past; he would gladly give up his new life—reputable job, family, house, car, holidays in Hawaii—if he could only travel back in time to his days as a poor student, when he sat around 'on his bare arse' coming up with inspirational ideas. The music teacher tells him this can be organized, blindfolds him with a blue scarf and transports him to the homeland of his dreams by leading him through the window of the communal flat in St Petersburg. On the way, the blindfolded nostalgic laughs hysterically. 'Hey,' he says, 'why does my dream reek of piss? Are you taking me to a shithouse?' When at last—on the middle of a boulevard in front of a statue of Lenin—his friend takes off his blindfold, claps him on the shoulder and wishes him luck, the man loses his nerve. Howling like an animal, he runs after the retreating taxi where the music teacher is sitting with a smug smile on his face.

Daniel couldn't stop laughing; the friends who had gone to the cinema with them also rocked in their seats. Lena was appalled. It just wasn't possible, she said, that life 'over there' was such paradise—French women moisturizing their shaved legs at open windows—while this country was a shithouse that reeked of piss. But it was useless; she didn't believe her own objections. The meaning of the word *sovok* was now well-established: a dustpan for all the filth of history.

In late April a woman burst into Lena's surgery smelling of damp earth. Lena hadn't seen anyone like her for a long time—perhaps not since the funeral in Sochi. She looked at least a century old. She was carrying a bunch of lilac whose scent mingled with the smell of her sweat, and she was dragging a hessian sack over the floor which reminded Lena of the empty hazelnut sack that her grandmother pulled behind her like a defective parachute in Lena's dreams.

Lena's assistant stood sheepishly in the door and said she hadn't been able to stop the babushka. Lena sent her out with a nod and offered the woman a chair, but she declined to sit down. She straightened her headscarf and laid her gifts on the desk—a damp cloth was wound around the lilac stems. Kneading her hands, she looked Lena in the eye and said it had been predicted to her that Lena alone could save her. She'd been to another doctor who had told her she was seriously ill, but there was nothing he could do to help her, he didn't have the right medication, and she had a great-granddaughter to look after at home, who couldn't find work and had no parents, and she didn't have the money to pay for treatment. The other doctor had told her she had the wolf in her body and it had taken hold of her lungs. She was finding it harder and harder to breathe—could hardly get her breath sometimes.

'Don't send me away, daughter. It's the Lord's punishment, I know—I deserve it. But he let me come to you or I wouldn't be here now. I said to him, "Judge me, Lord, but if I make it to the doctor who is said to have medicines to cure all illnesses, then heal me. I'll tell her everything." So now, doctor, you must let me talk—you must hear my confession. Maybe then the illness will go away by itself and I'll be able to breathe again; maybe I won't need your expensive medication. I can't tell a priest; he'd only curse me. The priest was part of it all.'

Eyes yellow as egg yolks looked out from the old woman's face, which gleamed dully like a gauze bandage soaked in black tea. There were no red patches on her skin, but her voice was hoarse and hard to understand through the rattle of her breath. People shouldn't get old, Lena thought—not here, anyway, not in this cruel age where everyone watched you perish and felt nothing.

'You'll know nothing of those times, but your grandmother and grandfather will. Ask them. They'll remember. You'll see it in their faces. I'm talking about the times when the Russians decided to let us Ukrainians starve, and the farmers felled their fruit trees and slaughtered their livestock and sent their grain to Moscow. Everything went to Moscow. Every living thing vanished; the fields were empty. Only lookout towers stood on the bare land, so the children could spy on their own parents. If a child saw his mother hiding grain under the pillow, he was to report it. I was sent up one of those towers, but I said nothing. My parents disappeared anyway.

'I hid in churches; I stole icons from the village chapel and swapped them for food with people from the city. There was one fine lady who never took her gloves off when she handed me bread; she wanted the embroidered altar cloths and then the crucifix and then the pictures from the walls. I took her everything she asked for—what else could I do? But soon the church was bare.

'When they found me, I was so hungry I couldn't walk; they grabbed me by the arms and legs, as if they were ripping out a weed, and they threw me into the barracks where children like me were penned up. Those children tore the flesh off each other's bones; you fell asleep at peril of your life. I don't know how I got out of there, but here I am, doctor, I'm alive.'

The sun was setting; it was growing dark in the surgery. At the back of the room, Lena could make out the dim outline of a faun, pipes to his lips, torso twisted. He was the size of a full-grown man and stood staring at her and the old woman, hairy legs akimbo. Lena saw herself on her hands and knees on their balcony in Horlivka, trying to gather up every last fragment of the shattered figurine, lest even the tiniest splinter should escape and lodge itself forever in the runner or in her skin.

'Somehow we survived. Again and again. And we forgot—or at least no one talked about it. There was just that one time when my neighbour in the village was hit by it. I was a mother by then and the old woman started singing the Solovki song: *Solovki, Solovki, how long is the way? / The heart cannot beat...* It was suddenly everywhere. I heard it coming out of the ground and the walls; I heard it in my dreams. I went over to my neighbour's house. I sat down next to her and waited. She sang and she sang, and when she wasn't singing she talked. About the penal colony. She'd been taken there by train and learnt the song from the others in her wagon. The Russians made her dig graves in the forest; they threw people half dead into the pits. The old woman talked on and on, and then she started singing again.

'I didn't do any of that. All I did was take the icons; I didn't report anyone, I didn't dig graves or gnaw flesh from anyone's bones. But the Lord is full of wrath for me all the same; I can't breathe any more; my lungs will burn up if you don't treat me. Don't send me away, doctor. I have nothing to pay you with except what grows in my garden. It's spring; there isn't much yet, but soon I'll be able to bring you all sorts of good things... Don't send me away. I didn't survive all that to perish like this. Yulichka has no one but me and—look...'

The woman made to empty her sack, but Lena stumbled round the desk, took her by the shoulders and pushed her on to the chair. Then she crouched before her on the floor and stroked her hands over and over. She took a deep breath to speak, but nothing came out.

Lena sent her assistant home and stayed on in the office. She'd flung the windows wide after the old woman had gone, and they were still open. Gusts of wind tore down the streets and whistled round the buildings; her ears smarted as she leant against the window frame, staring out at the pattern of yellow oblongs in the darkness. She was ashamed of herself for being so keen to get the woman out of her surgery. She'd promised to make all necessary arrangements: medication, examinations—all free of charge, of course. It was too late to save her, but she hadn't told her that. She'd given the bunch of lilac to her assistant.

The air was still thick in the surgery, like spilt gouache in the beam of her desk lamp. Lena sat down and played with the light switch, on and off, on and off, on and off. Then she rang Edil. To her surprise, he picked up.

'It's your daughter's first birthday today,' she said, when he asked impassively how she was.

'And why are you calling?' he asked, still impassive, as if he were busy with important work while he was on the phone.

She wished she could hate his voice, but instead it brought back the smell of him, the smell she used to hunt for between his shoulder blades until the two of them were dazed with happiness.

'What would you say if I emigrated?'

Lena didn't know what she expected. She denied herself the fantasy that he would burst into tears and try to stop her, insist on his rights as a father, beg her not to go, confess his feelings for her, get angry with her for abducting his daughter, say something like, *In other circumstances*… Of course none of that would happen. But a short pause of surprise would have been nice. A few moments of hearing only his breath and imagining that he felt some form of pain or confusion—that they might end up arguing and say what had to be said.

But Edil reacted immediately. 'I'll help you. What do you need?'

Not wanting to sob into the phone like an idiot, Lena replied just as quickly. 'I need a buyer for my flat. I'm leaving everything here, furniture and all.'

And that was that.

The darkness chafed her skin as she set off for home. Dnipropetrovsk had become her town, but never had she walked the streets alone at night for so long. Lights streaked through the bushes like stalking cats as cars bumped over cracked cobbles; drunks lay on the pavements; a bus stop had been vandalized. Lena crunched her way through a lake of broken glass and thought of the scene in *Window to Paris* where the heroine—a French woman who has accidentally jumped through the window and landed in St Petersburg—roams the city at night in only a dressing gown and turban. On the pavement ahead of her, a man comes into view. A moment later, he stops in front of a phone box, runs up to it and kicks in all the panes, tears the phone from the wall with his bare hands, dashes it to the ground, rips the metal frame of the booth into pieces, jumps up and down on the debris and then ambles off, hands in his pockets, as if nothing has happened.

Lena thought of hailing a taxi, but she wasn't in the mood to speak to anyone—not to a taxi driver and not to Daniel either. It was Edita's birthday; he would have baked a cake and sung to her. To soothe herself, Lena hummed Edita's birthday song all the way home.

The people stream past
Like a horde of drowned rats
Along streets of dull black and dark grey.
They're so deep in their woe
That they seem not to know
How happy I'm feeling today.

Daniel rushed to meet her. She stood quiet and pale in the door and he asked what was wrong, where she'd been, why she was so late, he'd been worried. She said she'd been thinking things over. 'We can submit the papers.'

The worst wasn't the conversation with her mother-in-law, whose lips tightened when she heard of their plans to emigrate. It wasn't the endless visits to the authorities to get hold of the right documents (they were prepared to speed things up by slipping cash into their papers) or the phone call to her father, who only breathed faintly at the end of the line until Lena offered desperately to take him with them—'Goodness, no, I'd only be a burden to you. Just bring little Edita to visit now and then, so I can see her growing up. Will you do that?' The worst wasn't the looks of scorn and envy from her colleagues, or Inna's indifferent shrug. It wasn't wondering what clothes to take if they didn't want to look like weirdos from the taiga and what books they'd need *over there*, or agonizing over whether it was really a good idea to leave all their furniture behind and have their photos sent on to them in shoeboxes (and possibly go astray). No, the worst was that Edil really did get back to Lena some weeks after she'd called and announced that he maybe had a buyer for her flat—a business partner of his would like to have a look round; Edil's description of the rooms had made him curious.

You only ever saw the bedroom, Lena almost said with bitter humour, but stopped herself.

'When are you leaving? Do you know yet?'

'We can get the contract ready now, but the flat won't be free for another year or so, maybe even longer, I don't know. No one can say exactly.'

She would have liked to ask if they could meet alone before the viewing, at least once; it seemed a shame, after everything between them, that they should see each other just for business and then never again. But it wasn't the time for melodrama; that was only in the movies—and even there, times were changing. Fantasy was going out of fashion and Soviet schmaltz was giving way to a new realism. All over the streets, men in leather jackets stared from the film hoardings, their wrecked faces turned belligerently to the passers-by.

Edil's cronies walked around the flat with their arms behind their backs, inspecting the ageing paint on the walls and pointing out faults in the bathroom. Lena felt as sick as she had on the train to her grandmother's funeral, only this time it wasn't the pregnancy hormones that were making her feel queasy; it was Edil's indifference. He had shaken her hand at the door, Daniel at her side, Edita napping in her cot. It was afternoon. Light shone through the net curtains into Edil's face; he screwed up his eyes slightly. The difference in light between the hall and the two rooms made Lena think of sudden sunsets—his face by day, his face by night. He'd hardly changed—and why should he? It was all quite recent. What was a year and a half? Her daughter's life and a series of shipwrecks in her own. Lena had last seen Edil before she left for Sochi; she hadn't known then of her grandmother's death. They had lain fully clothed on her bed, only the edges of their hands touching, and Edil had come out with this talk about the dead never completely leaving you; their souls, he had said, stayed with you, protecting or cursing you, depending on the degree of love or wrongdoing. Lena had disagreed—if what he said was true, her mother must be stuck in the labyrinth of souls; she hadn't once returned to Lena, either to reprove her or to offer protection. Lena talked to Rita constantly, but she never got an answer.

That conversation with Edil came back to Lena the night after he'd called with his friends to see the flat. She crept into the other room while Daniel and Edita slept, and tried to remember the wallpaper of her childhood—the pattern she had stared at when she was made to stand in the corner after breaking the Leningrad china.

She searched the plain woodchip for the black stems that had wound their way up the walls in her parents' flat in Horlivka. Her mother had dragged her into the corner by her ear; now she stood in the corner again, speaking to the bricks and mortar and the thin skin stuck to the walls with lumpy paste. She spoke without waiting for an echo or an answer. She whispered to her mother, speaking into the cool of the corner, and the colourless wallpaper swallowed every syllable.

As they were leaving their coats at the restaurant cloakroom, Inna flashed an expensive-looking watch in Lena's face, a gift from a *biznissmen* she was seeing.

'You basically have to emigrate these days if you want to meet a man who doesn't drink or shoot heroin or smash other men's faces in for money. But not me. I was lucky!'

The watch was the colour of rosé wine; precious stones circled the face. Lena stared at the hands, trying to work out when she had started to lose her sense of time. Sense of place, too. Was she still here? And where was *here*, anyway? The dislocation, she supposed, must have set in during those days in hospital with Edita, when all she'd heard was the rattling breath of her baby greedily trying to suck air through an inflamed, swollen throat. Since then, Lena had woken each day with a sense of grievance; it seemed incomprehensible to her that her eyelids continued to pop open every morning and fall shut every night. The days went on and on, tasting of nothing. The nagging *that was that* warped and grew into another phrase, no less merciless: *this is it.*

'We'll come and see you!' Inna said as they sat down. She had begun to speak of the future in the first-person plural, and Lena decided to take this as a good sign.

'That'll be lovely. Once we've settled in.'

'Yes, it'll be hell at first, but then…'

Lena was in the mood for nostalgia and ordered cognac, which she didn't usually drink—in fact, she'd hardly touched alcohol at all since Edita's birth. Inna ordered champagne, and as she raised her glass, gripping the filigree stem between three fingers, she said in a rush, 'Let's not drink to anything. No toasts or speeches. We won't mention your going away next week, and at the end of the evening we'll just say, *See you tomorrow*. I don't want any scenes.'

Lena studied her friend's narrow face, her short nose, the blond hair that she now wore permed and bleached. Inna talked a lot about having her teeth straightened abroad, maybe in Turkey. Her *biznissmen* could have a hair transplant while they were there. It meant going around with your scalp flecked with blood for a while, as if you'd been tattooed by a swarm of mosquitos, but then not long after you had a magnificent head of hair, like a Hollywood star.

Lena listened to this elated talk and realized that Inna wasn't going to ask whether she planned to come back if there were unexpected problems *over there*. She wasn't going to ask if Lena knew the name of the town where the refugee home was or if she was planning to re-sit her medical exams in Germany so she could keep working as a doctor. She wasn't going to ask if she'd started to learn German, or if she ever thought of chucking it all in at the last minute and running away.

'Do you remember the time I smuggled Oleg into the halls of residence and hid him under the duvet? We were crazy in those days.'

Of course Lena remembered.

'What an arsehole that guy was! I feel like all the men who made my life hell were leading me to the man I'm with today. It was all worth it, every step. I spent my life turning down offers, but not any more. You get lucky in the end.'

Lena had seen Inna's new boyfriend only once. He didn't seem like a bad man; if he looked like a creep, that was the alcohol weighing on his eyes. He'd been very polite, and Lena hoped that he wasn't like the others who had made Inna promises and then turned out to be married, or told her they'd leave their wives and then moved on when they got bored. Inna would call Lena and let loose a torrent of obscenities, some of which Lena had never even heard before. A new jargon was taking hold, full of vulgar words. Lena was not always convinced, but she couldn't pretend not to understand. 'Those male sluts should stop whoremongering,' Inna would rant. 'They and their mothers should go and get…' But when things went wrong, she invariably blamed herself.

'You know, Lena, my mother died young; she never told me how you go about finding a great guy like my dad. Instead I had my aunt as an example, who was basically a free cleaning woman for the men in her life. She thought she'd been sent to this planet to be unhappy, so she stuck with the wife-beaters, the drunks, the egomaniacs. I'm not like that; I want a good life.'

Inna drank and seemed befuddled, but not from the alcohol; she'd got out of the taxi in a daze. She was in love. So that's how it looks from the outside, Lena thought: you talk rubbish, look glassy-eyed and have nothing in your head but your next date. Everything around you is beautiful and luminous; everything bizarre seems normal.

'I've always wondered about the difference between genuine hope and servile patience.' Lines like that spilt from Inna's mouth.

'And? Have you found the answer?'

They topped up each other's glasses; Lena felt her brain cloud over. She would have liked to hug Inna and say something, but she couldn't think what.

'The ones who are quick to adapt are the ones who survive. Nothing new there. You'll have a great time in Germany. I'm happy for you. Really. I always knew Daniel was a good match.'

She said no more about Lena's impending departure, but went back to talking about their life in hall and what an amazing time they'd had. Lena distinctly recalled how much they'd cursed the vile communal kitchen, the filthy washrooms, the thin walls, but there was no stopping Inna—everything had been better in the past, in that golden age before they'd worked out that things cost money. Before money even existed. When a tin of goulash was all it took to make friends. They'd lived on top of each other, but it hadn't been the end of the world; now people lived on top of each other and wanted to wring each other's necks. Everyone was devoured by envy and jealousy; she had to take her watch off before going into work, so that her colleagues wouldn't talk behind her back. She wanted to travel. That was the only good thing about the times they were living in—that you could go where you liked. You just had to know the right people, and she did. She wanted to go to Miami and Singapore. Apparently there were palms hanging over the pools; the water was body temperature and flowed into the ocean, or up to heaven. Of course she wanted to come and visit Lena and Daniel in Germany too. Definitely. 'Let me know when you've settled in. And say if you need anything, money or anything. I'll always lend to you.'

Lena listened to the flood of words, nodded at everything, thanked Inna for her offer of help. The only thing she would have liked to ask of Inna was that she drop in on her father now and then, but he lived far away and Inna hardly knew him. Lena decided not to mention it.

Before leaving, Lena took the sleeper to Horlivka. She arrived early in the morning and was surprised to see her father standing fresh-faced on the platform; she'd expected to find him drowsing over a crossword puzzle in the kitchen. Roman Ilyich's narrow body listed to one side when he carried her suitcase to the car; his cap hung lopsided and his silhouette was the shape of an open clothes peg, but he wouldn't let Lena do the carrying. On the drive home Lena suggested a picnic in his favourite clearing in the woods. He shot her a cautious glance, without turning his head.

Once home, they set to work almost immediately and packed a small camping stove, a frayed rug, two tins of soup, a tin opener, aluminium cutlery, a bit of honey, a piece of salami and some hurriedly cut bread and butter. They were excited, as if they were late for something. They poured tea into the turquoise thermos with pink tulips, just as they'd been doing since Lena's childhood. Then they drove off and headed out of town. Little seemed to have changed in Horlivka, and Lena had no inclination to see more.

They parked the car at the foot of the hill and walked into the woods; Lena was allowed to carry the lighter of the two picnic bags. She remained a few paces behind her father so that she could see him better, remember him better.

The woods grew cooler and there was a bitter smell. Lena reached up an arm and let the orange beads of the rowan trees slip through her fingers, each one tickling her palm.

'They're sour, but good,' her father said. 'But don't eat them. They're for the birds. The squirrels eat them too, when the frost thaws at the end of winter. Apart from anything else, you have to be careful with unwashed berries. Sometimes I take blackberries back for the children. "Always rinse them in warm water first," I say. But do they? Do they hell. Stuff everything straight in their mouths. The robins come for them. The berries, I mean, not the children. The woods are tired. Can you see? The trees are still green, but they've given up; they're through with the year.'

Lena had the impression that her father was spreading outwards, as if wings were unfolding from his ribs. He could, she was sure, have walked these paths blind without tripping over the serpentine roots or bumping into the massive trunks, whereas she kept getting caught up in the branches; they left bits of bark and leaves in her hair, which she picked out as she went along. She remembered reaching out for Alyona's hand in the woods around the Pioneer camp, so as not to fall behind on the way to the lake, and she remembered Alyona running away from her with that lilting walk of hers. Lena had been sure that Alyona's face would fade with the years, but now she saw clearly the thick, untamed hair bouncing out from behind her ears, the flat nose, the oniony-yellow eyes, the inward-looking gaze.

When they sat down to eat in the clearing, her father's body collapsed again like a paper doll folding in on itself, yielding to gravity. Lena dropped on to the rug and stared at the zigzag of treetops stamped on to the piece of white sky. She didn't sit up until the smell of gas mingled with the smell of chicken fat and she could hear her own stomach rumbling; she hadn't been so hungry since childhood. She burned her mouth on the soup, but went on swallowing it down, blowing quickly to cool it.

'Do you remember the story about the dog and the wolf, Dad?'

A grey, floppy-eared dog was chased from the village because he was too lazy to guard the chickens when the fox came for them. He was old and good for nothing, walked with a limp and could barely see, so his owners gave him a kick in the backside and shut the gate behind him. For a while the dog roamed the nearby fields; then, not knowing how to go on living, he went into the forest to hang himself.

But just as he was tossing a rope over a branch, a sleek-looking wolf appeared, folded his arms and said, 'What do you think you're doing?'

The dog explained his plight, and the two of them came up with a plan: the wolf would go into the village and try to steal the newlyweds' baby, and the dog would waylay him, rescue the child and become the local hero.

No sooner said than done. The wolf pretended he was going to eat the baby, the dog pretended to attack him and save the baby's life, and soon he was back in his old home, fed and petted and allowed to lie undisturbed by the warm stove.

Then winter came. It was bitterly cold and the wolf howled so loudly that the dog took pity on him. He sneaked out and found him hungry and shivering under a fir tree.

'Come with me,' he whispered, and he smuggled him into the village feast that was being held that evening and hid him under the table which was laden with all kinds of delicacies and covered with a cloth to the floor. The dog fed the wolf jam and sausages and legs of lamb, and he told him that as long as he kept quiet he could have as much as he liked. And the wolf ate and ate. He ate until his belly was so round that he could hardly move, but only rock happily to and fro on his soft, fat haunches. He was happier and warmer than he'd ever been in his life—so happy that he let out a howl of joy. He howled along with the villagers who were crooning folk songs.

All hell broke loose. The banquet table was overturned and someone tried to shoot the wolf, but the dog intervened, and together they made it look as if the dog were chasing the wolf into the forest again. There, the wolf leant casually against a tree trunk, as plump as if he had a belly full of cubs.

'Well,' he said. 'If I can ever help, just let me know.'

And he trotted off into the starry night.

'Of course I remember,' her father said. 'Your stomach's rumbling like the wolf's in the cartoon.'

And Lena, feeling like a giggly five-year-old, threw back her head and howled—she howled to the moon although it was broad daylight, and her father poked her in the ribs.

'You're the dog, Dad! The dog with the floppy ears!'

She heard the faint whistle of the camp stove, and it occurred to her that her relationship to life and things was increasingly reliant on memories—films she'd seen as a child, vague images of Pioneer camp, a blond woman putting on make-up to listen to music. It was all so long ago, so far from the present. The present was hazy; the present was odourless gas in a mine shaft—you knew it was there because the canary fell off its perch, but you couldn't grasp it.

The next morning Lena suggested going to her mother's grave. 'Let's go and see Mum.'

Her father vanished into the bathroom to get shaved. He also gave his hands a good wash; Lena could tell from his red fingertips.

He must have tried to scrub the forest filth from under his nails—filth far older than the previous day's outing.

The cemetery had grown; Rita's grave was no longer at the edge. Lena filled a bucket at the trough and poured water over the stone slab to clean it of dust and leaves. Then her father laid the chrysanthemums they'd bought on the way on the gleaming surface. *Margarita Andreyevna Platonova*, it said. *Born*… *Died*… Nothing else. The engraved letters sloped slightly, like a handwriting exercise, but they were plain, without flourish.

Out of the corner of her eye, Lena saw people placing small stones instead of flowers on the next grave along. There were about four or five of them, all dressed in black, murmuring to each other and nodding. A very small child clinging to its mother's skirts waved at Lena with its free hand. Or at least it stuck its arm in the air.

I probably look as pale as them, Lena thought. Though it's almost the end of summer.

The Technical Museum, which they passed on their way back, was closed. They bought vanilla ice cream and sat in dappled shade on a bench in the park. Lena tilted her nose to the sun; the light glinted through the leaves. A little colour in her face wouldn't be a bad idea; she didn't want to arrive in the West looking like death warmed up. Music was coming from somewhere, a tune no one played any more—or was it in her head? Probably one of Okudzhava's old hits. Lena pulled her thin coat tighter around her, and her father started to talk about age. He had the impression, he said, that age wasn't measured in years, but by the speed at which you grasped things: the older you were, the quicker you understood what was going on in the world around you, and the quicker you could react and cope. Seen like that, he said, he was young, because he didn't understand a thing of what was going on—but before Lena could say anything, he'd changed the subject again.

'Will you take the washing machine?' he asked, holding out his empty ice-cream tub to her.

'Malyutka?' she said, looking around for a bin. 'Of course. I wouldn't leave a good friend behind.'

They set off along an avenue of oaks. The first leaves were falling on the path, but the treetops were still lush and strangely loud, as if the leaves were slapping against each other. Lena slipped her arm through her father's and tried to start a conversation with him, but he was already somewhere else, perhaps deep in the woods, and only made vague sounds of agreement, even when she hadn't asked anything.

Lena told herself she would come back regularly to visit him—maybe every few months, circumstances permitting. She would bring presents and eventually she'd persuade him to join her in Germany. She'd find him a small flat not far from theirs; she'd promise to return regularly to Mother's grave with him—at least once a year, on the anniversary of her death, to sluice down the gravestone. She'd promise to bury him next to Mother when the time came.

The pavement outside the House of Culture was in pieces; sand oozed out of gaping cracks, clumps of weeds tickled Lena's ankles. She heard her father drag his feet, and when she let him go on ahead she saw that his trousers were a little too long for him and that there was a brown line at the hem.

He wasn't yet sixty, but what did she know?

2015

'IT WAS SO DAMP, the trees soaked up the moisture like sponges. Ah, the smell of the woods. The leaves smell even stronger on an empty stomach. And everything dripping and gleaming, light dripping from the branches. I went straight to the oaks, and the chanterelles were everywhere, as if they'd been waiting for me—more than I could fit in my basket. You can make a lovely soup with them—did you know that? I don't have any cream, but I thought I'd be like the old woman in the fairy tale who makes soup out of an axe. You don't actually need anything but water and mushrooms. I'll share it with the woman next door, of course; we always cook for each other when there's something to cook. There were bay boletes under the copper beeches—a carpet of them—but you have to be careful with boletes, so I just took some bark to make tea. Then on the way back I noticed I'd lost my knife. A knife, can you believe it—I really must be getting old; it's not as if they give them away for free. The little one with the yellow handle. Luckily it's a very bright yellow, so I spotted it under the copper beeches when I went back, and I picked myself some leaves to chew while I was at it—'

'Don't you go to the food bank any more?'

'Yes, but it's a long walk and it'll soon be winter.'

'They don't bring things to you?'

'We can be glad it exists at all. But twelve miles there and back—it's tough on the legs…'

'And the young people?'

'The young people sometimes bring something, but stew's not so easy to carry. Plus, they're hungry themselves. The woman next door, clever old thing, has hoarded sugar, bags and bags of it; she boils it up in the evenings to make caramel for the young people. They love that. Do you remember Oxana? Her daughter's as tall as me now—no, taller, but then I'm shrinking by the day. Getting a hunchback, too—soon I'll be as bent as a sheathed woodtuft and I can go into the woods and join the other fungi. Don't cry, I'm only joking.'

'I'm not crying. It's my allergies.'

'At this time of year?'

'Sometimes.'

'Don't they have things you can take for it over there?'

'No, they do.'

'You're in good health otherwise?'

'Yes.'

'And Edita?'

'I don't know.'

'What?'

'Fine, she's fine.'

'Does she visit you?'

'Every weekend.'

'Bring a boy?'

'Sometimes. Not often. You'll see when you're here. Dad, we need to try doing this the other way round.'

'Don't you worry yourself. There really are mushrooms everywhere, and the young people haven't got a clue. Walk into the woods and walk back out again and haven't seen half what they might have picked.'

'Listen, I'm going to buy you a ticket from Rostov. I want you to cross the Russian border and from there I want you to take the plane to Frankfurt via Moscow. I'll meet you at the airport and bring you back to ours. We can let Edita know so she can join us from Berlin. Then we'll all be together.'

'And how do I get this ticket?'

'It'll be waiting for you at the airline desk when you get to Rostov.'

'How will you manage that?'

'I'll buy it on the internet. You just have to pick it up.'

'I don't think they'll let me into Rostov. If the Ukrainians won't let me through… This place is being sliced up like a loaf of bread. They put up borders where there were no borders before, and suddenly I'm not allowed across. If my own people won't let me through, the Russians certainly won't.'

'Yes, they will.'

'Why?'

'Because they have to.'

'Don't be silly, Lena.'

'I mean it. They have to.'

'That doesn't mean they will. Our people should, Lena, really they should. And what do they do? Tell an old man to go and die. Those rude brats with their rifles are younger than my granddaughter, but when I show them my passport at their supposed border, they laugh in my face. I'm not doing that again.'

'No, you have to go the other way this time—to the Russian border, not the Ukrainian one. Get a good night's sleep, drink your copper beech, eat some burnt sugar, but for goodness' sake make sure you get to Rostov. Hitch a lift; they won't say no to you.

And don't take a suitcase; all you need is your passport. Leave everything else behind.'

'And what about my things? Do I just leave them to rot? Let the fungi take over?'

'I'll come and pick them up.'

'And how will you get back in? Can you do that with your internet too?'

'Something like that.'

'And you'll pick everything up?'

'That's right.'

'Even the knives?'

'All the knives in the house. The one with the yellow handle and all the others too. Every single one.'

'I was only joking. What's got into you? I'm not daft.'

'Dad. I'll come in a few months and pack up anything you want and bring it back to Germany for you.'

'Mother's grave, too.'

'Yes.'

'Very funny. Do you know the name of the town where I was born? Its Soviet name? Stalino. After the man who tried to starve us. Our people ate each other. And now, on the very same soil, our own people are starving us out. Shutting down borders and telling an old man to go and die. And the Russians make us walk twelve miles a day for food. And what's the only country that'll help me? Germany!'

'Just don't forget your passport. It's the only thing you need. I'll fetch all the rest.'

'Do you know what I've been thinking? When you come back here, don't sell our flat. It's bad enough that you gave up the flat in Dnipropetrovsk. Edita might like to have it sometime. Or you. It's property, after all.'

'All right, Dad.'

'When everything's over.'

'When everything's over, I'll come and take care of the flat. But first you have to come to Rostov.'

'And Edita doesn't come and see you?'

'She's busy.'

'Wants to be a writer, did you say?'

'Journalist.'

'That's a good profession. Maybe I can tell her a bit about my life when I'm in Germany. About what's happening here.'

'You can. Definitely.'

'I'll tell her everything.'

'Yes.'

'Then it'll be in all the papers.'

'Absolutely.'

'And I can teach her to look for mushrooms. Do you think she'd be interested? It's an art in itself.'

'Yes. I think she'd be interested. I'm sure she'd be very interested.'

CIGUAPA

By day I sleep in the draught of the one-legged fan, but it only swirls the hot air around, so I help it along by filling the humidifier with water and angling its fibrous filter gills at my pillow. At night I'm awake. I sit in the hall, because it's more bearable there than in the bedroom or kitchen, and I wait for my computer processor to cool down, for the pressure in my head to ease off, for a sign that rain is on its way—this surely can't go on.

Sometimes the sky sounds like it's having palpitations. It gasps a couple of puny drops on to the windowsill, sucks itself full of electrical charge, grows yellow with tension. Did my mother have to move us to one of the hottest cities in Germany—to a valley where the kids on the playgrounds burn their fingers on the metal climbing frames summer after summer?

I often spend the day with my eyes closed. I have a recurring dream in which an endless line of people stand in a queue. They are naked. I can't see the beginning or end of the queue—only that the people are standing on a convex surface; you can see the curvature of the Earth beneath their feet. They don't resemble one another. They have long hair and short hair, curly hair and straight hair, green, blond and black hair—I even spot the flaky pink of some bald heads. Their arms are crooked or straight, sinewy or flabby; their legs knock-kneed or so stiff as to seem jointless. I know none of these people and nothing about them. All I know is that they're mothers and daughters, each woman the daughter of the woman in front and the mother of the woman behind. It isn't the lines on their skin that tell me this; these women are age-less. Or rather, their ages change depending on the angle you're looking from, as if they'd put their faces into that app that shows you what you'll look like when you're older—the same woman has a grandmother's face one moment and a little girl's the next. I can tell they're mothers and daughters from the way they look past one another. But they're looking *for* one another, too—seeking each other out with their eyes. Each touches the woman in front of her, trying to get her attention.

With a tightly curled forefinger, one woman taps the shoulder blade of the woman in front, like a woodpecker with its beak—*tock-tock-tock*, *tock-tock-tock*—while behind her another woman with a long, tightly curled finger taps *her* between shoulder and spine—*tock-tock-tock*, *tock-tock-tock*—and she in turn is clawed on her downy neck by the woman behind *her*—*krrr-krrr-krrr*. The skin is already starting to turn red, and she puts her hand to the itch and looks behind her, but just as she glances back, the woman who's been tapping or clawing her glances back at the woman behind *her*—her daughter—and so the women's eyes never meet, and they all stand there waiting for whoever's in front of them to turn her whole body, rather than just peering over her shoulder and swatting the offensive hand away like a mosquito.

None of these women moves from the spot. It's as if they're paralysed from the hips down; each one is simply a link in the chain. They stand there, the mothers in front of their daughters and the daughters in front of *their* daughters, with their backs beaten tender and their skin scratched raw, and they can't move—occasionally they swivel their torsos to and fro as if on hinges, but apart from that, not a lot happens in this dream.

I can't see myself in this chain—or at least, none of the faces seems to be mine. I'm not there. Nor is my mother. I know there's a chain of fathers too somewhere, but I can't see that either. It doesn't surprise me. I can't muster much interest in the concept of father; it has no associations for me. That's why it leaves me cold when Uncle Lev comes round and gets all paternal on me. He's pretty clumsy at it, maybe because he has no children of his own and feels the need to prove himself—to show he can actually do this: be there, care, understand. I prefer it when he just stumbles in as if by chance. He talks too fast, drops syllables—drops things, too—and is always losing stuff, but what's it to me if he has a new number every time I see him because all his phones end up in the gutter? I never call him anyway. Maybe yelling out after people with his new number is his way of saying he'd appreciate a phone call. I like him best when he's scatty.

I don't know if his wife left him because he couldn't have children, but he often talks to me about her—or rather, he talks to himself, and my presence spares him the embarrassment of telling his woes to the wall. Not everything he says makes sense, but he clearly misses her. I don't know anyone else in the *mishpocha* who's childless and alone. They're a close-knit lot, the Jewish community—make quite a thing of it, though all they have is a big flat on the second floor of a tower block, and as far as I know, the only Jewish thing about them is that they have a truckload of matzo delivered once a year. They pile it with smoked ham at all those parties of theirs—the ones with the Russian pop blaring and the singing so loud you can hear it on the street. One of the rooms in the flat is very large, almost a ballroom—that's where the dancing happens. Sometimes, after one of those parties, Uncle Lev rings at my door reeking of sweat and alcohol and tells me I ought to swing by too someday. I usually turn him away. On the whole, though, he's civil and comes in the evening because he knows I sleep during the day. I like him, he likes me; we talk about his new phone, his famous home-made schnapps, the keys he leaves with the neighbours because he's afraid of locking himself out. I don't tell him I think it's just an excuse to drop in on the neighbours.

The last time he came was different; I couldn't get him out of the flat. He started telling me about my mother—as if I hadn't heard the story a thousand times before, as if we didn't have an unspoken agreement not to mention her. He pulled the dad act, ignored my objections. As if he'd forgotten I'm old enough to make my own decisions. It was my decision to stay here when my mum moved away. It's my decision to be alone—not like my mum, who can't cope without other people. And it's my decision never to let anyone—and I mean anyone—tell me I don't understand what's going on. I understand better than most. I don't drink, I don't smoke weed; I've been medically certified as having above-average neural processing capacity; my visual and auditory perception are acute, and my long-term memory, unfortunately, works all too well.

I looked at Uncle Lev, his face softened by booze, and wondered whether life was better or worse when you understood so little of what was going on around you. He shuts himself away with his distilling equipment, watches the mash ferment and the alcohol evaporate and tells himself these stories. People from the community give him funny looks, but they're no better. How often have I met one or other of them on the street, reeking to high heaven and spouting drivel. It's the same whether they smell of spirits or perfume. Given half a chance, people spout drivel and act like idiots. As often as not, they blame it on the booze. 'I didn't mean it,' they say, 'I'd had a bit to drink.' Or: 'What can you do? Things are what they are.' The booze is always to blame. The booze and the kids. 'We did it for the children,' they bleat in the same hollow way they say, 'I'd had a bit to drink.'

People get drunk to provide themselves with excuses and they have kids to provide themselves with excuses. Their lives slip out of control, and so they add an extra link to the chain that shackles them. It doesn't stop them from being idiots, but at least they know they're not the last.

I'm not especially impressed by Uncle Lev's stories about how much my mum sacrificed for me. Of course you love your children, but that doesn't have to mean you like them.

At some point I understood that Uncle Lev had come to extend an invitation—a formal, almost ceremonious event, hence the clean shirt, only a little frayed at the collar. His face was a large-pored orange; he looked past me and rolled out the old story of my mum's sorrows, apparently seeing no other means of persuading me to show up at Auntie Lena's fiftieth. All those years ago, still with one foot in the refugee home herself, Lena had fetched my mum and me off the street. Now she was organizing a big party in the community flat; my mum was invited, of course, and so was I—and Auntie Lena, according to Lev, was hoping for a reconciliation. The party was planned for October, but here he was in August, already nagging at me to go. No excuses. Actually, it should have been clear to everyone concerned that I couldn't do it. I can't be in crowded spaces—I have medically certified proof of that, too—but people only believe what they want to believe; that's one of the reasons why my mother and I fell out. She wanted me to stop being difficult. Find a job, get married, have kids, God knows what else.

'You don't know what it was like!' Uncle Lev said, looking at me as if I was a baby again in my mother's arms, only a few weeks old, and my mum at the bus station with a bag between her knees. Auntie Lena, who'd never seen my mum before, recognized her right away, schlepped us home, found us a flat, gave me her daughter's cast-off babygros and organized a job for my mum and a crèche for me. Or so the legend goes.

I expect the expression on my mum's face when she got off the Berlin–Jena bus was enough to tell Auntie Lena who she was. They have a similar look, both startled by life. Lena had emigrated to Germany herself with husband and child not so long before; she was just starting to break free of the squalor of food vouchers, clothes vouchers, furniture vouchers and language lessons; the family had only recently got their first landline connection, and already the phone was ringing and there was a Tatyana on the line saying, 'You don't know me, you studied with my cousin in Dnipropetrovsk, I've got no one in Germany except my newborn baby and I don't know where to go.' We should come to Jena, Auntie Lena said. She had a small child herself. Her German wasn't much better than Tatyana's. They both came from a place people thought was somewhere in Russia. Soon they were on the phone daily and visiting each other regularly—even after a whole day together they would phone each other and go on talking as if they hadn't spoken for weeks. On the telephone table in our hall there was a photo of me clutching one of those paper cones of sweets that German kids are given on their first day of school. Mine was a present from Auntie Lena and, although I've never asked, I'm pretty sure that my mum had made one for Lena's daughter three years before—the one that Edi's clutching in the photo on Lena and Daniel's telephone table in *their* hall.

The daylight lay in pools on the PVC floor; morning clouds rippled the sky. Uncle Lev glared at me as if he was trying to pin me down with his eyes. 'You can't refuse Lena this!'

By which he meant, of course, that I owed her for saving us from a criminal all those years ago—a criminal who, sorry to say, happens to be my father. But that's not how things work. I'm really fond of Auntie Lena—at a distance and with plenty of silence between us—but I don't owe her a thing. I'm grateful to her. That's different.

Uncle Lev shook his head fiercely like he had water in his ear. The door handle behind him was a straight line of dull metal. It glinted when the sun caught it and jabbed at my eyes. Soon it would be hot in the flat; I must close the curtains.

'You should have seen your mother!' he went on, piling on the pressure. He's often described her to me, peering about her at the bus station, only a pair of trousers and a few changes of underwear in her sports bag. As if he'd been there. The way he tells the story, my mother was knocked up by a conman and abducted to Germany, but if I know my mum, there's no way anyone could have abducted her. She's stronger than any guy. If she grabs you by the collar, then good luck to you. I know what I'm talking about; I was dragged around plenty over the years. When my mum throws things, she leaves holes in the walls. Uncle Lev doesn't know that and he doesn't want to either. Just like he doesn't want to know that Saint Tatyana made me sleep on the doormat outside the flat for nights on end when I was kicked out of school for having weapons in my rucksack. In fact I'd only been lugging the knives around because I was stupid enough to believe her when she threatened to slit her wrists while I was flunking exams at school. She didn't slit anything. She didn't even smoke in the flat; she always made rice and vegetables for lunch, no deep-fried crap, and the bathroom cupboard was full of creams and lotions and supplements, Vitamin C, Vitamin A, Vitamins B and D, the whole fucking alphabet. I think you could say she looked after herself. I think she'll cope.

She might even be better off without me as her personal delusion breaker. Live your life in the delusion necessary to get you through the day. It's what most people do.

I know almost the whole of that Jewish community. You can recognize them by the looks of startled defiance on their faces; life hasn't been kind to them. They all have similar names too, Soviet chocolate-box names—Lyusa, Alyonka, Styopka, Masha. Luckily for me, I wasn't named after a brand of chocolates. I can't comment on my face. People think I'm older than I am, and I look nothing like my mother, so I guess when she looks at me she's reminded of things that aren't good for her.

There was a time, of course, when I asked a lot of questions about my father. My mum's replies were vague, and she generally ended the conversation by saying, '…a man, what can you do,' as if facing up to the diagnosis of a terminal disease. I don't have a photo of him or anything. But I can live with that.

Sometimes I'm out for a walk and someone from the community will ask me what's with the face. I always say the same: 'Guess it grew that way.' And they say, no, no, why do I look so angry? That's why I try to avoid hanging out with them. It's one reason, anyway.

I've had a bit of a look at this group of people around Auntie Lena and Uncle Lev. Not at their parties, of course—I steer clear of that ballroom of theirs—but on the internet, in features and news and documents from the online archive, and in eyewitness reports from a time that seems to have swept everyone away like an earthquake. The way I understand it, the colossus just disintegrated. Eleven time zones crumbled apart—how could that not have some kind of impact on people? But I wanted to know more, because that makes it sound as if something was in one piece and isn't any longer. I spent nights, weeks, months reading about what a shock it must have been. The only sure thing is that there are still aftershocks. And that those who experienced it at first hand are still trembling to their guts. Or else they suffer from a kind of phantom pain: the country they were born into has been amputated, but it still hurts. Little else can be said with certainty. I watched films, home videos, whatever I could get hold of, to try and understand what happened to them, into what parallel universe they'd been flung by the centrifugal power of history. To try and understand what they see when they stare through their net curtains with their Soviet eyes into the streets and backyards of a medium-sized East German town. Why they tilt their heads to the side. Why they wear those clothes. That make-up. Those shoes. And why they're always raising their shoulders.

I came across pictures of a huge inflatable caterpillar in Moscow. Some Hungarian artist sent it floating through Gorky Park to mark the centenary of the Russian Revolution. Apparently it was an allusion to an Antonio Gramsci quote: *The old world is dying and the new world struggles to be born; now is the time of monsters.* But over there it's always monster time.

I read my way through online dissertations and eyewitness reports; the contradictions were so blatant I almost went to a library. The historical studies tend not to tally with the announcements and reports in the news portals; the blogs about the Pioneer camps are written in a silly fairy-tale language, practically in rhyme—campfire sing-song stuff. I still can't make head or tail of it all. There was a housing shortage in the USSR, but some people had homes of their own; they were all Communists, but believed in God and money; they were Jewish and atheist at the same time. No one did their job properly, but everyone had a much better education than anyone in the West.

When I look at the reminiscences of former Soviets, I have the feeling they've never spoken to each other and have no idea how different their realities were—what totally different lives they led in a country where there was supposedly only one path, one possible way of life. They won't ever find out, either—not as long as their only communication with each other is through quotes by long-dead writers.

I have the impression they've committed themselves to a common narrative that says they belong together because no one else understands them. They've declared themselves history's unsung champions. Easily done, when history is over, done away with, the textbooks rewritten every year. Above their heads a caterpillar endlessly sheds its cocoon, but they still don't know what's going to emerge.

In one of the video games I play, there's a fantasy figure who's different from all the others. She has green skin and a mean look on her face, pointy ears and dark, seaweedy hair that hangs down over her bare arse. Her feet are back to front: her heels point the way her nose points and her toes follow the swell of her bum. You can find loads about Ciguapa online. She's a magical being of Dominican folklore who waits in the forest to seduce unsuspecting men and then devour them. Her footprints in the damp earth mislead anyone who tries to follow them. In one blog I read that they're back to front because they point into the past. Ciguapa goes neither backwards nor forwards; she's caught in limbo.

I promptly dreamt that the mothers and daughters in the human chain were standing on Ciguapa feet, their heels red-hot, quivering. I started up from the dream and wondered what feet would look like if they pointed neither into the past nor into the future, but stood firmly in the present. I supposed the toes would have to grow into the earth and put down roots. But would you be able to stand on feet like that, or would you keel over?

I wondered, too, if it was possible to speak to one's own mother without escaping into the past or future. To look her in the eyes now, in the present. Could we stop reproaching each other for what was over and done with, or complaining about what would never be?

I had to stop Uncle Lev in the end; he kept starting all over again. He seemed genuinely surprised when I told him I wouldn't be coming to the party.

After he'd gone, I got up and closed the curtains, filled the lung of the humidifier with water, lay down on my pillow and let the fine spray cool me.

II

I like the people in Kafka's parables. They do not know how to ask the simplest question. Whereas to you and me it may look (as my father used to say) as obvious as a door in water.

ANNE CARSON,
'The Anthropology of Water'

EDI

…*Y*OUR HOMELAND IS NOT *simply the land of your birth, a true homeland is the country that can kill you—even at a distance, the same way a mother slowly but inexorably kills an adult child by holding it near, shackling its every move and thought with her burdensome presence…* Edi glanced at her flashing phone, put it face-down on the sofa and went on flicking through the book. *Fieldwork in Ukrainian Sex*—a novel, if the publisher was to be believed—had been available only second-hand. The more Edi read it, the more confused she got.

> *GULAG—is when they drive an empty half-liter bottle*
> *Between your legs—after which they address you as 'ma'am.'*

She wasn't sure what to make of such statements.

The flimsy cover showed two Russian dolls, one of which—the one with female attributes—was leaning against the rotund belly of the other, the one with a moustache. It was a paperback, so there was no author photo, and the text itself was a dense, unindented wodge of scattergun abuse. Nobody came off well—not the Americans (the narrator lived in the US), not the Ukrainians (she came from Ukraine), not the Russians (logically enough) and definitely not the Jews (well, of course not, why would *they* get good press?). Edi's original plan had been to go to Kyiv to interview 'Ukraine's most important living writer' and claim it as a business trip. But that summer—the elections were still some weeks away—the editorial team had started on at her to give an opinion on *her people*; this was her chance to prove herself, make an image for herself, claim a niche. Someone used the expression *unique selling point*, and if Edi hadn't felt sick before, she certainly did then. She wasn't sure if she had a chance of a permanent post when her traineeship came to an end; maybe she was only a stopgap. But even if she was—a free flight to Ukraine and an opportunity to see the country didn't seem like a bad option. The trouble was that the editorial team didn't want her to write about Ukrainian culture; they wanted a feature on *her people* in former East Germany: quota refugees, straggler refugees, early repatriates, late repatriates, total repatriates, Volga Germans, German Russians, Jews with Stars of David round their necks, Jews with crucifixes round their necks, Armenian Jews, Circassian Jews, German Kazakhs with Jewish pets. A considerable part of this *mishpocha* had recently given their votes to a right-wing populist party, and Edi was expected to use the language she shared with these people to lure them to the microphone. At a recent editorial meeting, it had been suggested that it was time Edi said something about the *situation*. 'It concerns you, too.'

Of course it concerned Edi, but in what way? She wanted to become a journalist in order to travel, preferably westwards. She was interested in the US; she was interested in South America. Those were the places she wanted to specialize in, but her colleagues didn't seem to care. Didn't she have family in the former USSR? Wasn't she from…? Yes, she was from.

'How about we send someone out there and you go with them and take a few photos? People might be more likely to open up to you. Be a great opportunity to make some contacts.'

Edi had almost run out of the meeting, but she wanted the job; she wanted a desk of her own in the office, not half a wobbly table out in the corridor that had to be cleared whenever anyone else needed it. She wasn't doing badly. She'd been selected from over two hundred applicants; a traineeship was already half a job. She just had to grit her teeth and hang on in there. She pressed up against the back of her chair, made a vague motion with her head, neither nod nor shake, and tried to say something like, 'Not everyone who rejects socialism votes Nazi.' But she couldn't phrase it right. No, not everyone, not by a long way. Only her dad. And *Nazi* wasn't the right word, but she couldn't think of another. She could never find the right words when she needed them. Like the other day on the phone to her dad, when he'd happened to mention where he'd put his cross on the ballot paper.

Edi's Russian wasn't good enough for political discussions. The mix of German and Russian words squeezed into a more or less German syntax was a language all its own and it varied from one immigrant family to another, like the recipe for a well-known dish that tastes different at a friend's house. Not everyone used the same ingredients. Edi had hung up and decided that the conversation had never happened.

Sometimes, she had read in a book on the Donbas, *you come to an edge that just breaks off.* She would have liked to quote that at the meeting, but it hadn't come back to her until later.

Edi turned the phone over again; her mother's name was flashing on the screen for the fourth time. If only she'd switched it off—but she was waiting for a message from someone she had a vague date with. In the dating app chat, this person's name was just a series of numbers and hashtags; they gave no further information about themselves—only that they liked *music that scratches your ears* and *exhibitions that I can understand without having to read the bumf.* Also: *I'm top (never liked being bottom ☺), poly and fun.* Their profile picture was blurred; it must have been taken when they were moving. Edi saw only dark hair and no face; she wasn't even sure what part of the body she was looking at. Maybe Leeza would be on the doors at the club where they'd arranged to meet. That would be cool. They could share a couple of cigarettes.

The phone flashed and flashed. Edi couldn't play dead any more; each time she didn't pick up, the conversation got longer. Maybe she should take the call and tell her mum she couldn't come to her birthday party because she had to travel to the US—urgent work-related trip, highly sensitive investigative job, no way of postponing it. They always argued anyway, so why not about that?

'Have you been in touch with Tatyana?' Her mother jumped straight in. But she didn't play into Edi's hands by letting her anger show, so Edi, too, feigned indifference and said honestly, 'No'.

Instead of bombing down the grey autobahn to Jena, she'd cruise along a highway in Florida, Spanish moss dripping like green froth from the branches of centuries-old trees, Victorian buildings decaying like a crumbling stage set, faces bloated with damp and worry in the aisles of the malls. Maybe she'd even persuade her hashtag date to go along with her. Didn't people say the best way to get to know someone was to travel with them? Maybe by then the date would have a name she could call them by when they parked by the beach and headed to the ocean.

'You still there?' Her mother had been talking, but Edi couldn't have repeated her last sentences; she sensed only that she'd missed something important.

'Yes, I… My…' She trod aimless paths through the flat and stopped at the front door to examine the dented metal of the lock. The wooden frame next to it was in splinters; the door didn't close.

'My flat's been broken into.'

Edi touched the woodchips peeping out around the lock; they were soft, as if a tiny straw cushion had burst beneath the paint.

'You don't have to make things up. If you're not planning to come, I'd rather you just said so.'

Typical. Thanks for not asking.

'I'm not making things up, Mum. I came home this morning and the front door was open.'

'And before that? I've been asking you for weeks to arrange things with Tatyana. Is it really that hard?'

Edi stared at the strip of electric light shining into the hall through the gap between the door and the frame. It was early afternoon, but the sun didn't make it into her dingy backyard flat at any time of day.

'Chill, I'll call her in a second.'

'Did they take much?'

The question surprised Edi. She'd resigned herself to not getting a reaction from her mother unless she'd done something she shouldn't have. She looked into the sitting room. It was a mess, yes, but of her own making. No slashes in the sofa cushions. The blanket lay in a heap on the floor where she'd thrown it. The table by the window hadn't been moved. When she'd discovered the break-in that morning, she'd thought she'd find her laptop gone from the chest of drawers, but it was still there, plugged in, the pinpoint of light on the charger glowing green. The pile of magazines was also untouched—at least she thought it was.

'I—I don't know. I haven't checked yet.'

'What do you mean, you haven't checked yet?'

There was no point explaining to her mother that she'd done nothing since getting home and discovering the break-in. The burglars were gone; the flat smelt the same as ever. No open drawers; no books thrown from the shelves. That's what *she'd* do if she broke in somewhere, Edi thought—flick through every book in the bookcase and hurl them at the wall if she didn't find cash between the pages.

She'd tried to imagine what the burglars had been looking for—or had they just wanted to show her how flimsy the lock was? Maybe they'd just been practising on it; maybe they'd been surprised on the stairs and hadn't even made it into the flat. Then she'd gone into the bathroom and discovered the first sign that someone had been there. The toilet bowl was spattered brown; the burglar seemed to have relieved himself with force. Edi wondered if she should leave it like that until the police came, in case they wanted a sample. She imagined a policeman kneeling down in front of the toilet, reaching in an arm and depositing the evidence in a plastic bag. Then she flushed. She had to use the brush to get it clean. She flushed several times and scrubbed vigorously. Her face felt hot. She tried to imagine it was her own excrement—then wondered if she'd forgotten to flush before she went out. She couldn't tell her mother any of that. What would she say? *Someone shat in my loo*?

'I don't think they took anything.'

She couldn't tell her she'd poured all the cleaning products from the cupboard into the toilet bowl. Green detergent had dripped on to the tiles next to the bath; first she'd wiped it up, then she'd decided to clean the whole flat, then a terrible tiredness had come over her, a tiredness that ran down her face like tar. She'd stretched out on the sofa and reached for *Fieldwork in Ukrainian Sex*. That was when her mother had called.

'What do you mean, they didn't take anything? What about your jewellery?'

'What jewellery?'

She suddenly remembered the gold watch her mother had given her years ago, she'd forgotten when or why. Wasn't it in the bathroom cabinet, behind the mirrored door? First she avoided looking at herself; then she risked it. The peroxide blond didn't suit her pale complexion; she had the impression that her already broad, white face was leaking into her short, bleached hair. She tore open the door and immediately spotted the watch on the top shelf; she took it down and ran her fingers over the thin scratches in the glass. Was it even real gold? Did she have anything of value in the flat? Was there anything she'd miss if it were gone? She chased the thoughts away.

Had the burglars used her toothbrush?

She took it out of the tooth mug, ran her thumb back and forth over the bristles, tossed it in the bin and went back to the sofa.

'Sure they didn't take anything?' Her mother sounded strangely alarmed.

'Are you disappointed?'

It was a game they both knew well. Edi heard her mother take a breath, but decide against retaliating. Sometimes she would start yelling, which gave Edi an excuse to yell too. Today, though, she was offhand, as if there were someone else in the room. Edi thought of asking to speak to her father, but left it at vague noises through closed lips while her mother issued instructions.

'You ought to have a good look around, and then call the police and a locksmith. And when you've done that, you must ring Tatyana. A burglary's no excuse to stay away this weekend.' Lena spoke without drawing breath and then hung up.

Edi put her feet into the floral slippers at the balcony door—they'd been handmade by a friend of her mother who thought it barbaric to walk around the flat barefoot as Edi always did. She was convinced it was something you only did if someone had died.

The balcony was a narrow oblong with terracotta pots in the corners and a low wooden chair with its back to the door. Edi felt the chill of autumn nip her ankles and squatted down to inspect the plants. The roots of the mint had cracked the terracotta; she'd been meaning to repot it for weeks. She settled down next to the herbs on the wobbly chair, which was just high enough to allow her to look out over the railing. The trees in front of the stadium opposite were shedding their leaves, exposing the brick-red running track. Again she felt an urge to sleep. She laid her head on the railing and looked out along the black line to the balcony next door, and the one after, and the one after that.

At the end of the block, the sky was crumbly like damp flour. The metal under her temple made her pulse thud; the throbbing beat kept her from closing her eyes. She raised her head and looked in at the kitchen through the glass of the balcony door, grimy with dust from the road. What would her father say to the burglary, she wondered. Would it worry him? It was years now since he'd dropped her off at her first flat-share, a few cardboard boxes of books and clothes in the boot of his old Audi and two sports bags of groceries on the back seat—packet soup, pasta, tomato sauce, home-made jam. He hadn't been to visit since. They'd had the radio on at full blast all the way, but still talked non-stop. Daniel had made Edi promise to make the most of the traineeship she'd managed to land herself at the newspaper. Not to pack it all in because of some silly little thing, like when she'd dropped psychology after only two semesters, and sociology a couple of semesters after that. And no drugs, of course. She must stay away from drugs.

Barely a year later he'd phoned to say he was putting a small sum of money into her account so she could buy herself a car and go and visit them any time. It wasn't enough for a Mercedes, but she should be able to get herself a decent little motor that would at least make it from Berlin to Jena and back once a month.

'Once a month?' The question flew out of Edi's mouth like a tennis ball out of a ball machine.

'Yes, or as often as you want. So you can come whenever you like and aren't dependent on the train.'

Edi didn't argue with him. It must be easier for her father to believe that it was the bad train connections that were keeping her away from home. That it was the rail network that kept them apart, not the shame of not knowing how to justify their lives to each other.

Edi wrapped her arms around her legs and tried to balance curled up on the wooden chair. She sat like that until her eyes began to droop; then she decamped to the sofa.

I was a young, strong, stingy person of no particular gender—all traits advantageous to the pilgrim. So I set off… The thoughts weren't Edi's. But whose were they? In her half-sleep, the author's name had slipped her grasp. And where would she make a pilgrimage to, if she could? She wouldn't want to go alone, that was for sure—even the woman in the book, whose words had been in her head like an earworm when she woke up, had gone with a guy (though it's true, she hardly knew him and started off by giving him a new name). Edi glanced at the phone on the cushion beside her, jumped up and went to the wardrobe.

The black strapless top across her chest looked like a felt-tip line on her chalky skin. She added a brown men's shirt that was missing too many buttons to do up, and thrust her arms into her too-tight leather jacket. Then she reached for the cap stitched with the word *Xanax* and jammed it on to her head, hoping to give her face some kind of shape. If Leeza was on the doors tonight, she'd be sure to tease Edi about her clothes. Despite her bouncer's jacket, Leeza always looked as if she were about to appear on stage; even dressed in black she seemed to glitter in the dark of the backyards.

Night bus after night bus passed Edi, but she decided to walk to shake the tension from her bones. The club was in an old factory building beyond the railway lines; on the way she passed several of the houses where she'd rented rooms since moving to Berlin from Jena. Edi had been thrown out of her first flat-share for setting fire to her flatmate John's mattress when he'd said Israel should be razed to the ground, and she'd been thrown out of the last for tipping a box of washing powder over her flatmate Alex's head when she'd suggested the whole world should be like Israel.

Since then, Edi had lived on her own; the money she made as a trainee was just enough for rent and clubbing. Clothes were no big deal. Edi didn't see the appeal of jumpers that looked like saggy numbers filched from her dad, but were displayed in solitary splendour in boutique windows and cost a month's rent. She didn't stand out particularly, because in Berlin it was OK to look as if you spent your days rummaging through the bargain boxes in the cheap chain stores. She didn't get any more hassle for it than she had at school. Only her mother had a shouting fit whenever Edi showed up wearing lumberjack shirts over tie-dye T-shirts and trucker's caps over her bleached hair, but Edi just shrugged and said, truthfully, that it was what people wore in Berlin. That really set her mother off. Did Edi think she was going to let her treat her like an idiot? She might be from another country, but she wasn't lobotomized enough to believe that people would actually choose to go around in that get-up. She thought Edi was testing her. And on that point, Edi thought, she was right.

One thing was for sure, she couldn't take Leeza to see them. If she showed up at home with a Muslim woman, her parents and their friends would bombard Leeza with prying questions—if, that is, they deigned to speak to her at all and didn't just stare disparagingly. Because of this, part of Edi was relieved when Leeza said after their first night together that she wasn't looking for permanency because she didn't believe in it. Her parents had been separated by the war in their country; her brother was missing—the last thing she wanted was more people who might disappear on her. She was working on not needing anyone, she told Edi as they put their clothes back on. Edi gaped at her. Not for the first time she felt that desire was a muscle, throbbing and contracting. She stopped herself from saying, *I have so much to tell you*, because the words were a kind of warning that an *I love you* might be on its way, and she didn't want to scare Leeza off.

When the queue outside the club began to shorten and she spotted Leeza frisking jackets and rucksacks, Edi felt relief. Leeza rarely went in with Edi; she didn't like dancing and wasn't allowed to drink on the job, but when Edi was in need of a break herself, she would take her a bottle of alcohol-free beer and they would talk in the cold light of the headlamps that cast long shadows under their eyes.

The year before, at the end of the summer, Leeza had let Edi take her home. Edi had kissed her sweaty belly all morning until Leeza pushed her head away and suggested going out, somewhere with a bit of horizon instead of rows of houses. They got as far as the old airfield at Tempelhof. The trembling in their knees and the rollerbladers on the runways made it hard just to stroll; they were constantly having to dodge skaters and couldn't keep their eyes on each other's faces, so they stumbled off the concrete on to the grass and Edi gave a yell because she thought something was biting her bare calves, but it was only a patch of stinging nettles they'd wandered into. Leeza tore up a whole plant, complete with earthy, cobwebby roots, and tickled Edi's neck with it, and then Edi peeled her T-shirt over her head, stripped off her trousers and lay down in the prickly fire of nettles. She made an angel in the leaves with sweeping swimming motions; Leeza shrieked, pulled Edi's legs, grabbed her arms, but it was too late. A few hours later Edi's arms and legs were so swollen she could hardly get up. Leeza turned up at the flat with a litre-bucket of quark in either hand for compresses.

'Have the Hyenaz started yet?' Edi jumped the queue and went and kissed Leeza on the cheek.

That evening, as Edi lay on her mattress looking like the Michelin Man in swathes of cling film and dairy products, Leeza had told her she was studying Sinology and planned to get out of this place as soon as possible, leave the country and everything she knew. When Edi asked why Sinology, she said, 'Because of the mysterious signs.'

That was some time ago now, but Edi didn't probe; she didn't say, 'You're still here!' Apart from anything else, she was still here herself. She still hadn't decided where to make that pilgrimage to—if, that is, she ever found the courage to make one.

'They're not on till next weekend.'

'I won't be here next weekend.' Edi cursed, realizing that the trip to Jena for her mum's birthday was as good as decided. She would drive down with Tatyana. She hadn't spoken to her yet, but she'd sent a text and was relieved not to have heard back; she was keen to put off for as long as possible all talk of what to give and what to wear and who was coming. Her mum had insisted weeks ago that she needn't dress up, needn't bring anything but herself—but that was easily said. The place would be full of people subjecting Edi to scrutiny. They would air their rigid prejudices about her life in insinuations and self-absorbed monologues, and before long they would all be drunk and start to bawl Russian songs, and her father would sit down next to the pianist and try to strum away with him, though he'd never had a music lesson in his life. As for the guests' opinion on the colour of her hair—she didn't even want to know.

'I have to go to my mum's next weekend. Big birthday, big party, the works.'

'Happens to the best of us,' Leeza said without a spark of sympathy. 'When do I get to read something of yours? Didn't you have your first deadline the other day? I thought I'd be seeing your name in the newsfeeds.'

The zip was stuck on the shiny red bum bag that Leeza wore across her chest; it took her several goes to open it. She pulled out a soft pack of cigarettes and lit one; her face mellowed. When Edi had been little, she'd thought those glowing sticks warmed you up—that if people stuck them in their mouths all the time, it was because they were cold.

'I've got to rewrite it,' she said. 'They say I mustn't write everything in the first person, as if I'm just giving my opinion. They say I have to focus on facts and stuff…'

Her boss had put it more scathingly. Edi, she had said, should not imagine that the world around her vanished when she closed her eyes. It was very much still there. It went on turning just fine without Edi and all the others who thought they could cover up their lazy research by claiming to be constructivists, just because they'd once googled the word. This wasn't a lifestyle magazine and it wasn't some half-baked blog either. 'There's no I in the politics pages! We report on real things that really happen. I'm sick of your ego addictions! We train you, we give you a chance and all we get for it is I, I, I, I, I!' By then Edi had already staggered out into the corridor.

'You've got a date, haven't you?' Leeza flicked the cigarette butt away and ran her hands through her hair, as if she were ready to do something reckless.

'Is it that obvious?' Edi worried that her forehead was bright red; it generally was when she was excited. She pulled the *Xanax* cap lower over her face.

'Whenever you look as if you've no idea how to put an outfit together, I know someone's in there waiting for you.' The soft down above Leeza's lip tickled Edi's cheek as she kissed her, nearer to her mouth this time. 'Enjoy!'

Edi was tempted to grab Leeza by the waistband of her jeans and pull her close, but instead she pushed open the door, swept aside the plastic strips that separated the cloakroom from the club and headed for the smoking area.

Music that scratches your ears. Edi pondered the strange words. Her pulse merged with the thudding beat; her breath was shallow. She reached for a screw of tinfoil in her back pocket and began to grind coarse, dry crumbs on to the palm of her hand; then she looked up at the back dance floor. The light pulsed like hazard lights, then swept the floor like looming headlamps, as if lorries were emerging from the depths of the club and making for the crowd.

Like the kites silhouetted over Tempelhof, figures dived at Edi, but veered off before hitting her. She recognized her date by the elaborately messy mane that had featured on their profile picture; it fell over their shoulders and stuck out at the back of their head.

'Dea,' they said curtly, then leant against the unrendered wall, took the joint from Edi and sucked on it nervously several times. Under a baggy suit jacket they wore a dress the colour of onion skin; it fell over their body like water and for a moment Edi thought they were naked underneath. *I'm top, never liked being bottom*, she remembered, but Dea didn't look as if they were on the chase;

they looked exhausted, even if their face was only a cipher in the green-tinged light of the ceiling lamps.

'I'm always cold,' they said, holding perfumed wrists to Edi's cheeks as if to prove it. 'I'm shivering.'

'Bit early for that, isn't it? You've still got a few months to get through. It's only October.' Edi thought she recognized the perfume; she took a step towards Dea.

'I start to pack up round about late August. I hate it when things come to an end. My body gets colder and colder; it shifts down a gear or two.' Their voice was high, or perhaps they were shrieking to make themselves heard above the beat.

'Do you want my jacket?'

Dea looked at Edi for a little too long. 'Whisky's warming,' they said. 'I want whisky.'

Edi stared at the line of their lips until she was sure Dea could feel her gaze.

'I'll never accept that there are days when it gets dark halfway through the afternoon. It's like someone's stealing something from me. Soon there'll be frost on the grass in the mornings and my windows will look like someone's poured milk down the panes. Revolting.' Dea seemed content, working themselves into a pointless rage; they kept moving closer. 'I want the right to hibernate. Like a hamster. Or a hedgehog. I've decided I'm going to march into the Bundestag and demand two things: unconditional basic income and the unconditional right to bury myself in a pile of leaves every October. No one would be allowed to wake me. My heart would only beat once or twice a minute; I'd shut everything down and wouldn't wake until the blossom came out in the parks.'

'So I guess you're already studying law?'

'To win the right to shut down my heart? Oh, yes!'

Dea looked very pale in the light from the dance floor, as if their cheeks were powdered white. When Edi had given herself nettle rash, her face had looked similar—like a stencil roughly filled in with white chalk.

'And how are you going to keep warm until the Bundestag grants your request?'

Dea blinked. Their black-rimmed eyes blurred in the smoke.

In summer, Edi thought, or maybe even spring, the two of them could go to a lake together. She suddenly longed to take the plaid rug from the boot of her car and spread it on a sandy bank. She and Dea would lie on it side by side, eating brioche and staring at the bobbing heads on the lake. They would think about jumping into the water too, but instead they would hide out in the bushes. The undergrowth would leave a red print on Dea's shoulder blades.

They were standing close; Edi could smell the sweet, tangy bourbon on Dea's breath. Dea raised their glass and their jacket sleeve slid up to reveal a tattoo of an animal's legs—hooves and pasterns done in fine black lines.

'How far does that go?'

'Pretty far.' Dea took a step back to show Edi more of the tattoo. 'Pirosmani's giraffe. Do you know him? He never saw a giraffe in his life. There weren't any in Georgia and he couldn't travel; he was so poor he ended up starving to death under a pub table in the First World War. But he'd heard about this animal called a giraffe and he decided to paint it. He got it all wrong—the proportions, the colouring—but it doesn't matter; what matters is that he wanted to paint it and he did. I saw the picture in an exhibition, completely by chance. Just wandered in and…'

The supposed giraffe covered their entire arm, their shoulder too, presumably—and who knew what part of them was graced with the animal's head?

'I like it when people take risks. You don't know a place, you've only heard about it, but you try to form your own image of it. In the end, it doesn't matter how long the giraffe's neck really is, because Pirosmani doesn't say: *This is how it is*, but: *This is how I think it might be.*'

Edi wanted to object, but instead she reached out an arm and stroked Dea's neck.

They drank another two shots and staggered on to the dance floor, but soon headed off to the cloakroom for Dea's coat and walked out, hands intertwined; Leeza winked at Edi as they passed. On the way home, the fear grew in Edi that Dea would take one look at her smashed-in door and turn right round. But where else could she take them? They couldn't go to a lake. It was too cold and Dea was shivering. Maybe they were just the person to run away with to a hot country.

Dea didn't ask about the broken door and didn't seem surprised that Edi got in without using a key. They looked about them, studied the postcards in the hall mirror and ran a casual hand over the books in the bookcase. Edi saw the movement reflected in the glossy spines.

Edi's improvised bed without a bed frame didn't seem to bother them either, nor did the heap of clothes next to it. Nothing seemed to bother them. They accepted a glass of stale wine from the fridge, suddenly subdued; there was no more talk of the cold or slow heartbeats or short-necked giraffes. They sat down on the sofa and didn't move.

Edi gulped down her wine and knelt down in front of them, ran her hand under the waterfall dress, peeled the wet synthetic material from the skin around their knees, grabbed their jutting ribs. They fell back together into the sofa cushions. Edi crawled right under Dea's dress and Dea laughed, their body shimmering beneath the onion-skin fabric. Everything went quiet; the only sound Edi was aware of was the nervous chirp of a watch at her ear when Dea pushed her head between their thighs. They tasted of maple syrup and something more elusive that Edi kept searching for until Dea pushed her head away. She laid her cheek in the soft dip between the hair on Dea's mons and their pelvis. It would be nice to stay here, she thought. Here all was calm.

She woke with the smell of wet leaves in her nose—and because she was cold. She'd left the window open, and the air in the room felt damp, as if dew had settled on all the surfaces. Dea was right; it would soon be time to hibernate. Edi thought of the stinging nettles and wondered if they'd stay green under the snow. Her eyelids were trembling—probably a combination of the THC still circulating in her veins, the wine she'd drunk and the fluttery feeling she often had in the mornings, which she kept at bay with weed on the days she didn't have to go to work. She ran her eyes over the black lines on Dea's sleeping body; the tattoo travelled from their lower arm over the vague swell of their biceps to the bottom of their neck and then down to their breastbone. It looked like a horse craning over the bars of Dea's ribs, its head turned to the viewer.

Although it had been hot and smoky in the club, Dea gave off a smell of freshly ironed laundry. The smell came from their body; it had nothing to do with their clothes.

Edi groped for her phone; the beginning of a text from Tatyana glowed on the screen: *Sorry not to get back to you sooner…* She opened it and read, *Please come.* Tatyana was in hospital; no one else knew and she wanted it to stay that way for the moment. Neurological ward, room number so-and-so.

Sometimes *See you* can sound like *Go and break your neck.* Their goodbyes were perfunctory. Edi must have looked awful; Dea stared past her into space, their coat tucked under their arm, the undone buttons at the collar of their dress jutting out like thorns, their long hair moving as if it were an animal. Edi had woken them and pressed their bag into their hand, without coffee or brioche or even the offer of a shower—as if she had to leave right away, as if Tatyana's text had conjured her mother into the room, as if Tatyana and her mother were looking down at the two bodies half asleep, barely touching. Onion skin over the stranger's bum and a swathe of black over Edi's chest.

The smell of freshly ironed laundry had vanished. Dea flew from the flat like a stunt kite; Edi slammed the door shut; it sprang open again. Edi gave up on the door and grabbed her phone. She checked the coordinates in Tatyana's text, held her clammy hair under the tap in the bathroom and threw on some clothes that didn't reek of sweat and smoke. That would have to do. On the way to the hospital she looked up locksmiths' numbers, but the first couple she tried didn't answer. She couldn't go away for the weekend with her front door wide open.

Urban Hospital, on the canal. She'd often lain here on the steep grassy bank, arms under her head as she watched the swans trying to peck glinting bottle tops out of the earth, but she'd never dwelt on the thought that the block-like building behind her was a hospital where people were born, had broken bones fixed, died. It took her a while to find the entrance, but she had no qualms about going in. Far from it: Edi felt a kind of lightness as she stepped through the automatic doors; for her, hospitals were childhood places associated with her mother who had worked nights in a clinic to make a living and to have some time for Edi during the day. It wasn't until Edi had left home that she began to think about what it must have meant to Lena to slog away as a nurse in her new life when she was used to working as a doctor. As a little girl she'd sometimes made such a fuss about not being able to sleep without her mum that Lena had relented in exasperation. 'All right,' she would say, with a withering look at Daniel, 'I'll take you. But you have to pack some toys and get dressed by yourself.' Had it been a bone of contention between her parents that Daniel hadn't been able to cope with Edi on his own, although he had no work and little to do, while Lena had to bring in money for the whole family? Edi didn't know. Nor did she know whether she'd ever been too much for Lena on the walk to the hospital, chattering non-stop all the way: 'Look, Mummy, I'm a pony! Look, here's my ponytail! Here are my hooves! Mummy, you're not looking. Mummy, look!'

Without a fidgety child at her side, her mother would have had a few minutes of quiet to herself on the way to work—this thought often came to Edi as she lay on her sofa in Berlin, trying to imagine what those first years in Germany must have been like for Lena. She'd never asked—the opportunity hadn't arisen; Lena thought it unnecessary to talk about herself. They were here, all was well, end of story. And Edi could never have brought herself to ask whether her mother wouldn't rather have been alone, without the responsibility of a child and an out-of-work husband.

In the nurses' room, Lena's colleagues would bring Edi a blanket for the fold-out bed, and sometimes a cup of hot chocolate. One evening the sky turned purple and raspberry-red; yellow rays slanted through the clouds and on to the estate silhouetted outside the window. Edi was a little spooked—her mother was out of the room—but then she smelt cocoa powder and hot milk; a nurse came over, handed her a cup, ruffled her hair and said, 'Look how lovely. End of the world! Is often end of the world! Whenever you see is end of the world, you must stand at the window with hot chocolate and watch it.' She smelt of warm skin and aromatic oil in lukewarm water—and these smells mingled with the scent of chocolate.

Some nights Edi would set off down the corridor to look for her mother. She wasn't scared; she just missed her. She would wake up, see that Lena wasn't there, kick off the blanket and slip out.

Once, the door to a patient's room was open and the patient was asleep. Edi scurried past his bed, clambered on to the windowsill and closed the curtains so that no one would find her. She had no idea how long she sat there or what she did other than fiddle with the curtains. She only knew that her hiding place was discovered when she cried out instinctively at the sound of her mother's voice. Her mother yanked the curtain open and pulled her off the windowsill.

On the whole, though, Edi didn't see much of Lena. She rarely came into the nurses' room to lie down or make coffee, and when she did, she didn't say much. Edi would try to climb on to her lap and Lena would tell her to sleep or she wouldn't be allowed to come again, but as soon as Lena vanished into the corridor, Edi would pad off after her, anxious not to miss even a moment. That, at least, was how she remembered it.

Those nights in the hospital with her mother must have been rare, but it seemed to Edi that she'd spent her childhood there. She thought of them as her best times. It wasn't until afterwards that things had soured between her and Lena, stagnating like a pond starved of oxygen by algae.

Tatyana had been a constant in Lena's life, but Edi didn't feel she knew her well. She'd kept her distance from her, as from all her mother's friends. When you moved beyond small talk, you always risked getting caught up in a kind of interrogation, at the end of which you felt guilty, or at least bad about something, though without being able to say what. No, she didn't have a boyfriend… No, she wasn't studying medicine, or law, or economics… No, her hair wasn't an accident… And so on.

In Edi's memory Tatyana was always on the go. Even when they'd had her round to theirs, it had been Tatyana who'd cleared the table, fetched clean cutlery or transferred salads to crystal bowls, talking constantly to everyone, regardless of whether or not anyone was listening. Lena and Tatyana had spent a lot of time on the phone to each other, and in the photos taken on Edi's first day of school, Tatyana was laughing into the camera next to Lena, while Edi stood off to the side looking at them. Sometimes she and Tatyana's daughter had been bundled into a room together, but Nina had been too young, and later too weird. Or was it Edi who'd been too weird? Since puberty, if not before, she'd felt that she was the one who couldn't connect with the outside world.

Edi knew that Tatyana also lived in Berlin these days; someone saw fit to inform her of this whenever she found herself at one of her parents' parties. People seemed to imagine some mysterious connection between them, just because they lived in the same city—but no one knew, or wanted to let on, *why* Tatyana had moved away from Jena. Or had someone told Edi and she hadn't been listening properly? Not impossible. It was barely newsworthy anyway. Most people moved somewhere at some point, and a good number of them moved to Berlin. Didn't mean you had to be friends with them.

A sudden shriek tore Edi from her thoughts. Just the other side of the automatic doors she had spotted the hospital cafeteria and decided to sit down for a moment to brace herself. Now she spun round and saw that the shrill cry was directed not at her, but at a child of about five or six who was shovelling chocolate cake with a fork. It was a moment before she realized that the flood of words coming from the woman was in Russian.

'I told you to stop that! Don't eat it all now, it's nearly lunchtime!' The woman's gelled-back ponytail stuck out like a gun barrel and quivered as she shouted. Her cheeks were paler than the skin on her neck and forehead, almost blue. She must have noticed Edi's gaze; her head whipped round and she glared at Edi, even as she went on shouting at the child. 'What is this? What's the idea? Why won't you stop? Why does no one do as I tell them?'

Embarrassed, Edi stared at the floor and then at the child in denim dungarees who was bent over his plate, almost standing, gobbling the cake as fast as he could. Only a few tufts of black hair peeped out from the hood of his grey jacket; crumbs and bits of brown cake clung to his mouth and cheeks. The child chewed, his eyes on Edi, chewed and stared, chewed and stared.

There was another woman with them, an older woman in a thick cardigan, who sat and stroked the little boy's back. She turned on the woman with the sticking-out ponytail and said, 'What do you buy him cake for if you're not going to let him eat it?'

With one hand the younger woman jiggled the pram next to her; with the other she gesticulated towards the boy, her fingers grotesquely elongated by her glued-on nails. She looked about her and caught Edi's eye again; then she gave a snort and went back to nagging her son. 'I told you not to eat it all at once. What is this? Why are you doing this to me? Why is everything such a mess?'

She shuffled on her chair, as if she were thinking of throwing herself at something, but didn't know what—maybe at the child, who was now shovelling cake so fast that he was starting to choke; maybe at Edi's face. The child coughed and gasped for breath. Edi leapt to her feet. She stood wavering between the glass front of the cafeteria and the squabbling family; it felt as if something were moving under her feet.

... *'take me'*, she had read in the Russian-doll book, *always means: 'take me together with my childhood'*...

'Get that fork out of your mouth!' the younger woman yelled, and the older woman pulled the boy on to her lap and thumped him on the back like a cushion; the sound echoed dully in the otherwise empty space. The child's mother had gone quiet; the child made only a dry, wheezing sound.

Edi tore herself away and bought a bunch of gerbera at the hospital florist, more to calm herself than from any sense of courtesy or duty. She felt the need to do something hands-on. The flowers were white at the edges, becoming pink towards the centre. Edi remembered that her mother attributed meanings to flowers and their colours: hope, love, grief and God knows what else. Maybe Tatyana did too—maybe even the woman who had almost choked her child on a piece of cake; it was like bare feet in your own home meaning that someone had died. But Edi knew nothing of the language of flowers and hoped desperately that pink gerbera stood for something innocuous.

The sour smell couldn't be coming from the sheets; everything in the room looked clean and fresh. The curtain had been pushed aside; the windowsill was empty; the voices of men arguing drifted in from the courtyard. Two beds stood at opposite ends of the room; there was space for a third in between. Tatyana was sitting in the bed by the door; Edi walked in and found herself right in front of her. She tried to smile. She tried to hold the smile. Eye contact, mouth turned up. Chances were, it looked awkward, but she hoped it looked friendly too, or at least cheerful.

'What *have* you done to your hair?'

Edi felt the muscles tighten in her face. Tatyana was clutching her phone. *Her* hair, reddish in hue, shimmered silver at the roots—Edi hadn't noticed that before, but maybe she'd never looked so closely. All she could have said offhand about Tatyana was that her hair was bronze-coloured and probably dyed; she had no idea how high her forehead was, how full her lips, how fleshy her earlobes, which today were adorned with glinting clips.

'They for me?' Tatyana jerked her head at the flowers.

'Yes. I'll get you a vase.'

'Later. Sit down.'

Instead of taking the gerbera, Tatyana folded her arms behind her head. Edi heard her breathing deeply, and felt her eyes on her as she sized up her clothes. Tatyana had pressed her chin into her neck so that it wrinkled like a concertina, ageing her considerably. Today, anyway, Edi thought. Today she looks much older than I remember. She waited for Tatyana to say something. Maybe she needn't ask her anything; maybe it was enough that she'd come. The bunch of flowers in her hand felt as heavy as a baseball bat.

Edi perched with half a buttock on the foot of the bed; the metal frame pressed into her spine.

'Do you have the room to yourself?'

'I do now. The other woman was carted off yesterday.'

Edi couldn't bring herself to ask what Tatyana meant by *carted off* and decided to believe that the patient had been moved to another bed, possibly even discharged.

'So, is everything OK?'

'Oh yes, everything's just great.'

The sarcasm wasn't fair, but then, what was? Maybe being in hospital gave you a free hand to take the piss out of everyone who was fit and well. How else were you supposed to amuse yourself?

Television was an insult to intelligence; the hospital Wi-Fi was a joke, and reading a book was hardly an option when your arms and brain were jelly.

'So what's wrong with you? Why are you here?' Edi's lips twitched towards her ear in an attempt at a smile.

'They say in a worst-case scenario it could be fatal. But it doesn't have to be. And maybe I'll recover my sight completely, maybe I won't.'

For a moment, Edi heard only the buzz of the ceiling lamp, which was on even though it was broad daylight. Neither woman looked away. Those silvery threads in Tatyana's hair make her look like a superhero, Edi thought. Like a cartoon character, an anime figure. Someone strong and immortal.

'You'd rather not talk about it?'

Only the buzz of the lamp again. Tatyana took a deep breath.

'First they thought it was MS, then NMOSD; then they started calling it NMO and sent me for a CT and an MRI; then Professor X came and prescribed Y, to make sure it didn't develop into Z. "Chernobyl!" I said to them. "It's the delayed effects of Chernobyl." But they won't hear of it.'

A friend had once suggested to Edi that German hospitals were called *Krankenhäuser*, sick houses, because you stayed sick in them—otherwise they'd be called *getting-better houses*. Edi wondered if she'd manage to get Tatyana out for the weekend. Was it even a good idea?

'I had what they call an *episode*, and since then I've been almost blind in one eye and it hurts to move my eyes around—you'll have to forgive me if I look ridiculous. They're pumping me full of cortisone and still trying to get to the bottom of these spasms I had. Meanwhile I have to put up with being snapped at by burnt-out nurses who can't cope at work or at home—and the woman in the bed next to me, the one they turfed out yesterday, banged on the bedframe all night. She was a mouse during the day, a complete mouse—I sometimes wasn't sure she was still breathing—but as soon as it went dark, she'd start banging her bony hand against anything that made a noise. *Tock! Tock! Tock!* All night long.'

Edi stared at the empty space where the woman's bed must have been. And although she was still sitting at Tatyana's feet, she suddenly saw the room as if from the windowsill—the view of a little girl who had once hidden curled up behind the curtains, like in the porthole of a ship's cabin.

'I was standing in my kitchen and I couldn't see the microwave on top of the fridge. Then the next thing I knew, I couldn't see the fridge either, or the sink, or anything in the kitchen. Then the cramps in my legs started; I couldn't get up from the floor. Just managed to dial 112—after that my head was mush.'

Edi slid off the mattress, strode to the window and flung it open. She went back to the bed but didn't feel like sitting down again.

'And you still want to go to Mum's birthday party?'

'Yes, and this'—she pointed at her eyes and jerked her chin into the room—'must stay our secret.'

Edi folded her arms, squeezing the baseball-bat bouquet in her fingers.

'Listen, Nina isn't to know any of this. The girl has enough problems of her own, so I don't want anyone in Jena finding out, OK? It would get about in no time; no one in that place can keep their mouth shut, as you know, and we'd be in a real mess if it got out. Can you imagine what it would do to your mother? I don't want to ruin poor Lena's birthday.'

Edi squeezed the gerbera even tighter. They'll wilt, she thought. I ought to get up and fetch some water. I ought to leave.

'Now, don't make that face. That's exactly why I didn't want to talk to anyone about this; faces like that are the last thing I need. Do you know what I could do with now?'

Edi almost offered her a joint; she wouldn't have minded one herself. But she stopped herself in time.

'An Allan Chumak,' Tatyana said. 'You don't know who I'm talking about, do you? Back in the eighties, nineties, he was as famous with us as Madonna in the West, but you young people don't know anything any more. Chumak was a healer, a faith healer. A man who cured masses of people just by appearing on TV and waving his hands around. '*Have you prepared everything? Is everything ready?*' Tatyana spoke in the voice of a spirit from the underworld, or someone very drunk. '*Water, cream, oils... Are you sitting comfortably?*'

She seemed to think it funny. Edi thought of slipping out of the room without a word—or saying she'd got the wrong room and running out, mumbling apologies. She'd phone her mum and say she hadn't been able to get hold of Tatyana. She'd tell her Tatyana had disappeared.

'Just imagine, these self-proclaimed saints were on air for fifteen minutes a day—on *state television*—telling us to relax.'

'Did it help?' Edi choked out the words like something flabby that left a thick coat of slime on her tongue.

Maybe she'd tell her mother that Tatyana had gone mad. No way was she going to spend hours in a car with the woman in this state. It wouldn't be good for anyone's health.

'Goodness, yes! I can see him as if it were yesterday: striped jumper, starched collar, white hair flopping over his glasses, though he had a very severe parting. My grandma fancied him like hell; as soon as his face appeared on the screen, she'd jump up as if her hips had never given her any trouble and schlep a gallon of water into the living room for that quack to bless telepathically. The energy just flowed out of our TVs. Good, pure energy. Everyone believed the guy. People used to camp in their hordes outside his house in Moscow wanting to bathe in his aura or just touch the hem of his coat—he had a following like the Messiah. He made these circling movements in the air with his arms and moved his lips without any sound, and for most people that was enough; it convinced them. You should have seen my grandma. That gallon of water was much too heavy for her, but it didn't stop her holding it up to the TV—she probably felt the healing powers at work in her. Once, Chumak told people to soak the Moscow evening paper in the water he'd blessed and then eat it to strengthen their body and soul. And people did it. Not in Mariupol—we didn't get the Moscow evening paper. But we watched Chumak and Co. hypnotize people before a stomach operation over a distance of several thousand miles. That's what I could do with now. Not these Western doctors who can't think of anything more intelligent to say than they'll have to do more tests and they can't confirm anything or rule anything out yet. Can't, can't, can't. That's the trouble with the West—they can never confirm anything and they can never rule anything out.'

Edi pressed her lips together. No way. No way would she drive Tatyana to Jena, where there'd be even more like her. More of *Edi's people.* And no way would she ever write about them. Over her dead body. Not even if her job depended on it. Not even if it meant she never published a word. These stories about *her people* were her personal kryptonite.

'My father was a big fan of the other psychic, Kashpirovsky. Partly because he was better-looking—more like a pop singer than a demented wicked uncle—but also because he supported a party that promised to *board* America, pirate-style, and sink it in the ocean. That was straight talk. That was talk everyone understood.'

Edi put the gerbera down on the sheet and ran her hand through her hair. The permanent labour pains of these people who'd never-really-arrived made her itch all over. Florida—she had to get to Florida. No one could make her spend a weekend in Thuringia with these screwed-up post-Soviet whinge bags, these perestroika zombies. Thuringia, where the party that had just come second in the elections was promising… what exactly? To *board* people like Edi and her friends and all they believed in and sink them in the ocean.

'So you're waiting for someone to bring you a newspaper to eat, soaked in healing water?' Edi asked as calmly as she could.

'That's right. Did you bring me one? Or do you expect me to munch your flowers like a cow?'

Tatyana laughed so loudly that the mattress began to shake. She pulled herself up in bed and suddenly looked much taller and wide awake. She smoothed her hair and tied it in a ponytail with a scrunchie from her wrist.

'Another thing—about your mother.' She leant forward conspiratorially. 'We have to dye your hair back before we set off. I'm afraid Lena won't let us in otherwise. She'll throw birthday cake at us.'

She roared with laughter again. She laughed for so long that Edi ended up joining in from sheer bewilderment.

Ignorance and escapism. That's all it was. Tatyana was possibly at death's door—her illness, at any rate, seemed serious—but when she phoned after discharging herself for the weekend, all she could talk about was which dresses and trouser suits she should pack for the trip. When Edi asked tentatively if her state of health called for any particular action—was she perhaps on medication that she needed reminding about, or should they allow more time for breaks on the journey—she told her not to be ridiculous. Everything was fine; she didn't want to hear another word.

Edi lay in the bath, staring at the two Russian dolls on the front of Oksana Zabuzhko's book and wondering whether to pack *Fieldwork in Ukrainian Sex* for the weekend—or would it be embarrassing if her parents discovered that she read books in German with titles like that and Eastern-bloc kitsch on the cover? She probably wouldn't have time to lounge around reading anyway.

In the oblong of window over the washing machine, the clouds turned the colour of processed cheese. Edi opened her mouth, as if to swallow the sky, or at least take a bite out of it. When she was little, 'cheese-slice tower' was her favourite game with her mother. They would pile the pre-packed squares between them, count to three and then throw themselves at the stack of cheese, tearing open the plastic wrappers, kneading the flabby slices into balls, stuffing them into their mouths: chew, swallow, chew, swallow—who could eat the most? They would laugh so much, they both ended up spluttering bits of cheese on to the table. Once Edi got sick from all those cheese slices. She choked and gasped and spewed everything on to the floor. She couldn't remember what happened next. All she remembered was the yellowish-white mess under her little feet and on the knees of her tracksuit bottoms. It was her first memory of the feeling of choking. Since then, an image had often popped into her mind: some silly little thing like a tea leaf got stuck in her windpipe, and that was that. Wham, bam, end of story. A stupid, pointless death, but not unheard of.

She slid under the water and felt her hair turn light as feathers. It was still white-blond and probably invisible against the enamel of the bathtub—just like her pale plate of a face. Only two apricot-kernel eyes floated on the bottom. She would have to ignore a lot of what was said at the weekend. Her hair was bound be a topic; politics, too, of course. 'The thing about us…' the guests would clamour, and: 'They just don't understand…' 'They don't know what it means…' Sometimes *they* was the Germans; sometimes it was people who'd fled from countries other than theirs—and sometimes it was their own children who'd be dragged along to the party with them. Edi knew most of them; they'd run around on playgrounds together as kids, they'd bumped into each other in school. They hadn't always ignored one another, but at some point Edi had stopped responding to their calls and invitations. She had nothing in common with them. They had nothing to say to each other any more. Most of them hadn't moved far. They wouldn't dye their hair until they spotted the first grey streaks, and they were already doggedly continuing their parents' lives, as if following some predetermined plan—as if, by conforming, they could reassure their parents that they'd done the right thing, despite everything. Despite the lousy jobs, the lack of jobs, the sneaking suspicion that something had been irretrievably lost, even if there was money to spare at the end of the month. It seemed wrong to go against your parents when they'd been through so much. Edi would feel tired just listening, and the effort of pretending to agree with everyone about everything turned her limbs to lead. She always had trouble keeping her eyes open and staying upright on her chair.

The only person she didn't have to pretend with was Grisha, Dora-next-door's only son. Edi's mother had fallen out with Dora; she said the family was slovenly and that Dora drank schnapps with every meal. There were even rumours that she'd occasionally spiked Grisha's porridge when he was a baby in order to stimulate his appetite—that would explain, people said, why the boy had turned out so funny-looking, with his too-short nose and straggly hair and centre parting. But Grisha had never drunk more than Coke when Edi offered to bring him beer from the petrol station. Together with a few others, they would climb the folding ladder on to the flat roof and stand around in little groups, looking down over the estate. Grisha tended to stick close to Edi. He drank his Coke in tiny sips and neither of them said much.

Once, Grisha was away for a few days. He came back, beaming like a twelve-year-old, and the next time they met on the rough tar-and-gravel roof, he drew Edi aside and it all came gushing out. He told her he'd run off to Prague with Rüzgar and spent the nights in clubs with her. Edi was the only one who knew about Rüzgar. She was also the only one who knew about Rüzgar's abortion.

It was years now since Edi had last spoken to Grisha—and, as usual, she hadn't let him know she was coming to Jena. She had his details, but when someone had seen you being pushed across the playground and forced into a corner and made to pull your pants down, you weren't inclined to get in touch with that someone, even if you did have his number. She knew Grisha wouldn't be at the birthday party, because her mother had made a big thing about not inviting the undesirable neighbours.

Edi couldn't even remember what Dora's voice sounded like—only that she had eyebrows that looked like they'd been drawn on with a spent match, and a cat that had been trained to give its paw.

A black cat on your way
Brings bad luck, people say.
But so far, in fact,
The unlucky one is the cat…

The Russian song buzzed in Edi's head, its rhymes coating her mind like stewed tea. She hummed the tune underwater.

Then she heaved herself up and got out of the bath, taking care not to slip on the tiles. A tense, throbbing feeling filled her jaw and spread over her scalp like hot porridge.

She really must call a locksmith.

Tatyana knocked on the frame of the open front door with a curled finger—in front of her, the locksmith was crawling about on all fours, his rump sticking out on to the landing; she stepped over him as if he were a puddle. Edi saw her glance at his bald pate, then march on into the kitchen.

'You've got Gorbachev here?' she said, opening the doors of the wall cupboards.

'Why Gorbachev?' Edi spluttered. 'And what are you looking for?'

'Didn't you see the birthmark on his head? Like a continent.'

Edi watched as Tatyana took a large glass from one of the cupboards, filled it at the tap and drained the water in big gulps. There were little beads on her upper lip when she set the glass down, and she gave a contented sigh.

'No, apparently you didn't. Did you notice his thong, at least? What? What are you looking at me like that for? You think I made it up? Go and take a walk round him and have a look at his bum cleavage. Well worth it. A red lace thong. *Du bist so wunderbar, Berlin!*' She sang these last words—the jingle of a cinema ad for mineral water that was shown before every film in Berlin.

Edi went out into the passage, shot a wary glance at the locksmith, then took a few steps on to the landing and wondered whether to tiptoe down the stairs and run away.

'Ah, your ears are red. So I was right. What did I tell you?' Tatyana was gulping her second glass of water. 'All packed?'

Edi had tossed a bleached denim jacket and a pair of navy-blue crease-free trousers into her sports bag—also a black shirt that her mother would disapprove of, but it couldn't be helped; her wardrobe didn't run to elegant. She would drive in her no-longer-white Adidas trainers—her mother would force other, *better* shoes on her anyway, to make sure she didn't show up at the party looking like a passing jogger.

To Edi's surprise, Tatyana nodded approvingly at the battered trainers. She'd had a pair like that, too, she said, back in the day—though they hadn't lasted long. Only as far as Moscow, where the soles dropped off in the snow; it had been minus twenty-five, if not colder, and everything had turned to ice: her eyeballs, the inside of her nostrils—even her buttocks had frozen together. She'd worn her Adidases because she was so proud of them—her first pair of Western-brand shoes. She wasn't from Moscow and didn't want to feel like the country cousin, so she'd come in the smartest things she had, not realizing how cold it would be in the capital.

Tatyana was still gabbling away as they approached the motorway. Edi wondered why she referred to Moscow as *the capital* when she came from Ukraine—but she didn't ask. Tatyana, she thought, was like a jukebox: you threw in a question or comment and off she went, droning away to herself, regardless of whether anyone was listening.

The car was filled with Tatyana's perfume; it was only a matter of time before they both had headaches. It wasn't a long drive—only two and a half hours if the traffic was OK—but already Edi felt as though they'd been on the road for days, with no notion of where they were going.

The gnarled clumps of mistletoe in the trees behind the noise barriers looked like swamp-green balloons stuck in the treetops. Mistletoe was a parasite that put down roots into the host plant to drink from it, but Edi also knew that if you cut it with the right tool (a golden sickle) it took on magical powers. That, at least, was what it said in the comic that Edi's father used to read her at bedtime. His hairy finger would point at the old man with the long beard and red cloak who stood over the steaming cauldron, stirring up the ingredients of the magic brew. This potion, her father explained, made you *unbesiegbar*, but not *unverwundbar*—invincible, but not invulnerable. Over time, it had dawned on Edi that he was learning German from Asterix and Obelix. Sometimes he would repeat the words several times before explaining them in Russian, though Edi couldn't always have said where one language left off and the other began. For her it was all one sound; it was Dadspeak.

Like the knives in a hand blender, the rotor blades of the wind turbines chopped the sky into little pieces. Signs announced the approach of a Kullman's Diner, a McDonald's, a petrol station. Edi glanced at the fuel gauge and took the turning, mumbling something about needing petrol. Tatyana seemed only too happy to stop.

'I'm going for a cigarette, do you want one? Oh no, you pretend you don't smoke.'

The moment Edi cut the engine, Tatyana flung open the door and tripped away from the petrol pumps, the clapper-like tassels swinging on her suede boots.

Edi tried to breathe calmly, wondering whether to unpack her weed and go and join her. The sky was shades of washed-out grey, and light filtered hazily through the treetops. Edi shivered, though it was warm for October. She pulled her checked flannel shirt tighter around her neck and went into the building to pay.

Newspapers and magazines jostled for space on a shelf that ran along the window, and an extra stack of the local daily lay on the counter alongside chewing gum, condoms and liquorice. *Thuringia* leapt out from the headline in bold letters. What an ugly word, Edi thought. You couldn't make it sound melodious if you tried. Thuringia made her think of cheese-slice contests and of the hills that sheltered Jena from the wind and from reality in general—whenever it rained in the rest of the country, the sun shone in Jena, and whenever it was sunny up in the hills, monsoons descended on the valley. It made her think of the station called Paradise where the fast trains no longer stopped, so that anyone wanting to get to or from Jena, who didn't drive and didn't trust ride-sharing, was forced to make complicated travel arrangements involving several changes and long waits at provincial stations where the toilets had been out of order for decades. Thuringia was eleven-storey blocks with windows like arrow slits; it was the view of the University Hospital from her parents' sixth-floor flat, tower blocks dotting the landscape like dominoes, the view from the roof, her mother calling her from the yard.

Edi handed her debit card to the spaced-out woman at the till and walked to the door—then turned back, picked up a paper from the stack next to the till, folded it down the middle and put change on the counter. She couldn't remember when she'd last bought a print newspaper. The word was little more than a metaphor these days. No one ever sent her a printed copy of the 'paper' she wrote for.

She tossed the local daily on to the back seat, ignoring Tatyana's look.

'I've stopped reading the news,' Tatyana said. 'When I don't read about the world, I feel like it falls apart more slowly.' She made no move to get back in the car, and stared defiantly at Edi. 'I'm hungry. I haven't had anything all day except a couple of cigarettes.' She pointed at the fast-food restaurant next to the petrol station; heavy wooden tables and benches were fixed to the ground outside.

Great, Edi thought. Only just set off and already they were at a standstill. Then again, she'd only had a gooey peanut bar for breakfast herself.

Edi bit into the imitation-meat burger that Tatyana had sneered at when she'd ordered. Tatyana, meanwhile, was delicately dipping chips into the pool of ketchup on the paper mat of her tray and staring into the distance, as if there were a mountain range out there rather than a six-lane motorway.

'I can't face it either,' she said, wiping the corners of her mouth with finger and thumb.

Edi looked up, but went on chewing. Since discharging herself from hospital, Tatyana had grown younger again; her cheeks looked firmer, her eyes shone. Maybe she wasn't sick after all—or not seriously, anyway. Maybe she was almost better again; she seemed sprightly enough.

'You don't want to go because of what people will say about your hair and your silly clothes, and I'll have to listen to people going on at me about how worthless I am without a man—that's no fun either, believe me. Not that I don't understand them. A woman my age without a guy—you can practically hear the nails being hammered into the coffin. Apparently a woman in her late forties is more likely to be abducted by terrorists than find a long-term partner. You don't have these problems, do you?'

Edi listened to her grinding molars. Behind Tatyana was a kind of claw machine where adults (*No Children*, a sign warned) could try their luck. Edi wasn't sure, but it looked as if the only prizes were cuddly toys, goggles and mini footballs. The woman at the counter had been rubbing her glasses on her apron for some minutes, staring out through the glass front to where a sandwich board advertised *World Heritage Region Anhalt–Dessau–Wittenberg*. The combination of the distant roar of the motorway, the gurgle and hiss of the coffee machine and the flood of words from Tatyana's mouth made Edi's head lurch.

'Men! What can you do? They're impossible to live with, and impossible to live without. I'm telling you, it's no fun being in hospital with no one to bring you slippers and clean underwear. Do you know why women are the more robust creatures?' Tatyana paused for a beat, as if she were telling a joke. 'Because they have to put up with men.'

Edi knew she was trying to provoke her, but she couldn't say nothing. 'That may be how it is in your world,' she said, struggling to control her breath. She concentrated on the silhouettes of the couple outside at the clunky wooden table who were passing each other handfuls of home-made sandwiches. If they had a child with them, she thought, you'd call it a family; as it was, it was just two people.

'Not in yours?' Tatyana asked.

'I don't have to put up with men. My life's so much better now I'm lesbian.'

There. It was out. She'd given Tatyana what she wanted to hear. Edi hoped she'd made the word sound harsh and sleazy enough to end the conversation. But Tatyana laughed so loudly that people turned to look.

'Of course,' she said. 'I can believe it. Not every man can be such a sweetheart as your dad.'

She was right, Dad was a sweetheart. All those lullabies and bedtime stories, the Asterix comics, the long walks, the cooking. The way he defended her against Lena when they got in each other's hair. He was a dream of a man. A dream of a father. There was just the small exception of that afternoon when she'd felt her heart pumping in her throat and heard nothing for a moment but a high-pitched whistling tone. She hadn't heard the words coming from Daniel's mouth; she'd only seen his lips move and the fear in his face as he approached her. Then she'd crumpled to the floor.

She had told him that the girlfriend who was often round at their house and sometimes stayed the night in her room wasn't just a mate she did homework with; they did more together than buy Haribo in the shop across the road. Daniel's face went the colour of dead skin. Very quietly, and stressing every word, he told her that, first, he didn't want to know *that kind of thing*, and second, *what she had* could be treated; there was a cure. He'd find her a doctor or a clinic. Edi was so taken aback she forgot to breathe. Then the anger frothed up inside her and instead of starting to yell, she turned and ran into her room, and when Daniel tried to follow her she slammed the door. But it wasn't enough; she had to do something with the rage in her head, and so she tore open the door and slammed it again, this time so hard that the milky glass pane in the upper half of the door shattered. She kept on like this, opening and shutting it, opening and shutting; glass splinters rained down on her and on the floor. Only a few jagged shards were left in the frame. She stared at them and then into Daniel's horrified face. Then everything went black.

They'd never talked about it since and there were times when Edi doubted that the row had ever taken place; her dad really was such a sweetheart. The glass was replaced and everything went on as ever—but Edi no longer mentioned her girlfriends. That was the reason her last relationship had been so short-lived—her partner hadn't felt appreciated, because she'd never been invited to Edi's parents', not even at Christmas. That had annoyed Edi; the woman just didn't seem to get it. What Christmas, for fuck's sake?

As she and Tatyana left the burger place, Edi felt a sharp jolt in her knees, like when you reach for the bar above your head in a swerving bus and miss it. She swayed for a moment, grabbing at the air. Tatyana seemed amused. 'Aren't you feeling well? Would you rather I drove?'

'Why aren't you driving? You usually drive down by yourself,' Edi said, and immediately wished she hadn't. Of course Tatyana couldn't drive in her state. But the words were out. Tatyana looked her in the eye, the rouge on her cheeks luminous.

'Because I'm broke. I sold my car.'

She walked past Edi, as if she were abandoning her in the middle of the car park, as if Edi didn't have the key in her trouser pocket. As if she had some intimation of how the two of them were to make it through the hours and days to come.

Back on the motorway Edi made several attempts at conversation, but Tatyana ignored them all. She stared through the windscreen as though watching a film on TV, only glancing down at her hands now and then, or at the sandy filth that had gathered in the footwells, or the folded safety jacket in the passenger door, like a streak of orange in an otherwise black outfit. When had Edi last needed a safety jacket? She needed one now. Right now.

'And—how come you don't have any luck with men?' Edi cursed herself for not being able to ask something more innocuous, something that wouldn't offend this woman who smelt caustically of lilac. Tatyana moved her fingers, but she didn't make a fist; it looked more as if she was trying to grasp at something.

TATYANA

THE SHOT WAS FIRED just as she got the window open. The handle crashed into the tiled wall and dust rained down into Tatyana's eyes. Standing on the toilet lid in the locked cubicle, she put her hands on the grimy windowsill and thanked her dance teacher at the arts centre for the ruthless training—her arm muscles didn't let her down; she hauled herself up. Outside the narrow window, on the roughly rendered ledge, there was barely room to sit—and no room for second thoughts about jumping. She stuck her head out and looked down into the night; she would roll away, she decided, as soon as she felt the ground beneath her. Like in the previous year's dance choreography, only that then she had jumped from the top of a human star, not from a window three metres from the ground. But she had no better plan. She heard herself breathing through her mouth. Pull in your arms and legs, tuck in your shoulders, fold them in front of your chest like wings, roll sideways—you can do it. She heard more shots and voices; they were getting louder, or seemed to be. Then she jumped.

She hadn't been waitressing at Yalita long enough to have saved anything worth mentioning. Most days she started in the afternoon—tied the starched apron round her waist and tried to ignore everything except the orders, concentrating on serving the shashlik kebabs and the schnapps so discreetly that the customers didn't even think of talking to her. Business was good; Mariupol in general was in a bit of a slump, but Yalita was usually lively. The customers were rarely people Tatyana knew. They talked all kinds of languages: Russian, Ukrainian, Georgian, Greek—and probably also, though she wasn't sure, Bulgarian, Albanian, Serbian, Turkish and Turkmen. Sometimes, very rarely, she'd hear some English. They ate a lot and boozed a lot; some prayed like Christians, others like Muslims. Tatyana was never sure how serious the men were when they solemnly wiped their fingers one by one on their napkins, then joined or spread their hands and reeled off grace as if they were proposing toasts.

Until recently, everyone here had been dyed-in-the-wool Communists—certainly no one had gone to church. Now they evoked Jesus at every opportunity or bandied about the name of Allah, which, to Tatyana, sounded like a girl's name—and that of her favourite singer, Alla Pugacheva. She hummed 'Arlekino' softly to herself as she went back and forth between the dining room and the kitchen:

I'm just a clown, a harlequin, a joke,
I have no name, I barely have a fate.
Don't tell me that you care about such folk—
We make you laugh and there's an end to it.

Tatyana dodged the chef's glances and her boss's remarks like a slalom skier.

On this particular evening there was a private party in the restaurant. Tatyana had been harassed in the cloakroom corridor by a man who had later crossed himself about ten times and said a long grace before starting to eat. He made an unequivocal pass at her, and when she looked at the floor and tried to give him the slip, he pulled her by the ponytail as if she were a recalcitrant animal. She managed to get away, but for the rest of the evening her throat burnt with the reek of male sweat mingled with fried mincemeat.

She was glad not to catch more than a few snatches of Russian and the odd Ukrainian word; she didn't want to know what was being negotiated at the long table. Two of the men had come in with rifles which now hung by their straps from the backs of their chairs. Their voices grew louder and louder—Tatyana couldn't work out if they were arguing or spurring each other on. She was about to carry yet another tray of kebabs into the dining room when the other waitress, her eyes popping with fright, pushed her back into the corridor and signalled to her, hand to throat, fingers squeezing.

'What is it? What's going on in there?' The woman clearly understood more languages than she did.

They peered into the dining room through the glass window in the door. Two of the older men were talking loudly at each other, their eyebrows dripping with sweat. They continued to eat. One of them sprayed little bits of meat from the corners of his mouth; the other kept mopping his brow with his hand. Tatyana saw him put down his fork and reach for the rifle behind him; he pulled it off the back of the chair and threw it on to the table among the still half-full dishes. A man with his back to Tatyana gave a shout and leapt up from his chair; another yelled a reply. Chairs fell to the floor. Tatyana didn't move until she felt her colleague's cold hand on her arm; she pulled Tatyana to the toilet and pointed up at the little window. You had to stand on the toilet lid to reach the handle.

Tatyana thought about how much she needed the work, how much her family needed the money. Maybe all this wasn't as bad as it looked; maybe it wasn't even as bad as it smelt—the schnapps, the sweat, the fried mincemeat: it would all wash out. But then a shot was fired and the next thing she knew, her colleague was up on the toilet seat fiddling with the window catch. Floury plaster dust rained down on Tatyana and pricked her eyes. She hauled herself up.

The jump on to hard ground left her limping. The drop had felt further than she'd expected, but at least the window hadn't been any higher up the building, and at least she'd landed on grass, not on an asphalt road or in a construction pit bristling with planks. She and the other waitress ran gingerly, their aprons still round their waists, nothing to cover their thin blouses and bare arms. They went together as far as the crossroads, then separated in silence.

When Tatyana had been part of a troupe of dancers at the arts centre and still in regular training, a twisted knee or sprained ankle had been nothing unusual. This was different; whenever she put weight on her right foot, an electric pain shot up her spine. But she kept going, one step at a time, trying to hold herself as straight as possible. She didn't want to scare her parents by coming home with a limp; it was bad enough that she was dirty and dishevelled.

When she got home, though, no one came into the hall to greet her. A glance in the mirror told her that her ponytail was coming undone and that her bare arms had turned blue in the October chill. She was white in the face and felt as if she might throw up. Maybe it was the fright she'd had, or the pain in her foot. She tried to push away the thought that she might have witnessed a shooting and need to be interrogated. She wouldn't testify. No way. She hadn't been there, had seen nothing, heard nothing. She knew no names—that was the truth. But what use had the truth ever been?

Her father, mother and grandmother were shouting at each other in the kitchen; she'd heard them as soon she put the key in the lock, but had hoped it was only the lingering noise in her head. The shock, perhaps. Then she heard the sound of broken china and recognized the loudest voice as that of her grandmother. Her mother's mother had never been a peaceable woman; she could gnash her few teeth so fiercely you didn't dare look at her. But Tatyana had never known her to smash plates on the floor.

'Your mother wants to sell the flat and we've only just paid off the mortgage!' she yelled as Tatyana pushed open the kitchen door. Then she cursed her wasted life in such strong language that Tatyana didn't know whether to laugh or cry. So her parents had told her. The decision had been made some time ago, but her mother had wanted to put off the inevitable tantrum for as long as possible. What was the good of arguing sooner than necessary? The rows would come soon enough—best to put them off as long as they could.

Tatyana's grandmother had been weak on her legs for a while. These days, to get to the flea market behind the garages she had to lean on Tatyana's arm, a walking stick in her other hand, a woollen headscarf over her white hair. When they stopped to let her catch her breath, she stood swaying slightly, like a crooked branch with a coat thrown over it. Recently she had started to talk a lot about her childhood; the memories came in waves and were all variations on the same theme. She spoke of empty pastures and fields left fallow, of fruit trees felled by farmers who couldn't afford the taxes; she recalled how her family's house and garden had been seized and how people had formed packs and hunted small children in the forests. Tatyana tried not to listen; she soon knew the horror stories by heart, but her grandmother kept coming up with new images to describe the starved corpses that filled the roads because it was forbidden to dig graves—corpses that didn't disappear until the snow came and buried them. 'The only good thing,' she would say, 'was that the Party members grew fatter and fatter—at least the cannibals got something out of it.' She would give a hoarse laugh and turn clear eyes on Tatyana, her gaze still for once.

Now, though, she was yelling at her daughter and son-in-law. She refused to have everything taken from her again, she said, and swept the sugar basin off the table. Tatyana's parents ignored her bedraggled appearance—her wrecked hair, her chalky face—and appealed to her to take their part. She was in favour of moving to Kryvyi Rih, wasn't she? She was eager to get away from this place, where the only job that paid was serving vodka to boozed-up bandits?

Tatyana's cousin, Inna, had planted the idea in her parent's heads some months before, on a visit from Dnipropetrovsk. Mariupol, she said, had nothing more to offer; soon they'd all be out of work—but in Kryvyi Rih business was flourishing and attracting hordes of Western speculators. It was true that the metallurgic conglomerate—the one-time symbol of Mariupol's prosperity, the factory that had once employed the entire town—was on the brink of closure. Tatyana's mother, who was an engineer there, had been underoccupied for years; she would come home with a shrug in the middle of the day, and although she had a second desk in another office, she hadn't been paid for months. Tatyana's father had taken to catching the bus to Turkey, where he bought fake brand clothes to flog on a market in Poland. Tatyana, with her waitress's earnings from Yalita, was the only one who brought home a regular income.

Inna had given up her doctor's job in Dnipropetrovsk State Hospital, claiming that every builder earned better than her these days. She'd studied medicine because she'd thought it would bring her influential contacts and respect, and she'd know where to turn if she had kidney failure. But her only contacts, she said, were the inflamed genitals of former Party members who now preferred to be called *biznissmeni*. And the pay wasn't worth getting out of bed for. And she wouldn't want to rely on her colleagues to save her if her kidneys failed—chances were, she wouldn't have enough cash on her. And don't even start her on respect. So, change of plan.

Together with her boyfriend she'd gone in for all kinds of business ventures, until he conned her out of the last of her savings and disappeared without trace. When she travelled to Mariupol to persuade her aunt and uncle to sell their supposedly oversized flat and move with her to a place where, with enough starting capital, you could set up a lucrative business, she had nothing left but a watch the colour of rosé wine—and a lot of energy.

Tatyana's grandmother cursed, her fingers fidgeting with a valuable collector's plate. All her life, she said, she'd suffered, and now she was being driven out of her home again. Yet again. Her eyes were all red; you could hardly see the whites. Tatyana slipped out of the kitchen in silence.

In the bathroom she stared in the mirror. Bags bulged under her eyes. They look like prunes, Tatyana thought. Soon I'll be all shrivelled up and I'll fidget with the china like Grandmother and lose my hair. She shifted her weight to the side that didn't hurt and threw her filthy apron on to the stool next to the basin. Then she squatted down to open the cupboard that was stuffed full of green soap, took out a new bar and got in the bath with it. As the water scalded her neck, she ran the edges of the brick of soap over her legs.

The last time she'd received a compliment was when a customer in Yalita had pinched her thigh as she served him *yuvarlakia*, and the man at the next table had grabbed his fingers, pointed at Tatyana and solemnly announced that she looked like his sister and was therefore inviolable.

Her parents must have made up their minds to sell, otherwise they wouldn't have told Grandmother. Tatyana had been hoping it wouldn't come to anything; she'd fantasized about going to the arts centre and asking her dancing teacher to take her back; she'd dreamt of finishing the trouser suit she was sewing and applying to the local fashion school, which hadn't—yet—closed down. But now it looked as if she didn't even have a job to pay for her studies and keep her in bread and meat.

She slid deeper into the scalding water. Maybe Inna's idea of opening an off-licence wasn't so bad. Apparently whole shiploads of certified alcohol from the West arrived every day at the port of Odesa, and the stuff was in greater demand than family jewellery. Watches and earrings were no longer worth a thing, but genuine whisky was, and Inna knew someone who knew someone who could get hold of it, and of other spirits from the West—but in Kryvyi Rih, not Mariupol. In this day and age, when anyone wanting to open a business had to negotiate first with the police (for a permit), then with the tax authorities (for the right papers), then with the police again (who would drop in from time to time), genuine whisky was the best gift to go with that wodge of cash in an envelope. Sometimes the booze alone was enough, if it wasn't rotgut in a juice bottle with a home-made label and an unsealed screw top, but genuine Jim Beam, Johnnie Walker or Jack Daniel's. No one these days did business without slipping someone a suitably pricey bottle. The other good thing about alcohol was that it didn't have to be kept in fridges or freezers, which were hard to come by and inclined to break down—like in the co-op across the road recently, where the manager had got his face smashed in by customers whose kids had been poisoned by rancid cream cheese. All you needed were shelves, display cabinets and enough light to make the precious bottles twinkle like stars.

Tatyana lay in the bath, imagining people in decent clothes, maybe even tailored jackets, pushing down the door handle to the shop with one hand while they smoothed their hair with the other and asked Tatyana politely for a bottle of Jack Daniel's.

Then it occurred to her that maybe she could study at a fashion school after all, maybe even in Kyiv. She just had to make some money first. Right now she couldn't finance it even if she camped out in the hall at her old schoolfriend's. The girl had been intrepid enough to move to the capital, where she shared a one-room flat with three others.

Tatyana had been to Kyiv only once, when she changed trains there on the way to Moscow, and apart from the outside of the station building, the grimy platforms and a guard who'd yelled at her to hurry up as she boarded the train—*this isn't the slow train to the provinces*—she'd seen nothing of the city. She imagined it smaller than Moscow, quite a lot smaller, but built on firmer ground—Moscow had seemed to her like an abyss that swallowed everyone sooner or later. Escalators carried you miles under the earth, and the crowds in the metro carriages ruffled your hair and ripped the last buttons from your coats. One such crowd had swept her into the maw of a station. She couldn't have said which sleeves and briefcases and headscarves and backs belonged to which bodies; the Muscovites around her blurred to a buzzing swarm that bore her down to the platform. It was so stuffy that she had to undo her coat, and then the hurrying passers-by got caught up in the flapping material. The noise swelled like worsening rain; nobody screamed or shouted, but there was a whistling in Tatyana's ears. She opened her mouth as wide as she could to ease the pressure in her head; then she was caught up in a tide of people. It felt as if she was washed into the arriving train without moving her legs. She couldn't see the other women who'd come with her from Mariupol to audition as dancers at a new Moscow agency; she couldn't even turn her head. She concentrated on breathing and tried to remember the name of the station where she was supposed to get off—something with Dostoevsky. When at last she made it back out into the daylight and examined her reflection in the station window, she thought she looked like a clown with her smudged eyeshadow, missing buttons and windblown hair.

That was her memory of Moscow—that and the Arbat, of course. The houses that lined the famous pedestrian street must once have been painted salmon and peach, but the colours had long since disappeared under a grey film. The three-armed street lamps looked to Tatyana like harlequins with puffed sleeves, holding their hands up to call a halt. Street sellers accosted passers-by; a girl was having her picture drawn. In real life she didn't have plaits like in the picture, but wore her hair loose with a beret on top. She also had a much larger nose than the artist had given her and wasn't smiling at all but had a serious, intent look on her face. Tatyana hurried past so as not to disturb them. The other dancers from her troupe had joined a group of people further down the street. Tatyana heard a whipping sound as she approached. A short man in beige trousers hitched up with string was dipping rags into a plastic bucket of red paint and whacking them on to a canvas as if to slash it to shreds. He wore no shirt in spite of the cold, and the paint splashed on to his bare chest and into his weather-beaten face. His eyes were black; his short hair stood on end. At first Tatyana thought he was an actor performing a scene from a play and would soon turn to his audience with a joke or a bow. But the man stood there on bent legs, slapping on layer after layer of paint with a vacant look on his face.

'Children's tights,' someone whispered.

Tatyana couldn't take her eyes off the bloody stain that was taking shape on the canvas; birds seemed to shoot out of it in every direction.

'Those red things he's swinging around are children's tights. He dips them in paint and then waves them about. What's the idea? Is it supposed to be art?'

Tatyana hardly dared move. She peered at the rag that the painter was clutching in his fist. It looked like a wrung-out cloth, but then she thought she spotted heels sticking out at one end and was reminded of the girl who'd been sitting for her portrait; she'd been wearing white cotton tights just like that. And as if from nowhere, Tatyana felt a terrible anger at the artist for distorting the girl's appearance, giving her a smaller nose, plaits, a smile. She threw back her head to stop her brimming tears from running down her cheeks and stared up at the sky.

She never heard back from the agency, and soon after returning from Moscow she decided to get a job that would make her some money. Her plan was to apply to fashion school, and so she transferred her ballerina's foot on to the sewing-machine treadle and pedalled furiously—especially when her father and grandmother started arguing again because they'd run out of money, or because no one wanted fake Adidas clothes any more, neither in Poland nor in Mariupol. Tatyana hoped to make a trouser suit for her mother—a surprise birthday present that could double up as a portfolio piece for the fashion school. The flat wasn't small, but because they were all on top of each other it was hard to hide anything from anyone, and so Tatyana made warning noises whenever her mother approached—coughing and hissing and hiding the lilac-coloured fabric as best she could under the sewing table. Her mother would turn and leave, pretending she'd been meaning to go into another room anyway.

Tatyana hauled herself out of the bath; her throbbing ankle sent another electric shock through her body. She dried herself, washed the remains of make-up from her hot, red face and went to her grandmother in the kitchen, who was on her own now, sitting with her chin propped on her fist, her face streaked with tears, her sagging cheeks pulling down the corners of her mouth. She was staring at the empty table. She'd thrown a grey cardigan on over her green jumper; its thick collar bolstered her neck. Her hair was almost completely covered by a headscarf; only a few white strands peeped out at the temples. Her small mouth hung open and her dough-coloured face with its huge ears seemed to go on forever. Tatyana took a deep breath to tell her that arguing wasn't a bad thing—people argued when they loved each other; arguing was just another form of hugging. But when she put her head on her grandmother's shoulder, all she could manage to say was that it would all be OK. It would all be fine.

She was sick of it, Grandmother replied. Sick of it. All her life, people had been shooing her from one place to another. They wouldn't even let her choose the earth she was to be buried in.

She got up and left the kitchen.

Tatyana's mother made all the arrangements for the move single-handedly. Every dusty crystal vase was held up to the light and examined—was it fit to be given away? There wasn't much worth selling. The samovar under the sink was new, still in its original packaging, but what would anyone want with it? Who would be interested in it apart from foreigners—and no foreigner ever made it as far as Mariupol; they all stayed in Kyiv or went south, to Odesa or Crimea, and if Inna was to be believed, to Kryvyi Rih. All Tatyana knew about Kryvyi Rih was that the Germans had once made a film there, but that was in a bygone world, before everything had begun to fall apart, not least the much-vaunted friendship among nations.

Her mother refused help with the packing too. She turned out the cupboards, as if looking for things that had been missing for years. Sometimes she stopped and spoke to something as if it were a child. 'What am I to do with you?' she said to a much-darned pair of trousers. 'What are you doing, all neatly folded in cellophane?' she asked her old school uniform. She'd always been a practical person, trusting to categories like *useful* and *serviceable*, but the old flat had little of use to offer—nothing, in fact, apart from the furniture. The net curtains had been yellow even when Tatyana was a child, and her mother's only comment on the carpet that someone, at some point, had seen fit to glue to the fishbone parquet was that she was glad she didn't have to rip it out.

Her grandmother, meanwhile, sloped off to the nearby park, which local residents had started to convert into a vast vegetable patch and parcel out among themselves. They tore up the shrubs, dug over the lawn, fenced in their little plots of land with branches, planted seedlings in the raked soil and raised cucumbers and tomatoes and whatever would grow. Grandmother stayed out all day, tending her cabbages and carrots in spite of her aches and pains; only when the sun had almost set did she return to the flat, where the cupboards were getting emptier and emptier and the stacks of boxes in the hall taller and taller. If she didn't come back, Tatyana's father was sent to look for her, and if he didn't come back either, Tatyana went out to look for them both. She usually found them side by side on a bench with a bag of vegetables at their feet, their arms folded in front of their chests, their eyes on the dusky sky, like birdwatchers waiting for migrating birds.

Tatyana would look at them as if they were exhibits in a museum—people who had been surprised by a flood of lava from an erupting volcano and would remain porous statues forever. She thought of her mother clearing out and packing up the flat, and wondered if it wouldn't be better for her parents if they had a daughter like Inna—an enterprising daughter who went to see far-flung relatives to suggest they sell up and leave, a daughter with ideas about making life better and easier, about *getting to grips with things*. Inna had come with no more than a holdall and a glitzy watch, her white face thick with rouge, her eyes round and blue, a loosely braided plait curled round her neck like a cat's tail. She looked like something out of a fairy tale. And, like someone in a fairy tale, she claimed to have answers to the family's problems in this age when everyone was out of work and people were starting to live in abandoned cars and convert parks into vegetable patches. A daughter like that was worth something—not one like her who jumped out of windows, threw in the only job available to her and spent her days casting wary glances at the sewing machine.

Inna had known what was to be done: they must sell their unnecessarily large flat, move to Kryvyi Rih and make a living from import-export like the Americans. 'People want to pickle their livers with Western-brand booze, not with our home-made shit.'

To lend force to her business plan, she had told them about Bruce Willis. 'You know those American porno pools, the ones that are lit up from below? Me and my ex once watched this dirty pool movie with Bruce Willis—completely sick, the way they do it in front of the cameras... So, yeah, a pool like that is everyone's dream, and I saw this film and I thought, hey, the Americans swim in their pools and fuck in them and do whatever the hell they want, and we just don't have the guts. We don't have the guts to really *own* something. To really *be* something. But we have the pools! It's not like everything here is just desert and mirages, is it? It's just that in our pools, there are these little pieces of shit floating around all over the place. Shit wherever you look. You're in the pool and you want to swim, but you don't dare open your mouth in case something floats in—you don't even dare spread your arms because, yeah, what if you stir up the water and those little bits of shit come swimming towards you? I ask you—what kind of a life is that? Playing dead in a pool because you're too scared to swim laps? Fuck that! We should be swimming too. If they can, we can.'

There had been a fixed gaze on Inna's face; she'd avoided catching anyone's eye. It came back to Tatyana now—that and the way she'd held out her glass for more wine and wiped her lips with the back of her hand and laughed. Her laugh had sounded so free you wanted to believe every word she said. Her pale, almost white face had reflected the light from the ceiling lamp like a fortune teller's crystal ball. She had ended her case by announcing that she'd already found suitable premises for a *bizniss*—and a small flat just round the corner. She would take care of everything. The shop had windows on all sides; all they needed were shelves and a till.

The image of the filthy illuminated pool came back to Tatyana six months later when Inna staggered into the off-licence with her face covered in blood. When she tried to speak, her voice seemed to come not from her mouth, but from somewhere deep inside her. Her lips opened and shut, but they formed no words.

On the day of the move, Tatyana had been charged with seeing Grandmother safely to the new city on the train; it was more comfortable for an old lady and there was no room for them in the lorry anyway. Her parents took care of everything else. Tatyana was secretly relieved that the new flat was on the ground floor. At least, she thought, as she put in her shifts at the off-licence, Grandmother couldn't jump out of the window; the old thing seemed to be getting more deranged by the day. The two-room flat was too small for the four of them, but they'd never meant it to be more than a place to sleep. A temporary solution, they told each other, until their new, American-style life began. The two bedrooms, kitchen and hall were soon chock-a-block, mainly with shelves and racks for the shop and various tools. There was a strong smell of gloss paint and glue. Tatyana had no time to settle in because she was immediately assigned shifts in the off-licence, and on the whole that seemed like a good thing. Flat, shop, flat, shop. She was told to stand at the till, and she did as she was told. She knew the way to work and the way from work back to bed, and the routine helped her cope with the upheavals, the cramped quarters—even with her grandmother's misery. She missed Mariupol, but couldn't have said what exactly she missed. Maybe only her old habits. The prefab-lined streets that she walked every day on her way to work might just as well have been in Mariupol, and the grim faces were no different either. Both places smelt bad; you kept your breathing shallow and your eyes on the ground.

In the shop, too, Tatyana avoided the customers' eyes as far as possible, looking at the till or her hands when she totted up the bill. As a general rule she tried not to raise her eyes until she heard her father's voice at the end of her shift, when he arrived to guard the precious bottles through the night. He also received the deliveries—another night job. Tatyana was never told where they came from, and she didn't ask. The business was going full throttle. Word had got round that the off-licence was open twenty-four hours a day, and Inna was proved right on all counts: certified foreign whisky was the grease that oiled all negotiations and a lucrative investment at the same time.

When Inna dropped in to check on the stocks, she took almost no notice of Tatyana, only calling out if something needed ordering or seeing to, and then dashing away again. This time was different.

Inna had definitely spoken to her. Tatyana looked up. Inna's thick plait lay curled around her neck as always, but it was bedraggled. She was even paler than usual; the skin under her left eye was mottled red, and her lower lip was torn and bleeding. Tatyana ran over and pushed a stool towards her. Inna collapsed on to it and stared into space, threw back her head and then jerked it forward again, as if she were starting up from sleep.

'No, no, everything's fine,' was all she said.

She resisted Tatyana's attempt to help her out of her coat and looked around the shop as if seeing it for the first time.

'Yes. No. We can handle this,' she said, as if drawing a conclusion from unspoken thoughts. Tatyana asked question after question and tried to stroke Inna's hands, but Inna brushed her off like a pesky animal and eventually got up and left.

Tatyana rang her parents to ask them to look for Inna in town; then she went to the shop door and peered up and down the street—maybe Inna would come back, maybe she was lying on a bench with internal bleeding, maybe she needed cold compresses and something to drink. Tatyana thought of Inna's battered face, as proud as ever in spite of the bruises. Where did she get that faith in the future? Inna believed firmly that great things were in store for her, and perhaps it would turn out to be her salvation when the rest of them foundered.

Inna didn't return that afternoon, but two foreigners appeared in the shop. Tatyana had seen them there before; she recognized their funny Russian. One of them didn't draw breath; the other was quieter. Tatyana stared at the plastic dish for change, through the glass counter to the floor below, and then down, down, down through the floor.

The soles of the men's shoes made mousy squeaks on the linoleum; Tatyana didn't look up.

‘Why does everyone in this country say, “These hands have never stolen?”’ the windbag asked, clearly in a good mood. ‘Like it’s a mantra?’

‘A what?’

Tatyana hated his nasal voice and the way he tried to sound like a real Russian. Guys like him bought from her almost daily; the amount they spent on alcohol would have kept her family for a week. They had a habit of walking into the shop as if they owned it.

‘The usual? Jim Beam?’

‘Yes. And the box of chocolates in the window.’

He reeked of perfume—not aftershave, like most men these days, who smelt as if they’d been tippling from the cologne bottle; this man’s perfume was sweet and cloying. Tatyana found this strange. She leant over to reach for the chocolates in the window and a song popped into her head.

Alain Delon speaks French,
Alain Delon doesn’t drink cologne,
Alain Delon drinks double bourbon.

She hummed softly to herself.

The windbag asked what she was singing. Tatyana didn’t reply, but only put the chocolates down on the counter. He pushed the box towards her.

‘They’re for you. You need to eat more. Since I’ve been coming here, your hips have been getting smaller and smaller—it’s a shame!’

Tatyana felt as if she’d been given a hook to the chin—as if her jaw were out of joint. She took the chocolates and put them back in the shop window among the other boxes.

'No! What are you doing? Get them back out. Don't be like that.'

Tatyana tried to breathe calmly. 'I don't need chocolates.' She kept getting whiffs of his perfume and it was making her feel sick.

'Come on, let me treat you. Or let me take you out for tea in the café next door. I won't try anything on, I promise. I like listening to you, you have such an erotic voice. Has anyone ever told you that? Maybe you'll tell me a bit about yourself?'

Tatyana thought of Inna with her bloody lip, collapsing on to the stool and looking about her like a startled rabbit. Poor woman, she'd have liked to smash in the face of the bastard who'd done that to her—preferably with a broken whisky bottle. But she'd probably never find out who it was. Instead she had these sleazy guys here, one of whom thought he could buy everything in the shop, including her. She wondered what would happen if she whacked him over his shaggy head with the bottle of Jim Beam's she'd put next to the till for him. It filled her with a sudden fury that the man hadn't even combed his hair before sauntering in with a grin and talking as if they knew each other.

'Your hand's burning,' she said to him as casually as possible.

'What?'

She pointed at his wedding ring. 'Isn't that why you're so red in the face—because of that ring burning on your finger?'

The man's lips went very narrow, then popped open like a fish's mouth. He probably couldn't find the Russian words to reply. He tossed a few notes down next to the plastic dish and grabbed the neck of the bottle as if it were a gun; Tatyana thought about taking cover.

'That's for the whisky and for you, for bending over for me. Do what you want with the chocolates,' he stuttered in bad Russian. He pushed open the door and started cursing in German, and his mate, who'd been standing silently in the corner, followed him out.

The next day, when Tatyana arrived to take over from her father for the morning shift, there were flowers outside the off-licence door. Her father had stolen a few hours' sleep—*quiet night, hardly any customers*—and knew nothing about the metal vase on the doorstep with its skimpy bunch of red roses, so puny that they drooped over the edge of the vase. Tatyana's first impulse was to chuck them in the dustbin in the backyard, but she thought better of it and handed them to her father, telling him to give Mum a nice surprise.

Tatyana found out who the flowers were from a few days later when the quieter of the squeaky-shoed Germans brought her an identical bunch. This time he came into the shop instead of leaving the roses on the doorstep, but she couldn't take them from him because two men and a woman were busy laying waste to the little corner that served as an office. Sheets of paper sailed to the floor from the files they'd pulled from the shelves; Tatyana watched them seesaw down and thought to herself that it would soon be spring—there would be pools of sunlight for her to bask in and all her listlessness would melt away, the rubbery feeling in her bones, the taste of cardboard in her mouth; she would begin to live again. Soon the cherry blossom would be out—the region was said to be famous for it—and they would get a bus into the countryside, go for walks, get to know the city at last.

The intruders were all talking at once. Tatyana didn't even try to follow what they were saying; they were from the tax department and that was as much as she needed to know. They claimed that Tatyana was running an illegal business, and Tatyana assumed there was some truth in this. She didn't contradict them or speak at all, but she noticed that they fell silent when the German appeared in the door, clutching his bunch of droopy roses. Hasty glances were exchanged and the older of the two men said in a high voice that he thought that would be all for the moment—they'd be in touch next week. The woman, who was sitting on a chair behind the counter, flicked through the accounts book as if she were checking one last detail, and the younger man fingered the slack knot of his tie and stared at the stranger with gleaming eyes, as if at something forbidden and indecent.

Tatyana reached for one of the sheets of paper that had landed on the counter, turned it blank side up and pulled out a pen.

'By all means. What did you say your names were again? And your address?'

The woman gave a cry of outrage and got up from the chair; the older man took her by the arm and pulled her away from the counter. The German walked slowly into the shop, laid the roses down by the till one by one as if they were banknotes, and looked all three in the face, each in turn.

'Can I help?' he asked in English, and then added calmly in Russian, 'Your ID, please.'

The older man buttoned up his leather coat and reached for the briefcase between his feet; his colleagues followed him to the door. Before it closed behind them, the woman shouted back into the shop, but the noise of their winter boots was so loud that Tatyana didn't catch what she said. She and the German were left on their own.

She heard her breath, then his. She thought, fleetingly, of cherries—plump, black fruit whose stones you could shoot through your teeth like bullets, yards and yards. Then she saw the face of her Kyiv friend and wondered if the camp bed in the hall of her tiny flat was still up for grabs—if she could run away right now, without even packing. Then she reached for the phone. Inna picked up almost immediately, listened to the whole sorry story and then asked, after a pause, why Tatyana thought she, Inna, could tell her what to do.

'Because all this was your idea. Now you can fish the pieces of shit out of the pool. I'm not eating them.'

She saw the German watching her, hung up and offered him the chair where the supposed tax official had sat a moment before. She fetched two glasses from the cupboard and an open bottle of Johnnie Walker that she never touched herself, but which she knew her father drank at night to keep himself warm. Sometimes she'd arrive for the morning shift and find him with his head on the counter, a soft gurgle coming from his throat; she always wished she could cover him with her coat and leave him to sleep. The shop would smell of earth and wood and her father, and a little of hay and gloss paint. The remains of whisky in his glass would sparkle like resin and she would pour it away, sit down beside him and watch as he gradually felt the warmth of another body next to his, opened his eyes, looked about him in bewilderment and then smiled and yawned.

Tatyana hated whisky and pulled a face as she put the glass to her lips after clinking glasses with the German. It tasted rough, almost furry, like a film of ash coating her mouth. She sucked in her cheeks; then she asked the German his name.

He took a gulp, as if it were lemonade. 'Michael.'

Tatyana nodded. 'Thank you, Michael.'

'No problem.' He straightened himself and ran a hand through his blond hair. 'They'll be back.' He smiled.

As if I didn't know, Tatyana thought, suddenly annoyed.

'But maybe I'll be back, too.'

The whisky made Tatyana burp.

'Everyone has some kind of talent. My talent is being in the right place at the right time. People say I'm like a chameleon. I'm easy to miss and I have a habit of showing up unexpectedly.'

A chameleon. He even looked a little chameleon-like with his long head and big, slightly bulging eyes. But Tatyana only glanced at him and then stared past him through the shop windows to the other side of the road where the street-sweeper had fallen asleep in a doorway. He hung there lopsidedly, his trapper hat over his face; it looked as if he might collapse into the slushy snow at any moment. Further down the road, a group of young people on a bench were trying to keep a lighter lit, holding up their arms to protect the flame from the wind; they were probably heating up a spoon. A thickset figure hurried past them towards the shop, almost tripping at the bottom of the steps. That idiot Inna must have called her father.

'Did they hurt you?' he yelled, throwing open the door. Tatyana hadn't heard him in such a panic since the time he'd accidentally scalded her with boiling water when she was little. The nurse had pulled a piece of skin off with her tights and her father had cried.

Tatyana poured more whisky into her glass and pushed it towards him.

'No, they didn't. Because *he* was here.'

She jerked her head towards Michael. She wasn't sure how much Russian he understood. 'He acted the big shot, even spoke English.'

Her father followed her gaze to the man on the chair, clearly seeing him for the first time. Michael's blue eyes were so pale they were almost transparent; they shimmered colourlessly in the light. Tatyana's father took a step towards him and he jumped to his feet, tugged his jacket straight and pressed the hand that was held out to him.

'Thank you.'

'You're welcome.'

'Can I offer you anything? Anything you want, it's on me.'

'Thank you, that's very generous of you.'

Tatyana watched the two men clink glasses and size each other up as they exchanged first names and patronymics. Michael's sheepskin-lined leather jacket looked new; the roll-neck collar peeping out clearly belonged to an expensive jumper. Her father turned his attention to the limp roses on the counter, their stalks as floppy as shoelaces.

'What's all this? Why are the flowers being left to wilt? Don't we have any vases?' He smiled at her, trying to cheer her up with his eyes, but she wasn't in the mood to smile back. He changed his tone. 'Come on, girl.'

By the time she returned with a bucket of water, he'd invited Michael to dinner.

The table had been pulled away from the wall into the middle of the living room and covered with a new cloth, but the cloth was hardly visible beneath the dishes of beetroot and garlic, mushroom caviar, sausage salad, dill gherkins, stuffed eggs, herring and onions, grated potatoes in mayonnaise, beef in cream sauce, pickled vegetables, aubergine purée—beneath the plates and silver cutlery and crystal glasses. Tatyana's parents argued about the dinner service. Was it really the best they had? Hadn't Grandmother's cousin from Lviv—dead three years now, would you believe it—left them a better one? And where the hell was it? Hadn't they brought it with them when they moved?

Michael was their first visitor in the new flat. An uneasy feeling crept up Tatyana's throat. The family had kept themselves to themselves for so long that they'd developed a jargon all their own, a language incomprehensible to outsiders, especially foreigners, even if they did speak Russian. Her parents' half-spoken sentences were stuffed with allusions to past times and old films they'd watched together—some of them before Tatyana was born—and to one-time celebrities like that singer who was shot dead on camera just as he was about to say something that was of great significance to them, but only sounded hollow to Tatyana.

Waiting for Michael to arrive, Tatyana felt, for the first time, embarrassed by her parents. She tried to imagine what he would see with his pale-blue eyes: an array of salads in fancy crystal dishes, heavy, dark-red goblets with see-through stems alongside plainer glasses for vodka—and presumably the TV would be on all evening. She was suddenly glad that no one in the family played a musical instrument—but they would try to impress their German visitor, of course, and since there was nothing impressive about the family, they would regale him with stories of the wonderful city of Mariupol which they'd left for the wonderful city of Kryviy Rih.

Tatyana looked on as her parents begged her grandmother to put on a new housedress, just this once, for this special occasion. The whole country, she thought, was like her family; people had been isolated for so long that when they tried to make themselves understood to foreigners, they ended up in a kind of echo chamber of the past. Outside, people drove Western-brand cars and wore elegantly cut suits under sheepskin-lined leather jackets; they drank whisky rather than vodka and listened to American pop rather than Soviet bards who died futile deaths on camera for slogans that no longer meant anything to anyone. But Inna had been right to describe life as a swimming pool with pieces of shit floating in it—that, at least, was how people saw it; they shut their eyes to avoid seeing what lay before them, preferring to hark back to a past that they lied about until the lies came true. They'd all agreed on a common illusion; they raised their glasses and drank to a world that had ceased to exist.

The evening didn't go as badly as Tatyana had feared. Michael kept the family entertained with his clumsy Russian, which didn't seem to stop him from waxing lyrical about the virtues of the provinces. Anyone, he explained, could make it big in Kyiv or Odesa; there was no shortage of opportunities in the cities, but at the same time, competition was high—you could just as easily lose everything again. In Kryvyi Rih it was different; if you made money here, you had lifelong security and peace of mind, and that was what he wanted: peace of mind and a family. There was a pregnant pause. He was an ordinary guy, he went on, a small-town guy; he was suspicious of big cities and he knew what he was talking about; he came from Berlin which, post-reunification, was a noisy, chaotic place—unbearable, the riff-raff it attracted. He worked in the construction industry, but it was hard to explain the details—something to do with the transport of materials, though he couldn't say what materials. He was a kind of logistics manager, only different.

Michael didn't drink excessively, and Tatyana's father held off too and didn't keep trying to top him up. They laughed at Michael's pronunciation and he happily repeated his mistakes when he saw how much it amused them. Then Tatyana's grandmother confessed that she could remember a little of her school German, and Michael clapped his hands and asked her to say something for him.

Tatyana's parents had prevailed. Grandmother had been persuaded to put on a new, pale-pink housedress for their guest; she had also left off her headscarf, and her white hair was neat and tidy. Tatyana had never seen photos of her as a young woman, but she was sure that, had she been born today rather than half-way through the Five-Year Plan, she could have modelled for the fashion magazines. Neither Tatyana nor her mother had inherited her straight nose, full lips or chiselled eyebrows. Sometimes, when Grandmother dozed on the sofa, her eyes only half closed, Tatyana felt the urge to run a finger over her well-cut profile, but she was always a little afraid of her long, almost transparent eyelashes, quivering like the legs of a frenzied insect.

Grandmother turned to Michael and said something in German. All heads swung to look. Her son-in-law in particular stared as if he were seeing her for the first time in years.

Michael reached for his glass and gave a polite reply. His face had softened over the course of the evening and he was sitting less stiffly than before. His light-blond hair blended almost seamlessly with the doors of the sideboard behind him; the skin of his hands was the same colour as the tablecloth, and the cloth was the same colour as his shirt. White. Bone-white, yeast-white, cloud-white; as white as if there were nothing underneath—no veins flowing with blood, no muscles, no flesh. Tatyana felt she could have put her hand through him.

Her grandmother took a deep breath, hesitated for a second and then asked a question. She and Michael exchanged a few sentences in a language that none of the others understood. Then Grandmother cried out, almost triumphantly. There was a pause; then Michael burst out laughing. He pressed his bony fingers to his mouth and waved an apology with the other hand.

Grandmother looked offended. 'I messed that one up,' she muttered in Russian, staring forlornly at the half-empty crystal glasses.

'No, not at all!' Michael, too, switched languages. 'Forgive me, I'm not laughing at you. It's much better the way you put it. Much, much better! It captures it so well. Really! You don't know how good it is! I'm grateful to you. That was a fantastic thing to say. I hope I say such clever things when I speak Russian. That would make us almost a family.'

Tatyana saw her grandmother smile awkwardly and gaze over the salad dishes; she saw her father make a satisfied face and her mother dab at the corners of her mouth with her napkin, then look at her hands; she seemed to be trying to suppress a loud sigh of relief. Tatyana wanted to say how much she loved her grandmother, but thought it would sound weird if she blurted out something like that. She wanted to tell Michael everything she knew about her grandmother's life, but thought better of it. Why would she vie for the attention and affection of a stranger?

'I don't want to go to Germany! I don't want to go to Germany! I don't want to go to Germany!' Every time they met, their conversations began and ended in the same way.

Michael would treat Tatyana to coffee with evaporated milk, and Tatyana would tell him how much she loved Kryvyi Rih, a city she knew only from the walk to work that took her through dingy backyards and past sixties blocks whose tiny, many-paned windows made them look as if there were grids over the façades. She spoke of the park that was named after the newspaper *Truth*, of the bumpy paths edged with boulders where young people carved their names and dates, the pavilion where you could rent pedalos and glide a little way down the river. She spoke of the heady scent of azaleas in the botanical garden and even rhapsodized over the billion-year-old schist rocks glowing bronze in the furious gaze of the setting sun—here, if not before, she realized that she was repeating, cliché for cliché, the yarn recently spun for her by a young man, a native of Kryvyi Rih, who had come into the shop and asked for five whole bottles of White Label, a brand they didn't often sell. He'd also mentioned that he was head of the 'Club of the Funny and Inventive', an artists' collective that appeared regularly on TV. Soft-eyed and quick-tongued, this not particularly tall guy in a polo neck was, it seemed, a local celebrity, used to having an audience.

When Tatyana told him she'd only recently moved to Kryvyi Rih, he painted the virtues of his home town in such brilliant colours that she hardly noticed him pay and go; the money lay untouched in the dish, and azaleas danced before her eyes. Tatyana had stared at the door as it closed behind him, wondering if all that talk of pedalos and name-carving had been some kind of come-on, but the head of the local Funny and Inventive hadn't returned to the shop since, and Tatyana had neither time nor reason to walk in the park alone.

Now, sitting in the café with Michael, she parroted Mr White Label in the hope of making Michael realize that she wouldn't let herself be bought with promises of Western-brand nylons; she wasn't going to let him whisk her away from Kryvyi Rih. She was happy where she was and content with what she had; he could buy her coffee if he wanted, but that was as far as it went.

The discovery of her pregnancy tore at the backs of her knees like claws and brought her to the ground. She couldn't face her shift at the off-licence; her father had to step in for her. She sat listlessly on the living-room sofa, knees pressed together, arms folded, eyes fixed on the liquid pattern of the carpet under her bare feet, her toes rising and falling in slow motion, her grandmother's slippers coming and going. *Mishka... Mishka...* The name rang in her ears like an echo—her family's name for Michael since he'd been to dinner with them; her father had clasped him by both shoulders when he left.

An abortion was no big deal, but Tatyana had no idea what clinic to go to. She would have liked to reach for the phone and call her friend in Kyiv, ask if the camp bed in her hall was still up for grabs, if she'd mind putting her up. She thought of her studies, of her mum's trouser suit that was still in pieces in a bag, brought to Kryvyi Rih in the hope that her plans might come to something after all, that she might make something of her life. She sobbed so hard she could barely string a sentence together and her mother said, 'This isn't a bad gut feeling, my girl; it's the pregnancy hormones. You're going to feel like this for a while.'

And Michael, pale-skinned Mishka, with freckles even on his earlobes, was as happy as a child. He brought her yet another bunch of wilted roses and assured her that he didn't want to leave Ukraine; his life was here with her; he was learning her language (Russian, that was, not Ukrainian); he had a job. She still didn't know exactly what he did, what logistics he managed, but he drove a new car and had a flat of his own. And her parents approved of him because he was ten years older than her and a *biznissmen*. For weeks Tatyana felt so nauseous that whenever anyone congratulated her on being pregnant, she could have vomited in their face.

When she was three months gone, she stopped being able to pee; her heart raced as if she were running a marathon and she could hardly get up the stairs. Her ankles swelled like wet dishcloths. She wanted to sleep but couldn't keep her eyes shut; she stared as if through water at the faces that appeared before her, oblivious to almost everything but the cramps in her belly—it felt as if the little person inside her were trying to get out through her belly button. Her breath came in staccato gasps and didn't begin to steady until she was in hospital and diagnosed with nephritis; then at least, under the cool sheets of the hospital bed, she knew it wasn't the child inside her that was trying to rip her apart.

She was pumped full of antibiotics and didn't resist. Maybe, she thought, the baby wouldn't come after all. Maybe it had all been a misunderstanding; maybe it was over now. Nothing but one big inflammation, a misdiagnosis, a phantom pregnancy, another woman's life. Every day her mother sat at her bed with hot mushroom soup, bringing love from Tatyana's grandmother, who was so worried that she prayed daily to one of her TV healers, asking him to make Tatyana better. Her father came at the weekend and so did Michael, but her mother ushered them out with brisk, nervy gestures almost as soon as they arrived; she wore more rouge than usual, muttered to herself all the time—something she'd never done at home—and grumbled at no one in particular. Everything seemed to annoy her: the nurse was late to check on Tatyana, the sheets hadn't been changed for weeks, the floor was sticky with God-knows-what, the medication wasn't given on time and didn't have any effect. And what was this mush they called lunch? She went out to the nurses' room to find someone to do their job for once, but returned with pale lips and sank down on the mattress at Tatyana's feet, patting her knees and staring into space.

'When I had you,' she began, so softly that Tatyana could hardly hear her, 'the woman next to me on the maternity ward had twins. They were premature. Two months or so, which is nothing out of the ordinary for twins, and they were very weak, but they squawked, they made noises—I heard them, and their mother… she heard them too, of course—but the nurses and the doctor decided to declare them dead. There were no ventilators or anything in those days—no incubators or whatever you call them. One of the nurses took the babies and, right in front of their mother's eyes, she put them in a bucket of water and clapped a lid on it. I was in the bed next to her, giving birth to you. That poor woman screamed all the time I was there, day and night, day and night, and then suddenly she went quiet and they took her away or something. I don't know, I can't remember everything. All I know is that when I got home with you, I told my mother about the woman with the twins, and she just waved her hand and said, "The fields. That's the place to give birth. Out on the fields."'

Tatyana wanted to reach out and touch her mother, but her arms felt as if they were filled with lead. Her mother surely hadn't wanted to tell her all that now, when she was three months pregnant and in hospital with nephritis, but there, the story was out and presumably it was the reason why Tatyana found herself asking a question she'd never thought of asking before. 'What was it like, giving birth?'

Her mother looked up, not startled or surprised, but defensive.

'It was pretty typical, really.' The hospital staff had greeted her with the usual phrases: *Used to spreading your legs, eh? Well, you can close them again for now—no one here wants to see that.* The contractions were well under way by then. After that, everything went very fast; she saw the doctor's hand disappear inside her, fainted and was woken by slap after slap on her face. '*Don't go and die on us, you stupid bitch. You've got a baby here, so you'd damn well better stick around and look after it.*' She was discharged with green and purple bruises all over her face. 'I was glad when we were home.'

It was only much later, when her mother mumbled a goodbye and hurried out with the soup pan after what felt like hours of silence, that Tatyana allowed herself to cry. You had children or you didn't. That seemed to be all there was to say.

Even when she'd finished the course of antibiotics, Tatyana had swollen limbs, blurred vision and a head that seemed to be made of thick glass. She was glad that Michael's jabbering reached her only as a distant murmur when he lay next to her at night, talking politics. He talked about how much it meant that everyone was voting and there was more than one party on the ballot paper, how alarmed he was that the Communists—those criminals—were standing for election again, how important it was not to harp on the past. What was past was past and no longer mattered; the main thing was not to live like a serf any more, but to stand on one's own feet. Every man was the architect of his own fortune. Tatyana wondered whether she should press a pillow to his face or hers.

But it wasn't just Michael; everyone seemed to be a political pundit these days. When had it started? People knew something or read something and immediately had to pass it on. They ran up to each other and prattled away, like people handing hot bread around before it went cold, like kids whispering in class. At other times they sat silent and astonished, side by side on a backyard or pavement bench; whenever she passed them, Tatyana had the feeling she was walking through a cinema past a row of gawping spectators.

The first time she'd heard the obsessive, Tourette's-like political talk had been in Moscow; it was only a few years ago, but already it felt like a scene from a parallel universe in one of the science-fiction books she'd loved as a child. After sauntering down the Arbat, Tatyana had asked her way to the Soviet Union's first American diner and found herself walking past a mile-long queue of people, her Adidas trainers gradually disintegrating in the cold and slush of the Moscow winter. She couldn't believe a queue could be so long; people stood in twos and threes in a line that went all the way round the block. How many were there? A thousand? Two thousand? Jacket sleeves, gloves, felt galoshes, hats and scarves, jacket sleeves, shoulder pads, beanies and scarves, jacket sleeves, ties, fur collars, shoulder pads, leather coats, beanies, jacket sleeves, gloves, felt galoshes… Tatyana felt dizzy and kept her eyes on the ground until she came to the crowd barriers at the entrance. All the women queuing here wore furs and fancy hats; they teetered on high heels, their faces made up as if they were waiting to be let into an opulent ballroom, not a one-storey concrete block with an illuminated yellow M on the roof, sticking up like a pair of dog's ears. Tatyana hardly dared approach these women in her filthy shoes. One of them, who had almost made it to the entrance, had an elaborately set sapphire in her earlobe and Tatyana must have stared for longer than she meant to, because the woman turned her head and asked what she was looking at.

'Um… is the food good?' Tatyana stammered.

'The end of the queue's down there,' the woman retorted; then she gave Tatyana the once-over and added, 'Those greasy strips of potato in a paper bag? You must be joking. But my husband asked for them and he's in hospital, so I can hardly refuse, can I? I told him my sautéed potatoes are far superior, but he insisted on French fries—*and* a McDonald's flag. What can you do? I don't even know if he'll make it home.'

Tatyana asked what had happened, and the woman replied brusquely that her husband had been driving the wrong people through the wrong district at the wrong time. 'They wouldn't pay for the vodka, you understand?'

Tatyana didn't.

'Are you from Mars or something?'

'No, Mariupol.'

Well, that explained everything, the woman said crossly, but she pulled Tatyana into the queue, slipping an arm through hers as, with her other hand, she lit a cigarette. Complaints swelled behind them; the woman turned with the cigarette in her mouth and shrieked so loudly that the protests immediately subsided. 'This is my cousin from the provinces, you bastards. Any more from you and there'll be trouble.'

Tatyana recalled the woman now, her eyes the same sapphire-blue as her earrings, her bulbous nose glowing like a cherry in the biting wind. Even in those days, she thought, people had talked about nothing but politics. The woman outside McDonald's had gone on and on, telling Tatyana who was a liar and who was a thief and who was a complete nutcase; she had wound up by saying, 'What good is it to me if for the first time in the history of the country the Party criminals aren't rigging the results to the last decimal place before we've even voted, but I get to cast my vote for Candidate Don't Know-the-Guy Number One or Candidate Don't-Want-to-Know-the-Guy Number Two? Where does that get me when my husband's in hospital beaten half to death and I don't even know if there's going to be a tomorrow, let alone what that tomorrow's going to bring?'

'It's funny, I can remember exactly what she looked like. I can see her as if it were yesterday.' Tatyana stared searchingly at the overcast sky ahead, as if it contained a message for her. 'She was the one who said the world falls apart more slowly if you don't read about it in the papers. I got that from her.'

Edi felt the urge to stop the car, leave it at a service station and continue on foot, set off into the surrounding hills, take in all the sights that were signposted along the motorway. *Leuchtenburg Worlds of Porcelain*. Indeed. *Nebra's Ark: Experience the Nebra Sky Disc.* Well, why not? This fairyland was crying out to be explored. Another signpost announced a graduation tower. Saltwater was said to have healing powers. Beside her, Tatyana talked on and on, apparently unaware that Edi was holding her breath.

'Then Michael said he wanted me to meet his parents in Berlin before the baby was born—also he had urgent business there. Maybe he even told me what this urgent business was and I just didn't understand or wasn't listening properly—I'd got used to not understanding how he made a living. I was six months pregnant, I didn't really care, I didn't even mind that he was determined to drive the whole way. He got me a visa—didn't ask if it was what I wanted. Twenty-seven hours on the road? With potholes the size of construction pits? Sure, no problem. So what if my belly got a bit shaken up? Who cared about me?

'All I remember about that journey is that the engine started to smoke somewhere in Poland. We were on a main road, nobody stopped, we didn't have mobile phones in those days. I stood at the side of the road and watched Michael fiddling around under the bonnet. He fetched a bottle of Coke from the car and tipped it over the engine. We made it to Poznań in a car that smelt of burnt sugar. I sat in a little booth while Michael talked to the mechanic in the garage next door; I could see him through the steamed-up glass—windows that looked as if someone had taken a paintbrush and slapped dirty water all over them. It was like looking at a ghost. A ghost who was taking me to Germany. If I'd known it was for good, I'd have packed more trousers.'

Edi was trying to imagine what burnt Coke smelt like, when Tatyana said wasn't it time for a cigarette break. She needed a pee too.

Edi got out of the car and stared at the bushes next to the toilets; a few yellow flowers still clung on. Tatyana dashed off, almost at a run, lighting a cigarette as she went. The motorway roared, as if planes were landing right next to them. On the other side of the car park lorries were parked nose to tail like long beads on a necklace. One of them had a satellite dish attached to the cab; whoever was in there must spend their weekends parked in service areas like this. Edi wondered what else they had to help them through those empty hours in the cab, apart from an antenna connecting them with home.

In the toilets, Edi washed her hands in a steel basin set into the brick wall. The water was so cold it was like plunging her fingers into crushed ice, but it felt good. Her eyes looked out of the steel plaque above the tap like bullet holes; the rest of her face was a blur. There was a smell of sulphur and charred coffee grounds. How did burnt Coke smell? Like bitter caramel?

Clouds scudded across a white sky, tinged with green and purple. The cars whizzing past sounded as if they were driving over potholes filled with stones, but Edi was sure it was all in her head. In her mind she was still on a Polish road with Tatyana, heading for Germany in a car that smelt of burnt sugar; she was sitting in the back seat, staring at the backs of two heads, a light-blond one at the wheel and—what colour had Tatyana's hair been twenty years ago? Was it copper beech then, too? Did Tatyana chemically recreate the fading colour of her youth?

The lonely table on the grass was clunky, like it was made of dark-brown Plasticine. Tatyana leant against it and lit another cigarette. Edi jogged on the spot, shook out her joints, stretched her back, sucked in her belly and bent over.

'Sure you don't want one? I won't tell.' Tatyana held out the packet of cigarettes to Edi, who hung there, head down. She squinted up: Tatyana loomed, cone-shaped, against the white sky, her gleaming hair a darker red than the painted nails in front of Edi's nose. Edi couldn't see her face. She wasn't going to tell Tatyana that in the inside pocket of her rucksack she had five grams of weed that she'd been thinking about for a while, but had no intention of sharing with anyone.

She straightened up, fished her phone from her trouser pocket, swiped the screen at random a couple of times and put it away. The cigarette between Tatyana's fingers burnt quickly, the ash curling like a caterpillar. Something in the air felt sticky, maybe the dust from the road mixed with the approaching rain.

'I'll shut up now; you look a bit pasty.'

Tatyana was right, Edi would have liked to interrupt her story, but she couldn't, because… well, because she couldn't. When Daniel was opposed to something that Edi obstinately insisted on, he'd say, *It's no good, because it's no good.* End of story.

How much of this did her mother know? Presumably all of it. Those endless conversations. And Tatyana's daughter? Presumably nothing. But then, Edi thought, what did *she* know of anything? What had anyone ever told *her* about her mother and father? Nothing like that. It was always other people's numbers that were dialled when something was up.

'No,' she managed to get out. 'I mean… you don't have to stop. Telling me stuff. You don't.'

Tatyana looked Edi in the eyes; the last time she'd done that had been in hospital when Edi had stood in front of her with the gerbera.

'Sure? You look so startled.'

'Yes, I…' Edi began to stutter. Then she saw Pirosmani's giraffe on palely gleaming skin—that strange, haphazard creature born of the belief that it wasn't worth trying to see the world as it was, that it wasn't even possible. How could she explain to Tatyana that her perception of everything around her had, until now, resembled that picture; she would hear about things that had happened, pick up snatches of information here and there, and then do her best, using guesswork and intuition, to assemble it into a whole. If she'd tried to draw or paint that 'whole', it would have ended up as a short-necked giraffe with black spots on a white coat.

They walked back to the car and rolled past the string of lorries; wobbly antennae reached out to them like feelers. After a while, Tatyana started up again, speaking into the silence that had begun to fill the car as soon as the first signs announced Jena. She spoke casually, as if she were talking to herself.

'I'd expected more. More than what I found. More than the life on offer to me. That surprised me—after all, I'd always been adamant that I didn't want to move to Germany. But as soon as I found myself in Berlin, I realized I was disappointed. It wasn't that I'd been expecting flying cars or skyscrapers with flashing lights… I'm not actually sure what I thought I'd find, but I remember thinking the bombed-out Memorial Church drab and unspectacular—and the shopping centre opposite could have been in Kryvyi Rih. The same grubby white façade, the same empty oblong balconies, the same plastic tables on a terrace around a broken fountain. And there I was, my neck covered in pimples, my swollen belly pushing my breasts out to either side—big, flat breasts, wide as frying pans; I hadn't seen my knees in months. I stared out of the car window and noticed how cagey people looked and it suddenly struck me that Michael's watery, expressionless eyes were nothing out of the ordinary here. Everyone had them.

'Before we left for Germany, I'd asked my father why he thought this man, his Mishka, was right for me, and he said, "Look how serious he is. Sits there all quiet; that means he's clever and thinks more than he speaks—and when he's not thinking, he's running from one job to the next. What more do you want of a man?"

'Now I was on Kurfürstendamm, staring at these numb-looking faces, and I realized that the soon-to-be father of my child didn't actually look serious at all; he looked indifferent, absent; he wasn't with me and he wasn't anywhere else either. I noticed that no one was walking arm-in-arm and hardly anyone was holding hands; the passers-by were all so far apart it was impossible to say which of them belonged together. Everyone was wearing conspicuously plain clothes, as if to hide the fact that they had more than all the rest of the world. More than the world I knew, anyway.

'People in this country like to say *less is more*, but what do they mean by it? They stroll down Kurfürstendamm or Friedrichstrasse, stepping over the homeless people as if they were piles of dogshit. That's what struck me most—or what shocked me most—that there were tramps in Germany just the same as in our country. I suppose I must have thought it was just us who had tramps, ragged and yellow-faced and rotten-mouthed, holding out their paper cups to passers-by—and these Germans who pretended not to be rich didn't even glance at them; they acted as if they didn't see them, didn't hear them. When people who have more of everything, more time, more money, more leisure—when people like that say *less is more*, how is that any different from spitting in the face of people like me?

'Michael's flat was also *less is more*. There was practically nothing in any of the three rooms; the walls were bare expanses of white, like sheets of polystyrene. No photos on the sideboard, no rugs on the laminate, no throws on the sofa. No greasy fingerprints on the glass doors of the cupboards, no teacup rings on the pale-wood surfaces, no old magazines on the shelf under the TV. In the kitchen, there were two plastic chairs leaning folded against a square table. The shelves in the fridge were spotless as if they'd never been used; the balcony door stuck; the radiators didn't warm up properly. Michael said he hadn't bled them for a while, and that made sense, because he'd been in Ukraine. But then he got the rooms mixed up—said he'd show me the bathroom and opened the door to the broom cupboard: a few empty shelves and a bucket of cloths under a bare lightbulb. There was no shampoo in the shower, and the towels next to the bath smelt very new. I can't remember exactly, but maybe it was then I began to sense something.

'I lay on the futon, watching the sunlight reflected in the windows to the yard and wondering how I'd make myself understood to Michael's parents with no common language and a tongue that hung out like a dog's—I panted my way through that pregnancy. No matter what I asked Michael, his answer was almost always the same: "You're so sweet." *Du bist so süss.* It was the only German I knew then.

'I'd assumed his parents would welcome us with a meal when we arrived in Berlin, or look in on us the next day, but even when we'd been in the city almost two weeks there was no sign of them. Michael had his *bizniss* to attend to, so I was on my own all day. If I asked when he was coming home or what his plans were, he'd tell me how *süss* I was. When I asked about his parents, he said they were moving house and would have us *kids* round as soon as they'd settled into the new place in Spandau. When at last the day came for our visit to Spandau, I had a sour taste in my mouth and a terrible sense of foreboding—but what had my mother said? *It isn't a bad gut feeling; it's the pregnancy hormones.*

'I wore my best, my only pair of real maternity trousers—navy-blue cotton with a lot of elastane. I was so sick of wearing old jeans let out at the waistband with the fabric that, long ago, in another life, I'd planned to use for a trouser suit for my mother. All that morning I cooled my cheeks so they wouldn't look like bottled fruit, and I made up my face twice. When I came out of the bathroom Michael was on the phone and I realized at once that something was horribly wrong and had been for quite some time—all along, in fact.

'He was speaking in a soft, slow sing-song, as if to a small child, clutching his neck and sweating; red blotches appeared at his throat and spread down under his collar. I sat at the window watching his eyes grow more and more transparent, and when he hung up I asked straight out if his parents had cancelled because they didn't want to meet a stupid foreigner who couldn't even make small talk with them.

'He went even paler than usual and said what he always said. "Du bist so süss." But then he said something else. "That wasn't my parents." He jumped up from his chair and then collapsed back on to it, like one of those toys where you push a button at the bottom, releasing the springs and elastic bands so that everything flops down. "That was my son," he said.

'When you burn yourself, it feels very cold at first—know what I mean? The pain doesn't kick in till later. I tried to say something, but I felt as if I'd been punched in the throat; then I thought the light in the room had gone out. I found myself standing by the wall; somehow I managed to stay on my feet. No way was I going to crawl around in front of him on all fours—though it did occur to me that the laminate might cool my forehead.

'"He's ten," Michael said eventually. "I'm divorced."

'I closed my eyes and leant against the wall, trying to work out the quickest way out of that flat and away from this ghost, this evil spirit. I didn't have a word of German, I couldn't even walk down the street and ask for help.

'Not so long before, I had pounded the streets of Moscow without a map. I'd let a strange woman take me into the first McDonald's of the Soviet Union. I'd jumped out of windows. I'd stood at the top of a human star, contorted my body into the most fantastic positions, landed on my feet, spread my arms and smiled at the audience. But now, with my huge belly and swollen legs, my numb arms and a head that felt as if it had been doused in scalding water, I allowed myself to be led by the hand to the plasticky-smelling sofa. I allowed myself to be comforted. Once I'd been so brave; now I was just pregnant.

'I wanted him to take me home as quickly as possible, and for that I had to trust him. He told me he'd kept it a secret from me because he was embarrassed about fathering a child so young, and with the wrong woman—and I believed him. He said he'd only married her because she got pregnant (though she'd said she was on the pill), and two years later he divorced her because he couldn't imagine a future with her—and I got that. He said he wanted to be there for his son, as far as possible—and I nodded. I'd only heard of it happening the other way round: the guy got the woman pregnant and then took off, with or without explanation, and as soon as the baby was out of nappies and sleeping through the night, back he came and told the kid its mum had made his life hell—she'd chased him out of the house and banned him from getting in touch; he would have stayed, if he could, and taken responsibility for his own flesh and blood, but, given the circumstances, it hadn't been possible. As Michael talked, I compared him with the men I'd heard about from my friends and my mum's friends, and I decided he was different. He wanted to be a good father to his first child, so he'd want to be there for the second too. Wasn't that a reason to love him?

'Then we were in another new flat with more bare walls, but Michael's parents really had just moved in—I saw the boxes in the hall; he hadn't lied to me about that. The furniture was already in place and the dining-room table was heaving with salads and cold cuts; there were even heavy crystal glasses like at my parents'.

I was relieved and would have liked to call home from the phone I'd seen in the hall and tell my mum and dad all about it—tell them everything. I hadn't spoken to a single relative since leaving Kryvyi Rih.

'Michael's mother was so tall I had to look up at her. She had a very straight back and a pointy head, and scurried back and forth between kitchen and dining room like a marten on its hindlegs. She barely paid me any attention, but she barely paid Michael any either—only stared at the bowls and plates, and threw a few words at us as she passed us with a basket of bread. Michael translated for me: we could leave our shoes on if we liked. His father greeted him with a handshake. The old man had no hair on his head, not even eyebrows; he looked like a reptile, but at least he talked—to Michael anyway. He talked non-stop, producing a kind of background noise like water gurgling in a radiator.

'I didn't understand a word, so I kept my eyes on the tablecloth, watching it go into ripples when plates and glasses were moved. I stared at the patterns on the silver cutlery and on Michael's new shirt—a light-blue one that cooled his complexion. His freckles were very pale, like shadows on his cheeks; I'd never examined them so closely before. His face looked fleshy, although he was so thin that I felt his ribs at night when he tried to hold me and I pushed him away because my fat belly made me so hot. I thought of something my mother had said to me before we left—that it wasn't love that connected people, but a common consensus on what mattered in life. She told me I should learn to breathe, because as long as I didn't start panting and gasping I'd be fine. I sat there, feeling myself pant and gasp.

'Michael's mother's voice set in like pelting rain; she kept pointing at me. I desperately needed the toilet, but didn't dare get up. Michael began to shout. He pushed his half-full plate away and jumped to his feet, then sat down again, almost missing the chair. As I grabbed his arm as if in a reflex action, I felt my trousers growing wet. I had to get out, but I didn't know where the bathroom was and I couldn't ask. The upholstery of the chair I was sitting on was sopping-wet too, and I could feel my shoulders moving closer and closer to my ears. After a while, all went quiet. I didn't know if the argument was over or if I'd gone deaf, but I stood up slowly and slipped out of the dining room, trying to squeeze my thighs together. I found the bathroom on the other side of the hall, sat down on the edge of the bath and stared at the wet patches on my legs. Michael knocked, flung open the door without waiting for an answer and knelt down in front of me to help me out of my wet trousers. Then his mother burst in and started to shout. By then even I'd worked out that it was time to go to hospital.

'I asked Michael for my trousers, so I wouldn't have to leave the house in nothing but wet underwear; his mother threw me a dressing gown. She's burying me under a pile of cloth, I thought. She's going to suffocate me, tie the dressing gown up like a sack and throw me out of the window.

'At the maternity-ward reception, Michael kept his distance, as if I smelt bad or something. In front of us was a woman in a cream coat that must have been camel hair—soft but sturdy. She was holding a broad-brimmed ochre-coloured hat in one hand and gesticulating over the counter with the other. She was alone. I thought she must be visiting someone, but then I saw the elegant overnight bag at her feet and caught a glimpse of her pregnant belly when she turned round. We exchanged glances; then, very slowly, she began to walk away, putting one foot in front of the other. She was clearly in great pain. She was so beautiful that I caught my breath and then couldn't breathe at all. A couple of nurses pushed a wheelchair under my bum; I lost sight of

Michael altogether. I pulled the dressing gown tighter, and my only question was not, will I ever be able to breathe again or, will I make it home or, will I ever have a camel-hair coat like that? The only question gnawing at my brain was, what language am I going to scream in?

'They stuck a needle in my spine and I can't tell you what happened after that. The next thing I knew, Nina was asleep on my chest. I felt like weeping, but I didn't cry until Michael's father came to pick us up—not Michael, his father. At that point I realized what I ought to have known all along. But what do we really know about what we *ought* to have known? Everything makes sense in retrospect. Of course I believed the father of my child when he said he was divorced; it was what I wanted to believe. I believed he was a *biznissmen*, because my father said he was, and somewhere deep down inside I must also have believed that there's a happy ending for people like me, though I'd never seen any evidence of it—just the opposite.

'Michael seemed to have disappeared without trace, and either his parents didn't want to tell me where he was hiding, or they didn't know themselves. A chameleon—what can you say? *Everyone has some kind of talent*, he'd said, as he laid the limp roses on our shop counter. *My talent is being in the right place at the right time.* That meant that, just now, he wasn't in the wrong place at the wrong time, namely here with me; he was somewhere else, maybe with his wife and son. It wasn't impossible.

'Dark followed light, night followed day, but I couldn't have told you whether it was morning or evening; my time was measured in feeds and nappy changes. I nursed Nina and weighed her, changed her and carried her around, nursed her again, checked on her when she was asleep. One day, the man who was now my daughter's grandfather took me by the arm, signalled to me that I should leave Nina with Michael's mother and drove me to a shop where the entire first floor was filled with prams of all shapes and sizes. He wanted me to choose one. We could barely make ourselves understood to each other, but we pointed at various models and tried some of them out; we even had quite a laugh. I grabbed the handle of a pale-blue pram, like something in a picture book. I walked up and down the aisles with it; the wheels squeaked on the linoleum, and I arched my back like a pole dancer and then drew myself in as if preparing to leap from a human star: arms and legs close, shoulders folded like wings—you can do it. Michael's father stared at me; the places where his eyebrows must once have been shot up. He clapped; I attempted a half-pirouette. My legs didn't quite do what I wanted, but it didn't matter.

'We paid and bundled the pale-blue shell into the back of the car; it took up so much room I had to slide the passenger seat all the way forward. I sat with my knees tucked under my chin and stared through the windscreen at Berlin, as if seeing it for the first time. There was suddenly so much I wanted to do. Eat ice cream, push little Nina along the Spree in her new pram, walk in the Schlossgarten. Maybe, I thought, Nina's grandad could drive us there now and then; Charlottenburg didn't seem too far from Spandau. I would stroll along the gravel paths and look at the crazy topiary. I imagined all kinds of things. I wondered if there were lakes nearby where I could park the pale-blue shell on a sandy shore and doze next to it in the shade. All I needed was a swimsuit… It would soon be spring, and that meant it would soon be summer. On that drive back with the pram, I even thought of taking dance classes again—a place like Berlin must be full of arts centres.

'When we got home, Michael's mother was sitting in the kitchen with a woman who looked as if she'd been crying. There was a child standing next to her. The woman was very slim with blond hair tucked behind her ears; she was cradling a teacup in her hands as if to warm herself. She stared at me like I was a hallucination, a vision. The boy at her side was wearing jeans and a yellow sweatshirt with a picture of some superhero aiming a catapult at me; the freckles on his cheeks were much more pronounced than Michael's.

'I ran into the room where Nina was asleep. I picked her up and jiggled her up and down, and she immediately started to cry.

'"Sssh. Sssh. Sssh. Sssh."

'Maybe I was saying it more to myself than to Nina.

'Nina's... you know... When she was growing inside me, I thought it was me who didn't want her; later, I realized it was the other way round. She was the one who rejected me. She left me out in the cold, cut herself off; it was like she was asking me to get out of her life—not to talk to her or look at her or pass comment on her or anything. It took me a long time to understand that she really meant it. And that there was no point asking myself where I'd gone wrong. What I'd done to hurt her. What I'd done to deserve being treated like that. Sometimes it just happens. Someone rejects you, and you have to accept it, you have to let go. It was painful being with someone who so vehemently didn't want me. I couldn't bear it. Michael abandoned me like a dog. And in her way, Nina did the same.

'When you're one of the losers of your generation, you don't realize at first. You go around yelling this is unfair and that's unfair, because you believe in justice. You believe things will change. That you won't be a loser forever. And that even if you are, you'll at least stop feeling ashamed of yourself.

'Hey, what are you doing? Do you want to miss the exit?'

PIROSMANI'S GIRAFFE

HER MOTHER KISSED HER first on both cheeks, then on the top of her forehead, and Edi was suddenly afraid that in the months since they'd last seen each other and the years since they'd last properly hugged, she might have started to smell different—because of the bleach in her hair or the reek of grease from the fast-food place on the motorway. She waited for her mother to say something—object to her clothes, tell her she was late, but she only ran a hand through Edi's white-blond hair, took her jacket and pulled her out of the hall.

Tatyana was still taking off her boots and Daniel called from the kitchen, 'I hope you're not hungry; there's nothing to eat!' He paused for effect before adding, 'Except quark pancakes from the day before yesterday.'

He was small and pale; his hair was thinning; Edi could see his red scalp showing behind his sticking-out ears. But he was smiling. He would, of course, give no sign of remembering that their last phone call had been a disaster and she'd ended it by hanging up on him. There was nothing threatening about this weedy little man. OK, so he had some crazy views sometimes, but who didn't? He watched the wrong TV channels, but the others were in German. She'd felt like yelling down the phone at him, *What planet do you think you're on?* But how did you say that to a father so consumed with worry he hadn't slept properly for years? So what if he sometimes stammered nonsense down the phone? He'd heard on TV that Arabs had been abducting underage girls, surrounding them in groups and attacking them. Edi should take care, for heaven's sake—maybe Berlin wasn't such a good idea after all.

Now they were together for the first time in a while. They were the same diminutive height, both about five foot three, and they had the same helplessly dangling arms. There was no resentment between them. Why would there be?

Everything was in its place; nothing had changed. The oval table stood against the wall, covered with a cloth; the fridge gave off its low-pitched tinnitus; the television in the corner showed a mute panel discussion. Edi didn't know any of the faces. Somewhere she had read that the constantly running televisions of the East were eternal flames whose purpose was not to entertain the living, but to remind them of what was gone. Her parents' TV was a real gherkin jar; it showed an era pickled in brine, distorted behind murky glass. It must have been here that Daniel heard about the girl allegedly abducted by 'Arabs'. In fact the child had been hiding out at a friend's house because she was afraid to go home, but neither Edi nor the Berlin paper that had reconstructed the case—with GPS data from the girl's phone, medical examination reports and statements from the girl and her friend—could cure her parents of their taste for programmes about rape and retribution.

The embroidered black cat gave Edi a sidelong grin from its rose bush. There was a clatter in the hall and a plump woman with a brush and a newspaper squeezed past them into the kitchen.

'Let me do that, Anna,' Lena said. 'You've no need…'

But the woman began to sweep the kitchen floor with rapid strokes, mumbling a hello without looking up as she manoeuvred dustballs and hair clippings on to the open newspaper. It must be Lena's hair, Edi thought; her father didn't have much left to trim.

She remembered the funeral pyre of newspaper bundles on the landing outside the front door and wondered whether people here used newspapers solely for sweeping up dirt and wrapping up fishbones and vegetable waste—and what impression it made on them when she told them it was her job to write for these papers. They probably couldn't care less.

The woman called Anna scrunched up the newspaper and stuffed it noisily into the bin.

Edi glanced at her mother again. Lena's forehead was tense, her shoulders hunched, her lips two straight lines. She hadn't made up her face yet—there were still a few hours to go before the party started—but Edi could tell from the way she jiggled her foot that she was already nervous. Tatyana marched past her and helped herself to a quark pancake.

'I'm starving. Are these *syrniki* all you have? Where are the cakes and salads?'

'Do you know the joke about the dying Moishe, Tatyanush?' Daniel always spoke in jokes. He had no other means of expression, but explained everything that went on around him with reference to Moishe and his exploits, or the Jews' continued wanderings in the desert—the reason, as he saw it, for everything that ever went wrong in the world.

'Which one? There are so many. A Moishe or a Shmuel dies in every other joke you tell.'

'The one with the latkes.'

'I don't even know what latkes are.'

'Moishe's dying, right?'

'Mhmm.' Tatyana nodded; the raisins from the pancake made rubbery noises between her teeth.

'And he knows he has only days—ach, hours, maybe even minutes—to live. All the family have come, his children, his children's children, the whole *mishpocha*. They're busy divvying up the inheritance while his wife cooks for them all. And Moishe lies there with one of the great-grandchildren playing at his feet, humming to himself, and he smells the latkes frying in the pan, the onions, the hot fat, the—'

'But what are latkes?' Tatyana was on her second pancake.

'Potato cakes. Let me tell the joke. So—Moishe smells these delicious latkes, these potato cakes, and he imagines his wife Sarah—'

'Seriously? She's called Sarah?'

'...his wife Sarah pouring home-made apple sauce over them from the preserving jar, sauce made with fruit picked with her own fair hands, and his eyes grow moist and his mouth starts to water; for the first time since he's been dying, he actually wants something—he wants those latkes! If he could eat just one before he kicks the bucket... So he calls the great-grandson who's playing at his feet and he says, "Ruben"—yes, that's his name, don't interrupt me—"Ruben, go in the kitchen and tell Great-grandma to bring me one of those potato cakes. I have a real craving for one." And the boy runs out and Moishe is already weeping for joy at the thought of his last latkes, but when his great-grandson comes back he's empty-handed. "Great-grandma says the latkes aren't for now," he says. "They're for afterwards!"'

Tatyana forced a laugh. The most embarrassing thing about her father, Edi thought, was the way his nostrils flared with pride when he told a joke, like a teenager who'd been allowed to put his hands under a girl's blouse for the first time.

'So, the good food is for afterwards. It's going straight to the Community Centre—Anna's taking it there. The fridge here is empty. But I made the *syrniki* myself and they're good. Only Lena won't touch them—says she's too nervous. She's been fasting like a zealot for days and blaming it on her nerves.'

The clattering woman called out from the hall—she'd see them later at the Community Centre. The door slammed shut behind her.

'Community? Are we all Jewish this evening?' The sugar had made Tatyana's cheeks red.

'Since when have you been against partying in the Community Centre, you anti-Semite, you?' Daniel didn't wait for an answer. 'By the way, Anna has a job at the hairdresser's where you used to work. Did you two never meet? She ran the café in the University Hospital until management decided to build that massive canteen. I went to have a look the other day—they've done it very nicely, I must say. Long tables, classy lamps hanging from the ceiling. Pretty impressive, and it seats a lot more staff, of course. So Anna's had to close down Babushka's Cake Shop. She's still cooking and baking, of course—before work, after work, at the weekends. She's doing all the catering for the party and we've got about forty people coming, maybe fifty.'

'Unless no one shows up.'

Even when Lena smiled, her mouth never turned up at the corners but formed a straight line level with her earlobes. Her jiggling foot made the glasses on the table clink and for a moment Edi imagined her, rather than Tatyana, pedalling away at a sewing machine. She shook her head to get rid of the image. It was no wonder she mixed up the two women when she remembered practically nothing of her childhood except squares of processed cheese and the occasional night in the nurses' room, and had never been told anything of substance by anybody. All her family told were jokes.

She choked on the water that she had poured greedily down her throat. Still spluttering, she said, 'I'll go and see how Grandfather is.' Grandfather was asleep, she was told. 'Then I'll go out for a bit. Stretch my legs after the drive. Do you need me for anything? Is there anything I can get?'

'Don't be long, I want you to help me decide what to wear this evening,' Lena called after her, but Edi was almost out of the door. Instead of running down the stairs, she ran up to the top floor, unfolded the ladder and opened the hatch to the roof. She ought to bring Tatyana up here sometime, she thought, and as she climbed out she promised herself she would.

The sky was a chocolate biscuit cake, spread out in layers over the surrounding hills. *Leuchtenburg Worlds of Porcelain*, *Nebra's Ark*, *Heavenly Paths*. From here you could see the square tower of Binderburg Castle—at least, Edi thought it was Binderburg. In all those years in Jena, watching the others move away, she'd never once been interested in going there. Fairyland. This was no Florida, or if it was, it wasn't the Florida of white-painted verandas overhung with orange trees; it was the highway motel version—and the motel's permanent residents had all been thrown out by the manager for failing to pay the rent and then got their revenge by trashing the manager's office and smashing all the windows.

Round here, though, windows were still intact, façades had been renovated, new tower blocks had gone up. The yellow and green buildings looked like something out of a colouring book, shaded with coloured pencils in spring-like tones. *Heart roots push up paving stones, / sending coins flying gutterwards*, Edi had read in a collection of poems that an editor at the paper had thrust at her, suggesting she try to write something about it. Something about brick specials in the GDR, a relief element in East German architecture that made the prefabs look as if they were raising their hackles. There was a bit of it here; a narrow, windowless wall on the next building was studded with pyramid tips. Otherwise the estate was face-lifted, unrecognizable, no longer the place where Edi's father had dragged her by her wrist through the yards, her feet catching in the heart roots of the paving stones. She turned round in a circle. The balconies jutted out like empty drawers that someone had forgotten to close. Far below she spotted a low-slung BMW painted with a pattern of bright-pink and silver lozenges. *German Heritage*, it said on the back window in Gothic lettering over a picture of an eagle. The car had been parked outside the tidily fenced-in dustbin area for years. It had always been there, Edi thought, and probably always would be.

She felt a metal disc in her trouser pocket and pulled it out—a twenty-cent piece. She placed it on the tip of her index finger and flicked it into the air. Not a glimmer from the columns of the Brandenburg Gate in the dim light.

Make a wish, Edi told herself.

But what?

Anything! People throw coins in water and make a wish. The yard's your wishing well. Make a wish!

I don't have any wishes.

That's not true.

I don't.

Bullshit, you have way too many.

I don't feel like making a wish. It hurts, wishing for things that never come true.

You're up to your ears in bullshit, do you realize that?

'You're not thinking of jumping, are you?'

Grisha's voice tore Edi from her quarrel with herself. He must have been sitting watching her for a while, out of sight at the edge of the roof; even now he didn't get up, but sat with his arms round his knees, squeezing the soft metal of a Coke can in his hand. For a moment Edi thought of taking it from him and setting fire to it; she would breathe in the smell and know what Tatyana might have smelt all those years ago, pregnant and jolted by the bad roads. What she might have felt. Edi took a few steps towards Grisha.

'Of course I am; you can't not think of jumping when you stand so close to the edge.'

'Some people manage. Some people just take a step back.' He took a swig from the can. The Coke fizzed.

'Ready for the *party*?'

He said the word in the fake Russian accent used by actors playing shady characters in the pre-prime-time soaps. Edi stared out over the countryside, then back at her childhood friend with his child's face. Grisha was a few years older than her, but he looked as if he'd never grown up—the same broad-nosed pimply face, the same centre parting that had once been an embarrassment. Now everyone in Berlin Mitte wore a centre parting, but Grisha couldn't know that—he'd never been to Berlin, or if he had, he'd never told Edi. No, Grisha wouldn't go to Berlin; there was nothing there for him. Edi wasn't sure it was the right place for her either, but Berlin had one clear advantage: no one asked questions about it. Berlin was a sign saying *All Directions*. A runway for people waiting to fuel.

'What's wrong?' Grisha asked. 'You look flustered. It must be the joy of returning home.'

'Utter joy. Takes my breath away.'

Once, a bare eleven or twelve, Edi had run away from home, over the nearby fields and into the hills. When the drumming in her ribs became painful, she'd sat down under a tree and fallen asleep. She was woken by astonished joggers whose fluorescent jackets reflected the light shining through the treetops. What was the matter, they asked. Where was her home? But she couldn't reply; her mouth felt like it was welded shut. Her home was here. That was why she'd run away.

Now her breath was shallow for the same reason: this was her home.

'What's Anna's problem, do you know? Anna from the Community?'

'You have a problem with Community Anna? What's she done?'

'I didn't say I have a problem with her. *She* has something against *me*. First she almost knocked me down, then she said hello like she thought I owed her something.'

'Probably nothing personal. She might just be having a bad day.'

Edi thought of squatting down, so that Grisha didn't look quite so small, like a trussed-up bundle at her feet. But she didn't move.

'Maybe you're not the reason why people are cross or sad or whatever. Maybe they have feelings independently of you.'

'Have you taken up philosophy without telling me? Are you a student?'

'I am, actually. I've enrolled at university. Not in philosophy, but I have health insurance and get a discount on rail travel.'

'Cool for you.'

'Anna's lost her son.'

Edi's ribcage felt like the can that Grisha was crushing in his hand.

'I mean, he's still alive. But she's lost him to the war. He's fighting somewhere in the Donbas. He may even be dead by now. Anything's possible.'

There was a pause. Then Edi said the only thing she could think of. 'What side's he fighting on?'

'No idea.'

'Is he a Vatnik?'

'How should I know?'

'But is he Russian or Ukrainian?'

'I tell you, I don't know.'

Edi wondered whether she'd ever met Anna's son. She pictured a pale, red-headed man with a dull gaze, broad-shouldered in an improvised khaki uniform, rifle in hand, knife and cartridge case at his belt. One of those young men you saw in online portals and whose life stories sometimes—rarely—appeared under the rubric of *Human Interest*.

'That must be the worst, losing a child.'

Edi remembered the evening when Grisha had told her of Rüzgar's abortion. She didn't dare ask if they were still together, but suspected that it hadn't ended happily. Then it occurred to her that Grisha was the only person round here she could tell about Leeza. She took a deep breath, but couldn't get the words out. Maybe later. Grisha had got up at last; he was fiddling with his Coke can. A fine line of dark purple clung to the top of his upper lip; with his long, thick lashes and blotchy red skin he looked as if he were halfway through removing make-up. They hugged at last.

'Everything all right with you?'

'Yup.'

'Everything the same?'

'Yeah.'

'Your mum too?'

'Couldn't be better.'

'Long time no see.'

'Been a while.'

'And you're at university now?'

'It would be more accurate to say I use my student pass to go to the cinema, but it works well.'

'Cinema's amazing.'

'Yeah.'

'Cinema's great.'

They stared out at the countryside, throwing half-sentences at each other, making jokes about *Heavenly Paths* that led everywhere but Jena. Edi ran through a list of people they both knew. Most had moved on—disappeared—and if they'd stayed behind, Grisha had lost touch with them. Another form of disappearance. It was always the same. Edi noticed that Grisha's voice sounded older than she remembered; it was the only thing about him that had changed. If she'd listened to him without looking, she probably wouldn't have recognized him. Maybe that was a good sign. She was about to say goodbye when something stopped her.

'Tell me…' How do you ask when you don't know what you're asking? 'Have you ever… Do you ever talk to your mum—I mean, has she ever told you about coming to Germany and stuff? Do you talk about it? Have you asked her what it was like? For her, I mean?'

Grisha looked amused.

'What's got into you? Has coming home made you all emo?'

'No, no, this is for work. Research. Investigative research.'

'Yeah, right.' Grisha looked out over the tower blocks that lay strewn beneath them.

'My teacher in Ukraine was once beaten up in front of the entire class. I didn't see it happen; my mum was organizing our visa papers and had already taken me out of school. But she told me afterwards that two guys came into the classroom and started to lay into this Larissa Vladimirovna until she couldn't stand up any more. Apparently one of the kids had complained about her at home. His parents were pretty well off. The hitmen they hired called the woman a Communist cunt—she lay there writhing on the floor and they hurled abuse at her. I don't know why my mum told me about it in such detail. And so often. It really got to her.

I think she was trying to explain why it was time to leave. Time for us to leave.'

'Probably.'

'Yes… Larissa Vladimirovna taught me in pretty much every subject; I saw more of her than my own mother. I remember once—I must have been in Year One because we left before I started Year Two—the classroom door opened and these guys in uniform appeared and Larissa Vladimirovna went white in the face. I don't remember her screaming, but she fell forward on to her desk and I remember the noise when her head hit the wood—or maybe I'm only imagining it, but I do know that her glasses flew off her nose, because they landed right at my feet. I always had to sit at the front so the teachers could keep an eye on me. When I got home that day, Mum explained that Larissa Vladimirovna's son had died in the Chechen war—that was why the soldiers had come. And she told me that we were going to move away so that *she'd* never have to have a visit from men in uniform like Larissa Vladimirovna had.'

'Your mum couldn't have known then there'd be a second Chechen war.'

'If it hadn't been Chechnya, it would have been somewhere else. Dagestan, Ossetia, Transnistria, Ukraine. Does it make a difference where you're shot down?'

'But people's sons go anyway, even from here.' Grisha's pupils were very small. He took a few steps towards the edge of the roof and looked out at the grey light over the hills. Then he suddenly changed his tone.

'And you're going out with Tatyana now, or what?'

Edi felt as if she'd had her ears boxed with a saucepan lid. She wanted to laugh, but was too surprised.

'I saw you getting out of the car together. You looked knackered, Edi. Could hardly walk straight.'

Edi wanted to make a joke but wasn't quick enough; she wasn't like her father, who had a quip for every situation.

'Very funny,' she muttered.

Tatyana told me something that has some bearing on my life, but I don't know what. That's what she would have liked to say, but instead she looked down into the yard as if into deep water. Somewhere in the depths lay the coin with the Brandenburg Gate on it; she still hadn't come up with a wish. And it would have been silly to ask Grisha what he wished for.

Maybe she could ask her grandfather; at his age, you must have a pretty clear idea of what you wanted: good health, nice weather, jobs for your children and grandchildren.

She smelt mothballs and lavender as she nudged open the door to Roman Ilyich's room. He was lying on his back like a baked fish with its fins flat at its sides, and seemed to be just waking up. 'Roman Ilyich sleeps a lot lately,' Daniel had called out after her, maybe to stop her, or warn her. She hadn't seen much of her grandfather in the two years since he'd fled to Germany from Horlivka. Her mother had met him in Frankfurt and driven him to Jena, where he'd lain down on the spare-room bed and seemed hardly to have moved since. Certainly, he'd been lying in the same position in the same room when Edi had taken him tea on the day of his arrival; she'd straightened his pillows and he'd told her of his journey, complaining about the Ukrainians who'd refused to let him across the border and extolling—of all people—the Russian president and his supposedly life-saving soup kitchen. Edi pretended not to hear a word, and it suited her very well when, not long afterwards, Roman Ilyich began to say that his hearing aid didn't work on the phone.

Now he made a sound like someone waking from a nightmare.

'I'm sorry, Grandad,' Edi whispered, 'I'm sorry. I didn't want to...'

Roman Ilyich smiled and groped for his glasses on the yellowish-white surface next to the bed—not, Edi knew, a bedside table, but a mini washing machine that hadn't been used for years. It was a mystery to her why they hadn't got rid of the ugly thing ages ago and bought the old man a decent piece of furniture.

He blinked behind his thick lenses; his smile began to freeze.

'Editochka! What's that on your head?'

'That? That's hair.'

'I see. Hair.' His voice was gravelly. He sat up. 'Let's have a look at you.' He turned his eyes on her, but seemed distracted, as if there were someone else in the room, visible only to him, someone he was asking for understanding or forgiveness.

'And why have you stopped eating? Is there a new law against it? Did you know they almost starved me? Twice in my life they almost starved me, once at the beginning and once at the end. I'll never understand why you youngsters choose to be so skinny. I worry that you might fly away—and what would I do then? What would I do without you, eh?'

He looked like a stickman himself, a stickman in a pair of baggy paper trousers fastened to him with paper tabs.

'How's Mum?'

'I was going to ask you that.' They smiled at each other.

If nothing else, Edi thought, she'd inherited her fleshy earlobes from him. Maybe she'd look like him in her old age; it was a more attractive legacy than the stories of near-starvation and the flat gathering dust in a region that would probably never be inhabitable again in her lifetime.

'I think Lena's nervous.'

'I think she's happy.'

'Let's make sure she is. Are you writing anything interesting at the moment?'

Edi nodded warily. 'An article on Florida,' she said, before Roman Ilyich could launch into the next chapter of his memoirs.

'Florida? That's nice. What do they have there then?'

'Alligators.'

Her grandfather heaved his stickman legs off the mattress, took a sip of limescaly water from the glass on the washing machine, exhaled, as if it were the first drink of his life, and slid his feet into a pair of floral slippers.

'Alligators, eh? We have them here, too, you know. A real terrarium tribe, your mum's friends.'

'I'll go and see how she's getting on and you take your time waking up. Come and sit with us in the kitchen when you're ready—or shall I bring you something?'

Her grandfather seemed to appeal to the invisible person again.

'Do you have everything you need?'

Roman Ilyich looked at his granddaughter in confusion.

'Oh yes, I have more than I need. Stay and we can share it if you like? Why don't you just stay here? It's no less exciting than Florida, I assure you. We have alligators too. We have everything you want.'

Edi hadn't seen her mother in underwear for a long time; she wasn't prepared for it and tried to keep her eyes on the pile of clothes on the chair.

'This… or this?' Lena held up a black dress with transparent sleeves and an emerald-green trouser suit. 'Or maybe…' She showed Edi skirts, blouses, boleros; she flung open the wardrobe doors; she threw trousers on to the bed where Edi was sitting cross-legged. Edi gave no advice, but waited for her mother to make up her own mind—she would nod and give her the thumbs-up when she did.

Anna had cut her hair into a pageboy and dyed it blond. It looked peculiar, as if Lena were sixteen. Her movements and gestures, too, were those of a young girl; only the crow's feet around her eyes didn't quite fit the picture. She prattled away and then, in the same prattling tone, she asked Edi about the break-in and whether it was normal practice in Berlin to break down a door and not take anything? And what about if you had your flat broken into? Was it normal to do nothing—not to report the break-in, but to get on with your life, all calm and collected? Was that *something German* or was it *a Berlin thing*, this making light of everything and not letting stuff get to you?

She still seemed angry that the burglars hadn't considered anything Edi possessed valuable enough to steal. 'Not even the watch I gave you for passing your exams? It was your grandmother's, you know.' Lena pulled on a pair of tights that crackled with static as she rolled them over her legs. The sight of her thighs, hipbones, breasts was too much for Edi; she screwed up her eyes and ran her hands over her face. The wormy blue veins behind Lena's knees appeared on her closed eyelids. Seeing her mother's body meant that her mother was a human being; it meant she was alive and growing old and would one day die, and *that*—especially the last bit about dying—was out of the question. The folds in the curtains cast a shadow on the wall like a heart-rate curve.

'Mum, there's something I have to tell you. Tatyana's ill. She's been in hospital, on the neurology ward. That's why it took so long to get hold of her.'

Everything went quiet; only the mattress beneath her creaked softly. Lena stared at her. Edi told her what little she knew: suspected MS, suspected NMOSD, CT, MRI, X, Y, Z, no clear prognosis.

'She doesn't want anyone to know, especially Nina—crazy, eh?' Edi explained that she'd promised Tatyana she'd keep her secret, but that she felt her best friend ought to know. 'You've been through so much together, haven't you?' (*Come on now, say something. Say something meaningful for once.*)

Lena went back to working the treadle; her round, nylon-covered knee jiggled up and down, the surface lumpy and dimpled, as if there were little pockets of air under the skin. 'I'm not just her best friend, I'm a doctor, she has to tell me! I specialized in neurology for a while, I might be able to help.'

In your past life you were a doctor, Edi thought. Now you're a nurse. And what's all this about neurology?

Lena threw on a pair of jogging trousers and a T-shirt, but Edi was at the door before she could run out. 'No, don't… She has to tell you herself. Please! I promised. And what about Nina? I think *she* ought to be informed. I know she's got her own diagnosis to worry about, but she's still an adult. It's not right that Tatyana was in hospital all by herself and I was the only one who visited her. I hardly know the woman. I didn't even know what flowers she likes.'

Lena looked at Edi, as if seeing her for the first time since kissing her in the hall when she arrived. She didn't often look at her like that. The last time had been years ago, when she'd visited Edi in Berlin for a weekend. They'd wandered the streets around Clärchen's Ballroom together and laughed at the designer clothes in the shop windows—until Lena had spotted the words SOLDIERS ARE MURDERERS sprayed on the wall of a squat. She'd kept walking, but she folded her arms in front of her chest and said she thought it was wrong to say that—after all, someone had to defend them, and OK, killing wasn't right, but she personally would protect her family with a gun if she had to; she was prepared to kill for her daughter if it came to it. She'd do anything. Anything.

And Edi—because she couldn't think of anything better to say, or because she wanted to provoke her mother, or hurt her—had said, 'I don't believe you.'

They'd spent the next two days arguing. Edi's flat was small and Lena had refused to go out again; she'd walked from the kitchen to the sitting room as if pulled on a string, vacuumed dramatically, then walked back and scrubbed the fridge shelves several times over. Edi had been afraid that, of the whole visit, this was the image that would stay with her.

'An adult… An adult… If Tatyana doesn't tell me today, I'll ask her tomorrow.'

'Yes, fine. But what about Nina? She lives round here. Can't we give her a call?'

'You know how it is when we mothers phone you girls. Nothing but aggro—and that's assuming you pick up. I asked Nina to the party. She made it quite clear she didn't want anything to do with any of us. Let's talk about something else.' Lena turned back to the heap of clothes on the bed. 'What are you working on at the moment?'

Not knowing how to reply, Edi held the emerald-green trouser suit up to her mother. She told her it went well with her glamorous hair—and her grey eyes, of course—and Lena spun round with it in front of the mirror and pushed gold studs into her earlobes. 'They were your grandmother's. I wish you could have met her.' Lena had mentioned her mother a lot lately—as a blank, as someone who should have been there and wasn't.

Now she asked again what Edi was writing about and, like the day when Lena had made the remark about the graffiti, something tightened in Edi's chest and—not as part of any plan, but simply because she couldn't bear the way their conversations broke off just as they were getting interesting—she said, 'About the Donbas. I'm planning to travel there and write about the Russian mercenaries. I'm in touch with an NGO.'

Lena's shriek must have been heard all over the flat. She seemed, Edi thought, to turn transparent; then she wheeled round and stared at Edi as if she couldn't believe the person in front of her was her daughter.

'You will not do that.' She stressed every word, driving in the syllables as if with a hammer, then repeated the sentence, clearly struggling to keep her voice down. 'I'd sooner kill you myself. If you're thinking of inflicting violence on yourself, then let me know and I'll put you out of your misery. Understood?'

This was the Lena Edi knew. It was, at least, the Lena she remembered. She found it so much easier to deal with an angry woman than with the woman who'd kissed her on the forehead in the hall and then sat at the kitchen table trembling like a rabbit. Lena had a powerful voice with remarkable shifts in pitch, up and down.

Edi ratcheted things up a notch. 'Yes, well, to be honest, I haven't decided yet. Maybe Ukraine, maybe Chechnya. It's all connected anyway. Perestroika, the collapse of the Soviet Union, the wars that followed. I have to understand all that, I'm a journalist, I have to go where the action is.'

'You're bored, aren't you, craving adventure? Just look at yourself—the way you look, you wouldn't make it out of the door unscathed over there. Do you want to be beaten to death in the middle of the street with a stone? Because if that's what you're after I could do it for you here and save you the travel costs.'

'I—' Edi would have liked to go on, but she couldn't; Lena had started to yell, loudly, frantically. Words spilt out of her, she'd switched to Russian, Edi couldn't keep up. Daniel came running in and tried to put his arms round Lena, but she spat curses at him—Edi couldn't work out why. Lena waved her arms around wildly, as if she were trying to cast out evil spirits; then she sat down on the bed, stared grey-faced and silent at the emerald-green trouser suit in her hands, sneezed several times, very quietly, like a child, and burst into tears.

Edi wanted to get out. On to the roof or into the car and away—not back to Berlin, but right away, over the ocean. Somewhere without internet, where no one could track her. But instead of shunting Daniel aside, running down the passage, grabbing her bag and pushing open the door without glancing back—door after door after door after door—she looked into his sheepish face and asked him to leave. He obeyed without a murmur, without having to be coaxed. And Edi knelt down on the floor beside her mother.

'I'm sorry, Mum.'

Lena didn't look up.

'I'm sorry, I didn't want to scare you. I don't know why I say stuff like that, I don't really know what I'm doing… The thing is, I can't answer these questions about what I do and what I'm working on and what good my life is. I'm not like all of you; I don't have a nice self-explanatory job. Every two months I'm transferred to a different department and given assignments no one else wants—writing a newsletter or going to the zoo because there's a new baby penguin. I hate writing about things like that. I just waffle. You shouldn't take me so seriously.'

Lena made a sound that might have been a snarl, but Edi knew she was laughing disparagingly.

'That's just it. You don't care. Penguins, the war in Ukraine—it's all the same to you, it's all just names, places. Chechnya, the Donbas, the zoo. Whatever's happening, it's not happening to you. It's other people's lives and you think you can make fun of them.' She took a very long breath in, and as she breathed out she clasped Edi's head in her hands. 'Do you think that just for today you could act like a normal person?' she said. Then she stood up and left the room.

Edi climbed on to the ridiculously soft, bouncy mattress and pulled in her arms and legs. She could suddenly feel the drive in her, every mile, as if she'd walked all the way. The service-station burger and all Tatyana's stories rose in her gorge. She smelt something—not lilac or mothballs; something burnt and sulphurous—and she felt as if she'd never be able to get up again; her eyelashes were glued together, and a quiet, heavy hand switched off the light inside her head.

Edi dreamt she was standing in the middle of a housing estate. She'd never been here before, but she knew that over there, behind the houses with roofs like open storks' beaks, was the river. A landscape of allotments stretched out before her like sagging squares of cloth; in her allotment a pile of sawdust loomed, taller than her, taller than the shack she had stepped out of. The hazelnut trees had been spared; they craned their bare tops into the washed-out sky, but the oaks had been felled and chopped up for firewood; now they were getting their own back and setting themselves on fire. Edi sucked in the smell.

Her felt boots sank into the snow as she tried to walk. She leant forward as if struggling against a strong wind, stretched her arms out into the cold, damp air, pulled on an invisible rope, pulled herself along as if out of a swamp, stopped in front of the blazing pile of sawdust and stared at the billowing smoke.

Then she threw herself on to the pile, kicking and thrashing, as if she were fighting waves, then an animal, then herself. She flailed about, felt the fire singe her trousers, slapped her arms and legs and swam and swam until all the sawdust was flat, spilling out over the allotment like a lake; the ground looked as if it were growing a coarse-haired coat. She pulled herself up, panting rather than breathing. The allotments around her lay under deep snow, white and strangely peaceful—were they asleep? Was everyone asleep, while the ground throbbed beneath her feet? It gave a sound like a stifled groan.

When Edi opened her eyes, it was still light; she had no idea where she was or how long she'd been asleep. She started up and ran into the hall. Her parents and grandfather were on their way out. They looked elegant; her mother had looped her arm through her father's. They glanced back at her; Edi had trouble reading the expressions on their faces. She gestured to them that she would follow.

'I'll just change my shirt, I'm all sweaty, I won't be a second.'

The more daring of the children, most of them older than Edi, stood outside the entrance to the tower block, smoking. All the others sat in the big room like good boys and girls or allowed themselves to be herded around. Parents sang the praises of their particularly successful offspring:

'...skipped a year at school!'

'...just started studying medicine!'

'...spends every spare moment playing the piano. I call him whenever I have a headache and he comes round and plays all evening, just for me. It's wonderful!'

Edi noticed that she was looking for Grisha in the crowd, although she knew he hadn't been invited and that, even if he had, he'd rather watch series with his mum, stroke the performing cat or play video games in his cubbyhole of a bedroom. She was glad she hadn't inflicted all this on Leeza.

Anna pushed past Edi with a tray of brimming glasses of sparkling wine; she was wearing an apricot-coloured jumper glittering with sequins, but she had the same weary look she'd had that afternoon, and Edi decided that later, when the party had got going and it was easier to talk, she would ask her about her son. It must somehow be possible to have a proper conversation in this place. It must be possible to do more than exchange clichés.

A small, noisy group at the buffet was discussing the correct way to make *forshmak* and arguing about the quality of the stuffed chicken neck.

'Of course you use green apples, what else?'

'The cook forgot to chop the chicken skin into the paste, that's why it doesn't taste of anything.'

Then they got down to basics. 'No, the reason it doesn't taste of anything is that nothing ever tastes of anything in Germany!'

'Yes, but nothing grows here either except potatoes and cabbages; everything else has to be imported!'

'The other day in the supermarket I came across a packet of *salo*, and what do you think it said on the label? *Italian Speciality!* I was so furious I almost bit the shelf—since when is *salo* an Italian speciality?'

'What do you want them to write? *Salo, a Ukrainian national dish*?'

'Yes!'

'No one would buy it then. People associate Italy with la dolce vita; Ukraine they associate with Chernobyl.'

'That's presuming they know Chernobyl's in Ukraine, which is not necessarily the case.'

'Oh come on, it's not that bad!'

'I tell you, it is.'

Edi hurried past before they could rope her in.

The large room and the kitchen had filled rapidly; the guests had arrived on time (before Edi) and were scurrying back and forth with bowls and bottles; someone called out in a loud voice, asking for help opening a big bottle of Crimean champagne. 'Like liquid gold!' Edi reached out for the bottle, but a hand shooed her away. 'This is a man's job.'

She looked around, hoping to make herself of use somewhere, but no one showed any sign of needing her. Her parents seemed elated. Daniel's suit was a little too tight for him—when had her dad started getting a belly? Edi's fingers itched to pull his collar straight. Lena beamed in her emerald-green trouser suit, smiling in all directions, nodding and nodding, distributing hugs and kisses. 'What? That's for me? You shouldn't have!… Gosh, no, it's not a… Just what I've been wanting…'

Flouncy curtains, spotless white tablecloths phosphorescing like glow-worms in the dimly lit room, plates and glasses for four, five, six courses—hors d'oeuvres, soup, cold first course, hot first course, main course, dessert and then back to the beginning. Soon people would get up, say nice things, raise their glasses. People would sing and strum at the piano; there was even an old guitar in the stand on the small stage. The only thing there wouldn't be was comedy; Lena had been quite clear about that. 'I want to dance with you!' Edi had heard her shout. 'Music only! No nonsense, no silly skits, no politics!'

Edi hadn't prepared a speech and didn't have a present with her. Her father had called in the summer and suggested they give Lena a cruise for her birthday, something they could do together, *the three of us, as a family*—only a few days, a whole week was too expensive. Edi said over her dead body. Daniel said she'd make her mother very happy. Edi said cruise ships polluted the oceans and were helping to destroy the world with their selfish swank; if it were up to her, those boats would be sunk in dock while their investors popped champagne corks on board. Daniel said that for once this wasn't about what Edi thought; it was about her mother, who deserved a lavish gift for her big day. The upshot was that Edi was empty-handed at her mother's party, desperate for occupation.

Uncle Valeri put her in a headlock. He wasn't a proper uncle, but insisted on being treated as one of the family—as, in a way, did everyone here, with their powerful hugs and genial clichés. Some may even have been genuine relatives or in-laws; certainly, they all shared a family resemblance when they delivered their presents and good wishes, and they all laughed in the same places at things that were a mystery to Edi.

Daniel had once tried to explain to her that telling jokes had been easier in the past, when everyone had the same canon and there was only one version of the world. 'You didn't even have to tell the jokes; you could just say, "Joke twenty-three to twenty-five," and everyone knew the score and laughed.' Edi had stared at him in bewilderment; she knew it was supposed to be a joke, but she didn't get it.

Uncle Valeri released her from the headlock and thrust his heaped plate into her face. 'Look, Edita, chopped *pelmeni*, circumcised *pelmeni*. Ever see such a thing? Very kosher!' The buttons of his shirt moved all the time, as if little animals were burrowing underneath. 'Open wide.' He circled his fork in front of her face.

'No, thanks, they've got meat in them.' Edi pushed him away as best she could.

'Oh, great.' He laughed and moved closer again. 'The know-it-alls from Berlin are here. I ask you. These know-it-alls. Shall I tell you how it was in our day? You said thank you for whatever was put in front of you, and you kept your opinions in your handkerchief.'

He lowered his fork. Edi couldn't retaliate in Russian, so she had to satisfy herself with an impatient glare. The know-it-all had no answer and the uncle noticed.

'So tell me, what's it like in Berlin? Fancy car? Big apartment? *Biznissmeni* lavishing you with jewels? Manage to keep away from the riff-raff stranded there? Want us to come and pick you up? We'll come! With full artillery! We miss you! You should see the look on your mother's face when she talks about you. Pitiful. You're her only child. That's the trouble with not having enough progeny. You're off before we know it.'

Edi didn't know much about Valeri, only that he was a teacher in a secondary school—PE and another subject. She'd heard he was good at his job, let the kids run around outside and stuck up for them to their furious parents when they didn't have the marks to move up at the end of the year. But that was only what she'd heard. What she saw was that he'd had one over the eight this evening, although they were only on starters.

'Are you well? I mean, are you happy?'

Edi opened her mouth and closed it again. Valeri went on talking, chewing noisily in between words.

'Berlin, Berlin! You know what they say where we come from: *Don't come home if you drown*. Either you make it in the big city or you don't. But don't come back and moan if you can't cope. That's not how it works. Tell me, Editush, tell me really—what good is it to you, being up there with that filthy *mishpocha* when your parents are down here on their own? You got a man up there? What kind of a man? Or is it your work that's so interesting? Do they pay you that well? Or don't you like us? Is that it? Do we smell? Why aren't you down here with us, somewhere nearby, where we can look after you and you can look after us? We don't get any healthier as time goes on, and all the young people are moving away, it's not right, do you think it's right?' He popped another forkful of *pelmeni* in his mouth and chewed. He was serious. 'I don't think it's right. Imagine something happened to your parents, imagine they had an accident. How long would it take you to get here from that Berlin of yours? They'd kick the bucket before you could hit the motorway.'

Edi shook her head as if to throw off a load of rubble that had been dumped on her. Nothing would happen to her parents. Nothing. What could go wrong? They were strong, they had each other. As for her grandfather, he'd almost starved or been killed so often—Earth would leave its orbit before he bailed out on them. No, there'd be no emergencies, only the permanent emergency of emotional blackmail, which people here seemed to consider part of polite conversation.

'And you?'

'What about me?'

'Are you happy?'

The muscles of his face relaxed; only the slug-like bags under his eyes trembled slightly, and for a moment Edi almost liked him. His high forehead, his moles, the stray stubble on his round cheeks, his helpless outstretched arms, his splayed fingers sifting the light that fell from the lamps on to the small dance floor. The piece of *pelmeni* on his fork wobbled, but he soon recovered.

'Happy... I don't know. But I don't think we smell. I think we deserve as much respect as anyone. I don't think we should be left behind.'

Edi lowered her head and fiddled with the tablecloth, as if she were cleaning a pair of glasses.

'*Sometimes you come to an edge that just breaks off.*' She looked up again; the slugs under his eyes twitched.

'What's that?'

'Something I read in a book.'

'Say it again.'

'*Sometimes you come to an edge that just breaks off.*'

'The know-it-all again. What book is this?'

'About the war in the Donbas.' She knew, even as she said it, that it was a mistake.

'Which side?' The words shot out of him.

'What do you mean, *which side*?' Edi was playing for time. But what was the point? The battle was already lost.

'Which side's the hero on? Which side's the author on?'

Edi bit the flesh inside her cheek, pretending to think.

'Not sure. It isn't clear. Neither, probably.'

'Oh no. That's not possible.'

'Why not?'

'Because it isn't. You can't live without taking sides and you can't write without taking sides. The author of your book will know that. If he's any good.' Valeri wrinkled his nose. 'Is he from over there or is he one of those democrats from the West who have no idea what they're on about?'

'He's from there,' Edi mumbled into her shirt collar.

'Aha. Then he knows. And next time you'll know too: *you have to take sides*. Otherwise what you write is mush, drivel.'

Drunk adults sound like teenagers parroting their parents' words, Edi thought. They use other people's opinions until they become their own. Adults are children who think they know everything better.

'You know what side you're on, don't you? You know what blood flows in your veins?'

Edi breathed. It was all she could do. Breathe. Say the alphabet backwards, count the moles on Valeri's face.

'The same as in mine,' he said, then added, 'We're of the same blood.'

Edi wanted to say, *Let's not open our veins to check*, but she didn't have the words in Russian.

She couldn't go forwards or backwards, but she saw a strange movement outside the window, partly concealed by Valeri's bulk. The Jewish Community Centre was on the second floor of the tower block, so it could only be the treetops swaying in the wind, but what she saw looked more like part of an animal, maybe sticking-up ears, rabbit's ears making a victory sign, waving at her. Edi blinked. She hadn't drunk a thing and it was a while since her last joint. She squeezed her eyes till they hurt, squeezed them until crystals of light flew at her; then she peeled the lids apart and saw a slanting oval eye, about half the size of her face. The eyeball was very white and the pupil very black; it looked at her through the closed window, questioning, almost alarmed. It had no eyelashes.

As a child Edi had loved dinosaurs. She'd had a dinosaur rug on her floor that she would drag herself across on her belly, going from a creature with long claws to another with a spiky crest, trying to memorize every detail. Sometimes, lying outside on the grass gazing up at the clouds, she would think she spotted a Tyrannosaurus rex or a pterodactyl, and, realizing how small she was on the scale of things, she would feel so freaked out that she'd have to run home and read comics all afternoon to calm herself down. But this animal outside the window was no dinosaur; its gaze was too soft and the second floor was too low for a brachiosaurus. It could be bending down to her, of course—but even on her childhood rug the dinosaurs hadn't had bunny ears.

Edi left Uncle Valeri and went to the window. The skin around the animal's eye was slightly grey, as though smeared with soot or charcoal. The eye vanished and two short horns came into view, a hard V of woody stubs between little pointy white ears. Edi pushed down the handle of the window; the creature didn't seem startled, only swayed its head languidly. Edi saw more of the white fur with black spots, but before she could open the window completely, someone behind her started to whoop and soon others were joining in; the room filled with noise. Edi held her breath and turned round. A woman was walking through with an accordion, followed by several more women, all singing as if bunches of flowers were sprouting from their bosoms. The guests clapped and whistled; they, too, turned to look. Edi spotted Tatyana in the crowd. Her red hair was elaborately piled up on top of her head; she was wearing something dark. Edi hadn't seen her since they'd arrived and she began to move towards her, but Tatyana stared past her; she stared right through her into the room of people, grabbed a plate and set off in the opposite direction.

Edi felt stung. She looked out of the window again, but the white giraffe had gone. Only the edges and lines of the tower blocks were visible in the dusk, separated by patches of grass. On one of these a small group of youths had gathered; smoke rose from a fire that was out of sight behind them. Above all this, the sky was a blur of blues and purples, like a sloppy tie-dye.

Edi leant out over the windowsill; she could smell the chill of the air, but not a whiff of smoke. She thought of Tatyana turning her face away, averting her eyes like they were strangers. The little group huddled closer together; more smoke rose, but Edi couldn't see what they were burning. Maybe those bundles of newspapers.

A few tinkling notes sounded; someone was warming up at the piano. The round tables had filled up; full plates were doing the rounds. A first toast: 'To Lena! They say youth is a flaw that passes. May that flaw linger on and may we all look as young as you, Lenochka, no matter how much time goes by. To you!'

A second toast: 'May our misfortune be as great as the number of drops we leave in our glasses!'

Toast number three: 'Do you know about the admirer who gave his beloved three cinema tickets? "Why three?" she asked in astonishment. "Well," he said, "one for your father, one for your mother and one for your brother. To get them out of the house." Let us drink to inspired presents!'

Edi was unsure whether to raise her glass. It didn't seem to matter; no one was paying her any attention. She wasn't expected to join in—that much she had understood. It was enough for her to be there. You're not a trophy daughter, Edi told herself. No one's going to show you off or pass you around. Relax.

She peered at the window again, hoping for another glimpse of the lashless eye.

At one of the tables Edi spotted her grandfather. His head was propped in his hand, as if it might fall off at any moment, but he looked cheerful enough, his shirt clean, his trousers ironed, his feet jiggling up and down. A crystal glass stood in front of him, brimming with fizz. Edi pulled up a chair.

'You all right, Grandad? Can I get you anything?'

'Deda. You used to call me Deda.'

'Deda.'

He beamed at her. 'I must admit, it was all my doing. The first time I came to see you in the flat in Dnipropetrovsk I sat next to your cot and said, "Say Deda, say Deda, say Deda," until you did. You were an obedient child. Still are. A good girl.'

Edi felt a rasping in her throat; she reached for the full glass and took a great gulp as if it were water, then choked and gasped, spluttering sparkling wine all over her grandfather's freshly pressed trousers. He slowly raised a hand and patted her with little muffled movements on the part of her back he could reach from where he was sitting.

'Goodness, you coughed when you were a baby. Coughed and coughed. I wasn't there, but I heard it over the phone when Lena rang before she took you to hospital. You weren't yet a year old. "She's choking, Dad, I don't know what to do," and then the two of you vanished into intensive care, and for days all I had was the occasional phone call from Daniel, telling me you were still alive—that was as much as I knew. Goodness, we worried about you.'

Edi tried to ignore the lingering urge to cough and the sting of alcohol in her nose. She'd expected the Crimean champagne to get her grandfather talking about the Donbas: how cold and damp the rooms had been; how their own people had shut off the gas in the middle of winter; how the Russians had fed them while the rest of the world watched them starve—was still watching, in fact; even three years into the war, the world was still gawping and shrugging. Grandfather liked to tell how he'd ripped up his Ukrainian passport after arriving in Germany, and Edi always wondered whether it was as easy as he made it sound to tear a rubberized booklet to pieces. Maybe it was. Anything was possible. This story, though, was new to Edi. It wasn't one of Grandfather's old chestnuts; these were things she'd never heard before.

'Even when you were out of the clinic, your mother carried you around all the time—said you'd choke if you were lying down. Imagine, she didn't put you in your cot; she walked up and down with you in her arms, holding your little head; she held you tight, didn't want to let you go. Didn't want to lose you. And when it was clear you'd pull through, I said to Lena, "This means our little girl will survive everything. She's tough; no one can hurt her. Children who dodge death so early in life will still be dodging it when they're a hundred; you'll never have to worry about her again, you can send her into the world now." She still worries about you, of course, but that's mothers for you—you have to forgive her. She's worn out. It's hard, you know. Just don't listen when she says things that sound stupid to you. That's something you have to learn when you grow up: not to take things to heart.'

Edi felt a quivering inside her, like the surface of a lake before a storm. She saw her mother as a young woman—the woman she knew from photos—a baby pressed to her chest, the little head cupped in her hand like an apple; she saw her pacing the room, hushing the baby. *Sssh. Sssh. Sssh.* Edi had known nothing of this illness; she'd had no idea her mother had carried her around till she was sure she wouldn't *lose her*. What was this illness she'd had? Why had no one ever told her about it? Why did no one speak to her?

She excused herself, telling her grandfather she was going to get something to eat. He kissed the back of her hand and patted it. She staggered off, as if her feet were tangled in the tablecloth.

Tatyana's bronzy-red head caught her eye; she was smiling nervously with a hint of panic in her eyes, and Edi wondered what would happen if she had a seizure now and keeled over in front of all the guests. What if she had more of those spasms, started hyperventilating, lost her sight completely? How many here knew she was already almost blind in one eye? How many would be able to help in an emergency? A few had medical training, but no one in the room was sober. Edi had done a first-aid course for her driving test, but all she could remember was that you mustn't pull a motorbike helmet off someone with a broken neck. Come to think of it, Tatyana looked a little like someone who'd been in a road accident; she had the fixed gaze of a person staring at disaster. Suddenly it hit Edi like a wave: Nina. Tatyana was searching the crowd for her daughter. That was why she was so absent and distracted—she'd been hoping to find Nina here.

Edi hadn't seen Nina for years. She didn't know where she lived, but she decided to seek her out the next day and shake her until she came to her senses.

Edi sat down next to Tatyana. She topped up Tatyana, herself and everyone else at the table; some of the guests raised their glasses to her—'Only alcoholics drink without toasts!' A lot of them looked as if they'd worn expressions of suspicion for so long they'd become ingrained in their faces. They talked about work and holidays and what they watched on TV. When Edi joined them, they were discussing a series in which an ordinary teacher from Kyiv was elected president because of his honesty, perseverance and selflessness. Once he'd reached this position of responsibility, things began to get complicated for the young man—politics being politics, and apparently always complicated—but he rose to the challenge, as he rose to every challenge, because he was pure of heart, and the good guys prevailed and you could tell the villains by their ill-fitting suits and loutish behaviour. Everyone was wondering how the next season would end.

'And I know him!' Tatyana shouted. 'The lead actor. I actually met him! You won't believe it, but I used to sell him whisky in Kryvyi Rih!'

There were loud cheers and laughter; more details were demanded.

'He was captain of the local Funny and Inventive team! He bought whisky from me, White Label, an unusual choice—I still remember the exact brand! He always wore polo-neck jumpers, just like he wears on TV, and he talked to me about pedalos and invited me for a walk in the park. I made eyes at him for a while, but it didn't come to anything. He was very modest even then, a nice ordinary guy. Now he's a star. A TV president.'

'You should have made bigger eyes at him, Tatyana!'

'And gone for that walk in the park. You'd be a TV first lady!'

'Wouldn't be pedaloing on your own now.'

'Ah well, you're a soloist, it's the fashion.'

'Have you given up looking?'

'Or is there somebody? Do you have someone?'

Tatyana's face didn't budge; her painted mask didn't shift a millimetre. She seemed to stiffen, unsmiling, for a moment, and in that instant Edi called out, 'Yes! She has me!'

Knives, forks and glasses froze in the air; then everyone relaxed and laughed and patted Edi's cheeks. 'What a love! Isn't she sweet?' Tatyana didn't look at her; she reached for her glass and drank in hasty gulps, pretending to watch the crowd of people dancing by the piano, hips waggling, fists pumping the air, voices blaring the words.

'No, seriously,' Edi said.

Not this time. This time she wouldn't let them treat her like a child just because she had a turned-up nose and spoke funny Russian.

'She has me. What is there to laugh at?'

'But Editochka, a friend isn't the same as a man.'

'Oh, really. Why not?' Edi was talking too loudly, but she didn't care.

'Because a man keeps the mattress warm beside you no matter what, while friends come and go.'

'You're young. One day you'll understand.'

Tatyana was still staring at the people dancing. She was quite pale; she was probably in pain and didn't want to let it show.

'Tatyana? Will you dance with me?' Edi looked at her, daring her. 'Come on, come with me. Let's get out of here. Let's leave. We don't have to stay here. You don't have to listen to all this.'

Tatyana's eyes were like needles sewing her lips shut; Edi said nothing more, but a whisper in her head kept it up: I'll drive you into the hills, to the *Heavenly Paths*; we'll look down over the valley and get off our faces on weed. I have a rug in the boot; we can sleep in the car and when the sun rises we'll go and look for Nina, or I will. Or we'll just drive away—to the beach, the ocean, somewhere where it's warm in October. So much is possible if we leave this party...

Tatyana touched the woman next to her on the back of her neck and whispered in her ear; the two of them disappeared in the direction of the hall, handbags pressed to their bellies. Those left at the table tucked into chicken in aspic. No one spoke. Edi sat there, listening to the buzz in her chest; she imagined a swarm of mosquitos trying to break through her skin and chuckled soundlessly to herself, briefly amused. She seemed to have turned into a character in a Soviet film; everything was following the plot of that famous New Year's Eve comedy: a misguided courtship, too much eating and drinking, disgraceful behaviour, howls of self-pity. Edi helped herself to more wine and gulped at it.

Then she headed for the table where her parents and a few others were sitting. She found them in a state of excitement; someone shouted that Allan Chumak, the great national healer, was dead. They read aloud from their phones: the doctor, philosopher and author of the best-selling *For Those Who Believe in Miracles* had died today, on 9th October 2017, surrounded by his family. Eighty-three years old. Lena and Daniel's friends all spoke at once.

'I thought miracle healers lived forever.'

'They don't even say what he died of. Why didn't he heal himself?'

'Raked it in, didn't he, with his mass hypnosis!'

'No, no, he raked it in with *our* mass *psychosis*!'

'Do you remember he used to recommend putting a photo of him on the place that hurt? I actually did that. A classic case of *kiss my arse*.'

Salted gherkins and buttered caraway bread were passed around. Lena beamed as Edi approached.

'Come here, my Chechen girl, come and sit with us!'

Edi allowed herself to be hugged and pulled on to a chair. She wanted to ask something, but the sight of her mother's happy, tipsy face turned her thoughts to mush. She poured herself some hard liquor and knocked it back. Without a toast.

'This girl here wants to go to Chechnya. What do you say to that, my dears?'

There were sounds of general outrage. Someone laughed.

'What do you want to do that for?' a friend of Lena asked. 'Got a yen for wild animals?' Someone else burst out laughing.

'Seriously, Edita, what do you want to go there for? Aren't the savages in Berlin enough for you? Do women actually dare go out on the streets there these days?'

'Maybe she wants to go back to her origins.' Lena's voice sounded too high.

'What do you mean, *her origins*?'

'They're all brutes there. Natives!'

'Yes, they do act as if they came down in the last shower. But Edita's not like that!'

'No,' Daniel agreed, 'but she's still wet behind the ears, you know.'

The others nodded; some sighed agreement.

'She's young for twenty-five, doesn't know what she wants yet. We were proper people at that age, adults with responsibilities and children of our own, but the kids here need spoon-feeding till they're forty. She still gets childhood allowance. Do you know this one? A rabbi, an Orthodox priest and a whatchamacallit—parson, vicar—are debating when human life begins. The Orthodox priest says, "The moment the egg's fertilized." The vicar disagrees. "That's a bit strict," he says. "I'd say from birth." But the rabbi waves them both aside. "Oh, come on!" he says, "Human life begins when the kids are out of the house!"' Daniel waited for the laughs. Then he gave a sigh and ran a hand through Edita's hair as if to pull her out of the earth like a carrot. 'This one left home years ago, but we're still waiting for her life to start.'

And when no one said anything, because they were all busy chewing and ruminating, he added, 'She needs time, you know. The heart's like the engine of a Lada; it has to warm up. You can't just get in and drive off—'

Edi looked at him, remembering the afternoon when she'd slammed her bedroom door until the glass shattered and only a few shards were left in the frame. She thought of her racing pulse, the roaring in her ears, Daniel's pale face. Like now. How pale he was. Poor Dad.

She leant forward and kissed him on the cheek.

'I'm going.'

'What do you mean, *you're going*?'

Lena didn't even look surprised; her eyes had glazed over. Edi got up. People can die of loneliness, she thought. Even with a man beside them to keep the mattress warm.

She stood uncertainly between the tables, feeling the alcohol in her blood; then she grabbed a bottle of Coke, and, clutching it by the neck, she walked slowly through the room, people's gazes bursting on her like paintballs. She saw Anna coming out of the kitchen and started to head towards her, then turned without a word, pushed open a door, and another, and yet another—door after door after door—on to the landing, down the stairs, into the cool of the yard.

It was dark. The purple had washed out of the tie-dyed sky, giving way to a handful of stars. The youths were still standing around their improvised bonfire. Edi shoved past them, ignoring their comments, what did she think was she doing here. Someone pushed her, she lost her balance for a moment, but kept going and squeezed her way through to the heap of burning newspaper. Someone said she should piss off, must be crazy barging in like that, must be off her head… Edi ignored it all: the voices, the hands on her shoulders, the angry murmurs. Someone pushed her again. She didn't care.

She unscrewed the bottle top and poured the Coke on to the fire; it hissed like a woodland sprite and gave off a bitter, slightly salty smell. The youths yelled. She continued to ignore them. Any moment now and she'd get in the car and drive away.

I'll be gone in a sec.

NINA

All my life people have tried to prove to me that I'm no good at anything except maybe physics. My diagnosis came too late to save me from my hellish journey through the school system. It was sheer chance that I found myself with a doctor who referred me to a colleague who sent me to specialists who put me on an MRI table. By the time the protruding tongue drew me into the maw of the scanner, I already knew; I didn't actually need the follow-up talk with the doctor. Still, it was useful to be given a medical explanation for why I can't be in a room full of people without my kneecaps jumping and my jaw popping out of joint.

When I see too much at once, my scanners go on overload; I have to stare at door handles to get it under control. The cramp in my jaw is the first sign—so bad I can't open my mouth. Unfortunately, it seems that I also see too many images in my sleep; more often than not I wake with my teeth jammed together like I was a hatchetfish. I feel the knots of tension travelling up and down the muscles in my neck, all the way to my shoulders, tearing into me like vicious animals. When the cramp subsides, a wailing sound starts up inside me, like the roar of the fan on my PC.

I have all I need within reach on the table next to the keyboard, even food. Anna defrosts the fridge now and then when she drops in to check on me. 'What's the point of it, if it's just humming away to itself with nothing in it?' she asked the other day, and I quoted my favourite blogger at her: *refrigerators the best proof against fire, against earthquake, against almost everything.* In an emergency, a fridge is a panic room. You can't just get rid of a sanctuary like that. Anna shrugged, but I think she was smiling.

At first I didn't want to let her in, because I thought my mother had sent her, but she doesn't peer pryingly into the corners or bring love from Berlin. She helps me tidy up, puts the mouldy cups in the dishwasher, opens the windows, asks if we should strip the bed. She uses the we-form a lot and we both pretend I don't know what she means by it.

Anna has a son who left to fight in the war without a word to her, so I have to turn off the gunfire effects on my PC when she's around. Sometimes this son sends videos saying he loves her. She shows them to me. Usually the picture's blurred, and I wonder whether he does it on purpose so you can't see he's wounded, or whether he's so stoned on the stuff they take out there that he hasn't even realized you can't see him properly. But Anna's happy. She doesn't care. Mothers see what they want to see. Mine didn't notice what was wrong with me because she'd decided to see something different from what was there.

For years I came home from school exhausted, like I'd been sitting in a swarm of bees pulsing with information. I'd sit there clenching my teeth and staring at my desk—it wasn't till later that I came up with the door-handle trick. My schoolmates seem to have sensed that I didn't feel at ease with them. On my first day of sixth form there was a handmade sign waiting for me: FUCK OFF PSYCHO. The teacher saw no problem with the sign, but she didn't like the grim look on my face—enough to scare a person witless. OK, so maybe it was an overreaction to pull a knife, but I didn't lunge at anyone; I only rammed the blade into the sign.

By the time my mum was called away from the hairdresser's in the middle of the day to talk to the head teacher, it was blatantly obvious that I was going to leave school empty-handed.

At first it felt good when the doctors diagnosed me as having a brain that's differently wired from everyone else's, but soon things were the same as ever between me and my mum. That was the awful part. We fell back into the old patterns of mutual disappointment, as if nothing had changed.

She'd hoped the medical certificate would mean I'd get special assistance in finding a job, but I didn't show up to my appointments at the job centre or open the envelopes with the support application forms; I put my AKG K-701s on my ears and played video games. My life was already happening; I didn't need anyone trying to help me live.

The other day on the internet, I saw a Soviet film that must have been on at the cinema before my mum was born. The main character has gills and lungs; he can't walk around the harbour for long, but he doesn't feel properly at home in the sea either, and of course everyone thinks he's a weirdo. I sat there, fingers poised on the keyboard, ready to send the link to my mother with the subject line *this is how it feels*. But I didn't bother in the end because I reckoned it wouldn't get me anywhere. Apart from anything else, an email like that can send the wrong signal if you haven't been in touch for a while. I don't want her thinking I'm keen to talk to her about Amphibian Man's scaly costume. And I don't want her knowing that I trawl the internet for films she might have seen as a child. That I think about her all the time. Every day.

The last time we spoke on the phone she said I had no reason to throw my life away. I didn't even try to explain that what I have isn't a throwaway option; it's a decision I make with a clear head. Because that's all I have: my clear head. I heard her bang something against the wall at the other end of the line. She'd already been away from Jena a while and if I'd told her once, I'd told her a thousand times—no way was I going to follow her to my *native city* with that ugly television tower jabbing the relentless grey sky like a syringe.

In the same conversation she claimed that the country she comes from can't be grasped rationally. I knew we didn't mean the same thing, but I thought maybe we could agree that there is no determinable or predictable relationship between cause and effect—only ever a spectrum of possible relationships. Physics is helpful here, and I suggested that Heisenberg's Uncertainty Principle provided a better model for understanding the Soviet era than politics or history or her feelings: the more precisely you can define one property of a quantum object, the more uncertain the others become. You never see the full picture. That's the most important part of Heisenberg's discovery—that there's never a tangible reality, only the desire to understand and define something in its entirety. That would be Einstein. But even he couldn't dispute Heisenberg's theory.

My mum said I should stop *spitting in her soul*, and hung up.

I can't explain myself. I don't try to hurt her, but she can't see it any other way. I do care about her; I don't know why she's decided that it's nobody's business but hers if she's dying.

That's the only reason I let Edi in when she turned up at my flat the day after Auntie Lena's birthday. Because she knew something. The doorbell woke me. I pressed the buzzer. We stood in the hall staring at each other. Edi blinked like she had midges in her eyes.

We grew up together, we can see right through to each other's bones. We're MRI scanners to each other. But we can't always process what we see. Just because I crawled around in her babygros doesn't mean we were friends. I remember catching up with her and then overtaking her, in height and width. She started out small and stayed that way. Boys from my class used to push Edi around the playground like she was a chair in their way—and they were three years younger than her.

I told her she could leave her shoes on and showed her to the sofa. Her face wasn't bruised, but she didn't exactly look fresh. With her chalky skin merging seamlessly with her short, bleached hair, she reminded me of Amphibian Man. Her face looked tense, like someone was pulling her back by her hair, or like she was holding it under a steady flow of water.

She seemed disoriented. She'd been sitting in the same place only a few hours before, but maybe she'd been in shock then. This is actually a peaceful neighbourhood—it's unusual for anything to happen here. Sure, we have skinheads in town wandering around with sawn-off table legs—who doesn't? But I've never seen any on the estate and I've never known the kids from here to beat anyone up.

For a while we didn't speak.

'They just suddenly went for you?'

'I put their fire out.'

She nodded slowly, like in slow motion.

I tried a different tack. 'Yesterday you said you'd seen giraffes.'

'Only one. White with black spots, like a Dalmatian.'

When Edi lay in the dirt last night raving about wild animals I thought she was taking the piss out of us. But apparently not.

'You must have knocked back a few too many glasses of Uncle Lev's schnapps. That home-made stuff can really fuck with your nerves.'

'Other stuff fucks with my nerves.'

That was pretty obvious.

'I keep trying to get away from here, but I always end up coming back.' She made it sound like we lived together, and she was trying to tell me she wanted to move out and start a new life.

'No one's stopping you, are they?'

'Actually I wanted to move to Florida, settle there.'

Maybe she was permanently high. Giraffes. Florida. The weird hair.

'What do they have in Florida?'

She said her grandad had asked the same.

I know her grandad; he sometimes shuffles up the path to the woods, sits down on that little bench by the clearing and talks to himself—I've even seen him there quite late at night. Once he was singing. It sounded so sad I decided it could only be the Russian birthday song, which is basically a dirge. Maybe it was his birthday. When I got closer, though, I heard the words 'Victory Day! Victory Day!' Like he was calling a dog that wouldn't come.

'And what did you tell your grandad they have in Florida?'

'Everything but you people.'

She has a hurt laugh—has had since she was a child. But she used to laugh a lot and talk a lot when she was a kid. Mumbled, too—her parents were always hassling her about it. 'Speak more clearly. Speak more slowly.' She tried to say too much at once. Today she looked like a hologram, choppy because of a dodgy connection.

In a kind of reflex, I reached for the chicken wings on the table. I took one and offered them to Edi. She shook her head, watching me lick my fingers.

'Someone broke into my flat just before I came away. But they didn't take anything. Nada.'

She told me about the broken lock, but said nothing had been touched otherwise. 'Only the toilet…' She laughed again. 'Is that weird? To be upset by that?'

'That nothing was taken?'

'That there's apparently nothing in my flat worth taking.'

When I realized that all she wanted from me was an audience for her self-pity, I regretted having let her in.

'Then I got Gorbachev round to mend the lock. Your mum called him that, because of the Europe-shaped birthmark on his head. He was wearing a red lace thong. You could see it above his waistband when he bent over his toolbox. *Berlin, du bist so wunderbar!*'

So she and my mum were close enough to get together and watch Gorby bend down for them in lace underwear. I hadn't even realized they were in touch.

'Tatyana has these episodes. They think it might be NMO. Do you know what that is?'

She tossed the words out, then asked, in the same casual tone, if I smoked weed, and when I said I didn't, she began to roll herself a joint.

'Your body attacks itself. You can go blind, be paralysed and a lot of other stuff too. If you're really unlucky, it can kill you.' Her face was so smooth I thought I could see mine reflected in it, so I rocked my head to and fro a bit, fighting the urge to sit down at my PC and type *NMO* into the search engine. Later.

'Did you know that?' she said.

'What, about her illness?'

'No duh. What do you think? About the BMW she wants to buy?'

'Did she ask you to come and see me?'

That might have been nice, but she shook her head and crossed her legs.

'You were round at ours so often—all those afternoons, sometimes even late in the evening, after dark. You'd ring the bell and Mum would let you in and you'd sit in the kitchen together, or you'd sit there on your own—we never really talked and I still don't know where you slept when you stayed the night. Even back then I tried to pay as little attention as possible to what went on here, to make it easier to leave when the time came. I realized when I was only twelve that I wanted to get away, as far away as possible. But look at me—I'm still here. I keep coming back. I can't seem to leave the place.'

I remembered the Ciguapa dream and glanced at Edi's feet to see if they were back to front. For a second I was sure they must be, but her Adidases were entirely unsuspicious, one foot hanging rootless in the air.

'I saw you in the yard yesterday and then here in your flat and I thought, maybe...'

'What did you think, maybe?'

I stared at my kneecaps, waiting for them to start jumping. But they didn't. Only the sound of Edi's trouser legs rubbing together was beginning to grate on my brain. I watched her smoke. The invisible hand that was pulling her back by the hair loosened its hold and her face relaxed.

'You can still go to Florida, you know,' I said.

She looked at me in surprise, her fishy mouth gaping, as if I'd said something indescribably stupid.

'Yeah, I know. I just don't know who with.'

It was pretty clear that she wasn't seeing anyone, but she wanted me to ask, so I did. She said she was in love with a bouncer who wouldn't let her in. Very funny.

Then she started to mumble, like her grandad on his bench. 'I'm reading this book—I can lend it to you, if you like, I have it with me. It says things like: *"take me" always means "take me together with my childhood"*. That jumped out at me, because... I don't feel like telling anyone about myself. There's too much to explain. Too many unknowns in the equation. I can't even solve the equation myself.'

Then it was her turn to ask me if I was seeing anyone. Totally unnecessary. We've known each other too long for that—and how many times must she have heard my mum's tales of woe about her useless daughter? I can't have anyone in my life. Don't want anyone either.

I looked at Edi. I wouldn't have been surprised if she'd invited me to fuck off to the US with her.

I guess loneliness is always plural. When you're lonely, there's someone else lonely next to you, but that doesn't mean you get together. That's not how it works.

Edi's joint had gone out. I could tell she was nervous from the way she kept flicking her thumb over the flint wheel on her lighter. *Krrr-krrr, krrr-krrr*—until, at last, a thin flame appeared.

The smell of weed filled the room. I went to the window to open it and almost fell over backwards. A black, lashless eye was staring at me, two horns, ears, nostrils. A fuzzy white forehead pushed against the glass that separated it from us.

Acknowledgments

For the polyphony, thank you to: Toni Morrison, Anne Carson, Maria Stepanova, Serhiy Zhadan, Polina Barskova, Masha Gessen, Oksana Zabuzhko, Junot Díaz, Lauren Groff, Eugeniusz Tkaczyszyn-Dycki, Maya Angelou, Lutz Seiler, Esther Kinsky, Tommy Orange, Marion Poschmann, Benjamín Labatut, Valery Tarsis.

This book is full of the voices, misgivings and suggestions of: Nadja, Vita, Natascha, Lena, Wera, Sabine, Ilona, Andrii, Necati, Kirill, Emre, Nadine, Sivan, Mareike, Marie, Karin, Yoko, Martina, DP.

Thank you for every thought.

Then there's the question of how to thank DP. When my manuscript had a different title—a silly title, I knew it even then—when the voice was all wrong, the composition of the chapters out of kilter and I had no idea what story I was trying to tell, you said to me, 'You have to inflict yourself on yourself.' In a way, it sounded like a paraphrase of Ingeborg Bachmann.

I wrote your words on the imaginary cover of a version of the novel you'd never set eyes on. I'm still looking at them today and intend to look at them forever.

There must be an adequate form of thanks for what you've given me, but I haven't found it yet—and I couldn't ask you—so I'm still searching.

List of Sources

The quotation on p. 66 is from Ivan Valeriy (Valeriy Tarsis), *The Bluebottle*, translated from the Russian by Thomas Jones (London, 1962), p. 9.

The quotations on pp. 191 and 214 are from Oksana Zabuzhko, *Fieldwork in Ukrainian Sex*, translated from the Ukrainian by Halyna Hryn (Las Vegas, 2011), pp. 29–30, 60 and 72.

The quotation on p. 193 is from Anne Carson, 'The Anthropology of Water', in *Plainwater: Essays and Poetry* (New York, 1995), p. 191.

The quotation on p. 199 is from Anne Carson, 'The Anthropology of Water', p. 123.

The quotation on p. 285 is from Marion Poschmann, 'Kindergarten Lichtenberg', *Geliehene Landschaften* (Berlin, 2016), p. 24, my translation.

The quotation on p. 320 is from Junot Díaz, *The Brief Wondrous Life of Oscar Wao* (New York, 2007), p. 330.

FORBIDDEN NOTEBOOK
ALBA DE CÉSPEDES

COLLECTED WORKS: A NOVEL
LYDIA SANDGREN

MY MEN
VICTORIA KIELLAND

AS RICH AS THE KING
ABIGAIL ASSOR

LAND OF SNOW AND ASHES
PETRA RAUTIAINEN

LUCKY BREAKS
YEVGENIA BELORUSETS

THE WOLF HUNT
AYELET GUNDAR-GOSHEN

MISS ICELAND
AUDUR AVA ÓLAFSDÓTTIR

MIRROR, SHOULDER, SIGNAL
DORTHE NORS

THE WONDERS
ELENA MEDEL

MS ICE SANDWICH
MIEKO KAWAKAMI

GROWN UPS
MARIE AUBERT

LEARNING TO TALK TO PLANTS
MARTA ORRIOLS

THE RABBIT BACK LITERATY SOCIETY
PASI ILMARI JÄÄSKELÄINEN

BINOCULAR VISION
EDITH PEARLMAN

MY BROTHER
KARIN SMIRNOFF

ISLAND
SIRI RANVA HJELM JACOBSEN

ARTURO'S ISLAND
ELSA MORANTE

PYRE
PERUMAL MURUGAN

RED DOG
WILLEM ANKER

THE COLLECTED STORIES OF STEFAN ZWEIG
STEFAN ZWEIG

AN UNTOUCHED HOUSE
WILLEM FREDERIK HERMANS

WILL
JEROEN OLYSLAEGERS

MY CAT YUGOSLAVIA
PAJTIM STATOVCI

BEAUTY IS A WOUND
EKA KURNIAWAN

BONITA AVENUE
PETER BUWALDA

IN THE BEGINNING WAS THE SEA
TOMÁS GONZÁLEZ

TRAVELLER OF THE CENTURY
ANDRÉS NEUMAN